Praise for Enchanted, Inc.

"With its clever premise and utterly engaging heroine, Shanna Swendson has penned a real treat! *Enchanted, Inc.* is loads of fun!"
—JULIE KENNER, author of *Carpe Demon*

"A totally captivating, hilarious and clever look on the magical kingdom of Manhattan, where kissing frogs has never been this fun."
—MELISSA DE LA CRUZ,
author of *The Au Pairs* and *The Fashionista Files*

"Light and breezy, but not without substance . . . a bit of the sense of a screwball comedy, only updated for these times that we live in . . . with a hint of *Sex and the City* and maybe a dash of *Bridget Jones.*" —CHARLES DELINT, *Fantasy & Science Fiction*

"Lively . . . a pure and innocent fantasy . . . a cotton candy read."
—*Publishers Weekly*

"This is a witty, unique approach to the familiar story of a young woman working in modern Manhattan, and the laughs are plentiful."
—*Romantic Times*

"Swendson offers a quirky twist on supernatural powers, suggesting that not having any can actually be an asset. This appealing novel offers a charming cast of characters and a clever premise, and readers will hope that Katie's skills will be needed in New York City again soon."   —*Booklist*

"A totally fresh approach to chick lit that's magical and fun."
                                                    —freshfiction.com

"From the moment that you pick up *Enchanted, Inc.*, you know that you will have fun. . . . A marvelous world populated with the most interesting people."   —aromancereview.com

"Ms. Swendson does a marvelous job of bridging our world with the world of fantasy, in such a way, as to be completely plausible. . . . This book, if you'll pardon the pun, enchanted me from the first page."   —romancejunkies.com

"Light humor, a bit of magic, a dash of danger and adventure, and an engaging heroine add up to a recipe for a really enjoyable novel."   —BooksForABuck.com

"Lots of likeable characters (and potential romantic interests) that leave you wanting more."   —*Locus* magazine

"[Katie is] like the Harry Potter of adulthood. Author Shanna Swendson pens a delightful, whimsical tale about an unlikely heroine who saves the day against all odds—and oddities. *Enchanted, Inc.* offers a wonderful escape from the ordinary."
                                                    —*Dark Realms*

Once Upon Stilettos

Once Upon Stilettos

A Novel

Shanna Swendson

Ballantine Books
New York

A Ballantine Books Trade Paperback Original

Copyright © 2006 by Shanna Swendson

Published in the United States by Ballantine Books, an imprint of The Random House Publishing Group, a division of Random House, Inc., New York.

BALLANTINE and colophon are registered trademarks of Random House, Inc.

Library of Congress Cataloging-in-Publication Data

Swendson, Shanna.
  Once upon stilettos : a novel / Shanna Swendson.
    p. cm.
  ISBN 0-345-48127-5
  1. Young women—Fiction. 2. New York (N.Y.)—Fiction. 3. Women—Employment—Fiction.
[1. Magic—Fiction.] I. Title.

  PS3619.W445O53 2006
  813'.6—dc22

2006040721

Printed in the United States of America

www.ballantinebooks.com

9 8 7 6 5 4 3 2 1

Text design by Meryl Sussman Levavi

Dedicated in loving memory of my aunts, Marie Swendson and Frances Ryan, who were always so supportive of my literary aspirations.

Special thanks to

Mom and Rosa for the reading, feedback, nagging, and encouragement as I wrote; my agent, Kristin Nelson, and my editor, Allison Dickens, for helping me whip this book into the best possible shape; Barbara Daly for New York location research assistance; Jim Loats for giving Arthur J. Lansing (the very important businessfrog) his name; Stuart Weitzman for designing a very inspiring pair of red stilettos; The Browncoat Army, which knows a thing or two about guerilla marketing; all the readers who wrote to me, told their friends, showed up at book signings and otherwise made the release of *Enchanted, Inc.* so much fun. I hope you enjoy this one as much.

Once Upon Stilettos

one

It all began with the red shoes. I just didn't know it at the time.

I was out shopping with my roommate Gemma on a Saturday afternoon. That wasn't unusual. The unusual part was that we were shopping for me. Even more unusual was the fact that we were shopping for something for me to wear on a date—a real date. Not a blind-date setup, but an honest-to-goodness date with a guy who'd asked me out for a second date after a first date that could have made the record books for weirdness.

Any guy who asks you out for a second date even though he nearly had a nervous breakdown caused by your friends and co-workers on the first date has to be pretty special. He deserves a little extra effort. And that's why Gemma and I were in Bloomingdale's that Saturday.

"Let's go upstairs and look at shoes," she urged me, tugging at my sleeve.

"But we haven't found anything for me to wear yet," I protested. "How are we going to figure out what shoes I need?"

She looked at me with pity in her eyes and shook her head sadly, like a doctor about to tell me I had two weeks to live. "Oh, Katie, honey. You have so much to learn. We need to find the ultimate pair of shoes, and then we'll build an outfit around them."

When she bypassed the moderate shoes and continued up the escalators to the designer boutiques, I got the impression that her "ultimate" would exceed my budget. "Gemma," I warned, trying not to whine, "if we buy shoes up here, then I'll have to wear a plastic garbage bag as a dress, and I'll only be able to afford that if we already have some under the sink."

"We only have clear ones, so I doubt you want to go there," she said, not breaking stride. "And relax, I'm not going to make you buy designer shoes. We just come here for ideas and inspiration, then we'll buy the closest thing we can find at a more reasonable price."

I knew her well enough to know what she was doing, and it had nothing to do with putting together a great outfit for my date that night. She couldn't go into Bloomingdale's without making a pilgrimage to the holy shrine of shoes. Her pace quickened as we bypassed the designer boutiques and headed straight for the upscale shoe department. There she paused reverently at each display, lightly touching certain shoes. Every so often, she picked one up, held it to her breast, and closed her eyes in silent contemplation. I tried not to look at any of the shoes because I knew I couldn't afford them and there was no point in developing longings for things I couldn't have.

Not only was that a wise philosophy where shoes were concerned, it was also the reason I was going on this particular date. It only made sense to go out with the guy I could have, who fit every requirement I could think of for a man, rather than pining over someone I couldn't have. Ethan was good looking, intelligent, nice, and had a good job. He also wasn't the most powerful wizard of his generation, unlike someone else I could mention but didn't want to think about. *Blinders, remember,* I warned myself.

Then Gemma let out a gasp of awe mixed with longing. "Katie, look at these. You have to look at these."

I lifted my eyes from the carpet to see Gemma holding a red shoe. Not just any red shoe, but a high-heeled stiletto pump that looked like it was made out of candy apple coating, all rich, shiny, red, and good enough to eat. "Nice," I admitted.

"Nice? Nice? That's all you can say? These are amazing. These are shoes that say, 'Worship me.' You have to get these."

"Do I really want men to worship me?"

She gave me another one of those pitying looks. "Why wouldn't you?"

"Because I'm not the kind of girl men worship. And I'd prefer a more equal relationship."

"Wear these shoes, and you get the worship. And then you can have the relationship on any terms you want—equal or otherwise."

"But I don't have anything to go with them," I said, changing tactics.

She gave me a "what will I ever do with you?" sigh. "You don't find clothes that 'go with' shoes like these. These shoes aren't just accessories. They're an outfit that you accessorize with a simple black or gray dress. This is what you should wear on your date."

"I can't afford to buy shoes that don't go with almost everything I already own."

She flipped over the shoe she held and checked the price tag. "These are only two hundred dollars. That's half the price of a pair of Manolos. They're a bargain."

"They look like I could click my heels three times and get back home to Kansas."

"Oh, no, honey," she said, shaking her head. "These are the shoes that get you out of Kansas. Go on, at least try them on."

"You're the one who likes them so much. You get them."

"They'd make me look like the Jolly Green Giant. I'd tower over Philip." Philip was her boyfriend, and the fact that she'd given up towering heels for him was a sure sign of true love. Philip also used to be a frog, but she didn't know that. It's a long story. Suffice it to say, there was more than a hint of weirdness to my life. "But Ethan's really tall, and you're not all that tall, so you could totally wear these."

I could probably even wear them and still be shorter than a certain someone who wasn't quite as tall as Ethan, but I'd promised myself I wasn't going to think about him all weekend. "Gemma, I don't think so. Not yet. This is only a second date. I don't want to look like I'm trying too hard, and those shoes scream 'pulling out all the stops.' I don't want to give him that impression."

"So we're playing it cool?"

"Yeah, playing it cool. A strategy taught to me by a certain person named Gemma."

With a deep sigh, she replaced the shoe on its display. I grabbed her arm to drag her to the escalators so we could look at clothes I could actually afford, but when I turned around, I saw something that made me do a double take: two women with wings looking at shoes in the adjacent boutique.

For most people, the wings would be the cause of the double take. That's not something you see every day. But the fairies caught my eye because I knew them, and they didn't strike me as the kind of people who shopped at Bloomingdale's. I had them pegged as the type who wouldn't think of buying anything north of Fourteenth Street.

I was trying to think of a way to get Gemma to another department, fast, when one of the fairies said, "Katie! What are you doing here?"

"I was about to ask you the same question," I said, trying to keep my voice light and casual even as I glared at them. I was pretty sure Gemma couldn't see that there was anything odd about them—other than that they were so obviously downtown girls who probably wouldn't wear most of what was in that store—but I still wasn't comfortable mingling my work life and my personal life.

I work for a company called Magic, Spells, and Illusions, Inc.—it's kind of like a Microsoft for magic users, only not as into world domination. I'm not actually magical myself, but I have this strange immunity to magic and illusion, which in the magical world counts as sort of a superpower. I hadn't yet shared this information with my nonmagical friends, who thought I was just another administrative assistant at a boring corporation.

"We're out shopping," said the taller fairy, whose name was Ari.

"Same here," I said.

"Oh yeah, tonight's the big date," said the smaller fairy, whose name was Trix. "Getting something special to wear?"

"I'm trying to, without much luck."

"Friends of yours?" Gemma asked.

Remembering my manners, I made introductions. "Gemma, this is Ari and Trix. We work together. And this is Gemma, my roommate and fashion consultant," I said, watching Gemma's reaction to the fairies. I wouldn't have put it past Ari's twisted sense of humor to let her magical veil drop so everyone could see her wings, just so I'd have to scramble for an explanation to Gemma.

Fortunately, Gemma didn't seem to think anything was weird. "Nice to meet you," she said. "Maybe you can offer a second opinion. Don't you think Katie should at least try on these shoes?" She headed back toward the shoe boutique, and Ari and Trix followed.

"Katie can't afford these shoes," I said as I brought up the rear of the procession, irked at Gemma trying to get around my objections even as I was relieved that she hadn't questioned why I was talking to people with wings.

"Oh, fabulous," Trix breathed when Gemma held the sample shoe up for all to admire.

"Not your usual style," Ari said while staring hungrily at the shoes. "But there's nothing wrong with giving your image a little shake-up."

"See?" Gemma gloated. "Just try them on."

The three of them were practically drooling. Yeah, it was an eye-catching shoe, but I couldn't imagine it changing my life. I mentally added this to the list of popular things I just didn't get, along with George Clooney, designer-logo handbags, and reality television. As I watched them discussing the merits of the red shoes, I wondered once more what Ari and Trix were doing there. I had a very strong feeling they were following me. I shouldn't have been surprised; it was barely a week since I'd played a crucial role in giving the competition a major setback, so I probably needed a magical bodyguard or two. But I'd prefer it if I didn't have to face them when I was with a nonmagical friend. I could cope with fairies, people making coffee by flicking their wrists, and talking gargoyles at the office, but it still gave me a jolt when I saw those things in the "real" world when I was with people who weren't in on the secret.

"Come on, Katie," Ari urged. I felt like I was being recruited by the Cult of the Red Shoes.

"No, not this time," I insisted. "I need clothing, and I need to buy it soon so I'll have time to get ready. Gemma, we'd better get down to moderate dresses." She sighed and put the sample shoe down. "I'll see you two on Monday," I added very pointedly to Trix and Ari as I began walking toward the escalators, with or without my roommate.

"They seemed like fun," Gemma said when she caught up with me. "I can't believe you haven't talked more about your co-workers. You only talk about that one cute guy. Whatever happened with him, anyway?"

"Nothing. He's just a friend. Besides, with the gossip mill in that place, dating a co-worker would be suicide." Ethan fell in the gray area between co-worker and non-co-worker, since he was contracting his services to MSI and didn't have an office in the building. Also, I hadn't yet told my roommates that he was working for the same company, since I'd met him through them and explaining why he'd ended up working with me would have been more than complicated. To change the subject, I said, "So, what look should I go for—casual, sexy, trendy, sophisticated?"

With the opportunity to dress me, Gemma quickly forgot about discussing my co-workers. She picked out a simple black dress with an embroidered cardigan that fell within my budget. But she hadn't had the last word. "Those red shoes would go with this outfit," she said as we left the cash register.

"I swear, what is it with you and those shoes? You'd think they had you mesmerized. I've spent enough on this outfit as it is, and the black shoes I already own will do fine. Now home!"

Several hours later, I was dressed in my new outfit, my hair and makeup were done, and my roommates were getting on my nerves. "You don't have to wait around, you know," I told them. "You've already met Ethan, and I don't need anyone to help pin on my corsage and take our picture together."

"I wonder if there's any film in my camera," Gemma mused.

"No! Geeze, you act like me going on a date is a once-in-a-lifetime event."

"With you, it almost is," Marcia, my other roommate, said from her position on the couch.

"I've been on dates recently," I protested.

"Yeah, but this is the first time I can remember in a very long time that you've been on a second date with the same guy," Marcia replied.

She was right. After I went out with a guy once, he seldom wanted to see me again. Most of the time, it was because I was too normal, too boring, too girl-next-door, too much like a sister. That had changed lately, though. Now they were more likely to think I was too weird, and they'd be right. Take my last blind date, where a strange man appeared in the restaurant and serenaded me during dinner while claiming that I'd saved him from a lifetime as a frog. Really, all I'd done was rescue him from an illusion that made him think he was a frog. When he wasn't stalking me, he was an okay guy, and now he was dating Marcia. Gemma's boyfriend, Philip, was the one who really used to be a frog, but I had nothing to do with disenchanting him. I was only there when it happened.

Most of that crazy stuff wasn't my fault at all, since I can't actually do magic, but my job means I'm around a lot of weird things that I can't explain to normal people without them thinking I need to be medicated. It was tough living a double life where I couldn't talk to my closest friends about the things I saw or what happened at the office. It was kind of like being a spy, I guess, only a lot less glamorous.

Then there was Ethan. On our last date I'd discovered his magical immunity, then a couple of guys from work had shown up to test him by making increasingly outlandish stuff happen in the middle of the restaurant until he was forced to admit that he was seeing things, and that had dragged him into my crazy world when MSI recruited him. He'd asked me out again, anyway, even after he'd been involved in an all-out magical battle. It was the first step toward having a real boyfriend. But that would be more likely if he didn't have to run the roommate gauntlet when he came to pick me up.

"I don't suppose you two could find somewhere you have to be, oh, right about now," I said.

"You're trying to get rid of us?" Gemma asked.

"That, or you hide in the bedroom when he gets here."

"You're no fun."

"I don't want to make him feel awkward, and since he and Marcia were set up that time and didn't hit it off . . ." I let my voice trail off with the hint.

Marcia slammed her book shut. "Let's go get some coffee," she said. Gemma was still protesting as Marcia dragged her out the door.

That left me alone to wait nervously. I paced our tiny living room as I counted down the minutes until Ethan was due. All I wanted was a relatively normal date. Boring would be perfectly fine with me. Was that too much to ask? In my life, it usually was.

A knock on my front door startled me. I'd been expecting to hear the buzzer from the front door downstairs. I opened the door to see Ethan standing there, looking very *GQ* in a sweater, jacket, and slacks. "Hi, how did you get in?" I asked.

"I hit the wrong button by mistake, and your neighbor buzzed me in. You look great, by the way."

"Thanks." I felt oddly flustered, more nervous than I had been before my very first date back in high school when my entire family hid in the kitchen while I greeted the guy. "Let me get my purse."

I locked my apartment, then we went down the stairs. I had to hang onto the railing, my legs felt so watery with pre-date jitters. On the landing below my floor, a door opened and a grizzled head stuck out. "You could be more courteous to your neighbors, you know," the person said. "All that pacing in those heels—*click, click, click*. And then he has to go and push the wrong button."

"Sorry about that, Mrs. Jacobs," I said, feeling my face turn beet red. Great, now I sounded like a lousy neighbor, and Ethan knew I was nervous about the date.

When we made it outside, he said with a grin, "She seems charming."

"I think she's the designated building curmudgeon."

"Every building has to have one." He opened the back door of a cab waiting in front of my building. "Your chariot, milady."

I got in and slid across the seat to make room for him. He gave the cabdriver a nod, and the cab took off. "I planned something a little different. I hope you don't mind," he said as he settled back into the seat next to me.

"I'm sure it'll be great," I said, fingering the strap of my purse. This was why I wanted a boyfriend—to reach a comfort zone with a person so I didn't have to go through this kind of stress every weekend. But as my roommates never ceased to remind me, you had to date to get a boyfriend.

"And let's hope it doesn't go like last time," he said with a laugh. "I like Rod and Owen, but I don't want them showing up on all our dates."

I'd been so good about not thinking about a certain other person, and there my date had to go and mention him. I distracted myself by focusing on his casual mention of "all our dates." That was the kind of detail Marcia and Gemma would want to hear later when we analyzed every second of this date. There was a strong implication that he wanted to make this a steady thing. Then again, would he have asked me out at all if he already knew he didn't want to see me again after this date?

This dating stuff was way too complicated, and I was too old to be such a novice at it.

The cab pulled up in front of a Midtown restaurant. Ethan paid the driver, then got out and helped me out of the cab. He held his arm out for me to take—my mom would have been so impressed with such a gentlemanly show of manners—and escorted me inside. I was surprised to see one long table rather than the usual restaurant arrangement of scattered individual tables.

"It's a wine dinner," Ethan explained. "There's a wine selected to go with each course, all from the same winery. I thought it would be fun. We'll have other people to chat with and an automatic topic of conversation."

I was all in favor of having a topic of conversation that didn't involve magical intellectual property, which was what we'd talked about on our last date. I was nervous about the wine, though. In addition to being a total lightweight who's under the table asleep after a couple of glasses, I had the world's least sophisticated palate. I couldn't find anything wrong with white zinfandel, something that drove my room-mates crazy. They said no real wine drinker would go near that pink stuff. I'd look like a total hick among people who could discern a hint of oak in a full-bodied red, or whatever it was people said when they were analyzing wines.

We had to mingle with the other diners while eating appetizers brought around by waiters. I wasn't exactly sure what was in each bite, but the wine they gave us with that course was pretty good. I sipped at it, knowing I needed to pace myself.

The crowd, however, was enough to drive me to drink. These peo-ple reminded me of my old job, the one I left when I joined MSI. They'd all probably be shocked and horrified that a small-town Texas girl was in their midst. I was careful to suppress my accent while mak-ing small talk. These were the kind of people who'd automatically look down on me for not being a born-and-bred city slicker. I felt a bit bet-ter when I saw that Ethan looked stiff and uncomfortable, too. He didn't know anyone there, either.

He edged closer to me after one waiter passed by with a tray of what looked like liverwurst on toast. "Sorry about this," he said in a low voice. "I didn't realize we'd be dealing with the yuppies from hell."

"Just as long as you promise to defend me," I whispered back.

The host urged everyone to take their seats. Fortunately, Ethan and I were seated next to each other so we had a chance at private conversation. The array of silverware on the table was intimidating, not because I didn't know how to use it (my mother is a good Southern woman who taught us proper table manners, so I knew to work from the outside in), but because of the number of courses it implied. A glass of wine with each course would mean I'd be horizontal before we got to dessert. My bigger worry was that alcohol might lower my inhibitions enough for me to talk about work, which was not a good idea with a job like mine. Then again, everyone would probably write off any weirdness to the drunkenness. I vowed to myself that I wouldn't finish each glass of wine.

At the head of the table, a well-dressed man stood up and tapped his water glass with his knife. He reminded me of the man who'd tried to start a community theater group in my hometown. Even though he was in a tiny Texas farming community, he'd acted like a theater impresario. It took him a while to figure out that avant-garde surrealist drama didn't go over well in that setting.

This guy wouldn't have looked out of place wearing a sweeping cloak and a monocle. He was introduced as Henri, a representative of the winery providing the evening's selections. "Good evening, everyone," he said. In spite of his French name, his accent was pure American. "Welcome to tonight's dinner. You've already been enjoying our Estate Sauvignon Blanc with the canapés. I'm sure you noticed the lush texture and hints of passion fruit and pear."

Frankly, I hadn't noticed any of that. I pretty much just tasted wine. If it was all made out of grapes, how was it supposed to taste like passion fruit?

"With our first course," Henri continued, "we'll be serving our famous Pinot Gris. You may detect flavors of apple and lemon, with a midpalate burst of ginger. It complements the salmon with mango salsa we'll be serving."

Waiters brought out fresh wineglasses, then filled them with a wine that looked to me a lot like the one we'd just been drinking. I followed everyone's lead in swirling the wine—only sloshing a little over the edge—and sniffing it. Yep, smelled like wine. Everyone then took a sip and seemed to ponder the flavors. I couldn't taste anything but wine. No apple, lemon, or ginger. I was horrified when I noticed Ethan nodding sagely. Was he really into this stuff? On our first date, he took me out for hamburgers. This was a real switch.

Then again, was it so bad if he was a wine fanatic? Learning something new would be good for me. I complained all the time about feeling like a hick in New York, and here was my chance to do something to change that. I took another sip of wine and tried desperately to taste all those delicate flavors that were supposed to be there.

We went through another course that came with a wine Henri described as "creamy with citrus undertones." I had a hard time thinking of wine as creamy. Ethan leaned toward me and asked, "Are you enjoying yourself?"

After three glasses of wine—even if I didn't drink the whole glass—I was feeling pretty good, regardless of whether this event was my cup of tea—make that glass of wine. "Sure!" I said cheerfully, raising my glass to him.

If I was feeling good, that was nothing compared with the rest of the guests. They were practically swooning in rapture with each sip. I'd thought I'd be a lightweight in a group of real wine aficionados, but they were acting drunker than I was—a lot drunker. The woman seated next to me was nibbling on her husband's ear and halfway crawling into his lap, while he had a hand up her sweater. I fought back the impulse to tell them to get a room and turned to the other side of the table, where a man who'd introduced himself as a cardiologist was wearing his necktie around his head like a bandanna. This felt more like a frat party than a wine dinner. I appeared to be the most sober one there, except for Ethan.

I leaned over to him. "Do these things usually get like this?"

"I've only been to one other, and behavior there was a little more restrained. Frankly, this is a lot more fun."

They switched to a red wine with the main course, which meant I could finally tell the difference from the last few wines. I still didn't taste the clove, coffee, or wood flavors Henri promised, for which I was somewhat grateful. It seemed to me that if your wine tasted like wood or coffee, you'd throw it out. The other guests knocked back the wine like they were doing tequila shots, so I doubted they were noticing the flavor nuances, either.

By the time we got to dessert, I was barely registering the life story Henri told us about the wine. I thought he said something about moldy grapes, but that couldn't be right. It didn't sound like the sort of thing you'd brag about. I did like the wine, though. It was probably my favorite of the evening because it was so sweet. They served it with poached pears that would have been a challenge to eat under the best of circumstances. As tipsy as I was, it was nearly impossible. I spent about five minutes chasing a pear around my plate, only to have it leap onto Ethan's plate.

"Oops, sorry about that," I said, hoping my words didn't slur too much.

"No problem." He gently returned the pear to my plate with his fork. I thought I detected a wink behind his glasses when he added, "Want me to cut that up for you?"

"What, and then have multiple moving targets?"

He chuckled. "Good point. You're not used to having this much wine, are you?"

"Is it so obvious? I'm not even drinking the whole glass. Well, except this one. I like this one."

"Don't worry. It only looks like a slight bit of motor coordination difficulty. In this crowd, you look like the picture of sobriety. I'm not sure you could be obnoxious, no matter how drunk you got."

Aww, wasn't he sweet?

By this time, the party was in full swing. I shouldn't have worried about people noticing me struggling to eat my pear. Their attention was more likely focused on the female stockbroker standing on the table and doing a striptease. The things she wore under her pin-striped suit showed that there was a whole other aspect to her personality.

Henri and his cronies chose that time to swoop in with order forms, going one by one to the guests. I noticed that each guest stiffened, losing the looseness of intoxication for a second or two before taking a pen and signing the form. After the paperwork was completed, the host made a note on his clipboard, and the guest passed out. It reminded me of something I'd seen recently, but in my foggy state I couldn't quite remember what it was.

Fortunately, Ethan was practically sober, so I thought maybe he'd know what was going on. I tapped him on the shoulder and whispered, "Is there something odd about this, or am I just drunk?"

But before he could answer, Henri had reached me with his order form.

two

"And are you enjoying your evening, mademoiselle?" Henri smarmed to me.

"Oh yeah, sure," I said, trying to approximate the level of drunkenness at the rest of the table without resorting to removing my clothes. I sensed it would be best to play along until I was sure what was happening.

I must have done a good job (not that I had to fake being drunk) for he went straight into salesman mode. "Then if you've enjoyed the wine this evening, I'm sure you'd like to order several bottles so you can repeat the experience while dining at home. We offer discounts if you buy a case, and you can mix and match the wines in the case." He then handed me an order form and a pen and said, "Now, what would you like to order?"

"Nothing, thanks," I said cheerfully, handing him back the order form and pen.

"Are you sure?" he asked a little more forcefully, handing the form and pen back to me.

"Yeah. Not only can I not afford a case of wine, but I can't think of where we'd store it in our apartment, unless maybe we threw a scarf over it, put some candles and magazines on it, and called it a coffee table." That struck me as the funniest thing anyone had ever said, and I collapsed in hysterical giggles. I glanced at Ethan to see if he appreciated the humor. He just frowned.

But he wasn't frowning nearly as severely as Henri was. "I'm sure you'd like to order," he said in a commanding tone, and the hair on the back of my neck stood straight up. It wasn't his tone that had that effect. Magic was being used nearby. It might not work on me, but I could feel it. Suddenly I realized what it was I'd been trying to remember. The behavior of the guests when Henri handed them the pen and order form reminded me of when the people at MSI had tested the initial spell being marketed by Phelan Idris, a rogue wizard with very different ideas of how magic should be used. That spell made it possible to control the actions of others. Was that what was going on here?

When I still didn't order any wine, Henri moved over to Ethan, who was as immune to magic as I was. He had similar results, except for the witty quip about using the case of wine as a coffee table. Instead of making jokes, Ethan studied the form like the lawyer he was. "There appear to be some errors on this order form," he said at last. "Surely you aren't charging this for a case of wine? It doesn't match the market prices I'm familiar with. Maybe you accidentally got the decimal point in the wrong place."

A muscle jumped in Henri's jaw, and I knew we'd caught him doing something he wasn't supposed to be doing. I tugged on Ethan's sleeve. "I think something strange is going on here," I whispered.

Ethan smiled at Henri and said, "Would you excuse us for a moment?" Then he stood, reached around Henri to grab my wrist, and pulled me to my feet. "What is it?" he asked.

I forced myself to be as coherent as I possibly could be in my condition. "It's a spell he's using. I've seen one like it before. It's like the one Idris was selling, the one he signed papers saying he wouldn't sell anymore because it was based on MSI intellectual property. It lets you make people do things, and they don't even know what they've done."

"But he can't sell that spell—that contract was supposedly unbreakable."

"I don't know how it all works. Maybe these people bought the spell earlier. The contract might not affect spells sold before it was signed. Or maybe it's a slightly different spell and they were testing it. It seems a bit different. But I'm pretty sure they're using magic to make people order the wine, and I'm even more sure the wine was enchanted, especially considering I'm almost the least drunk person here and I'm a total lightweight."

"Okay, then let me handle this." We went back to Henri, me hanging on Ethan's arm, partly for support and partly because he was pretty hot when he was being all authoritative. "It does seem like there are some irregularities on these order forms that I'm sure you didn't intend."

Henri raised an eyebrow. "Oh, really?" he asked icily.

That set me off, in spite of Ethan's warning grip on my arm. "You don't know who you're dealing with here, do you?" I asked, unable to hold back a triumphant grin. "I know what you're trying to pull, and I'm not going to let you get away with it. Enchanting all those people with your magical wine, then hitting them with a spell to make them buy wine at inflated prices." I tried to keep my voice low, so it was just between us, but it seemed to echo loudly throughout the restaurant. I'd forgotten that I tended to talk louder when I was drunk. Oops. Not that anyone else noticed. The ones who weren't passed out were too busy doing the limbo under a curtain rod with the heavy velvet drapes still attached to it.

Ethan gripped my arm hard enough to cut off the circulation. I caught the hint and shut up. "I think she's had a bit much to drink. But I do think there's a problem with your forms. I'm an attorney and I'd be happy to correct the forms for you before anyone leaves. No fee, unless you want to send me home with a bottle of that Botrytised Semillon."

"Was that the sweet one?" I asked.

He looked down at me with a fond smile. "Yes, that was the sweet one." He pinned Henri with a steely gaze. "So, want to take me up on that offer?"

"Of course. Thank you. I'm grateful you caught my error." Henri didn't sound the least bit grateful, unless he was grateful to be given such an easy out. He'd still make out like a bandit on wine orders, since everyone was both drunk and enchanted from the wine, but he wouldn't be able to pull off the full scam.

While Ethan went around the table correcting the forms, I drained his unfinished glass of the sweet wine. It sure didn't taste like it was made from moldy grapes. If they were tricking people with enchanted wine, the wine was still good without the magic.

When Ethan returned to me, Henri approached him with a bottle of wine. "With our compliments, sir, and thank you again for your assistance," he said with a thin-lipped smile.

"Glad to be of service," Ethan said, giving no indication that there was anything out of the ordinary about the situation. "Now I'd better get her home. She seems to have had a little too much fun tonight," he finished with a laugh. "Come on, Katie."

The floor refused to cooperate, and if it hadn't been for Ethan's steady guiding arm around my waist, I probably wouldn't have made it to the exit without taking a bad tumble. The cool air outside made me a little more alert, but the moment we were safely ensconced in the backseat of a cab, I suddenly felt very sleepy. I rested my head on Ethan's shoulder, and he put his arm around me.

"Mmm, that's nice," I murmured.

"You're really drunk, aren't you?" I could hear the smile in his voice. "Sorry about that. It honestly wasn't my plan to get you wasted. I just wanted to do something nice."

"You were trying to impress me," I said, only realizing after I'd heard the words that I'd said them out loud. I was never going to drink on a date ever again.

"Yeah, maybe a little bit, since I don't think I impressed you so much on the first date."

"Why can't I have a normal date, one where magic isn't involved? Did I ever tell you about the frog guy?"

"No, you didn't. Maybe later. But wouldn't normal be boring?"

"That's what I used to think. Now it might be nice."

"Well, you can never claim there's no magic to our relationship," he said with a soft laugh. "I can't believe we still haven't managed a magic-free evening. You're sure they were using magic?"

"Yep. I could feel it. There's a little tingle. Besides, did any of that look normal to you?"

"I don't know. I've been to some law firm parties that looked a lot like that."

I must have drifted off to sleep, for next thing I knew I felt cold air on my face. I opened my eyes and realized that Ethan was carrying me from the cab to the front door. I then closed my eyes because the movement made me dizzy.

Ethan pressed the buzzer, then Marcia's voice said over the speaker, "What?"

"It's Ethan, bringing Katie home. She's a little, um, incapacitated."

"Come on up."

Ethan gave me a little shake. "Katie? Wake up."

I forced my eyes open again. "Huh?"

"If you lived on the second floor, I might be able to carry you up, but I'm afraid the third floor is beyond me. Can you walk?"

"Yeah, sure. Put me down."

He put me on my feet, keeping one arm around me to steady me while he opened the front door with his other hand. We made our way slowly up the stairs, with him supporting most of my weight. I must have been really heavy to him, for I felt like I weighed a ton. I could feel the gravity pulling me toward earth. "Just a few more steps," he urged.

Marcia was waiting with the apartment door open and a disapproving scowl on her face. Ethan would have been better off facing my father. "You got her drunk?" she snapped.

"I took her to a wine dinner. I didn't realize she didn't have a lot of experience with wine."

"I liked the sweet one, the one they make from moldy grapes," I put in helpfully.

"If my intentions weren't honorable, I wouldn't have brought her straight home," he pointed out.

Marcia had to see the logic in that, even if she wasn't overly fond of Ethan. "Well, let's get our little drunk inside," she said. The two of them walked me to the sofa, then got me settled onto it.

Ethan knelt in front of me, and I struggled to bring his face into focus. "We'll have to drink that bottle of wine I got some other time," he said. Then he stood up and told Marcia, "I'd better go. The cab's waiting."

"Did you hear that?" I asked Marcia as soon as the door shut behind him. "He wants to see me again."

"And why wouldn't he? You seem to be a pretty cheap date."

"Not cheap. I think this was expensive."

"You'd better start drinking water or you'll regret it in the morning." She disappeared for a moment, then I heard her voice coming from the kitchen. "Argh. Gemma forgot to buy water again." I heard water running from the tap, then she pressed a glass into my hand. "Drink up," she ordered.

I managed to get the whole glass of water down. My head was already clearing, though I still felt sleepy. "I didn't drink that much, really," I told her. "Only five little glasses of wine, and I only finished one of them. Most of them I just sipped. And that was with food, over several hours."

"You really are a lightweight, aren't you? Now, off to bed with you."

Before I fell asleep, I pondered which was worse, getting so drunk on a few glasses of wine and making a fool out of myself in front of Ethan, or having magic make yet another unwelcome appearance on a date. I'd once been the most normal person on the face of the earth, but almost everything in my life had become weird.

It said something about how my weekend had gone that I was ridiculously happy when Monday morning rolled around. Sunday was characterized by a nasty headache, grillings from nosy roommates about my date, and a depressing phone call from my mother, who remained convinced that I must be terribly homesick living in the big city. Going to work allowed me to escape all that. It was a relief going to a place where the weird was perfectly ordinary.

Well, there might have been one other reason for looking forward to Monday morning, and he was waiting for me on the sidewalk in front of my building. Owen Palmer perfectly fit the definition of the word "heartbreaker," without actually deliberately doing anything to break hearts or even knowing he was doing so. He was incredibly gorgeous, incredibly brilliant, incredibly nice, and every indication was that he'd filed me firmly in the "just a friend" category.

He was also an extraordinarily powerful wizard and a leading fighter in the magical war of good against evil. That may sound sexy and romantic, but in reality I suspected it didn't make him ideal boyfriend material. Besides, I was happy being friends with him. Really.

He greeted me with a smile. "Good morning, Katie. How was your weekend?"

"Good morning, yourself. And my weekend was okay." We fell into step together as we walked toward the subway station.

"You had a date with Ethan, didn't you?" The office grapevine at MSI was possibly the best in history. Or Ethan had told Owen. They were becoming pretty good friends. The casual tone of his voice when he asked about my date with another man was yet another piece of evidence proving he had no interest in me. Not that I was setting out to make him jealous, but would it have killed him to show the tiniest hint of it?

"Yeah. It was nice. The date part was, at least. But there was some other stuff that got kind of strange."

"Such as?"

"I'll probably need to talk to you about it at work." If I was going to have to discuss certain aspects of my dating life with him, I preferred to do it in a business capacity.

"Now you've got me intrigued."

"Trust me, it's not that interesting. Just something we might want to track. And how was your weekend?"

"Nothing exciting. I mostly rested."

"Good. You're not back working on counterspells, are you? The boss said you had to recover fully." Owen had been more than a little drained and banged up in his last encounter with our nemesis. He still had the faintest traces of a healing black eye, which stood out against his pale skin, and although he no longer carried his left arm in a sling, he wasn't using it much.

"I'm being good, trust me. I can't afford to let myself get run-down right now."

And with that, we'd exhausted our conversational supply. We didn't really hang out together beyond work-related situations. I didn't even know if we had anything in common. That didn't stop me from wanting to sigh dramatically whenever I saw him.

But then I saw something odd enough to distract my attention from the gorgeous man at my side. You see strange things on the streets of New York every day, and I see stranger things than most, but this was really strange. It was like a living skeleton was walking alongside us down the Fourteenth Street sidewalk. Nobody else who passed us seemed to notice anything odd, but with New York commuters, that didn't necessarily mean anything.

I moved closer to Owen. "You don't see anything weird, do you?" I asked him.

He raised an eyebrow. "Define *weird*."

"Walking skeleton on your left."

I admired his cool as he barely moved his eyes in that direction. If the wizard thing didn't work out for him, I thought he'd make a decent spy. He even looked like a young James Bond. "Hmm," he said after a moment. "There's definitely something veiled near us. I can feel the power in use. What do you think we should do?"

"You're the wizard."

"Well, it might make a scene if I unveiled it in public."

"If anyone noticed," I reminded him.

"Oh, right. Well, let's get him out of our hair." He mumbled something under his breath and twitched his wrist.

The skeleton creature suddenly flew up against a NO PARKING sign, where it remained stuck and struggling. I almost hit a light pole, I was so busy looking to see what happened while still trying to walk forward and look casual. Owen pulled me out of the way just before I broke my nose.

"Nice teamwork," he said with a satisfied grin. "You spot 'em. I spell 'em. I wonder how long it will take for someone to realize it's there and free it." I didn't need the reminder that his commuting with me in the morning had more to do with business than it did with affection or even chivalry. It was a form of mutual protection against our enemies. I could spot any magical threats that might have been veiled from him. As powerful as he was, his magic meant that magic could be used on him. Meanwhile, he could defend us against any magical attacks that I spotted. And if the motion of a crowded subway car happened to throw me up against him, well, that was a bonus.

"I wonder what that was about," I said, but before he had a chance to respond, I already knew the answer. There was a street musician near the entrance to the subway at Union Square, playing the bongos with no sense of rhythm. I grabbed Owen's arm, for the would-be drummer wearing a brightly colored Rasta cap that didn't go with his otherwise nerdy attire was none other than MSI's current nemesis, Phelan Idris. I was fairly certain he was using a spell to hide himself from Owen.

"What is it this time?" Owen asked under his breath.

"Let's just say there's a good reason that guy playing the drums has no rhythm."

He gave a weary sigh and walked right up to the bongo player. "Sorry I don't have any spare change on me," he said. "I know we messed up your livelihood, but couldn't you have found something a little less degrading to do? Your lack of talent is embarrassing."

Idris's beat got even more off as he looked up at Owen, then turned to glare at me. I gave him a cheery little wave. "So you're still using your girlfriend's eyes, huh, Owen?" he asked.

It would have been nice if Owen could have managed a hint of a blush at that point. He was so bashful that it didn't take much to turn him beet red, and surely if he secretly harbored any feelings for me whatsoever, the accusation that I was his girlfriend should have been enough to make him start glowing. Instead, he remained icily calm. "And you're still dredging up whatever abominations you can find. Or are you making them yourself? Magical bioengineering isn't just against the code, it's a bad idea."

"Oh yeah, the oh-so-holy code. Well, don't worry about me. I've got plenty to keep me busy, as you'll see soon enough."

Owen rolled his eyes and turned to head into the subway, muttering under his breath. I hurried to follow him, but paused to look back when I heard a loud bang. Idris's drums had exploded in a shower of silver dust, earning far more applause than his playing had. I got the impression that Owen hadn't been muttering curses. Well, not the obscene kind, anyway.

I caught up to Owen just past the turnstiles. "He's up to something," he said, more like he was talking to himself than to me.

"Isn't he always?"

"Well, yeah, I guess. But sending me a message like this means he's up to something new, and he wants me to know about it."

"Doesn't that sort of ruin the element of surprise? You'd think he'd accomplish more if he didn't give you advance warning."

"Yeah, you'd think, but he doesn't work that way. I suspect half the fun for him is watching us react." He frowned. "Unless maybe he isn't up to anything at all, and he just wants us to think he is."

"Owen, if you keep that up, your brain is going to explode."

He looked at me, then shook his head and laughed. "I am sounding paranoid. Okay, I won't let him get to me."

The rest of our commute went without incident. We got off at the City Hall station, crossed the park and a street, then headed down a side street to the castle-like building that housed MSI. A cheerful voice greeted us as we approached. "And a good Monday to you!" it said.

Both of us looked up to see a gargoyle perched on the awning over the front door. "Good morning, Sam," I said. Sam was in charge of security for MSI.

"How was the hot date?" the gargoyle asked with a wink.

"It was good, thanks."

"Everything under control, Sam?" Owen asked.

Sam saluted with one wing. "The building's still standing."

Owen grinned. "Keep up the good work."

Inside, Owen and I parted ways, him heading to Research and Development, me heading up to the executive suite, where I was assistant to Ambrose Mervyn, the chief executive officer. He's better known as Merlin. Yes, *the* Merlin, as in King Arthur and all that. He'd founded what had gone on to become this company, then was revived recently from a sort of magical hibernation to take charge once again as we faced the serious crisis of dealing with Phelan Idris and his dark spells.

I found Merlin at his receptionist's desk, fiddling with the telephone. He might be a legendary genius, but he was new to the twenty-first century. I had a feeling that within days, though, he'd know exactly how a telephone worked and might even have built one from scratch.

"Good morning, Katie," he greeted me.

"Good morning. Where's Trix?"

"I'm afraid she's out ill. Would you mind sitting at her desk today?"

"Not at all. I'll move my laptop out here."

"Thank you. I don't seem to recall fairies becoming ill that often, so I do hope it isn't serious."

It must have been serious, considering how eager she'd been to hear about my date with Ethan. I made a mental note to ask Ari if she knew anything. I got my computer from my office, then settled in at Trix's desk.

Merlin went back to his office, returning moments later with his calendar. "I have a meeting this morning at ten, very important. Amalgamated Neuromancy is open to joining us for the fight against Phelan

Idris and his upstart venture, but there are some details we need to discuss."

I made a note on the desktop calendar. "Will you need me for that?" In addition to being Merlin's executive assistant, I was also his personal verifier, ensuring no magical cheats or shortcuts were used against him.

"No, that won't be necessary." His eyes twinkled. "I intend to apply some personal persuasive techniques against their chief executive, so it would be best if there are no outsiders present."

I couldn't help but grin. "Okay, gotcha. I'll let you know when he arrives."

"Thank you." He started to head for his office, then turned back. "By the way, I understand you and Mr. Wainwright went out together Saturday night. How did that go?"

This place was worse than a small town. Even the thousand-plus-year-old boss knew about my dating life. "It was nice. He took me to a wine dinner. Come to think of it, have you heard of the Pegasus Winery? I think they might be magical. It looked to me like they enchanted the guests with magical wine, then tried to cheat them on wine purchases. The way people were acting, it reminded me of that spell Idris was selling, the one Owen was testing."

"I don't recall having heard of them, but you should probably ask around. I hope you and Mr. Wainwright put a stop to it."

"We did. Well, not the enchantment part, since it was too late for that, but we did stop the cheating."

"Good work. I must admit that I find the news disturbing. If our kind are so willing to use magic for cheating and other lawbreaking, will we truly have the will to stand against what Idris represents? Or will he find an even greater market for his wares than we realized?"

It was a sobering thought. Phelan Idris used to work for MSI, but got fired for developing spells designed to cause harm, an absolute MSI no-no. He went into business for himself to market those harmful spells. We'd put a stop to his first efforts with a little legal maneuvering and a big magical fight, but he was still out there.

Trying to cheer up both Merlin and myself, I said, "But haven't there always been cheats? Otherwise, why would you need people like me?"

"Cheating among the magical is one thing, and usually done only for amusement and one-upmanship, considering we always get caught. Using the nonmagical for gain is entirely another. Check with Sales and see if that winery uses any of our spells for its business, and let Mr. Palmer know what you observed."

He went into his office, and I got to work typing memos and reviewing documents for Merlin after sending an e-mail to Sales about the winery. The visitor arrived just before ten, and I escorted him into Merlin's office. He looked like the kind of person who would need a particularly strong form of persuasion to get him to do something for the general good.

Merlin must have gone straight to work on him, for I had to ignore the occasional odd sound and flash of light that showed through the crack under Merlin's door once the meeting started. As entirely nonmagical as I was, I could feel the tingle of increased power usage nearby.

I was just considering forwarding Trix's phone to my office so I could shut the door and tune out whatever was going on in Merlin's office when Owen came running into the reception area.

"Is he in?" he asked. He normally wasn't that brusque, so something had to be wrong.

"He's in a meeting. What is it, Owen?"

"I need to talk to him."

"He said he wasn't to be disturbed." Just then, a particularly loud pop sounded from within the office, accompanied by a flash of light and an odd smell. We both flinched. "No, disturbing him probably isn't a good idea," I added.

He nodded. "You may be right, but this is pretty urgent."

"What's wrong?"

"I think we've got a spy among us."

"What makes you say that?"

He waved a handful of papers at me. "Because someone's been into my notes on protective spells. Notes that were locked in a desk drawer, inside my locked office, inside our highly secured R and D department."

"But they didn't take them, right? How do you know someone was looking at them?"

"I, uh, booby-trapped the drawer before I left Friday. Nonmagically. And it's definitely been disturbed. Each page was looked at, probably copied."

"There's no legitimate reason for anyone to have been in that drawer?"

He shook his head. "I have the only key—that I know of—and the office is both locked and warded. No one outside the company can get in there when I'm not there. The cleaning brownies even have to work in there during the day instead of at night."

"Which suggests an inside job."

"Exactly. Either someone here is helping someone get in, or someone who works here is doing some unauthorized snooping. So, you can see why I think this is important enough to interrupt a meeting. He needs to know right away." There was another loud flash and pop that made us both jump. "Or I could wait out here until they finish killing each other."

"Good idea. Have a seat." He settled uneasily into the chair in front of Trix's desk. "You said you booby-trapped the drawer. Did you already suspect a spy?"

He shrugged and looked uncomfortable. "I had a feeling." Owen's feelings were uncanny and tended to be accurate.

"Who do you think it is?"

"I have no idea. I hate to make accusations at this point, with so little evidence. We just need to be aware that something is going on."

"It would explain how Idris seems to be right in step with us, like him coming out with a new spell as soon as you found the counter-spell for the last one."

"And since we beat him at that, I can imagine he's keeping track of everything we do. That's probably what he was talking about when he said I'd know what he was up to soon enough."

"How'd you do it?" I couldn't resist asking.

"Do what?"

"Booby-trap your desk."

A faint pink stain appeared on his cheeks. It made him look even cuter than usual. "I set up some film canisters in the drawer. When I open the drawer, I use a stasis spell to keep them in place. But if someone didn't know they were there and opened the drawer normally, they'd fall over. This morning they'd been disturbed. I also put a single strand of hair on each page, and they were all gone."

"Where'd you learn to do that?"

He turned even pinker. "I read it in a book."

I was about to quiz him on what kind of book—the personal details I knew about him were depressingly few, and despite my best efforts not to, I couldn't help searching for more—when Merlin's office door opened and Merlin escorted his guest to the spiraling escalator that led down to the lobby. Merlin looked as unruffled as ever. The CEO of Amalgamated Neuromancy looked like he'd survived a hurricane—barely.

"I take it that went well," I remarked as Merlin approached the desk.

"Quite. He was most cooperative. Now, Mr. Palmer, were you here to see me?"

"Yes, sir. It's rather urgent."

"Then come on, son. Let's talk. I could do with a cup of tea."

They disappeared into Merlin's office and I tried to get back to work, but I was troubled by what Owen had told me. We'd had intruders before—I'd caught one myself. The thought of one of our employees working against us was even more disturbing. What MSI stood for and what Idris stood for were polar opposites. We were all about finding safe ways for magical people to use their powers without revealing themselves to the rest of the world. Idris was all about using that power for domination. Had one of his henchmen managed to get a job here, or had someone at MSI gone to work for him?

About fifteen minutes later, Merlin's door opened and Owen

came out. He still looked troubled, but he flashed me a smile that would have made me lose my balance if I hadn't been sitting down. "I'll see you later," he told me as he left.

Then Merlin appeared in his doorway. "Katie, may I see you for a moment?"

I got up and headed to Merlin's office, a flutter of nervousness forming in my belly. He didn't suspect me, did he? I'd been instrumental in stopping Idris so far, even if I said so myself, and since I was nonmagical, I had no motivation for helping Idris use nonmagical people for his own ends.

"Please, have a seat," Merlin said when I entered his office. He remained standing as I perched on the edge of the sofa. "Mr. Palmer briefed you on the situation, didn't he?"

"Yes. Do you really think we have a spy?"

"It does seem likely."

"Do you know who it is?"

"Not yet. I will talk to Prophets and Lost and see if they have any insight, but it's very likely that this person would be veiled to their vision. No, this will require old-fashioned detective work to find the culprit." He then looked at me long and hard, to the point that I felt like his eyes were boring holes in me. "Katie, I have an assignment for you."

three

I had a feeling I knew what he was going to say, but rather than make a fool of myself by jumping to an assumption, I asked anyway. "An assignment?"

"I'd like you to help me find our spy."

"Me? But I'm not even magical. How am I supposed to track this person down?"

"Any magic a spy uses to conceal his activities will be useless against you. That makes you uniquely qualified for this project."

"And I'm sure he'll know that."

He gave me a sly smile. "Which is why I must ask you to tell no one about this assignment or otherwise give any indication of your task."

I stood up. Pacing seemed like a good way to work off the tension so I wouldn't freak out in front of my boss. "You want me to figure out who our spy is without anyone figuring out what I'm doing? That would make me a spy, and I don't know how to be a spy." Everything I knew about spying I'd learned from watching *Alias,* and I doubted I could solve this by putting on sexy lingerie and a fake accent. Sure, I'd had a few bits of luck that made me look good, like catching an intruder trying to sneak into R&D under cover of invisibility, but that had more to do with being in the right place at the right time with my magical immunity. It wasn't like I'd been out looking for invisible intruders. In fact, I was pretty sure if I'd gone looking for an intruder, I wouldn't have found anything.

I was clueless about surveillance, interrogation, and all that, which seemed pretty crucial for catching a corporate mole. I wasn't devious enough myself to think a step ahead of someone devious enough to do something like spy for the enemy without them figuring out what I was up to. It took all my wits just to keep the secret of my job from my roommates. I wasn't sure I could add another layer to all the secrets I had to keep.

"But you are discerning. You have a way of seeing the truth, magical or otherwise. And I trust you completely. It would hardly do for me to assign someone who might *be* the spy to help *find* the spy, now, would it?"

"That does make sense," I admitted. "But the fact that you trust me doesn't mean I'll actually be any good at this."

"Who else would you have me choose for this task?"

"Well, there's Sam and his security team. Isn't this their job?"

"And everyone knows it's their job. People behave differently when they know they're being investigated. Mr. Palmer, as the spy's apparent target, isn't in the best position to investigate, though he may be helpful to you."

I knew when I'd been beaten. I could keep arguing about this all day or give in now, all with the same outcome. I stopped pacing and folded my arms across my chest. "Do you have any suspects in mind?"

"Everyone in this company is a potential suspect until you have evidence to eliminate them."

"Even you?"

"If you find evidence implicating me, I would prefer that you not dismiss it without investigating further."

I gulped. I wasn't sure how many employees there were in total at MSI, and I doubted I'd met even half of them. My job as the CEO's assistant and head of our marketing efforts gave me some excuse for visiting other departments, but looking casual would be a challenge.

"Okay, then," I said. "I guess I'd better get to work."

"Good luck. Oh, and Miss Chandler? I'd prefer to keep the presence of the spy a secret for the time being. We may retain some advantage if this person doesn't know he or she has been discovered."

"My lips are sealed."

As I returned to Trix's desk, I mused that Merlin must not be aware of the company grapevine. Someone had to have noticed Owen's angry stalk from his office. That would then be discussed and analyzed, and the conclusion spread around the entire company. I figured I'd be hearing about it by quitting time.

It turned out that I'd underestimated the grapevine.

I'd barely seated myself in Trix's chair—which wasn't too comfortable for someone who wasn't hovering above it—when a voice startled me. "Lunch?" it asked.

I looked up to see Ari. "Sure. Just a sec. I'd better check the boss's calendar."

"Ah, they've got you filling in for Trix, huh?"

"Yeah. Do you know what's wrong with her or how she's doing?"

"Broken heart," she said, rolling her eyes. "She and that Pippin guy, the sprite park ranger, had a falling-out over the weekend. I imagine they'll patch things up by next weekend, but for now she's wallowing in her misery and said her eyes were too red and puffy for her to come to work."

"Poor thing. I probably ought to check on her."

"She'll be fine. I'm not sure she wants to talk about it yet. When she comes back to work, she'll want to discuss it in great detail, so you'd better save it for then."

"It looks like he doesn't have anything major scheduled for a while, so I can probably get away," I said, getting up. "I'll tell him I'm stepping out. Will I need my coat?"

"Nah, we've snagged a conference room and we can zap you something."

I stuck my head in Merlin's open door and said, "I'll be at lunch for a while. Is that okay?"

He looked up from the book he was reading—*Who Moved My Cheese?,* and if anyone needed a guide on coping with major changes, it would be Merlin—and said, "I think that sounds like a very good idea. You're lunching with other employees, I presume?"

"Yes, I am." It dawned on me that with this assignment, I'd never be truly off-duty. I'd have to keep my eyes and ears open even while I had lunch with my friends.

We met up with another member of our group, Isabel, the Personnel secretary, in an empty conference room. Isabel greeted me with a huge hug, like she hadn't seen me in months. The hug nearly cut off my breathing and circulation. Isabel was quite large—as in probably part giant. "What'll you have for lunch, Katie?" she asked.

"The usual," I said, taking a seat.

There was a zapping sound and a sandwich, a small bag of chips, and a cup full of what I knew would be Diet Dr Pepper appeared on the table in front of me. Two more zaps, and the others had created their own lunches.

There were a few perks to working for a magical company. Getting lunch to order was one of them. When someone at MSI said they were zapping some lunch, they weren't talking about a microwave.

I steeled myself to be quizzed about my date with Ethan, but Ari surprised me by asking, "What was Owen's deal this morning? He went tearing out of R and D like there was a crisis. I can only assume he was heading upstairs."

And thus the rumor mill began turning. I knew his actions wouldn't have gone unnoticed.

I gave what I hoped looked like a casual shrug. "Who knows? He just wanted to see the boss. You know Owen. He probably translated something exciting and had to share with the one other person in the company who would be as excited as he was."

Ari shook her head. "No, it wasn't his 'Eureka' look. He looked upset. But he did go talk to the boss?"

Damn. I'd confirmed that. As vague as I was, I hadn't been vague enough. "Yeah, but he seemed okay when he left."

"Interesting," Ari said, then took a bite of her sandwich.

"You guys see all the good stuff," Isabel said with a sigh. "Nothing interesting ever happens in Personnel." That "nothing interesting" meant Isabel had plenty of time to talk to people during the day, and as the one who handled all the employment paperwork, she knew everyone in the entire company. Now that she knew about Owen's attack of alarm that morning, I had no doubt that it would already be an old story by the end of the day.

I made a mental note to try talking to Owen about being a little more discreet, but the problem was that he so seldom made any kind of display about anything, the least little show of emotion was enough to set tongues wagging. If he'd been frowning slightly and walking a little faster than normal, his co-workers would have noticed it.

"And how was your big date?" Isabel asked.

"It was nice. We went to a wine dinner. Very classy." I left out the part about foiling a magical scheme. That would raise the juice level a bit too much. An uneventful date was less likely to be the lead story on the office grapevine.

"Somebody likes you," Ari singsonged. "Those things aren't cheap. He shelled out mucho bucks for that date."

I supposed that was true, but I tried not to rate dates based on how expensive they were. "It was very nice of him, then," I said neutrally before taking a bite of my sandwich.

Ari then spent the rest of the lunch hour regaling us with stories about her weekend. I could hardly believe she'd managed to fit in her visit to Bloomingdale's to interrupt my shopping amid all that activity, but I didn't have Ari's energy level.

While she talked, I tried to evaluate my friends as possible suspects. I hated thinking of them that way, but I knew I'd feel better if I could eliminate them from the list. Ari worked in R&D, but in the practical magic division rather than in theoretical magic with Owen, which still gave her access to the entire secured department. I got the impression that she had a thing for Owen, but he showed no signs of returning her interest. She had a devious streak and was the person to go to if you wanted a creative revenge plan against a cheating boy-friend. If she'd made a pass at Owen and he'd rejected her or—more likely—hadn't even noticed, there was no telling what she might do to get back at him.

But she was also a little on the flighty side—and not just because of the wings. I couldn't imagine her being driven enough to care about corporate espionage. Work to her was a way to earn money for going out and having a good time. She lacked the motivation and determina-tion for spying. The only way I could imagine her breaking into Owen's office was if she was looking for personal information or blackmail ma-terial to force him to ask her out. I couldn't eliminate her entirely as a suspect, but she wasn't high on my list.

Isabel was at the same time the perfect spy and the worst possible spy. She knew everyone in the company and everything that happened there, but she also couldn't resist telling everyone everything she knew. If she'd been the spy, she'd have already let it slip to at least one person that she'd been in Owen's office because she'd have to tell all about anything else interesting she found while she was spying. She was also the size of a pro-football linebacker, so she wasn't exactly in-conspicuous.

As Isabel zapped the remaining food wrappers and cups out of ex-istence, I reflected that musing wasn't going to get me anywhere. I had to find a reason to get out and about within the company to figure out what was going on, or my suspicions were likely to be based strictly on my personal feelings.

I'd barely made it back to my desk when Rod Gwaltney, the head of Personnel and Owen's lifelong best friend, stepped off the escalator and approached the desk, a stack of papers in his arms. "Hi!" I greeted him. "You're a few minutes early, but I can see if he's ready."

He flopped into the chair in front of Trix's desk and draped one leg casually over the arm. "I don't mind waiting. It gives us a chance to chat."

"Chat about what?"

"Just wanted to see if you'd heard anything interesting. Word has it that Owen's desk was broken into over the weekend."

Seriously, the CIA should have been recruiting at MSI. Finding one spy in a company full of them was going to be nearly impossible. Guiltily, I tried to measure Rod as a suspect. Deception was a way of life for him, given that he constantly wore an illusion that made him look outrageously handsome to those who were affected by magic while he put no effort into his real appearance. I generally considered that a harmless quirk, though. He might know everyone in the company, but he didn't have full access. Then again, that lack of access often irked him, and he'd shown signs of being jealous of Owen.

"Where'd you hear that?" I asked casually, with what I hoped was the right hint of curiosity. Whether or not he was a suspect, he was a good source of company information.

He waved a hand. "Oh, around."

"Did they steal anything?"

"That's what I was going to ask you." He gave me a grin that made him look appealing in spite of his greasy hair, bad skin, and unfortunate features. If he'd do something about his hair and skin and smile like that more often, he might be even more successful with women with his real face than he was with the handsome illusion and attraction spells he used. Or maybe not. He averaged about three dates per weekend; it would be hard to top that. I knew I'd find him more appealing without the façade, even if I only saw the real Rod no matter what he did. As long as I knew he was hiding himself, I had a hard time taking him seriously as a man. His spectacular social life was a sign that I was one of very few women who remained immune to his magic.

"Why would I know anything about someone breaking into Owen's office?" I asked with my own attempt at an innocence illusion. Since I didn't have access to magic, I suspected it wasn't very convincing.

"Because I heard he came to talk to the boss about it, which means he'd have talked to you."

I shrugged. "I don't have anything to tell you. Maybe you should ask him."

He laughed. "We are talking about the same Owen here, right? You can't get anything out of him that he doesn't want to give. He only clams up tighter. I've known him since he was four, and he's always been like that. All I know is that he's put some even stronger wards around his office. Nobody gets in there without being cleared. Next thing you know, he'll be taking DNA samples from anyone who enters."

"Seems like a reasonable precaution for these times."

He leaned forward, putting his elbows on Trix's desk and giving me a puppy-dog-eye kind of look that I was sure was particularly effective when combined with his favorite attraction spell. "Come on, Katie, surely you know something. Owen sometimes even talks to you, which is more than anyone else gets from him."

Fortunately for me and unfortunately for him, I was immune to both the spell and the puppy-dog eyes. "Sorry," I said with a shrug.

He turned off the charm like it came with a switch. "Oh well, I thought it was worth a shot."

"Why are you so worried about this?" I asked him.

"I guess it's old instincts kicking in. I always tried to look after Owen when we were kids, and I'm still doing it even though he's perfectly capable of taking care of himself. To be honest, he was when he was a kid, too. Bigger kids only messed with him once."

"I think these days we all need to look after each other."

"You're probably right about that. You'll let me know if you hear anything?"

I couldn't promise that without breaking my word to Merlin. "I'll keep you posted," I said instead, hoping that was vague enough for my conscience. I hated having to keep secrets from people, but I was getting better and better at it. If you can keep the secret about magic from the rest of the world, hiding a few things from your coworkers isn't that hard.

Merlin came out of his office. "Oh, good, Mr. Gwaltney, you're here. Please come in." Rod gathered his stack of papers, gave me a wink, then headed into Merlin's office. As I watched the door shut behind him, I considered the preposterous idea of Merlin as a suspect. He might have said he wasn't above suspicion, but the idea of him teaming up with Idris was beyond my comprehension. I wouldn't worry about him unless there was evidence.

On the other hand, his response to the situation was to assign a novice to investigate, and he probably had more access to the headquarters than anyone. He also lived in an apartment in the office building, so he was there all the time, even over the weekend when Owen's desk had been broken into. I shook my head. No, there was no way Merlin could be in on this. Idris had little respect for him, and quite frankly, I doubted Idris was a good enough actor to fake that. If I couldn't trust Merlin, I might as well quit my job and practice saying, "Do you want fries with that?"

Merlin's office door opened, and he and Rod emerged, Rod still carrying that stack of papers. "I'll get these distributed immediately, sir," Rod said.

Merlin nodded, then blinked and looked at me. A light sparked in his eyes, then he turned to Rod and said, "I believe I'll have Miss Chandler take care of the distribution. The message will have more authority coming directly from my office."

"Distribute what?" I asked.

"It's a document for the various department and division heads," Rod explained, "outlining company policy on intellectual property and the like—so we can avoid future Idris-like incidents. We enchanted it so that signing it is binding, which means it has to be distributed in person."

Right away, I knew what Merlin was up to. He was giving me an excuse to snoop around the company. "I'd be glad to help," I said, giving them both my perkiest smile. "Do I need to get someone to cover the desk here?"

"I don't anticipate your brief absence causing any problems," Merlin said, looking satisfied with himself.

Rod handed the stack of documents over to me and said, "Thanks for the help, Katie. I owe you one." And I owed Merlin one for setting that up so neatly. Then again, I shouldn't have been surprised. He'd apparently been quite good with the scheming back in his day.

I hadn't had to hand-deliver a memo since the dark days when I worked for Mimi, my evil boss at my old, nonmagical job. I hadn't minded it much then, for it gave me a chance to escape from my desk for a while. This particular mission was something else entirely. I felt almost dirty and dishonest, going around the company under false pretenses with the intent of scoping everything out. I had to remind myself that catching the spy was important and that honest people had nothing to hide.

I decided to start at the lowest level and work my way to the top. The design department was in the basement, but it was empty at the moment, not that I expected the company's designer to leave his video games long enough to spy on anyone. On the ground level, I dropped the memo off in the security office to the side of the foyer. Sam was probably outside in his guard position, but I couldn't make myself consider him a suspect. He was too busy moonlighting as a security guard at various churches around town to have time for corporate espionage. He was also intensely protective of the company. There would have to be a literal smoking gun to make me suspect him.

Next, I headed up to my old department, Verification. Just approaching that doorway made my stomach knot up. I hadn't been back since I'd been promoted to my current job, and I doubted anyone there would be happy to see me. I had good reason to look for suspects there, too, for a magical immune would be able to get past any wards. Gritting my teeth, I pushed the door open. "Gregor! I have a memo for you from the boss!" I said, heading straight for the department head's desk.

Even though he was in charge of the verification department, where most of the company's immunes worked, Gregor was magical. He was definitely on my list of suspects because he had a known grudge against Owen. He used to have Owen's job until an accident turned him into an ogre. He still tended to turn green and grow horns when his anger got out of control. That proved he had motive and a history of tinkering with questionable magic.

He barely looked up as he took the memo from me. "Do you need a response right away?" he asked.

"No, just sign it and return it when you get a chance. You will note that it is binding."

He groaned. "Of course it is." He put the memo aside on his desk. "Is there anything else?"

"No, not really. I was just wondering how things are going."

"Same as usual," he grunted. There were fewer verifiers working in the department than there had been a couple of months ago. They'd been scattered throughout the company to better spot any magical irregularities. That also meant they weren't too carefully supervised. Even so, I could probably eliminate most of them as suspects because spying was too much like real work for their tastes. They had a cushy gig and they knew it, so I doubted they'd do anything to upset that.

There was only one verifier I was suspicious about, and fortunately, she wasn't in the office. When I worked in Verification, Kim had been overly ambitious, taking far too many notes about what was going on in the company and showing far too much interest in company happenings. Her goal had been to get the job as Merlin's assistant, and she'd never gotten over me being appointed to that post. I'd been dreading running into her ever since I got the job she'd been scheming for.

As luck would have it, she came into the office just as I was leaving. "Kim!" I greeted her. If I acted friendly, maybe she wouldn't claw my eyes out, I hoped.

She gave me a look so frosty it made me wish I'd brought a coat on my errand. "What brings you back here?"

I waved my stack of memos. "Just delivering memos for the boss. At least I didn't have to type them this time." I hoped making the job sound like menial secretarial work would leave her a little less bitter. Her eyes narrowed and I waited for her to say something cutting, but she just headed over to Gregor's desk. Relieved, I left the office before she changed her mind and started a catfight.

Next, I headed to R&D. If my steps were lighter and my spirits boosted, it had nothing at all to do with seeing Owen. He must have known I was coming, in that uncanny way he had, for the usually locked door opened easily for me. I didn't know the head of the R&D department or even where his office was, but Owen was head of the theoretical magic section of R&D, so he was sure to be able to point me in the right direction.

Both Owen and his assistant, Jake, were at work in the theoretical magic lab. They had a giant book open on the table and a much-erased series of words on a nearby whiteboard. Owen said a few words that sounded like nonsense to me, there was a tingle of power in the air, then Jake yelped and dropped his clipboard.

Owen winced. "Sorry about that. And it looks like that one didn't work." He erased some of the words on the whiteboard, then bent over to look at the book again. "Hmm, maybe they spelled it wrong, and this is what they meant." He wrote a different series of foreign words on the whiteboard while Jake, still shaking his right hand, bent to retrieve his clipboard.

Jake was probably the one person other than Owen who stood a chance of getting into Owen's office without looking suspicious. He'd struck me as fairly loyal to his boss, but that could have been an act. On the other hand, he'd been the one to find the first commercial spell Idris had produced and had brought it to Owen for testing. Would he have helped like that if he'd been working for Idris? But that also meant he tended to frequent places where dark spells were sold. I left him in the "possible" column. His proximity to Owen made it too dangerous to write him off so soon.

I cleared my throat. "Before you zap Jake again, I need your help with something."

"Of course. What is it?" Owen asked, re-capping his dry erase marker and looking over at me with a welcoming smile that made my knees feel a little watery.

"Memo for the department head, from the boss. I don't think I know where his office is."

"I'll get it to him."

"It's no problem. I can deliver it myself if I know where to go."

"Let me take a look at it." His tone had gone from casual to the least bit commanding, so I handed over the memo. As he read it, I tried to contemplate the unthinkable. Owen had been the victim in this situation, and he was the one who'd reported the crime. That would generally leave him above suspicion. Then again, that sort of thing happened on TV all the time, where the killer was the one who "found" the body and reported the crime. Maybe he'd reported this so he could go on spying and we wouldn't suspect him.

I shook my head. It couldn't be Owen, and not just because he was so incredibly cute. Idris really hated him, so even if Owen went crazy and decided to become a spy, Idris would probably laugh in his face. I'd seen how freaked out Owen got over the idea of dark magic. He wouldn't go near the stuff, and that was what Idris was all about. For the time being, I put Owen in the "safe" column.

He finished reading the memo and looked up at me. "It's enchanted, isn't it? A binding spell, it seems, jointly cast by Rod and Mr. Mervyn."

"Yeah. How'd you know?"

He shrugged. "Magic has fingerprints. I'll get this to the director."

"Thanks," I said, wondering if I should be suspicious about his evasion.

I must not have hid it well, for he grinned and said, "Don't worry, there's nothing sinister going on. Mr. Lansing tends to avoid people in general. Almost everything for him goes through me."

"Oh. Okay. Well, thanks again. I guess I'd better finish my rounds."

As I left, I heard another zap behind me, followed by another yelp from Jake. "I don't think that's it either, boss," Jake whispered painfully.

On my way out, I was surprised to find Sam entering the department. "What's up, Sam?" I asked.

"Hey, dollface, nothing much. Just doing a routine security sweep of the department." He winked as he said the word "routine."

"Probably a good idea in these times. I left a memo for you in the security office."

"Thanks for the heads-up."

My final stop was the sales department. As far as I was concerned, the entire sales department was suspicious, but that probably had more to do with my personal experience with salespeople than with any actual evidence. Before I moved to New York, I ran the business end of my family's farm and ranch supply store, and I'd dealt with more than my fair share of slick sales guys. The MSI sales force seemed like good people/elves/gnomes/whatever, but they came and went often and interacted with a variety of people outside the company. As long as they could get the information from inside MSI, they could sell it to almost anyone on the outside without looking the least bit suspicious.

Most of the sales beings I knew were out of the office as I passed through the department. I went straight to the office of Mr. Hartwell, the director of sales, whom I was convinced was a giant Ken doll brought to life. He gave the memo a cursory glance, then put it aside as he said, "We need to have a meeting about marketing soon. It's time to shake things up again."

"Of course. Let me know and I'll put it on my calendar." While I kept up a cheerful front, I groaned inwardly. Great, more to worry about. I had my usual job, and now this spying thing, and then I'd have to do more marketing. I was going to be busy. Then again, marketing would give me more excuses for investigating. But I could put him to work, too. "Did you get my e-mail about the winery?" I asked.

"Yes, I did. We have them on record as a customer in the past, but they dropped off about a year ago. I'll get Corporate Sales on it to see what happened. It sounds like they found another supplier."

I knew who that other supplier might be, and it wasn't good. "Please let me know what you find out," I said.

I returned to Merlin's office suite and found myself wondering about Trix as I looked at her desk. She had access to Merlin, which meant she had similar access to the rest of the company through her association with him. She was also out sick on the day Owen discovered the spying. I'd seen her Saturday, and she hadn't looked particularly brokenhearted then, but she could have fought with Pippin on

Saturday night or Sunday and still not felt well enough to be at work Monday. I left her in the "possible" column until I had actual evidence, but I reluctantly admitted that I needed to check out her story.

Merlin's office door swung open, and he and his latest victim emerged. The chairman of the magical committee for something-or-other didn't look quite as shell-shocked as the Amalgamated Neuromancy guy had that morning, so he must have been cooperating. He and Merlin shook hands, then Merlin approached Trix's desk once his visitor was gone.

"How's it going?" I asked him. "Are we getting allies?"

He sighed. "They're reluctant to accept change, to acknowledge that the cheese has moved." Oh boy, he was now quoting from the business books. This was going to be fun. "I'm having difficulty persuading them of the threat inherent in one lone renegade. They seem to have forgotten the last few lone renegades who caused serious trouble in the magical community. They hide their heads in the sand until the danger is so dire they can no longer ignore it. Arthur was the same way about Guinevere and Lancelot and about Mordred."

It still blew my mind that he was talking about people I'd always considered fictional characters as people he knew and remembered. "Human beings haven't changed all that much in the past thousand or so years," I said.

"And how is your investigation coming?"

"It's difficult," I admitted reluctantly. "It's all rumor and personal impression at this stage. But if you wanted the fact that we might have a spy to remain secret, I'm afraid you're going to be disappointed. It seems like the whole company knows, or will know before long."

He rubbed his beard thoughtfully. "Now, that I find interesting. You, Mr. Palmer, and I are the only ones who know the full details— and the spy, of course. I haven't told anyone, I can assume you haven't told anyone, and I suspect Mr. Palmer has remained as guarded as ever."

"I think most of it is guesswork. Someone saw Owen tear out of R and D, and there's already some worry that we could have intruders or spies. Next thing you know, word has spread around the company that someone's spying, and they broke into Owen's office. Finding a real spy when everyone else is already doing their own spying is going to be nearly impossible."

"This is only the first day of your investigation," he said kindly.

The intercom squawked just then. "Katie-Bug, you there?" said Sam's voice.

"Yeah, I'm here. What is it, Sam?"

"I'm at R and D. You'd better get the boss down here, pronto."

Merlin and I looked at each other, then he headed toward the escalator. Without waiting for an invitation, I got up and followed him. I'd been there no more than fifteen minutes earlier. What could have happened?

Normally, the door into the research and development department was secured, with a hand ID and magic spell required for access. Even I couldn't get into that department unless I was accompanied by an employee or Owen was expecting me. But now the door was wide open. Sam and a white-faced Owen stood in front of the door. "What is it, Sam?" Merlin asked.

"The security to this department has been totally short-circuited. Kaput. It looks like it works the same way as always, but anyone could have walked in at any time."

"How long has it been like this?"

Sam shrugged as expressively as a stone creature could. "No telling. I wouldn't have even discovered it today if the kid here hadn't asked me to do a security sweep of the department." He indicated Owen with one wing.

"I thought it was a reasonable precaution," Owen said softly.

"And it's good that you took that precaution," Merlin said. "Can you fix it, Sam?"

"Sure. No problem. But first, we ought to run a similar sweep on the rest of the building."

Merlin nodded. "Do it."

"That would explain how the spy got in, huh, boss?" Sam said as he went back to fiddling with wires.

"It also means we can't narrow the suspects down to only people who have access to R and D," I remarked. Great, my job had just become even more difficult.

"Was this done magically or mechanically?" Merlin asked Sam.

"Maybe a little of both," the gargoyle replied. "I'll get someone down here to check people one by one as they enter. Then you'd better seal off the department for the night."

"I'll make sure everyone gets out on time tonight, then we'll shut down," Owen said.

While they were talking, I glanced over my shoulder at the corridor, then did a double take. I touched Merlin's elbow and said softly, "Somehow, I don't think our spy is a secret anymore."

four

A crowd had gathered, both in the outside hallway and in the R&D corridor. I noticed Jake peering wide-eyed over Owen's shoulder. Ari hovered over the group clustered in the R&D corridor, looking like someone who had slowed down to ogle the five-car pileup on the freeway.

In the outside hallway, there was an even larger crowd. It was as if someone had gotten on the company intercom and announced that there was free food outside R&D. Gregor and Kim were there from Verification. Minerva Phelps of Prophets and Lost stood in front of the group, like she'd been the first arrival. Dortmund, the accounting gnome, was elbowing people in the knees as he worked his way to the front.

If Merlin had been any other boss, he would have said, "Don't you people have jobs?" and sent them scurrying to stir up more rumors based on half-truths and guesses. Instead, he faced the crowd and said in a commanding voice, "It appears that we have a traitor in our midst.

Please be aware of the activity around you and report anything suspicious to Miss Chandler, who will be managing the investigation. Now you may return to your work. The situation is under control."

When Merlin went into ancient-sorcerer-who-built-an-empire mode, people tended to listen, so the crowd dispersed rapidly. When they were gone, I said, "I guess we're not investigating covertly anymore."

He sighed, and he was once again a very elderly man in a difficult position. "It didn't seem likely that we could maintain any secrecy, so I felt it best to adapt our strategy. You will surely be overwhelmed with reports of suspicious behavior, but it's possible that a germ of truth will be within. You'll have to use your discernment to sort through it all wisely."

"So you're not going to reassign the investigation to people who know what they're doing, now that we've been outed?" I asked hopefully.

"I see no need to make any changes at this point. Please continue your efforts."

I could see already that I'd have to sit down with Isabel to get the scoop on the entire company so I'd be able to tell who had a grudge against whom and for what reason. Without being up on all the dirty laundry, it would be impossible to sort the malicious reports from the possible facts. Then again, there was always the possibility that someone who had a reason for a grudge might be telling the truth.

This was a whole new kind of verification, and it had nothing to do with seeing past magic. It would take seeing the truth in each person's heart and soul.

Piece of cake. Yeah, right. I wondered if it was too late to opt out of my part in the saving-the-world-from-bad-magic gig.

By the time I got back to my own office, I had twelve e-mails and four voice mails. I checked to make sure there was nothing urgent in the mix, but they were all tips. I saved the voice mails and transferred the e-mails into a new folder I created for the investigation. It was almost five and I didn't feel like I could face sorting through all that negativity. It could wait until morning.

I moved my things from Trix's desk back to my own office, then got my coat and bag and headed out. I was surprised to bump into Owen in the lobby. "I don't remember the last time I saw you going home this early. I mean, other than when you'd had your shoulder ripped to shreds," I remarked.

"I suppose one good thing to come of this is the fact that sealing off the department means I have to go home on time."

"You could probably use the rest anyway."

Then we reversed our morning routine, walking to the subway station from the office, side by side and almost in step. "So you got the ugly job of sorting through all this," he said.

"Yeah. I wonder what I did to deserve it."

"You've got a level head and a knack for seeing through all kinds of illusions," he replied.

"I was being sarcastic."

"I wasn't. I think you're probably best for the job. You don't have any real ax to grind, unlike most of us who've worked there a long time."

I looked at him suspiciously. "You have grudges and enemies and all that, too?"

"Let's just say that there are people I don't trust. I wouldn't go out of my way to hurt them, and I wouldn't frame them. But I wouldn't be sad to see evidence pointing at them, and I might not be as discerning as I should be at deciding whether to believe that evidence." He shrugged. "The problem with a company this old and this stable is that not only have most of us been working there our entire adult lives, but our parents and grandparents also worked there. Some of these grudges and feuds go back generations."

"It's nice to hear that the company man isn't entirely a thing of the past."

"When you're dealing with inherited job skills, it's more likely. I suppose you could inherit a head for figures or a talent for art or music, but when the skill that makes you right for a job is a genetic trait, you get multiple generations in the same job. I'm one of the few outsiders in the company in a job that nobody in my family had before me. At least, as far as I know."

I remembered that he'd said he was an orphan who didn't know who his parents were. Although I was curious about his background, I didn't know if that was a touchy subject for him, so instead I said, "I guess you, Merlin, and I are in the same boat, then. He's not technically an outsider, since he was the founder, but he doesn't really know anyone else in the company."

"That's one of the reasons he was brought back. We didn't know if we could trust our previous leadership. We needed someone above suspicion with no ties to the current employees."

I was dying to ask him what he meant by that, but we'd reached the subway station, where a platform full of rush-hour commuters wasn't the best place to talk about magic.

I used to hate riding the subway at rush hour, but since I'd started commuting with Owen, I'd learned to like it a lot better. He could reach the overhead bar, and since I couldn't, he'd hold me steady with an arm around my waist. I had a feeling that was the only way I'd ever get contact that intimate with him, so I had to enjoy it where I found it. Standing like that with him made me remember every romance-novel cliché I'd ever read about weak knees and pounding pulses, while it didn't seem to affect him at all. Reason number seven-hundred sixty-eight why I was pretty sure he didn't feel about me the way I felt about him.

I felt a pang of disappointment when we lurched to a stop at the Union Square station and shoved our way to the doors. My daily time with Owen had nearly come to an end. I'd have to wait until the next morning when I emerged from my building to see him again.

Oh boy, did I have it bad. I thought I'd talked myself out of the crush that ate Cleveland, but no matter how many pep talks I gave myself about how an ultrapowerful wizard of mysterious parentage might make a great fantasy-novel hero but would probably make a lousy boyfriend for a girl like me, and no matter how many clues I found that proved he saw me as nothing more than a friend, the next time I saw him, it started all over again. If I didn't know for sure that magic didn't work on me, I'd have suspected him of using one of Rod's attraction spells.

We finally came aboveground and I took a deep breath of fresh (or what passed for fresh in the city) air. I started to head for the crosswalk, but Owen paused. He frowned as if in thought, then said, "Do you have any plans for dinner?"

"Not that I can think of. Both my roommates said they had late meetings this evening, so I'm on my own."

"After today, I don't even have the energy to throw something in the microwave. Do you want to get some dinner?"

My heart did back handsprings worthy of the Olympic gymnastics team while my brain reminded it that this didn't sound like a date. It was merely two single people who didn't want to eat alone. "Sure," I said with what I hoped looked like a casual shrug instead of a nervous spasm.

He smiled and his blue eyes lit up. "I know a great little diner down the street. It's nothing fancy, just good food and a lot of variety. I've been eating there for years, and I haven't had anything bad yet."

You could probably poison Owen and he wouldn't complain, but I'd also learned that he didn't give a compliment he didn't mean wholeheartedly, so I said, "I'll take that as a recommendation. It sounds wonderful."

He led the way across Fourteenth and then down a block to a little corner diner. It would have been nice if he'd held my hand, taken my arm, or even put a guiding hand to my back, but this was really the first time we'd been together in a nonwork capacity, so I reminded myself not to let my imagination run away with me. This was not a date.

The waitress who met us at the door appeared to know Owen, for she greeted him like an old friend. "Well, hey there, handsome. I thought you'd abandoned me," she teased.

He turned crimson and didn't meet her eyes as he said, "I haven't been eating out much lately."

"As long as you're not cheating on me with some other waitress. Would a booth work for you tonight?" she flirted.

"That'll be fine, thanks," he said mildly, his color gradually returning to normal.

The waitress put a little extra wiggle in her walk as she led us to our table. She was old enough to be Owen's mother, but he still seemed to have the same effect on her as he had on me. She plunked napkin-wrapped rolls of silverware and laminated menus in front of us with a warm "Here you go," then got a pad out of her apron pocket and asked, "Now, what can I get you to drink?"

We both asked for water, and I was surprised that she was as friendly to me as she was to Owen. Maybe she was merely enjoying having a good-looking man around without getting possessive about him. I liked her better already.

"You really must eat here all the time," I teased Owen as soon as she was out of earshot. "You've definitely made an impression." I was rewarded with a slight pinkening of his ears as he kept his eyes focused on his menu. Someday I'd have to catalog his various kinds of blushes and see if there was a correlation to the kind of embarrassment. "Any recommendations?" I asked.

"As I said, everything I've tried has been good. I like their burgers. The Greek food's good. The turkey and stuffing remind me of Thanksgiving at home."

There was yet another tantalizing mention of home. I was dying to ask more, but I'd have to know more about him to be able to ask him more about himself. From what little I knew of Owen, I had a feeling he'd tell me what he wanted to tell me, regardless of what questions I asked.

I chose to start at a broader level. We could get more personal later in the meal. "There's a café a lot like this in my hometown, except it's only open for breakfast and lunch, and the waitresses call you 'hon' and 'shug.' "

"There seems to be a place like this in just about every small town in America," he replied, his eyes still on his menu.

"Are you from a small town, too?" Now we were getting somewhere.

"I'm not sure where I was born, and I have the vaguest memories of living in a city when I was very young, but I grew up in a tiny old village up the Hudson."

The part of me that harbored the killer crush gloated at my more rational side as one of the possible barriers between us melted away. I'd thought of us as so radically different that we'd never be able to find common ground, but if he was a small-town boy, then on some level we might have a similar background.

"I imagine your definition of 'old' in this part of the world is different from mine," I said.

"Pre–Revolutionary War," he said with a nod.

"Yeah, very different. My hometown dates from not much more than a hundred years ago."

"These days, it's a suburb of New York, about an hour away by train, but it used to be a farming community. They still have a colonial farm nearby for the tourists."

"With the land prices around here, you probably can't afford to farm." Even as I kept up the small talk, I wanted to bang my head against the table. Did he even know what he was doing when he neatly deflected anything that might become personal, or was it an old habit? Or was he hiding something?

The waitress returned with two glasses of water. She set them down on the table in front of us, then got out her pad and pen once more. "Ready to order?"

Owen nodded toward me. "I'll have the bacon cheeseburger," I said.

"You want the full plate with fries and slaw?"

"Yes, please."

She turned to Owen, who said, "I'll have the same."

She noted this in her pad and said, "It'll be right out."

I felt like our earlier conversation had lost its momentum, if it ever had any to begin with. While I was still trying to think of another topic, he surprised me by starting one of his own. "You never did tell me how your date with Ethan went, other than that it was nice and that something odd happened. Where did he take you? He said he had something different planned."

My heart and my head went to war over what this question meant. Was this relationship recon, his attempt to see where my current relationship (if you could call it that) stood so he'd know when or if to make his move? Or was it casual interest because two of his friends were going out together and he was curious how it went?

While the battle raged within me, I decided to just answer instead of analyzing it to death. "He took me to a wine dinner, one of those things where they create courses to go with certain wines from a particular vineyard. It was interesting. The food was good, but I don't know enough about wine to say much about that."

"And what was the odd part?"

"I'm a total lightweight. I almost never have more than one glass of wine at any one time, and they served a glass with each course. I tried to only drink half a glass each time, but after five courses that's still a lot of wine."

"So you were a bit toasted," he said with a teasing grin. Even if it was at my expense, I enjoyed the sight too much to complain.

"No 'a bit' about it. And here's where it gets interesting."

He leaned back against the booth, now looking at me directly, still grinning. "Interesting, how?" He raised one eyebrow.

I glanced around to see how close any other diners were to us then leaned forward across the table. He got the hint and leaned forward until there was only a small space separating us. "I was the most sober person there, other than Ethan. It turned out to be a magical winery," I whispered. "The wine was enchanted, so everyone else there was even drunker than I was. After dinner, they passed out order forms so people could buy the wines, and it seemed like they were using a variation on that control spell to make people order wine at what Ethan said were outrageously inflated prices."

"So they were using a wine dinner as a cover for a magical scam?" He managed to scowl, look incredulous, and smile all at the same time.

"Yeah. So Ethan and I called them on it. I don't think they expected to find a couple of immunes in the party. He offered to fix their 'typos.'"

"Did you tell the boss?"

"Yeah, and Sales says they stopped being an MSI customer about a year ago."

"You think the spell was a variation on Idris's control spell?"

"I'm no expert, remember, but I did feel power in use, and there was something about it that looked similar, but it was also different. It didn't seem to be nearly as strong as the one I watched you test."

He nodded and frowned. "Interesting. I wonder if there's a connection. It's worth investigating."

"Are you ready to eat, or am I interrupting a private moment here?" The waitress's voice startled both of us. Owen blushed bright pink and my cheeks felt uncomfortably warm as we moved back so she could set down our plates. "You two enjoy. Let me know if you need anything else," she said.

"So, what happened after you foiled their scam?" he asked as he struggled to get catsup out of the bottle onto his fries. His injured arm must have still been bothering him, because he wasn't very effective at either holding the bottle steady or hitting it, so I reached across the table, took it from him, and poured catsup for him as I answered.

"I don't remember much else. It got blurry after that point. I remember being in a cab, then Ethan carried me out of the cab but woke me up before we had to climb the stairs. One of my roommates made sure he hadn't taken advantage of my condition, and that was pretty much it."

After getting enough catsup out for him, I went to work putting some on my own fries. Now that I thought about it, I was surprised that I hadn't heard from Ethan since then. He hadn't had any meetings at MSI, but that hadn't stopped him from dropping by before. He hadn't even called me. I knew guys didn't want to appear too eager by calling too soon, but Ethan hadn't seemed the type for that. Had I put him off with my drunken belligerence?

"It sounds better than your last date with him."

"And that one was no thanks to you." My first date with Ethan had been when Rod and Owen tested him for magical immunity. It got rather weird, to put it mildly. "Why can't I seem to have a social life without work getting in the way?"

"Unfortunately, this isn't the kind of job you can get away from. Once you become part of our world, it's difficult to truly escape from it."

"I notice you left that part out of the company recruiting pitch, along with the part where we have to save the world." He saved himself from having to answer by taking a conveniently timed bite of burger. I picked up a french fry and pushed it around in the pool of catsup on my plate. "That's the part that takes getting used to, the idea that things I do now really make a difference. In my old job I was lucky if anything I did still mattered a week later."

"It's taking some adjusting for me, too. I always hoped I'd make a difference, of course, but I thought my contribution would be hiding in a lab somewhere doing translations and research. I wasn't supposed to be on the front lines."

So our resident superhero was a reluctant one. That was a sobering realization. "I guess we all do our parts, huh?"

"We don't have much choice."

After that, we both concentrated on eating for a while. I had a lot to think about. On one level, I hadn't learned much new about him for my mental fact file other than where he grew up. But on another, it was like I'd gained a whole new insight into his personality.

"It was an interesting day at work, wasn't it?" he said after a while.

"Oh yeah. Was there anything important on those papers?"

"It was something I was working on directly related to the Idris situation. Now, of course, I'll have to go a different direction with it." He shuddered slightly. "I don't like the idea of someone going through my desk. Not that I have much to hide in there, but still . . ."

"It's your space."

He looked me in the eye. "Exactly." He held my glance for a while. This time, I was the one who had to duck and look away.

"You know what's really sad? When my roommates ask me what happened at work today, I'll have to say, 'Nothing interesting.'"

He laughed. "Can you imagine what they'd do if you told them the truth?"

"They'd think I was making things up so my work wouldn't sound too boring. I'm not sure I'd believe it if someone told me these stories."

"I suppose I'm lucky not to have any relationships outside this world. I seldom have anything to hide."

The part of my heart where the crush resided took a victory lap. I hadn't heard any rumors about him dating anyone at the company, and if he didn't have any relationships away from work, that meant he wasn't seeing anyone. Then my brain reminded my heart that he'd said "world," not "work." There were magical people who didn't work at MSI, and he could very well be dating one of them.

"Maybe you've got the right idea, though," he added thoughtfully. "You've got a sense of perspective. This world is all-consuming, and a taste of something normal must help keep you grounded."

I snorted. "If I were any more grounded, they'd have to dig me up."

"And that's what makes you so valuable to us. Are you hungry for dessert?" he continued, totally changing the subject. He had a habit of doing that. "They have the best cheesecake here. It's not chocolate, but it's still good." If he'd learned one thing about me, it was that I had a minor addiction to chocolate. I was flattered that he remembered.

"I'm stuffed," I moaned.

"We could share a slice."

"You're tempting me."

He gave me a mischievous grin and leaned forward. "Rich, creamy cheesecake."

I put my hands over my ears. "Stop it. I give in. We can split a slice."

The waitress came by with her pad handy. Her sixth sense must have been almost as good as Owen's. "Any dessert for you?" she asked.

"We'll split a slice of cheesecake."

"Coffee?"

"Decaf," I said.

"Me, too," Owen added.

"If my thighs are bigger tomorrow, it's your fault," I told him when the waitress left to get our dessert.

"I hope you're not fishing for me to tell you I don't think you're fat."

"Why, do you think I'm fat?"

"No. But you don't need to fish for compliments. Trust me." I wished I knew how to take that.

The waitress quickly returned with a slice of cheesecake, two forks, and two coffees. After one bite of cheesecake I was glad he'd convinced me to try it. I let him have most of it, though. I wasn't as worried about calories as I was about popping a button off my clothes. While he ate, I gathered the nerve to ask a personal question. It seemed a shame to finally be with him away from work and spend the whole time talking about work. But what did you ask a guy like this? "Read any good books lately?" The last book he'd read was probably written in something like Ancient Transylvanian.

"So if your work tends to suck you in and take over your life, what do you do when you're not working at all? Do you ever really get away from it?"

He frowned like he was contemplating the bite of cheesecake he'd just taken, then he took a sip of coffee. Finally he said, "I do the kinds of things anyone else does, I guess. I'll admit to reading work-related material in my spare time, but only because that's what I enjoy reading. Otherwise, I watch baseball, listen to music, go to movies. Mostly quiet things. I don't like noise and crowds, but I sometimes go out with Rod on the rare occasion when he doesn't have a date. Or two."

That didn't give me a lot to go on. He was the most difficult person to get to know that I'd ever met.

"What about you?" he asked.

"About the same as you, I suppose." I hadn't thought about it that way, but my list of outside activities wasn't all that interesting, either. "I do stuff with my roommates. A lot of the time that involves blind dates. Most of the time, I'd rather stay in if they'd let me. I read a lot when I have the chance—nothing literary or good for me, only fun stuff. I go to movies sometimes, but I prefer old movies, the kind that usually aren't at the theater. I cook. That's about it."

"When your work is as exciting as ours is, maybe you need your personal time to be quiet."

The waitress dropped the check on our table as she walked past, and he grabbed it before I had a chance. "This one's on me," he said.

"No, I can pay my part."

He shook his head. "No. I owe you."

"For what?"

"Well, if you don't count saving my life—which I do—I do owe you for a breakfast."

I felt like I should protest more, but I also got the impression I'd never win. I gave a sigh of defeat. "If you insist."

"I do." He grinned. "You should know better than to get in my way."

"Oh, like you could do anything against me?"

"I'm sure I could think of something."

I laughed at the mischievous look on his face. There was something familiar about the way I felt at that moment. It wasn't the crush. It wasn't even like anything I'd felt with a man before. Then I realized that it reminded me of the times when my brothers and I sparred verbally, all in love and fun. Great. Just what I needed, another big brother.

As he walked me home, I realized that if this had been an actual date, it would have been the best date I'd had since I'd moved to New York. Maybe even since before that. I couldn't remember a date where I'd had that much fun, been that at ease with someone.

It hadn't been a date, though, even if he had picked up the check. In spite of all the bonding we'd done, he still didn't come close to touching me—no hand holding or even near-miss brushing of hands as we walked, no arm draped around my shoulders. But did that really matter? I'd had fun. I enjoyed being with him.

When we stopped in front of my building, I said, "Well, thanks for dinner. I'm glad we did that. Otherwise, it was going to be mac and cheese in front of the TV."

"I'm glad you joined me. I think I needed to get out."

There was a long pause. I wondered if I should invite him up. I hoped he was wondering if he should kiss me good night. Before I made a decision about what to do, he said, "See you in the morning," then turned and headed off toward his place. He didn't even try to hug me or shake my hand.

With a deep sigh, I climbed to the third floor. The apartment was still empty when I opened the door. Both roommates must have made their own dinner plans. The light on the answering machine was blinking, so I hit the PLAY button as I removed my coat. "Uh, this message is for Katie," my mother's voice said. Someday maybe she'd get used to newfangled things like answering machines. "This is your mother. I need you to call me as soon as you can. I have big news for you."

five

My mother will wait to tell you about a death in the extended family so it won't ruin your day, and she hates answering machines, so the fact that she'd actually left a message and had said she needed me to call as soon as possible could mean only one thing: a death or serious injury in the immediate family. One of my brothers must have accidentally shot another brother while they were out hunting, or something equally dire.

I wished I'd invited Owen to come up with me so I'd have someone nearby when I got the bad news. My hand shook as I picked up the phone and dialed home. When my mother answered, I could hear a quaver in my voice as I said, "Mom, it's me, Katie."

"Frank! It's Katie!" Her voice sounded like she was talking away from the phone. Then she spoke into the phone. "Hi, honey, that was fast. I wasn't expecting to hear back from you tonight."

"You said to call as soon as possible," I reminded her. The fact that she'd left a message would have made me call back right away. If she just wanted to chat, she'd keep calling over and over again for hours instead of leaving a message. She always said she didn't want to be a bother or make anyone feel obligated to call her back if it wasn't important. "What is it, Mom? What happened?" I asked.

"We have some news for you," she said. She didn't sound grief-stricken, so I allowed myself to relax slightly.

I kicked off my shoes and sat down on the couch. There was no such thing as a short conversation with my mother, so I needed to get comfortable. "What kind of news?" I asked warily. I wouldn't be at all surprised if she told me she'd found an exciting new job for me or the perfect man for me to marry in a nearby town so I could come home from New York right away. My parents weren't thrilled about me being in New York, to put it mildly.

"Good news. We're so excited. Your brother Frank Junior won the Rotary Club raffle at the homecoming game."

"That's nice," I said. It certainly wasn't call-everyone-right-away news. They usually raffled off something like a shotgun or a duck blind.

"It was two round-trip airline tickets to anywhere in the country, and he gave them to your father and me so we could come visit you. Isn't that exciting?"

"Wow," was all I could say—literally. It wasn't that I didn't want to see my parents. I hadn't seen them in a little more than a year, and I still suffered the occasional pang of homesickness. I just wasn't sure I wanted to see them in New York in the middle of everything that was going on.

My parents in New York was a frightening enough idea. They'd never left Texas in their entire lives, as far as I knew. They found Dallas huge and intimidating. I couldn't imagine turning them loose in Manhattan. I wouldn't be able to hand them a subway map and tell them to have fun. I wondered if I could get away with booking them on one of those all-day bus tours that went all over the city—would that look like I was ditching them, or like I was being a dutiful daughter and giving them star treatment? Throw a magical threat into the mix, and things got a little too complicated for me to imagine coping with any degree of sanity.

"She's speechless," my mom said aside to my dad, who usually stood nearby while she talked to me. I didn't know why they didn't get a speakerphone. To me, she said, "Now, don't worry about having to put us up for the week. I know you said your apartment was small. We'll get a hotel."

I knew manners meant I should protest and insist that they stay with us, but with Marcia's sofa bed in the living room pulled out, nearly every square inch of our apartment was full. We might be able to put someone in the bathtub, but that could get awkward unless that person was an early riser. "I'll make reservations for you at a place near here that's not too expensive, but still clean and safe," I said. "When will you be here?"

"She'll find us a hotel," she said to my father before saying to me, "We were planning to be there for Thanksgiving. We can fly up that Monday, then back the next Monday. You don't think it'll be too hard to get a hotel then, do you? I mean, with all the people there for the parade?"

"I don't know, but I'll give it a try." My mind was still buzzing from the idea of my parents coming anywhere near my crazy world. Normal New York would be wild to them. Magical New York would be mind blowing. Not that they'd necessarily see it, but I didn't want to take that chance.

"You probably have to line up really early to see that parade, don't you?"

"I think so. You'll see it better on TV."

"Then it'll be just like home. We can make Thanksgiving dinner at your place for you and Marcia and Gemma. Won't that be fun?"

It did sound fun, in a way. It also sounded like something that could drive me stark raving crazy. I had exactly one week to prepare. Maybe if I got moving on that investigation, I could nail our spy, save MSI once again, and earn myself a day off while my parents were in town. I imagined myself having a burst of insight the next morning, calling a staff meeting, then outlining the evidence that led to the dramatic revelation of the culprit, just like Sherlock Holmes. Unfortunately, I seemed to be more Inspector Clouseau than Sherlock Holmes. At best, I was Jessica Fletcher with a slightly better wardrobe and a lower body count among my friends and neighbors.

"I'll make reservations for you tomorrow," I said. "Then let me know your flight details so I can meet you at the airport."

"Oh, you don't have to go to any bother."

"It's no bother, really," I said. It would be a lot easier to meet them at the airport than to identify them at the morgue or put up MISSING posters about them after they accepted a ride from an unlicensed cabdriver who seemed friendly. I wasn't sure either of my parents had ever been to an airport before, so they wouldn't know the drill.

"I can't wait to see you again, baby," she said. "I've missed you so much."

"I've missed you guys, too. I guess I'll see you next week."

I was still sitting on the sofa in shock when Gemma came home. "I hate dinner meetings," she said as she hung up her coat and scarf. Then she turned and saw me. "What's wrong?"

"My parents are coming for Thanksgiving."

"Then why do you look like they just told you your dog died?"

I shook my head to clear it. Of course, I couldn't explain the full reasoning to Gemma, so she wouldn't be able to understand my worry. "I'm mostly surprised. They spent so much time telling me how awful it would be here that I can't believe they're willing to come here of their own accord. And it's bad timing. I've got a huge project at work, and I can't take time off to show them around."

"I've got some time off next week. I can play tour guide at least one day."

"Really?" Gemma would make a great tour guide, and in spite of the fact that she was unknowingly dating a guy who'd spent decades under a frog enchantment, her world was a lot more normal than mine was.

"Sure. It'll be fun. I love your parents." She grinned suddenly. "I don't suppose your mom is planning to make Thanksgiving dinner, is she?"

"She's already got it planned. She'll die when she sees the kitchen, but she wants the big family gathering."

"Don't get me wrong, your Thanksgiving dinner last year was wonderful, but I still remember that year I came home with you from college for Thanksgiving. Your mom is an amazing cook."

"And she'll be delighted to feed you."

Marcia then came through the door. The starry look in her eyes hinted that her lateness had little to do with a meeting and everything to do with her boyfriend, Jeff, who also had some frogginess in his past. Only he wasn't ever really a frog. He just thought he was for a while.

"Guess who's going to be here for Thanksgiving?" Gemma asked her before she even had her coat off.

"Who?"

"Katie's parents."

Marcia's eyes lit up. "Is Mrs. Chandler cooking Thanksgiving dinner?"

"She plans to," I said. It said something about my mom's cooking that neither roommate had yet asked where my parents were planning to stay. For some of my mom's pumpkin pie, I imagined either one of them might volunteer to sleep in the bathtub. Before they had to offer, I said, "I'll need to make hotel reservations for them. Then I need to see if I can manage any time off. Maybe I can work half days."

"It's a holiday week. Nobody will get any real work done, anyway," Marcia said. "Do you think she'll make that sweet potato stuff with the little marshmallows?"

I was still so preoccupied by the impending parental visit that my heart almost forgot to flutter when I saw Owen waiting in front of my building the next morning. He greeted me with a warm smile, then frowned. "What's wrong?"

"Wrong? Oh, it's nothing. I've just been thinking."

He kept his usual slight distance as he walked alongside me. "About what?"

"My parents told me last night that they're planning to come here for Thanksgiving."

"That's great." Then he hesitated and added, "Isn't it?"

"Yeah. But I'm really busy right now, what with that investigation and all, and I don't know that I can take any extra time off. According to company policy, I'm not even eligible for vacation time yet. But my folks really shouldn't be left on their own in this city, trust me. I'm not sure who'd be in more danger, them or the rest of the city."

"Your boss probably doesn't even know we have a vacation policy," he said with a wry grin. "I'm sure he can be flexible with you. But other than the work issue, you're glad to see your family, aren't you?" He sounded almost concerned.

"Yeah, I'm glad. I'm mostly worried about what they think of the city and my life. They were so worried before I moved here. Part of me is afraid this whole trip is their excuse to drag me back home. It would be a lot easier if I went to visit them."

"Or they could see what you see in the city. They might be proud of you for surviving here, and seeing the reality instead of their fears may make them feel better about you living here."

"You obviously haven't met my parents."

He laughed. "They can't be that bad. All parents worry a little, and their worries are usually a lot worse than the reality could possibly be."

I turned to stare at him. "You mean they're worrying about worse things than me being caught up in a magical war between good and evil, in a company that has an enemy spy in it?" Then I thought for a moment. "Come to think of it, from what I know about my mom, she is worried about worse."

"And it's not like she's going to learn about the magical issues while she's here."

Before I could counter that, I noticed something in the sky, something larger than a pigeon and growing larger as it came closer to us. I grabbed Owen's arm and shoved him out of the way before an ugly half woman/half bird dove at us out of the sky. The last time I'd seen one of those things, it had been digging its claws into Owen's shoulder. The harpy swooped back up to the sky and began another dive.

"What is it?" Owen asked, his voice tense.

"Harpy, I think."

He frowned for a second, then nodded. "Got it." At that moment, the harpy seemed to hit an invisible brick wall in the sky, then fell to the sidewalk with a *splat*. A business-suited commuter casually stepped around the body, then continued on his way, as if dead mythical creatures on the sidewalk were something he encountered every morning. I wondered what he saw instead of seeing a harpy—a pile of trash, maybe? That wouldn't be out of place on a New York sidewalk, but as far as I knew, trash didn't fall from the sky or appear out of thin air. The ability of New Yorkers to focus on their own business and tune out everything else never ceased to amaze me.

I took a deep breath to steady myself. "Okay, that's why I don't want my parents in New York. How do you explain something like that—the street people are breeding with the pigeons?"

"Your parents likely wouldn't see anything extraordinary."

"So, what would they see when something dropped out of the sky and started ripping them to shreds? There's no way for anyone to make that look normal."

He took my arm and steered me back into the flow of pedestrian traffic on the way to the subway station. "I doubt they'd come after your parents. This attack was probably aimed at me, and if I know Phelan Idris, he wants to shake me up more than he wants to hurt me. If I'm thinking about ways to protect the city against harpies, I'm not working on ways to counter his spells."

"He nearly killed you with one of those things the last time," I reminded him.

"It was only a flesh wound. But just in case, I'll talk to Sam about getting a security detail for your parents."

"I know you're trying to help, and I appreciate it, but somehow the thought of a group of gargoyles following my parents around the city isn't what I'd call reassuring."

If the commute was unusual that morning, the office was even weirder. The moment we entered the building, I felt a changed atmosphere. Instead of friendly greetings from co-workers I passed on my way up to my office, there were cold stares. And it wasn't just me. Nobody spoke to Owen, either, and I'd noticed previously that he was generally well respected. Nobody made eye contact with anyone else when they passed in the hall. It was like everyone saw everyone else as a possible traitor. I ducked out of the way when I passed Gregor in the hallway. He was bright green and yelling at someone who was yelling back at him about using the verifiers to his advantage.

Trix was already at her desk when I got to Merlin's office suite. "Are you feeling better?" I asked.

"It's amazing what a ton of chocolate and three back-to-back viewings of *Thelma and Louise* can do for your outlook on life," she said grimly.

"That bad?"

"He filled up my voice mail with apologies."

"Sounds like a positive sign."

"Ari said to let him stew until Thursday, not go out with him this weekend, and then by Monday he'd be eating out of my hand."

"Or you could patch things up now and be back in swing by this weekend," I suggested. Ari's way seemed a little harsh to me, unless he'd done something awful enough to deserve it.

She sighed. "That's what I thought. Maybe I'll do that and not tell Ari. I miss him too much already to drag it out another week." She abruptly shifted gears. "I hear we had a little excitement yesterday."

There had to be an e-mail list for company gossip, and apparently I wasn't on it. "Yeah, a bit. R and D is in lockdown, with actual guards at the doors. The boss has turned my phone into a tip line, so you can guess what my day will be like. Speaking of which, I'm probably going to have to wade through about a thousand messages, so I'd better get to work."

I wasn't too far off the mark. Combining phone messages and e-mails, I had seven hundred seventy-five messages. How many employees were there? Somebody had to have left multiple messages.

I went through the voice mail first so I could clear out the mailbox for future calls. Most of the so-called tips were useless, just repeating information I already knew. I didn't need a tipster to tell me to check out the people who worked inside R&D, for example.

"You should look into Melisande Rogers from Corporate Sales," said a typical message. "She's been taking a lot of business lunches that no one else in the department knows about." The tip was anonymous, but it came from an extension registered to Outside Sales.

The next message said, "Dagmar Holloway in Outside Sales has been acting suspicious lately. I hear her sales numbers are dropping, too." The tipster had called from a Corporate Sales extension. This was starting to sound like the girls' bathroom at lunchtime in a junior high school.

The e-mails were even worse:

Hi, i'm writing this from my home account because i don't want you to no who i am but your should chek on kim in verification she's always taking notes and that makes me suspishus. She's also a stuck-up bitch and you can tell her i said so. She's also been staying late at teh office and i think she's up to something.

And that was one of the more literate ones. I felt like I had to read each one all the way through in case there really was worthwhile information buried in all the venom. While some of the intrigue was fascinating, in many cases I'd read economics textbooks that were more gripping. I didn't need a log of anyone's daily activities, including bathroom visits.

And the work kept piling up. While I listened to a message, at least one more came in. I had to turn my computer's sound off so the constant ding of incoming e-mail notifications didn't drive me bonkers. As I finished charting the tip from an e-mail, my phone would ring. Finally, I got caught up, but I didn't feel like I'd made any real progress on the investigation.

With a groan, I got up and staggered to the outer office. "Trix, coffee, please!" I begged. "This company may be too much for even Dr. Phil to help. We might want to go straight to beating each other over the head with chairs like on Jerry Springer." Then I noticed the person standing at Trix's desk. It was my date from Saturday night, the date I hadn't heard from since then, come to think of it.

"Hi, Katie," Ethan said. "Rough day?"

"You have no idea." I turned to Trix. "Coffee?" I whimpered. A steaming cup soon appeared in my hand. I was glad I didn't have to actually make pots of coffee. This way, I didn't know how many cups I was drinking, and I wasn't sure I wanted to know.

"I hear you've got some excitement going on around here," Ethan said, leaning casually against Trix's desk. "I tried to drop in on Owen, but Security wouldn't let me past the door. Then I thought I'd come up here and say hi and see what was going on."

I ignored the implication that visiting me was an afterthought to dropping in on his buddy. "We've apparently got a spy/saboteur/double agent, something like that. The boss put me in charge of collecting tips, and my phone is about to melt." I turned to Trix. "Doesn't anyone in this company like anyone else in this company? This is insane."

"I don't know," Ethan said with a shrug and a raised eyebrow. "It's no worse than some law firms I've worked with. Someone would drop the slightest hint of innuendo and it was like throwing a hunk of raw meat into a shark tank. It was sometimes kind of funny."

I faced him with a glare. "If you did this on purpose to see what would happen, now would be the time to confess. I might even let you live."

"I agree with Katie," Trix said. "I've been getting the overflow, and it's brutal."

"This seems to be the chance to settle all your old scores," I said. "Maybe we should just throw everyone into the conference room with some of those foam bat things and let them all get it out of their systems."

"You don't think they'd stick to foam, do you?" Trix asked.

"You're right. We'd be busy for months disenchanting the entire staff after they all turned each other into cockroaches and dung beetles."

Ethan stood up straighter and said to me, "Do you have time to talk? I know you're busy. This'll only take a minute."

He sounded serious, so I was instantly concerned. "Of course. Come on into my office." As I left I said over my shoulder, "Thanks for the coffee, Trix."

While I set my coffee down on my desk, Ethan closed my door behind him. I was on the verge of real worry when he stepped forward and pulled me to him in a big hug, then kissed me. He was grinning when he let me go. "Was that what you wanted to see me about?" I asked. The kiss had left me dizzy and breathless, most likely because it was so unexpected. In our extremely short relationship, we'd never come close to kissing.

He shrugged. "Maybe. I didn't think you really wanted that to happen out in the lobby."

"Us dating is the worst-kept secret in the company. Even Merlin knows. But thanks for the attempt at discretion."

He settled into my guest chair. "Sorry I didn't get a chance to call yesterday. How have you been? It wasn't too bad a hangover, was it?"

I sat down and took a sip of coffee. "I'm fine. I've had worse hangovers. Not many, granted. I'm not sure I have what it takes to be a wine connoisseur, though. You'd have to be able to get through one of those dinners without getting blitzed."

"It's like any sport. You have to train and work up to it. But I promise, no getting you drunk next time. And speaking of next time, what are you doing Friday night?"

"If the rest of the week goes like this, very possibly I'll be putting my head in the oven."

"Dinner with me might be more fun than that."

"I may be begging you to get me drunk by then."

"Only if you insist. So it's a date?"

I studied him for a long moment. True, he wasn't Owen, but if the night before had taught me anything, it was that as cute as Owen was, whatever it took to bridge the gap from friends to lovers apparently wasn't there for us—at least, not from his side of things. Even I was beginning to pick up on and maybe even welcome the brother vibe. It wasn't like Ethan was sloppy seconds, either. It was entirely possible that if I put Owen out of my mind for more than a few minutes, something might happen with Ethan. The kiss had been a good start.

"It's a date," I said. "Should we leave from here, meet somewhere later, or what?"

"We can leave from here. I'm not planning anything fancy you'd need to change clothes for."

"What are you planning?"

He gave me a wink. "That would be a surprise. See you Friday after work." Then he got out of his chair, opened the office door, and left.

Within seconds, Trix was hovering in my doorway. "Hmm, looks like the date last weekend went well."

"I guess so."

"He did come to ask you out, right?"

"Yeah, looks like it. Did he have any other business here?"

She shook her head. "Nope. He'd just shown up when you came out in a caffeine frenzy. I think he was here specifically to see you."

"Wow." I wasn't used to someone actually pursuing me—aside from the brief time when Jeff was stalking me, and that was part of an enchantment, anyway. I had to admit it was kind of nice.

"He's not bad at all, for a human."

"Yeah, I suppose I could do a lot worse. I have done a lot worse. And now I need to think of something to wear to work Friday that will carry over to a casual post-work date."

"Did he tell you where you'll be going?"

"He said it was a surprise."

She rolled her eyes. "Men! Don't they know we need to prepare ourselves?"

She had just fluttered away when Merlin appeared. "Have you made any progress on the investigation?" he asked.

"Just enough to know that all of our employees are entirely dysfunctional. Is there a company policy against magical duels during working hours on company property? I sure hope so."

"Have none of the tips been helpful?"

"No, not really. Most of them have nothing to do with the immediate situation." My phone rang and I ignored it, letting it add to the pileup of voice mail. "I'm starting to wonder if that might be the point to all this. Maybe it's more about sabotage than about spying."

"Sabotage?"

"Well, think about it. If everyone's making calls to rat out their co-workers, they're not doing their work. You can't have effective teamwork if people don't trust each other, and nobody trusts each other right now. We're at a standstill."

He stroked his beard in thought. "You may be right. How would you go about investigating that angle?"

Suddenly it struck me that this was something I knew all about. I was from a small town, so I was an expert in gossip. I might not know anything about investigating corporate espionage, but I knew all about how rumors spread. With increased confidence, I said, "Track the grapevine to its source. Find out who told whom what and when. You said it yourself yesterday—the only people who knew about the spying were you, Owen, me, and the spy. If we find out who was the first one so eager to let others know there might be a spy, it might lead us to our mole."

"Excellent deduction. I look forward to seeing the results. Please keep me posted."

Coming up with a reasonably valid-sounding theory made me bold enough to say, "Sir? There is one other thing I wanted to talk to you about."

"What is it, Katie?"

"My parents are coming to town next week, for Thanksgiving. I know we already get Thursday and Friday off. I was wondering if I could maybe take a little more time off that week, just a few hours here and there. I know we're busy, and I've got this investigation to work on, but if I'm spending time with them, then they can't be asking to visit me at work."

"I don't see a problem with that. We can see how things are going later in the week and decide then when would be best for you to take off."

"Thank you. I really appreciate it."

"In the meantime, continue your efforts. That was an excellent theory. Good work."

There was one possibility with my theory that I hated to consider. If the object was more to stir things up than to actually spy, it took Owen off my "safe" list. What better way to stir things up than to report spying that hadn't actually happened?

I wouldn't be able to bear it if one of the few people I absolutely trusted was actually betraying me.

six

Now that I knew I was tracking a rumor, I knew exactly how to approach the situation. It was like that old game of telephone—the message changed as it moved farther from the source, and the tone of the message shift gave you a pretty good idea of who was part of the chain. The closer the rumor got to the actual truth (or the obviously manufactured lie), the closer you were to the original source. I hadn't been a member of any particular clique in high school but had moved freely among all of them, and because of that I'd generally been tapped as the mediator in school rivalries. That made me an expert in figuring out who had said what to whom. I even had the "Miss Congeniality" picture in the yearbook to prove it.

This meant I'd have to leave the office. "I have to look into some things," I told Trix as I headed out. "All the calls should go straight into voice mail." Not listening to more gripes and whines was a price I'd have to pay for my diligence.

One thing I knew about gossip is that there's always someone who sees all and knows all, even if she's not involved in it. In this company, that was Isabel. If anyone in the company knew what the major feuds were, she'd be the one. She'd probably refereed most of them. The trick would be getting information out of her without giving her anything worth spreading. "Got a minute?" I asked when I got to her office.

"Rod's out right now."

"Actually, you were the one I wanted to talk to."

Her face lit up and I braced myself for a smothering hug, but she stayed seated. "Come on in, then. Can I get you anything?"

I'd had enough caffeine for the week, so I shook my head. "No thanks. But maybe you can help me with something."

"The spy investigation, huh?" she said with a knowing nod.

"It's turned into a massive grudge fest, and I need to know who has reason to hate whom so I can sort out the tips from the tattletales."

"You want a list of the grudges in this company? How much time do you have?"

"Not nearly enough. But anything you can do to help me narrow it down would get me that much further along."

She leaned back in her chair and folded her hands across her middle. "Well, you know about Gregor and Owen, of course."

"I know Owen got Gregor's job after that accident. Is there more?"

"Well, when he was in charge of that division, Gregor and Idris were pretty tight, and neither of them got along with Owen. The rest of the division took sides. It was like there was the Gregor faction and the Owen faction. One of the first things Owen did when he got the promotion after Gregor's accident and transfer was fire Idris."

"What happened to the rest of the Gregor faction?"

"The usual things that happen after a regime change. One or two quit. The rest changed which ass they were kissing. You'd have thought they were pulling for Owen all along."

I wanted to demand names, but this was already sounding too much like a police interview. "Was Gregor into the same dark magic stuff as Idris?" I asked.

"Owen thought so, but there wasn't any real proof. That spell that turned him into an ogre was definitely a gray area—assuming he was really working on the spell he said he was. Owen always thought that was a huge cover-up."

"Now I'm even more glad I got out of Verification. And it would explain the number of calls I got from within R and D. Any other big spats?"

"This is between us, right? You're not going to be telling who told you what?" She looked intensely uncomfortable, an effect the usual company gossip didn't tend to have on her.

"It's between us. I can't use gossip as evidence. Right now, I just need to be pointed in the right direction."

She leaned forward across her desk and dropped her voice. "I'm not saying this to be mean, but Ari has dated almost every straight, single male in the company—and even some not so single, if you get my drift. To hear her talk, it was all their fault it didn't work out. The ones she hasn't dated probably rejected her. I love her to death, but anyone she reported, you can dismiss outright."

"I don't think she's reported anyone."

Isabel looked relieved. "She must be growing up."

I was dying to ask where Owen fell on Ari's list, but to a gossip like Isabel, that was like adding my name to the day's hotsheet, proving I was interested in him.

"Corporate Sales and Outside Sales have a grudge match going on, but it's mostly friendly competition. This situation is hurting both of them, so I don't see either group getting caught up in it."

"How did word get outside the company?"

She shrugged. "Wives talk to husbands, husbands talk to wives. People talk to friends and lovers. Word gets out. You can't keep a lid on something like this."

That was exactly the opening I'd been trying to get. I hadn't lost my touch since the days when the drill team needed me to help find out which cheerleader had been spreading rumors about what they were up to and with whom under the bleachers after football games.

"How did you hear about it in the first place? You and Ari were asking me about it while it was still supposedly a secret."

"I heard it from Ari."

"And where did she hear about it?"

She cocked her head to one side. "You'd have to ask her to be sure, but I assumed she was close enough to see firsthand how Owen reacted when he figured out that someone had been into his notes. Or I guess she might have heard it from someone else who was nearby. All those labs have windows into the hallway, so you can see what's going on, and I doubt there's a woman in the department who doesn't have Owen on her scope."

"How did people hear about the security tampering? That word got out really fast."

"I heard it from Rod. I'm not sure where he heard about it. I think he knew Owen was getting Sam to look into things."

That narrowed it down to someone in R&D, it would appear. I got out of the overstuffed chair that I would have loved to lounge in all afternoon. "Do you think you could call down to R and D and tell someone I'm coming so they'll let me in?"

"Honey, I'm sure Owen knew you were coming before you decided to go there."

From the way Owen had described his occasional bursts of precognition, I didn't think he was quite that on the ball, and I was sure he had better things to do than keep an eye on my whereabouts.

It turned out that I didn't have anything to worry about. Owen himself was at the front door to the department, working with Sam on the security panel. I paused to admire the sight before making my presence felt. While Owen was a vision dressed up for work in a nice suit, there was something about the way he looked with his sleeves rolled up, his dark hair mussed and falling across his forehead, and his tie loosened that I found particularly appealing. Maybe it made him look a little less perfect, a little more attainable.

"Hey, dollface," Sam greeted me.

Owen jumped slightly, as if startled, then jumped again when he apparently hit something he shouldn't have. He sucked his index finger, then shook his hand vigorously, all while turning several intriguing shades of red.

"Sorry, didn't mean to startle you," I said.

"Sam startled me."

"Can I help it if you're so high-strung?" the gargoyle said.

"I'm high-strung because I'm working with both magic and electricity to try to fix the device that's supposed to keep this department secured," Owen snapped back. I'd never seen him this testy before. I'd seen him angry, but that was more of an icy-calm state that was scarier than any snarling. This was just normal human frustration. Then he sighed. "Sorry about that. Didn't mean to snap." He looked up at me. "Is there something you need, Katie?"

"I need to talk to you when you have a moment. And not here. Somewhere private."

He glanced at Sam, who said, "I'd probably get more work done with you out of my way."

Owen stood and absently brushed his hair off his face. "I'd feel better talking somewhere other than in this building, if you don't mind. Let me get a coat out of my office, then we can go outside. I could use some fresh air. We can get lunch while we're at it."

I followed him back to his office, which was a cozy den full of old books. He gestured for me to enter first, then paused like he was watching to see what would happen as I crossed the threshold. Nothing did happen. He frowned and came through the doorway.

"What was that about?" I asked.

"I'm testing something. I still don't have it right. I can block anyone magical, but an immune can get past the wards. It may take a physical barrier to deal with that."

"You suspect an immune?"

"Right now, I suspect almost anyone."

While he took his suit coat off the back of his chair, something up near the ceiling in a corner of the office caught my eye. "What is that?" I asked.

He followed my gaze, then shook his head. "What's what?"

"Did you have a verifier go over your office while you were doing your security sweep?"

He turned red. "I didn't think of it."

I kicked off my shoes and climbed up onto the armchair in that corner of the office. "It looks like one of those webcam things."

"Interesting." He climbed up beside me and waved one hand in the general direction of the camera. "Ah, there it is." The camera flew into his hand. He waved his other hand over it, then blinked. "Oh, I see what you mean." I assumed he'd magically removed whatever veil had kept it hidden from him. He raised an eyebrow and smirked. "It looks like someone's spying on me."

I tried to be as cool about it as he was even though my theory about the suspect being in R&D had been shot to hell. "Huh. Imagine that. Who'd have guessed it?"

He waved his hand over the device again, then it floated back up to its position. "Now it'll tell them what I want it to tell them. I'll track down where it goes later. First, lunch and talk."

Just then, Jake came rushing toward the office. "Hey, boss, glad I caught you before you went to lunch," he said, then cried out as he tried to cross the threshold. "Hey! What was that about?"

Owen's ears turned pink as he waved a hand and Jake took a tentative step through the doorway. "Sorry about that. I've been tinkering with the wards."

"You're blocking me out now?" Jake was the very picture of aggrieved innocence. He looked like what would happen if Jimmy Olsen from the Superman comics joined a punk band, and I still had a hard time imagining him betraying his boss, but it seemed like Owen hadn't cleared him.

"I'm blocking everyone. If I'm in here, I'll let you in. If I'm not, it can wait. Now, what did you need?"

While they talked business, I put my shoes back on and looked around for anything else that didn't belong. In Owen's cluttered office that was a challenge. I'd only spotted the camera because it was too high-tech for its surroundings. If it had been hidden inside a book, I never would have seen it.

Owen sent Jake off to correct something in the spell he was working on. Then he took his overcoat from the hook on the back of his office door and held it out for me. "Here, this way you won't have to go back to your office."

I shrugged into the oversize coat while he put on his suit coat. "You're going to freeze," I said. The wind cutting across the island was icy.

"I'll be fine, trust me. I have my own resources, remember."

Oh yeah, that. I knew what he was capable of, but he was so matter-of-fact in the rare times I saw him do magic that it was easy to forget what he was.

As we passed Sam, who was still working on the security device, Owen said, "Don't let anyone from outside the department in while I'm gone."

"With luck, I'll have this thing fixed before you get back to get in my way," Sam growled, shooing Owen away with one wing.

When we were out of the building, Owen said, "Talk first, then lunch? I doubt we want to discuss this at a restaurant."

"Sounds like a plan," I said.

He led the way to the park at City Hall Plaza, where we sat on a bench near the fountain. "This should be safe enough from eavesdroppers. The sound of the fountain muffles conversation."

Obviously, he'd put a lot of thought into this. Maybe he should have been in charge of this investigation. He knew a lot more about spying than I did. He looked at me expectantly, and I remembered that I'd been the one to ask for this meeting. I wrapped his coat tighter around my legs and asked, "What, exactly, did you do when you discovered that someone had been in your desk and looking at your notes?"

He frowned. "What do you mean?"

"Well, word got out pretty fast that there was a spy. I know you didn't tell anyone other than Merlin and me. So either someone saw you react and made an assumption—"

"—or it was the spy who spread the rumor," he finished. He worried his lower lip in his teeth as he thought. "I don't think I reacted all that visibly," he said after a while. "Not where anyone could see me. There may have been certain, um, well, words used in the privacy of my office." A stain of red that I suspected had nothing to do with the cold spread across his cheeks. I had a hard time imagining him cursing. He probably did it in some arcane language. "But after that I don't think I looked too different from any other time I think of something I need to talk to Mr. Mervyn about. Did I look all that different to you when I got to your office?"

"I could tell something was up because you didn't bother with the usual niceties before saying you needed to see the boss."

"Oh." He winced. "Sorry about that."

"But even that wouldn't have been enough for me to assume it meant we had a spy in our midst. That's a pretty big leap to take. To come to that conclusion, someone would almost have to have known why you were upset."

"So you think our spy was the one who started rumors about us having a spy?"

"Maybe." I wasn't likely to find a more receptive audience, so I plunged forward. "In fact, I have this theory that the spy isn't really spying at all. Yeah, if they find something, I'm sure they'd pass it on to Idris. But what would really help him is if we can't pull together right now, if we're so busy suspecting each other and worrying about who the spy is that we aren't actually getting any work done. How have you spent your time for the last couple of days?"

He closed his eyes and groaned. "I've been checking our security. If you're right, I totally fell for it."

"The security panel in R and D and the camera in your office could be more red herrings, or they could be proof that I don't know what I'm doing. We do know that someone tampered with the departmental security, got into your office, planted and veiled a camera, got into your desk, and looked at your notes. We don't know how much of that was really part of their mission and how much was just giving us something to talk about."

"The camera may have been to watch my reaction so they'd know when to start the rumors. They'd have looked stupid if they started spreading rumors before I noticed that anything was wrong."

"Before I found the camera, I was pretty sure I'd narrowed our spy down to R and D because they'd be the ones who would have seen you react, but now it could be anyone, as long as at some point they had a chance to plant that camera. It seems like every time I close in on a theory, something happens to make me doubt it. When we get back to the office, what do you want to bet that something important will be missing, or a bomb planted, or worse?"

"Don't talk like that."

"I'm trying to track the rumor to its source, but that's turning out to be a real challenge. I'm used to dealing with gossip, but not with technologically and magically assisted gossip."

"I'm sure there's a way to set a trap. I'll see what I can come up with."

"From your spy books?"

He blushed adorably. "You can learn a lot from Robert Ludlum."

I added to my mental list of the very few things I knew about him and said, "So, lunch? I'm freezing and I'm starving."

We found a nearby deli and had a quick lunch punctuated by small talk. He insisted on paying, which was good because my purse was still in my office. He said since we'd been talking business he could expense it, but I had a feeling he wouldn't. It was another one of those non-dates that was as good as any date I'd been on, and it was with great reluctance that I gave his coat back to him in the lobby and headed up to my own office.

"You can go to lunch now if you want me to cover for you," I said to Trix when I returned.

"No thanks." She made a face. "I still don't have much of an appetite."

"So you haven't made up with Pippin yet?"

She shook her head, and her wings seemed to wilt a little bit. "Ari talked me out of it. He sent me flowers, though."

"Forget about Ari. You know how bitter she is about men. If you want to be with him, talk to him. Don't punish him if you care about him."

"You're probably right, Katie. Thanks."

I went back to my office wondering what the world was coming to if I was giving dating advice.

Friday couldn't have come fast enough for me. The spate of complaints and tips died down, and no new obvious acts of espionage came to light. I hoped that our mole had done his or her job by making us all suspicious of each other, but I knew that sooner or later, something else was bound to happen. They weren't going to let us get entirely back to normal.

I had to admit that I was also looking forward to my date with Ethan. His kiss had left me intrigued, and by late Friday afternoon when I touched up my hair and makeup before I left to meet him, my nerves were tingling with anticipation.

I'd expected to meet him in the lobby or on the sidewalk in front of the office building, but when I stepped out the front door, a silver Mercedes was waiting on the street. I recognized Ethan's car. He got out, ran around, and opened the door for me. "Your chariot, milady," he said with a sweeping bow and a flirtatious grin.

With a grin of my own, I got inside. When he got back into the driver's seat and set the car in motion, I said, "I take it we're not going anywhere in Manhattan. If we are, you may have just lost the last available parking space."

"I thought it would be fun to get away from the city for a change of pace. I know you're not a native city girl, so you probably need to see green stuff every so often."

"Green is good," I agreed. "I've even been a little homesick lately, probably because my parents are coming next week." I noticed that we'd joined the line of cars entering the Brooklyn-Battery Tunnel.

"Really? When are they coming in?"

"Monday evening. I've made hotel reservations. Now I probably need to hire a car service so I can pick them up from the airport."

"I can drive you. Which airport?"

"You don't have to do that."

"Come on, if I don't use the car when it's truly helpful, there's not much point to having one in Manhattan. I'd be glad to play airport limo."

"You don't mind?"

"Not at all."

"I should probably warn you about my parents."

"Why? They're not going to start planning the wedding when they see you with me, are they?"

"That is a possibility. They may also be here just to try to make me go back to Texas."

"And I should try to stop that if they do?"

"Please."

We inched forward toward the tunnel. At the rate we were going, we might make it out of Manhattan before midnight. I reminded myself that Ethan tended to be as obsessively organized and prepared as I was, so I was sure he'd factored rush hour into his travel plans. I settled back against the leather seat, preparing for a long ride.

Ethan was as calm and unruffled about facing Manhattan traffic as he was about everything else. He even made Owen look excitable, though I supposed it was Owen's air of carefully suppressed intensity that made him seem less calm than Ethan. And why was I thinking about Owen when I was out with somebody else?

I deliberately faced Ethan and asked, "How was your week?"

"Not nearly as interesting as yours, from what I've heard. How goes the investigation?"

"Nowhere. I have some theories, but tracking them down may prove difficult. I'm hoping the Thanksgiving holidays cool down some of the paranoia. Right now, the atmosphere feels like we're not too far from tarring and feathering."

"Sounds like the Salem witch trials." Then he winced. "And that was probably in bad taste, considering who we're dealing with."

"Those weren't real witches, and the kind of magic we deal with has nothing to do with witchcraft. But yeah, similar atmosphere."

We finally made it into the tunnel and I almost had to hold my breath until we came out the other side. I didn't like dark, enclosed spaces. Plus, I'd seen too many movies with car chases taking place in that tunnel.

"Where are we going, anyway?" I asked, trying to keep my mind off the thought of all the water overhead.

"We've been invited to a party out on Long Island."

"Oh. Nice. Who's having the party?"

"Some people I've been working with."

He sounded deliberately vague, and I couldn't help but wonder if he meant lawyers or if he meant magical people. I wasn't sure which I'd prefer. "Am I dressed okay?" I'd changed into dressier shoes, but otherwise I was wearing my work clothes—a skirt and blouse.

"You look fine, very nice. I'll be the luckiest fellow there."

I breathed a sigh of relief when we left the tunnel, but the traffic didn't ease much. I glanced at my watch. We'd been on the road for an hour. I would have eaten more lunch if I'd known dinner would be this late.

As if reading my mind, Ethan said, "Do you want to stop and get a snack? This is taking a little longer than I'd planned."

"How much farther until we get there?"

"The directions say it shouldn't be long now."

"Then let's stay on the road."

An hour later, I wondered about the definition of "not long now." We were on the Long Island Expressway and officially outside New York City, but we were nowhere near what I'd consider the country— at least, I thought we were still firmly entrenched in an urban area. It was pitch black, so it was hard to tell. If I hadn't been so hungry that my stomach was about to climb my neck to see if my throat had been cut, as my mother would say, it wouldn't have been a bad drive. Trapped in the car together, Ethan and I had managed to have the kind of small-talk conversation we'd skipped on our previous dates.

"Ah, here's our exit," Ethan said at last.

I was surprised by how abruptly we went from city to country. Within a few miles, I felt like we were in a deserted area, even though

I knew civilization wasn't that far away, probably just beyond a stand of trees. Ethan squinted at a note by the light of the car's dashboard. "Okay, it says here we go another two miles, then turn right, and then we should see it."

"Great!" I hoped they had good food, and lots of it.

Ethan made the right turn, then the car came to an abrupt halt.

"Did you hit something?" I asked.

"I don't think so. The car just died."

I restrained myself from making a remark about how he should have bought American, and instead looked out the window to see where we were and what was going on. What I saw was unsettling, to say the least.

"Um, Toto, I don't think we're in Kansas anymore," I said softly.

seven

We were surrounded by a menagerie of magical creatures straight out of some of my more colorful nightmares. They weren't the relatively friendly types who worked at MSI. These were the kind of beasties who teamed up with the wicked witch in Disney cartoons. My old buddy Mr. Bones was there, freed from the NO PARKING sign where Owen had stuck him Monday morning.

"Whoa," Ethan said. "Now what? Magic shouldn't work on us, right?"

"Magic doesn't work on us, but they can harm us physically." I noticed a fireball forming in Mr. Bones's hand. "And your car isn't immune to magic. That doesn't rub off from the driver. If they do something to the car, we're in trouble."

He hit the button to unlock the doors and said, "Jump!"

Fortunately for Ethan's insurance company, the skeletal creature with the fireball held back once we were outside the car. It looked like they had us right where they wanted us.

Or to be more accurate, they had me right where they wanted me—on the passenger side of the car, separated from Ethan, who was still on the driver's side, away from the scary mob. They were all closing in on me. Ethan could have made a run for it if he'd wanted to. It was nice of him to stick with me, but I wished he'd run for help. There wasn't a lot two magical immunes could do against that bunch, other than spot them if they tried to make themselves invisible or normal looking.

I tried for the icy calm Owen usually displayed in a confrontation like this. "What do you want?" I asked.

Mr. Bones said, "You're becoming a problem." I wasn't sure if it was giving me an evil grin or if it just looked that way because of the way its face was formed.

I forced a laugh. "If y'all are worried about me, then you've got bigger problems than anyone can help you with and you may as well give up."

Out of the corner of my eye I saw Ethan edging toward the car's trunk while ducking behind the car. I hoped he didn't do anything stupid—unless, of course, it was both stupid and effective and didn't get him or me hurt or killed.

I kept talking in hope of distracting them from whatever it was Ethan had planned. "You're working for Idris, right?" I asked. "That pathetic geek must be getting really desperate if he's resorting to picking on me. Or is he afraid to go after the big boys?" I desperately wished I were out with Owen, and for a change it wasn't because of that silly crush I had on him. He'd be able to get rid of this bunch with a careless flick of his wrist. Then again, they'd be able to harm him in ways that wouldn't work on me.

Taking a deep breath, I moved forward, away from the security of all that solid German engineering. "Well, you can tell your boss that getting rid of me isn't going to do him much good. I'm just a glorified secretary, and he should know that. He's got his spy in our company. Or is that what this is all about? I'm getting too close to the truth?" If I was, I wished they'd let me in on the secret because I had no clue.

Mr. Bones formed another fireball in his hand and threw it at me. It took every ounce of self-control I had not to duck. I knew intellectually that magic couldn't hurt me, but my instincts saw a threat coming and wanted me out of the way. The fireball disintegrated harmlessly as it touched me. I felt the tingle of power, but otherwise was unaffected.

"Nice one," I said. "But obviously you don't have a lot of experience with immunes." I almost felt like that fireball had given me a surge of power. I knew I wasn't invincible, but I sure felt like I was. I folded my arms across my chest and said, "Got anything better you want to show me, or have you passed on your message? I have somewhere I need to be."

This was a really good time for the cavalry to show up, but I didn't know if any of my magical bodyguards would have followed me all the way out of the city. I should have noticed a fairy or gargoyle tracking us. Or did they have a network that passed us from one to the other as we traveled?

The monsters closed in again, and I couldn't help but back up closer to the car. Magic or not, they were big and scary. I tried to get to the trunk where Ethan was. Just when I thought they'd be on me, there was a loud whoosh of air and white foam sprayed everywhere, forcing the monsters to move back. I turned to look at Ethan, who defiantly held a fire extinguisher with its nozzle facing the crowd of monsters.

"You wouldn't happen to have a tire iron in there, would you?" I asked.

He dug in his trunk and came out with a cross-shaped lug wrench. "Will this do?"

I'd have preferred something with a little longer reach to it, but I took it anyway. It was better than nothing, and it looked like the sort of weapon Wonder Woman might have used. The mob made another charge, and I waved my lug wrench at them while Ethan gave them another blast from the fire extinguisher. The extinguisher ran out of foam, and Ethan threw it into the crowd, scattering them briefly. He handed me a crowbar and said, "Hold them off for a second," before going back to digging in his trunk.

I wielded the crowbar like a sword and waved the lug wrench back and forth as if it were an exotic martial arts weapon. The monsters didn't look too impressed. "What else do you have in there?" I asked Ethan.

"I'm looking for something that might help. Ah, there it is." A second later there was a loud sound like a gunshot, then a whistling and a burst of light overhead. Ethan, bless his overprepared heart, must have had a flare gun in the trunk of his car, along with the fire extinguisher, enough tools to take the car apart and reassemble it, a spare blanket, a first-aid kit that was better equipped than some ERs, and enough bottled water for a trek across the Sahara. My mother would love him at first sight.

The creatures all ducked and cringed. They must have been used to that kind of thing being far more dangerous and magical. I wanted to duck myself, but I forced myself to stand upright and stare them down.

Soon there were several popping sounds, along with the rustle of wings around us. Someone grabbed my elbow. I started to resist, but a voice in my ear said, "It's me, Ethan."

Another voice said, "Get in the car, hurry."

I looked around to see that we were surrounded by friendly-looking gargoyles, as well as some humans and fairies. I wasn't sure where they'd come from, but I was grateful. They formed a shield around Ethan and me. As we made a dash for the car doors, I caught glimpses of fights between two sets of magical people. My hair felt like it was standing on end from the surges of power around us. Ethan opened the driver's-side door and shoved me inside. I scooted across to the passenger seat so he could climb in and shut and lock the door. The engine roared to life on its own before Ethan had a chance to turn the key. A beaked gargoyle flew ahead of us as Ethan floored the accelerator and tore off down the road, leaving the still-raging battle behind.

We soon reached a large old mansion blazing with lights and looking like something out of *The Great Gatsby*. Music poured out of the open doorway. "And here we are," Ethan said, killing the engine and taking a deep breath.

"You know what you said about not getting me drunk on our next date?" I asked. "I won't hold you to it."

"I don't blame you."

"Nice work with the flare gun."

"Thanks. I've had it forever and never had a need for it, but I thought we were close enough to the party that we might be able to get help. You were amazing staring them down."

"Thanks." I took a deep breath to steady myself and tried to get myself back on track for a date now that the danger was past. "I take it this is a magical party?"

"Yeah. I was helping Corporate Sales with some contract negotiations this week and they invited me. I hope you don't mind, but I thought it would be interesting."

Did I mind? The real question was, after having just faced down an evil magical menagerie, would I be able to relax around more magical people, especially if I knew that one or more of them might be working for the enemy? How else did the bad guys know we were going to be there? Then again, what semi-corporate party with salespeople was ever fun? "It looks like fun," I lied, not wanting to hurt his feelings, but hoping maybe we could just go to dinner and a movie on our next date.

I waited for him to come around and open my door for me, not because I was playing Southern belle, but because my legs were still shaking from the close call. The gargoyle came to rest on the ground beside Ethan, and said, "You'll be safe here. This estate is warded. Invited guests only."

"Thanks," I said shakily. Ethan escorted me inside with a protective hand at the small of my back, the very way I'd wished Owen had escorted me earlier in the week. And there I went again, getting sidetracked.

A butler took our coats in the entryway and directed us to the ballroom where the party was being held. The room was packed with every kind of magical creature I'd ever seen—except for the scary sorts we'd met outside—and a fair number of humans I assumed were wizards.

"Look, food!" Ethan said, gesturing toward a loaded buffet table. We restrained ourselves from running at it, but we walked with eager rapidity.

We'd just started loading our plates when a business-suited woman approached Ethan. "I was wondering if you were going to make it."

"You're not the only one. It was a close call. And I think the directions you gave me were for flying carpet, not car. It took longer than I expected to get here."

She laughed. "I keep forgetting about that when I deal with non-magical folk."

He then turned to me. "Katie, have you met Melisande Rogers in Corporate Sales? She's the one who invited us."

I recognized the name as one of my many tipsters, the one who'd been ratting out an apparent rival in Outside Sales. She didn't look particularly happy to see me, but I put on a smile and held out a hand. "Nice to meet you. I'm Katie Chandler."

She took my hand in a dry, cool grip. "Yes, I know. The boss's right hand. I'm glad you could make it." There was something in her eyes that told me she hadn't expected Ethan to bring a date when she'd invited him to the party, especially not a date who knew what a backstabber she was.

Ethan seemed oblivious to the tension between us. His magical immunity may have allowed him to spot spells, but he was apparently blind to the workings of female jealousy. He said, "We're both starving after that drive—and all the excitement. I'll have to catch up with you later."

Judging from the look she gave us, if it had been up to Melisande, I probably still would have been on the side of the road chatting with Mr. Bones while Ethan was safely ensconced in the mansion, having drinks with her. I was lucky that most of the magical world respected Merlin enough to give me some degree of protection, and I made a mental note to ask around about Melisande on Monday morning.

A bedraggled group of magical folk came into the room, and a cheer rang out. I recognized a couple of the people who'd come to our rescue. One of the gargoyles flew over to us. "You shouldn't be having any problems from them for a while," it said. "Unfortunately, a few of them got away, but they were heading out so fast, I doubt they'll even look back until they're safe in their lairs. You should be able to get home without being bothered tonight."

"Thank you for your help," I replied.

It saluted me with a wing that managed to look leathery and stone-like at the same time. "Just doing our jobs, ma'am. And, um, you wouldn't mind putting in a good word with the boss?"

"I'll be sure to let him know."

Before anyone else could approach us and delay our dinner, Ethan and I found a relatively quiet corner with a table and two chairs and dug into the food. "Either this is the best food I've ever eaten or I was hungrier than I've ever been," Ethan said with a laugh after devouring half a plateful.

I was just about to respond when I heard a flutter of wings. I looked up to see Ari.

"Hey, Katie, I didn't know you were coming to this shindig."

"I didn't know I was coming myself."

She made a "tsk-tsk" motion with her fingers in Ethan's direction. "Now, is that a way to treat a lady? By the way, I'm Ari."

I remembered my manners. "Ari, have you met Ethan, our new corporate legal counsel?"

She fluttered her eyes and wings simultaneously. "We haven't met in person, but Trix has told me about you." She glanced at me and added, "And I've heard a little from Katie. She hasn't done you justice."

Ari was my friend, but she wasn't high on my list of people I wanted to run into when I was on a date. She'd been around during my last disastrous blind date, and although she wasn't directly responsible for the disaster, she hadn't helped matters. Unfortunately, there was no polite way to tell a friend to get lost. Ari wouldn't mind, but I didn't want to look like a jerk in front of Ethan.

It must have been my lucky night, for before I had to grab her by the wing and beg her to leave us alone, she winked at Ethan and said, "I'd love to stay and chat, but I'm sure I'll get all the details on Monday morning. Ta-ta!"

"She's interesting," Ethan remarked as she flitted away.

"You can say that again. Dessert?" I needed a chocolate fix in the worst way.

"Sure."

The moment we stood up, our empty plates vanished. "That's handy," I remarked.

"I wonder how they do that."

"I'm not sure I want to know. The less I think about how magic works, the less my head hurts."

"Then never ask Owen a question about something magical when he's got a marker in his hand and is anywhere near a whiteboard. I had to take an aspirin and lie down afterward."

I was going to ask him more about Owen's magical lecture, but I was saved from making the faux pas of talking about one guy while on a date with another by Trix, who stood forlornly at the dessert table, popping one chocolate after another into her mouth. "Trix? I wasn't expecting to see you here," I said.

She sighed deeply. "I wasn't planning to come. I was going to go over to Pippin's place and try to talk to him. But Ari made me come. She said it would be good for me to get out." A single sparkling tear trickled down her cheek.

"Nice of her to abandon you after dragging you here," I commented.

She sniffed. "I told her to go have fun. There's no point in both of us being miserable."

Ethan got that helpless expression men tend to develop when they're around a weeping woman. He awkwardly squeezed her shoulder, then directed a wide-eyed "what now?" look at me.

I put an arm around her, carefully avoiding her wings. "Come on, honey, if you keep eating chocolate like that you won't be able to fly." She let me lead her to the table where we'd been sitting. It was only after we got there that I realized I hadn't managed to get any chocolate for myself. Once the initial shakes from our frightening encounter had worn off, I no longer needed or wanted a drink. I had a feeling I'd need to keep my wits about me. I did, however, desperately need chocolate.

Ethan proved to be the consummate gentleman. With a glance at me, he held his hand out to Trix. "Come on, let's dance. That'll make you feel better." I watched him gently guide her to the floor, then I made a beeline back to the dessert table. I wasn't a good enough dancer to get on the floor in front of people I might need to respect me later at work.

Ethan and Trix seemed to be having a good time out there. She was even smiling and laughing, her wings perked up instead of drooping sadly like they had been all week. As I munched on a miniature brownie and watched them, I decided I'd found myself a pretty good man. He was prepared for everything, was good in a crisis, got along with my friends (with the possible exception of Marcia) and was kind to people in need. For the first time since I'd met him, I truly wanted it to work out between us, and not only because I doubted I'd ever have the man I really wanted. I was glad I had Ethan as a boyfriend.

When I got up to Merlin's office suite Monday morning, Trix looked significantly better than she had Friday night. She almost even looked happy. "Thanks again for coming to my rescue," she said. "It was sweet of you and Ethan to interrupt your date to help me."

"I think my enemies had already interrupted our date," I said. "Once a walking skeleton has thrown fireballs at you, it's hard to get into a romantic mood."

She fluttered her wings. "Oh, I don't know. Don't they say that the response to danger and sexual arousal aren't all that different? It could have made for some interesting foreplay."

"Trust me, that was the last thing on my mind when we got out of there."

"Do you have any idea who it was or what they wanted?"

"No clue. I doubt it was a magical mugging. They were specifically after me. But why me? It's not like getting me out of the picture will make that big a difference."

Merlin came out of his office, concern on his wrinkled face. "You're well, then?" he asked me. "I heard about the incident Friday night."

"I'm fine. They didn't do anything to hurt me. I think they just wanted to scare me, and I'm not entirely sure why, unless they're still trying to make me give up and quit. Fortunately, Sam's security team was on the ball, even in their off-hours."

"It would probably be safe to assume you're closer than you think to the truth about the spy."

"Or else I've managed to piss off the wrong person and this has nothing to do with work."

He cocked his head to one side, considering that idea. "Possible, but it seems like a great deal of effort for a personal vendetta. Those kinds of bandits don't come cheap. They didn't in my day, and I doubt that has changed with time." He started to go back to his office, then turned back. "I think you should take Wednesday off to be with your family," he said. "Getting you away from the office might give the spy a false sense of security."

"Thank you," I said. "I really appreciate that."

I left work early to meet Ethan in front of the building. While I waited for him, I chatted with Sam, who was back in his usual spot on the building awning. "My folks are flying in this evening," I told him. "Do you think you could increase the bodyguard detail a little bit?"

"Worried that Idris'll go after them?"

"Kind of. I mostly just want to avoid any situations that might make my parents worry. If they had any idea about the weirdness I'm caught up in, they'd have me hauled back to Texas so fast my head would spin. Heading off the bad guys at the pass would be a very good thing."

"Gotcha! I'll get my people right on it." Then he winked. "Besides, Palmer already talked to me about it. He said you were worried."

Even when Ethan arrived and we were on our way to the airport, I couldn't stop fretting. I'd already worried about what my parents would think about my dinky apartment over a nail salon in an old tenement building. They were guaranteed not to like that. But even if they couldn't see creatures with wings, flying gargoyles, and other magical oddities, they were still likely to see the effects of anything that got close to me. I wasn't good at coming up with explanations on the spur of the moment.

"It'll be okay," Ethan said mildly as he negotiated the traffic on the way to LaGuardia.

"Hmm?" I asked, distracted.

"Your parents. Most people are scared of New York the first time they come here, but after a while it becomes just another place. It isn't nearly so scary. In fact, I think that letting it become a real place instead of the bizarro world they imagined will make them feel better about it."

"The problem is, it's more a bizarro world than they possibly could have imagined. Muggers I think they could deal with. But magic?"

"These people have been hiding their magic from others for ages. I think your parents can spend a week here without discovering the secret. It took you a year, didn't it? And I'd lived here for nearly ten years before I figured it out, even as an immune."

I hoped he was right. It had been difficult enough to give Ethan, someone I barely knew at the time, the "magic is real, okay?" speech. I didn't think I could give it to my parents while remaining sane. I gave him a quick kiss before I got out of the car and headed in to the baggage claim area.

The longer I waited, the more nervous I grew. I hadn't seen my parents in more than a year. More important, they hadn't seen me. What would they think of me? I felt like I'd changed so much. What if they didn't like the new me?

When I saw the crowd of passengers arrive and head to the baggage claim for the flight from Dallas, I got so nervous I thought I'd throw up. Then I caught a glimpse of my dad's head towering above the crowd and I rushed forward. "Dad! Mom!" I called out.

It took them a second to find me, and in that moment I was astonished by how much older they looked. It had only been a year, but my mental image of them was one I'd retained from childhood, apparently. The current reality came as a jolt. My dad had silver hair, and there was more gray than blond in my mother's hair.

But then they reached me and hugged me like they never wanted to let me go. "Oh, my baby!" my mother said over and over again. My dad just kept patting me on the back. I was glad that Ethan had to stay behind with the car because I didn't want him to see me cry.

"It's good to see you," I told them when I'd regained enough control to speak. "I missed you so much."

My mom held me at arm's length. "Look at you! You're so thin. Are you eating enough? If you didn't have enough money to eat, you should have said something."

I felt like I was right back at home. "I'm eating fine, really," I said with a laugh. "You have to walk a lot in New York. That keeps me in shape."

"You aren't anorexic, are you? Like all those models?" She opened her tote bag. "Here, I brought some food with me since they don't feed you on airplanes these days. I think I still have some fried chicken."

I reached over and closed her tote bag before she could pull out an entire chicken dinner in the middle of baggage claim. "Mom, I don't need any fried chicken. We'll be having dinner soon enough."

"You've been living here too long. You always loved my fried chicken."

While we were talking, my dad had gone about collecting their bags. "Do you have everything?" I asked. "My friend is outside with the car. They probably made him circle around."

"You didn't have to come pick us up," Mom said.

"I wanted to, and my friend offered to drive."

Ethan pulled up almost as soon as we got outside. My parents took one look at the Mercedes, then looked at each other. When Ethan got out of the car to help them load their bags, they appeared even more intrigued.

"Mom, Dad, this is my um, friend, Ethan Wainwright. We work together. Ethan, these are my parents, Frank and Lois Chandler."

Ethan shook hands with both of them. My mom caught his hand

in both of hers and said, "It was so nice of you to offer to come pick us up. You must be a very special friend to our Katie."

An impatient cabdriver waiting to unload his passengers spared me potential further embarrassment by honking. Everyone had to scramble to get in the car so Ethan could pull away. It was only a temporary reprieve from embarrassment, though, for once we got on the road, we were trapped inside a car with my mother, whose potential-wedding-for-her-only-daughter radar was pinging loud and clear. She'd probably make Gemma scrap the sightseeing expedition and take her shopping for mother-of-the-bride dresses instead.

"So, Ethan," she asked. "What is it you do?"

"I'm an attorney."

"And you work with Katie?"

"Sort of. I have my own firm, but I'm on retainer for Katie's company."

"And that's how you met?"

I tried not to groan out loud. I hadn't even thought of working out a cover story with him in advance.

"Actually, it's kind of funny, but no. I'm a friend of Jim's, Connie's husband. You know Connie?"

"Of course. The girls were always coming home with Katie on weekends from college." Connie was my other college friend who'd moved to New York with Gemma and Marcia. When she got married and a spot in the apartment opened up, they'd persuaded me to join them in New York.

"Well," Ethan continued, "Jim originally set me up with Marcia, but we didn't hit it off so well. But Katie and I did."

I didn't have to look at the backseat to see my mother's satisfied smile. "So you two are dating?"

"Yes, we are." He said it like he was proud of it, and that gave me a warm glow.

If I could read minds, I knew at that moment I'd be able to hear my mom rehearsing the speech she'd give her friends back home. "Oh yes, and our Katie is dating a very prominent Manhattan attorney. He drives a Mercedes, you know."

"We only just started dating," I said, before she got carried away with thinking of how she'd tell her friends that she was expecting an engagement announcement any day now. I changed the subject by saying, "I got you a room at a hotel down the street from where I live, so it'll be easy for us to come and go."

"I hope you didn't go to any bother," Mom said.

"We'll pay our own bill," Dad added.

"It wasn't any trouble at all," I said. "I wish we had enough room for you to stay with us, but believe me, you'll be much more comfortable in a hotel. It's the same hotel where Gemma's and Marcia's parents stay when they visit."

"Then I'm sure it'll be fine," my mom said.

I glanced over my shoulder to the backseat and saw that both of them were staring out the window. It was dark already, so there wasn't much to see. It was probably for the best. That part of Queens wasn't the most scenic section of New York and probably wasn't the best way to introduce them to the city. "You can see the skyline ahead," I pointed out. "We'll be crossing the Triboro Bridge soon, and then you'll have a great view."

That cut off the personal questions for a while as they looked for landmarks. Ethan shot me a glance, a smile, and a wink, and I winked back at him.

We made good time heading down FDR to Fourteenth Street, so my parents didn't have a chance to start the truly personal questions. "I'll take you to your hotel so you can unload your bags," Ethan said, "and then I'll leave all of you to have some time together."

"You're very sweet to go to all this trouble," Mom said, a lilt of Southern belle flirtation in her voice. Was that what I sounded like when I pulled that stunt?

"It wasn't any trouble at all." I knew he was lying through his teeth. The tolls alone were outrageous.

"You'll have to come over for Thanksgiving if you don't have any other plans. Katie and I are planning a big feast for all her friends."

I felt a moment of panic. I wasn't sure I was ready to subject Ethan to that much of my parents. On the other hand, it would probably be the safest possible circumstances, with Marcia, Gemma, Philip, and Jeff there.

Ethan glanced at me, like he was getting my okay before responding. I gave him a slight nod. "Yes, we'd love to have you."

"Great then, I accept. I was just going to get a turkey TV dinner and watch football all day."

"You do get football at your place?" my dad asked, sounding the least bit panicked.

"Of course I do, Dad. It's on network TV. But they have cable at the hotel, just in case. I'm not sure whether or not we'll get the Texas game Friday, though."

"We'll be out sightseeing and shopping Friday," Mom declared. "And I'm glad you'll be able to join us, Ethan. But aren't you spending Thanksgiving with your family?" She was in full-on mother-hen mode. I could only imagine what she'd think about Owen, a true orphan.

"My parents are taking a cruise this year."

"Then it's good you don't have to be alone. You'll have to join us."

Ethan pulled up in front of the hotel, which was in a brownstone building much like my apartment, and helped unload the bags. "I'll see you tomorrow, Katie," he said.

"Thanks again for your help." I was relieved that he didn't try to kiss me. Not that I didn't want to kiss him; I just didn't want to have to deal with my parents asking me about the state of our relationship. As it was, things were nice and ambiguous.

I was watching him drive away when Mom said, "What's that?"

"What's what?"

She pointed toward a nearby tree. "That."

If I wasn't mistaken, I caught the briefest glimpse of a gargoyle's wing.

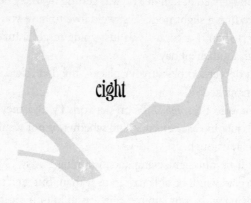

eight

I turned back to my mother, horror knotting my stomach. "What did you see?" She could not have seen a gargoyle. She just couldn't. Hell, she was in New York City for the first time in her life. There were any number of things she could have seen that would have shocked her. A careening taxicab with an ad for a strip club on top would have been enough to give her the vapors.

My dad gave a long-suffering sigh. "Don't mind her. She'll be seeing a mugger behind every tree. I had to confiscate her pepper spray before we left for the airport." He took Mom by the shoulders and turned her to face the hotel entrance. "Come on, Lois, let's get checked in." He caught my eye over the top of her head and gave me a smile as he shook his head in amusement.

With a great sense of relief, I stepped forward and picked up one of their bags. "In this part of town, we only have muggers behind every other tree, and that's only on odd-numbered streets, so you'll be okay here," I said.

I got them checked into the hotel, then led them down the street to my apartment building. "I live less than a block away, so this is the next best thing to staying with me," I said, trying to sound chipper, even as I dreaded them seeing the way I lived. My parents were nowhere near rich, but they lived in the lap of luxury, comparatively speaking. My whole apartment could easily fit into the living room of my parents' house.

I reached the doorway to the side of the nail salon. "Here we are. See, this key unlocks the front door to get into the building." I demonstrated. "Visitors ring the doorbell here, and we can then buzz them through. It's like an extra layer of safety."

Once we were all inside, I led them up the stairs. I was intensely conscious of the dingy paint on the stairwell walls, the worn dips in the stair treads, the stained linoleum on the landings. Seeing through my parents' eyes, I couldn't imagine how anyone would want to live in a place like this. I glanced over my shoulder at my mother and could see her eyes narrowing in judgment. Oh yeah, I was going to hear about this. I dreaded seeing her face when she got a look at our apartment.

"And here we are!" I said brightly when we reached the third floor. "See, another couple of locks here—just in case. It's actually a very safe neighborhood and nobody has tried to break in since we've lived here." I didn't tell them that my apartment had yet another layer of protection. It had been warded against magical attack. No one could use magic to break into or damage the building. Somehow, I doubted they'd find that bit of information particularly reassuring.

I flung the door open with a game-show-hostess gesture. "Marcia, Gemma, we're here!" I called out. My mother greeted my roommates with a big hug. My dad shook their hands and nodded silently.

"How was your flight?" Gemma asked.

"Long," my dad replied.

"Ready for dinner?" Marcia asked. "Our treat, since you're doing Thanksgiving for us."

"We made reservations at one of our favorite New York places,"

Gemma added. "It's not too far away, and it'll give you a look at the neighborhood."

My mother made a show of protesting that they didn't need to go to any effort, but she was helpless against the relentless force that was Marcia and Gemma. My dad and I looked at each other and smirked. Eventually, Mom gave in and we all headed out.

Mom walked with Marcia and Gemma, who gave her a running narrative on every place they passed. I followed behind with Dad. When we reached Union Square, Gemma said to Mom, "You'll have to come over here Wednesday morning for the market. It'll be the best place to stock up on food for Thanksgiving. Katie shops here all the time."

"The farmers bring their produce in to sell, and they're fun to talk to," I added. Anything that reminded my parents of home was sure to make them feel better about me living in New York.

"There aren't any muggers in the park?" Mom asked nervously, cradling her purse against her chest.

"It's pretty safe," Marcia assured her. "It's busy, and you're generally safe wherever you see a bunch of people."

The restaurant was on the other side of the park. We crossed the street and reached the awning-covered entrance. "And here we are!" Gemma said, before stepping forward to check in with the hostess.

"This is a typical New York bistro," Marcia explained.

It was a long, narrow room with mirrors on the walls to visually widen the space and a low ceiling made of old-fashioned pressed-tin tiles. The tables were close together, so we could overhear a hodge-podge of discussions about everything from politics to movies. I'd been fascinated by restaurants like these when I first moved to New York, for they were so different from the chain restaurants on the freeway that dominated dining out in my part of the world.

Mom looked nervously at the white tablecloth as we took our seats at the table. "You girls don't have to take us out for dinner," she said.

Gemma put her hand on Mom's. "Mrs. Chandler, we insist. We

simply demand at least one homemade pumpkin pie for each of us in return."

She knew exactly how to work my mom, who instantly looked better. If she could pay off a debt, she was much happier. After we'd given our drink orders to the waiter, Mom beamed at Gemma and Marcia. "You girls look so glamorous! You really fit into the big city." She then put an arm around my shoulders. "But I'm glad our Katie is still just the same. You haven't changed a bit."

"Mom!" I protested, but it didn't do any good. She was on a roll.

"You know, it wouldn't hurt you to wear a little more makeup so you don't look so bland. Maybe you should wear more lipstick, or a darker shade. I brought a few samples with me that might look good on you."

By that time of day, I was lucky if I had any lipstick on at all other than on my teeth. "Mom, New York women don't wear that much makeup," I said.

"It's true," Gemma agreed. "The natural look is the goal."

My mom, who never left the house without doing her face in the full Mary Kay lineup, looked horrified. "Really? Well, then, Katie, who knew? You've always been in style."

"Katie looks fine," Dad said from behind his menu.

"Of course she does. But it wouldn't hurt her to liven up her look. We don't want our little country mouse to fade into the background in the big city."

"Mom, I have a boyfriend. I think I'm doing okay," I said, trying not to cringe visibly. I felt mousy enough most of the time without any help. Then I realized how easily I'd let the word "boyfriend" roll off my tongue and hoped I wasn't overselling the relationship.

Gemma, bless her heart, came to my rescue. "So anyway, here's the plan for the week," she said. "I'm getting off work early tomorrow, so I'll show you around in the afternoon. That might be a good day to go to the Empire State Building. I know someone who works there who can get us past the usual lines."

"My boss gave me Wednesday off, so I'm all yours then," I said.

"Then Thursday and Friday are holidays, and we'll have the weekend." With any luck, I wouldn't have killed anyone or died of embarrassment by Sunday night.

Then again, embarrassment was a pretty minor consequence compared with everything else that might happen, I realized as I looked up and noticed a man walking across the restaurant toward our table. It was none other than Phelan Idris. I'd never faced him without Owen by my side, and while I knew he couldn't hurt me magically and I suspected I could hold my own against him physically—especially with my friends and parents close at hand—I didn't want to have to deal with him at all. I glanced around the restaurant, for once hoping for a glimpse of gargoyle or fairy, but there was nothing out of the ordinary. All I could hope was that an incognito human wizard was nearby.

I held my breath and willed him not to recognize me, to keep walking right out of the restaurant, but no such luck. With a smile that could only be described as evil, he came straight to our table, put a hand on the back of my chair, and leaned over me. "Well, now, if it isn't Katie Chandler," he said. "I almost didn't recognize you without your boyfriend nearby."

I should have come up with a witty remark while I watched him approaching us, but I was drawing a complete blank. All my snappy comebacks to him involved referring to magic, which left me with nothing to say in front of my friends and family.

And he knew it, I could tell. He smirked and said, "Boy, does he know how to show a girl a good time, walking her to and from work every day. I always knew he was dull, but I had no idea it was that bad." He patted me on top of my head. "Let me know if you ever want to try something a little more interesting. I did set you up with some friends of mine at that party on Friday."

Every head at my table swiveled to look at me. "Sorry, they weren't my type," I said. "But you know what they say about birds of a feather."

He laughed. "Good one. And speaking of birds, you know some

of my feathered friends seem to have a thing for that boyfriend of yours."

I shivered at the memory of the harpy tearing into Owen's shoulder and at the thought of the other one that had attacked us on the street last week. I dared a glance at my family and friends and saw that they looked utterly baffled. So far, he hadn't said anything that was outright about magic, but he'd said enough strange stuff that I was sure I was going to have to come up with an explanation.

"Well, considering the other options, I can hardly blame them," I managed to quip. When he didn't respond, I turned to look at him. He was staring at Gemma.

"Well, aren't you pretty?" he said, his eyeballs practically popping out of their sockets. "Are you a model?" She got that a lot, considering she was tall, thin, elegant, and worked in fashion. Still, I wondered what it said about me that even my mortal enemy couldn't stay focused on me for long. Maybe I did need brighter lipstick. Or a brighter personality.

Gemma rolled her eyes. "No," she said with the slightest of sneers. That was a pretty good sign she saw him as I did. He wasn't pulling a Rod and making himself look gorgeous.

"You could be, you know," he said, now sounding more like an overeager geek than a crafty, evil wizard.

"Thanks," she said flatly, picking up her menu and burying her face in it.

I was on the verge of reminding him that he was supposed to be threatening me, not hitting on my roommate, when I remembered that I didn't want him threatening me. I didn't want him hitting on my roommate, either, but Gemma was more than capable of dealing with guys like that.

"I know some people," he said. "I could pull a few strings, open a few doors."

"No thanks," she said, not looking up from her menu.

He looked more like the president of the AV club who had just been turned down after asking the prom queen to dance than like an evil wizard out to take over the world. I worried that he'd do something evil to make Gemma notice him, but apparently he found someone else much more interesting, for he crossed the room abruptly and began bothering that person. I wasn't sure what was more annoying, a nemesis who focused all his attention on me or a nemesis who couldn't seem to be bothered with me for more than a minute at a stretch.

"Okay, that was weird," Marcia said.

I chanced a glance around the table. Everyone was giving me funny looks. Mom looked like she was ready to go right back to the airport. "Friend of yours?" Gemma asked, looking up from her menu now that the coast was clear.

"Not really. He's just someone who knows someone I know, and I seem to have been caught in the middle. He pops up every so often to be a pest," I explained, trying to act like it was no big deal. But it was a big deal. If he was shadowing me, he had to be up to something, and I couldn't help but suspect that some of his scarier friends might also be around. And worse, he now knew what my friends and my parents looked like.

The next morning when Owen and I got to work, I let him go ahead while I stayed at the building entrance to talk to Sam. "Can you do me a favor?" I asked him.

"Sure, doll. What's up?"

"Well, Idris paid me a visit last night—when I was at dinner with my roommates and my parents."

His stone face looked astonished. "That shouldn't have happened. I wonder how he got past my people. What did he want?"

"It was just the usual bad movie-villain taunting. And hitting on my roommate. But I really don't want it to happen again. I'm trying to convince my parents that I'm safe and happy here, and I can't do that if I have evil geek wizards stalking me."

"I've got it under control," he said with a salute.

"Thanks, Sam." I glanced up at the doorway where Owen had disappeared into the building, then turned back to Sam. "You might want to have a detail follow Owen over the holiday, too. I think he's visiting his foster family, and if Idris is doing this to me, I can only imagine what he's got in store for Owen."

"Good idea. I'm glad you brought it up. The kid himself never would have asked for help."

"Of course, you didn't hear it from me," I said as I opened the door.

"Hear what?" he asked with a wink.

I was halfway up the main lobby stairs on my way up to my office when Trix flew toward me. "Oh, good, Katie! There you are! Come quick!" She turned and flew back the way she'd come without waiting for me to respond.

"What is it?" I asked as I ran to keep up with her.

"It's Ari. That girl in Sales she hates said something about her probably being the spy, and things went downhill from there. They're shooting magic at each other, so you're the only one who can get in there safely and break it up."

Well, actually there were a number of other magical immunes in the company who could do the job, but I knew what she meant. This was the kind of thing that was probably best left among friends instead of getting anyone more official involved.

The feeling of power in use became so intense it gave me goose bumps when Trix slowed to a halt. "There they are," she whispered.

Ahead of us, Ari and Melisande Rogers were slugging it out magically. It looked a lot like the last big fight between our guys and the Idris team, only with fewer people. They kept throwing power at each other in an attempt to knock each other out. "Watch what you say about me, bitch," Ari snarled, hurling something glowing at Melisande.

Melisande ducked it without mussing a hair on her perfectly coiffed head. "I must have hit close to home to get you this upset," she shot back, punctuating her words with a glowing snake of light that Ari easily sidestepped.

"Or I just don't like you," Ari replied.

I took a deep breath and threw myself into the fray, feeling like I was getting myself into a dogfight and wishing there was a water hose handy to use to break it up. My hair seemed to stand on end from all the power being tossed around. "Enough!" I shouted. "Do you two want to get in real trouble? Do you know what the boss would say if he knew what you were up to?"

The level of power in the air declined. They glared at me, but they seemed to have quit trying to kill each other. There was a tense moment as I waited to see what would happen next; then Melisande turned wordlessly and headed toward her office. Ari made as if to go after her, but Trix caught her arm. I hurried to grab the other arm, and the two of us marched her toward R&D.

"So, do you have any plans for the holiday?" I asked, forcing my voice to be bright and cheerful in an attempt to defuse the situation. "I've got the day off tomorrow, so I'm taking my parents sightseeing. And then on Friday, my mom and I are going shopping. She's always wanted to go to Bloomingdale's."

Trix caught on quickly to what I was trying to do. "Oh, you have to show your mom those red shoes."

"I should," I agreed, as chipper as a morning news anchorwoman. "Do you think you'll buy them?"

"What would I do with shoes like that? But they probably wouldn't even have my size. They always seem to run out of the sevens first. You can find fives and tens on the sale rack, but the sevens are usually gone as soon as they come into the store."

"Guys, I know what you're doing," Ari said. "And thanks, but you don't have to babysit me anymore. I've calmed down. I'm not going to kill anyone anytime soon."

Trix winked at me from the other side of Ari. "I knew it. Shoes always work. And they say music has soothing power." I knew everything was going to be okay when Ari joined in the laughter.

The apartment was empty when I got home that evening, but not for long. I'd barely changed out of my work clothes when the front door opened and my parents came in with Gemma. Their arms were loaded with shopping bags. "Did you have a good time?" I asked, then did a double take when I realized my dad had one of those foam Statue of Liberty crowns on his head.

"We had a wonderful time," Mom said. "I found the cutest snow globes at the Empire State Building. Now, where's your kitchen? I've already started shopping for Thanksgiving, so we stopped by the hotel on our way here to pick up the food I bought at the market this morning while your dad took a nap."

"Here, let me take these," I said, stepping forward and taking the shopping bags from her. "The kitchen's around the corner." As I led her to the alcove that passed for a kitchen in our apartment, I glanced into the bags. "These are gorgeous pumpkins. Which market did you go to?"

"The one Gemma told me about last night. While we were waiting for her to get off work, I wandered over there. You were right, they had the nicest vendors."

I hesitated, that far-too-familiar sick feeling forming in my stomach again. The Union Square market wasn't open on Tuesdays and Thursdays, as I'd learned not so long ago. On those days, there was only a magical market that most people couldn't see. No, she couldn't have been shopping there. Maybe she'd been turned around and had found the market in front of St. Mark's Church. That one was open on Tuesdays.

"Was it the market in front of the church?" I asked.

"No, the one in front of the big bookstore. And you call this a kitchen? How do you cook in here?"

I felt dizzy. My mother could not have gone shopping at a magical market. Then again, this was Thanksgiving week. Maybe the schedule was different. The early part of the week would be prime food shopping time. That had to be it.

Fortunately, my mom didn't notice my confusion. She was too busy complaining about the lack of counter space. "And is this even a full-size oven? Can you cook a turkey in this?"

"I did last year," I said, putting the bag of pumpkins on the dining table. "The one I bought this year is the same size, so it should fit."

Gemma joined us in the kitchen area. "I think Katie's the only person in New York who actually cooks, so they don't make very big kitchens here. We usually go out to eat or order in." She opened the refrigerator, then turned to yell at Marcia, "You forgot to buy water again."

She might as well have stuck my mother with a hot poker. "You buy water? Why on earth would you do that? You can get it for free from the tap." Mom shook her head. "I don't know what the world is coming to. Buying water."

Gemma took a can from the refrigerator. "Can I get you something to drink, Mrs. Chandler?"

"I don't suppose you've got a Diet Dr Pepper in there?"

"You're in luck. We Texas gals have a supply." She handed a can to Mom.

I took a glass out of the cabinet and filled it from the tap. My mom smiled approvingly. "See, I knew you wouldn't lose all your common sense when you moved up here," she said.

I took a sip of the water and fought not to make a face. While I agreed with the practicality of not buying water, I could see Marcia and Gemma's point. There was something off about the taste, probably the result of flowing through the ancient pipes in our building. I didn't want to think about what we might be drinking in that water. Something must have gone wrong in the system because I didn't remember it usually being that bad.

"Dad, can I get you anything?" I called to the living room.

"Just some coffee. Instant's fine if nobody else wants any."

It would set off a whole new discussion if anyone said that we usually got coffee at Starbucks, but fortunately Marcia, our resident coffee snob, was out. I found a jar of instant in the back of the cabinet—usually reserved only for dire emergencies—put on a kettle, and made him a cup.

"So what's on your agenda for tomorrow?" Gemma asked.

"I want to go to Macy's and I want to see Times Square," Mom declared. "That's the heart of New York."

"You'll want to go in the morning so you'll miss the worst of the parade preparations," Gemma said.

"Then, if it's nice, I was thinking we could go to Central Park," I suggested.

"I was hoping we could visit your office," Dad said. I knew what he was up to. He wanted to see for himself if my boss was an honest businessman.

"I don't think that'll be possible," I said. "We're in the middle of a big project, so there's a total security lockdown. I wouldn't be able to get you in the building."

"But we're your parents," Mom protested.

"Yeah, but if I can get you in, then everyone else's parents have to be allowed in, and then where would we be? I can't ask them to make an exception."

That did the trick. "Oh, well, of course not," she said. "We wouldn't want to be any bother." She was very big on not being a bother and not having anyone make exceptions for her.

All I could hope was that I could play that card the rest of the week.

The next morning, I met my parents at their hotel. They were geared up for a day of tourism, with cameras and guidebooks at the ready. "You don't need the guidebooks," I told them. "You've got me." While I hadn't run into much in the way of nonmagical mischief in my time in New York, being with two obvious out-of-towners might alter my odds. Anyone walking around with a guidebook was asking for trouble.

"You're probably right," Mom said. "We don't want to look like tourists. See, I even dressed like a New Yorker. I hear they wear a lot of black." She wore black slacks and a black turtleneck sweater under her overcoat. She actually would have fit in if she hadn't been wearing white sneakers with that outfit. I chose not to say anything. It was better if she was comfortable, and I tried to convince myself that she could pass as a commuter.

Once they'd put the guidebooks back in their room, I herded my parents toward Union Square. "The market's a lot bigger today," Mom remarked when we reached the park. "Let's see if that nice man who sold me the pumpkins is here again. I told him I had a single daughter he ought to meet." Before I could stop her, she'd headed off into the market. I hurried to keep up with her. "Funny, I don't see him here today. You'd think a pumpkin seller would be here on the day before Thanksgiving."

That now familiar sick feeling hit my stomach again. She was right. Any normal vendor who sold pumpkins would have been at the market that day. But my mom shouldn't have been able to see the magical market.

"Lois," my dad said, an edge of warning in his voice. "You wanted to see Macy's and Times Square."

"Oh, right. I already have pumpkins, so we don't have time for this. But Katie, make sure you look for him next time you're at the market. I'm pretty sure he was single. And he lives on a farm. He'd be perfect for you."

"Mom, remember, I have a boyfriend. You know, Ethan? The guy who picked you up at the airport in his Mercedes?"

She laughed. "Oh, right. I'd forgotten that. Sorry about that, sweetheart. Old habits are hard to break. I'm so used to you being alone and single. But it wouldn't hurt to keep that farmer in mind, in case things don't work out. You never know."

I finally got them onto a bus uptown, and then we walked across town to Macy's, where my mother had a religious experience before practically fainting at the price tags. All she bought was a shopping bag with a logo on it to take home to her sister. Dad and I then successfully pushed her outside.

"It's not that far uptown to Times Square," I said, once we were back on the sidewalk, "but let's take the subway. There's something about emerging right in Times Square that adds to the experience." That was what Gemma and Marcia had done to me the first time I came to New York.

Mom held her purse tightly against her chest and glared at anyone who came near her inside the subway station. Even my dad edged a little closer to me. I was sure I'd felt much the same way my first time on the subway, but it was such a daily part of my life that I didn't even think about it anymore. My concern had more to do with deranged wizard geeks and magical creatures that might be following us. In spite of what Owen and Sam had promised me about extra security, I hadn't caught sight of anyone or anything that looked like it might be guarding us.

A train came along and we boarded. "We don't need to sit down," I told my parents. "We'll be getting off at the next stop." The three of us stood around a pole, Mom glancing anxiously around the car and at all the people around us.

"You do this every day?" she asked.

"It's not so bad. You get used to it." My usual traveling companion didn't hurt, but I didn't share that with her.

When we reached the Forty-second Street station, we fought through the crowd to get off the train and head to an exit. "If everyone would wait their turn, that would be easier," Mom huffed. "They don't have to push and shove."

"It's a way of life, Mom," I said with a grin. "Now, we'll be coming up right into Times Square. It's even more impressive at night, but it's still something to see in the daytime."

I might have been used to New York, but I still got a little thrill of excitement when I went into Times Square. This was the noisy, chaotic New York that outsiders usually pictured when they thought of the city. In my relatively quiet neighborhood it was easy to forget that this side of New York was there.

I kept a hold on each parent, making sure we didn't get separated in the throng of tourists while my parents gaped at all the bright lights and flashing signs.

"I wonder what their light bill is," Dad said with a frown. "Seems like a waste to me."

"Would you just look at this?" Mom said, over and over. "Oh my."

I pointed out the building where they broadcast *Good Morning America,* the famous military recruiting station, and some of the theaters. "A lot of the Broadway theaters are actually on side streets," I added.

"So this is Broadway, then?" Mom asked, her eyes wide with awe.

"Yes, this is Broadway. Exciting, isn't it?"

"And look at all these people. Hey, that man's not wearing any clothes!"

I turned to see the guy who was famous for playing the guitar while wearing only his underwear and a pair of boots. "Oh, him. He's a street performer."

"Well, he's going to catch his death of cold. It's freezing here." I held tightly to her arm so she couldn't go tell him to put some clothes on so he wouldn't come down with pneumonia.

My dad stared at another person on the street. "Well, would you look at that," he said with a chuckle. "That boy must have fallen face-first into his tackle box."

I turned to see a teenager playing drums, his face covered with piercings. "Don't stare," I hissed at Dad as I held on to his arm.

Before I'd learned about magic, when I'd seen even stranger things on the streets of New York that nobody else seemed to notice, this was what I'd been afraid I looked like—a green tourist straight from the sticks. "This is probably the weirdest part of New York," I said. "The rest of the city isn't like this." Well, actually, there were weirder parts of the city, or so I'd heard, but tourists generally didn't go there, and I didn't plan to tell my parents about them.

Mom came to an abrupt halt, pulling Dad and me to a stop with her. "Now, she's good," she said. She released her death grip on her purse and opened it. "I want to give her a dollar."

I turned to see a fairy hovering above the sidewalk. She wasn't a street performer. She was the real deal, just going about her business. That sick feeling in my stomach came back in full force. My mother could see the fairy.

nine

It would have been nice if the fairy had been someone I knew, someone I could get to play along with me. Unfortunately, she was a total stranger. Before I had a chance to react, Mom tried to hand her a dollar. "I don't know how you do that, but I'm impressed," Mom said. "Lovely costume, too."

The fairy looked at her like she was crazy. "What the f—" she started to say.

"Mom!" I interrupted, dragging my mother away even as my head spun trying to think of what I could do for damage control. If she was magically immune, that would make things infinitely more complicated. Automatically, I scanned the area, looking for anything else magical I might have to explain, but Times Square was so full of oddities, it was impossible to spot the magical oddities in the midst of everything else.

"Kathleen Elizabeth Chandler, I did not raise you to be that rude," Mom protested.

"Mom!" I hissed. "Hush and listen. That wasn't a street performer. I think you insulted her." I glanced back over my shoulder to make sure a pissed-off fairy wasn't following us, but I didn't see anything. It wasn't until I was about to turn back to my mom that I thought I saw something out of the corner of my eye. I looked back again, and there was the fairy, a shimmering haze around her so that she looked like she was blurring. I grabbed my parents and pushed them into the nearest doorway, in case she was putting together a spell to use against us. I'd be safe and apparently so would Mom, but I wasn't so sure about Dad. What if she was one of Idris's people? Worse, what if she'd actually been stalking us on purpose?

The doorway turned out to lead into a souvenir shop. "Look! Postcards! You'll want to send one to each of the boys, right?" I said with forced enthusiasm. The huge rack of cheap postcards would distract my parents for a good five minutes while they argued over which ten to buy and which view of the skyline was nicer.

That gave me time to check out the situation and figure out what to do next. I ducked back out of the souvenir shop and looked up and down the sidewalk. It didn't seem like the angry fairy lady was going to come after us, so maybe I'd been overly paranoid to assume she was working for Idris. I was sure I'd feel better if I could spot one of my MSI bodyguards and verify the situation, but I didn't see anyone I recognized, human or otherwise. There was never a gargoyle around when you needed one.

That brought up my next problem: what should I do about Mom? My first instinct was to call the office and ask for advice. Rod knew all about immunes. He'd know what to do. Then I realized that would be a very bad idea. The company was desperate for immunes to help them guard against other magic users, and we were increasingly rare. I couldn't let them try to recruit my mother. If she knew what I was mixed up in, she'd haul me back home, magical immunity or not. We were going to get through this visit, and then I'd put her back on a plane to Texas where she could live a blissfully unmagical existence. All I had to do was keep the secret for a few more days. Fortunately, my mom was primed to think New York was exceptionally weird. I'd lived here a year before I learned the truth. Surely I could get my mom through a few days.

I counted to ten to steady myself before going back into the store. Mom and Dad were still arguing over postcards. "This night view is a good one," Mom said.

"But you can't see anything other than lights," Dad pointed out. "The sunset one's nicer."

"Get both," I suggested. They turned to look at me, and I realized they hadn't even noticed I'd been gone. They finally settled on ten cards, and I got them to the cash register before they could start discussing which card to send to which person.

As we left the store, Mom asked, "Now, Katie, what was that all about?"

Dad gave one of his long-suffering sighs. "Lois, you tried to give some girl on the street a dollar. I know she was funny looking, but if you tried to give a dollar to every funny-looking person you saw on the street in this town, you'd run out of money awful fast." He put his hands in his pockets and walked ahead of us, like he was ashamed to be seen with us in public. I couldn't entirely blame him. In fact, I wanted to join him.

"She wasn't a street performer, Mom," I said.

"But Katie, she had on wings. What kind of person wears wings, when it's not even Halloween? And I could swear she was flying."

I scrambled for an explanation and came up with something she wouldn't dare question. "Mom, there are all kinds of alternative life-styles, and they're pretty open about them in this city. I don't think you really want to get more into it than that, okay?"

She looked stunned, then frowned like she was trying to put together a mental image. Finally, she shook her head as if to clear it. "Okay," she said at last in a small voice I could barely hear over the traffic.

"Let's catch up with Dad," I said, relieved that I'd managed to get away with telling a version of the truth. All I had to do to get through the rest of the week was think of the places in the city where we were least likely to run into magic. Oh yeah, piece of cake.

Unfortunately, I'd already promised to show them Central Park. There was maximum weirdness potential there, as I'd discovered soon after joining MSI. Any enchanted frogs should have been hibernating for the winter by Thanksgiving, so that wouldn't be an issue. I'd hope there wouldn't be any pranks like the one played on Marcia's boy-friend, Jeff, when his friends cast an illusion that made him and every-one else think he'd been turned into a frog, so that he did things like crouch naked beside a pond in the park. I could probably explain any naked men squatting by ponds as deranged drunks. I was more wor-ried about the number of male fairies—they called themselves "sprites" because they thought it sounded less gay—and gnomes who worked in the park. Sprites could be more "alternative lifestyle" people my mom wouldn't want to talk about, but how could I explain living gar-den gnomes?

As I expected, my folks were charmed by the Plaza Hotel and the lineup of carriages they'd seen so often in movies. I led them to the Mall so they could look down the lane of elm trees. It wasn't as spec-tacular as it was during the summer when there was a canopy of leaves, but I thought it was still an impressive sight. Dad studied it for a while, then asked, "About how many acres do you think this place is?"

"I have no idea, but it is a huge park. If you get into the middle of it, you can almost forget you're in the city."

He nodded. "Hmm. That's good. You need something green around to keep you feeling alive."

"Hey, what's that?" We both turned when we heard Mom's voice.

"What's what, Lois?" Dad asked.

"That!" She was pointing at the base of a nearby statue, where a garden gnome was at work with a tiny shovel in the flower bed be-neath the statue. I did a double take, for I was pretty sure I recognized that gnome, which was odd. I didn't know too many magical people who didn't work at MSI, and I definitely wasn't acquainted with the park's magical groundskeeping staff. The gnome's look of sheer panic when he looked up at me was proof that this was someone I knew. After a moment, I realized who he was: Hertwick, a member of MSI's sales force. But what was he doing in the park during business hours?

Then I remembered that the more important question was how I'd find an explanation that would satisfy my mother without making my dad, who probably didn't see anything at all, suspicious.

"I don't see anything," I said. Hertwick looked indignant, but then I caught his eye, inclined my head slightly toward my mother and frowned. He got the message and jumped behind the statue while my mom was glaring at my dad.

"It's right there!" Mom protested, turning to point to the place where Hertwick had been. Then she frowned and looked puzzled. "Or it was. I could have sworn I saw something. It looked like one of those little statues in Louise Ellerbe's front lawn—which I always thought were as tacky as plastic pink flamingos—only it was moving. It was like it was digging in the flower bed."

This time it was my dad who took her arm and moved her away. "Maybe we'd better head back to the hotel," he said. "You're probably tired."

She jerked her arm out of his grasp. "I am not tired. And don't tell me my hormones are out of whack, either. I know what I saw." She marched right over to the statue, then walked around it. Hertwick ran around the statue base, keeping it between him and her. When she'd made a full revolution around the statue, she returned to Dad and me, a frown wrinkling her forehead. "Huh," she said, then looked up at Dad and wagged a finger in his face. "And don't you dare say a word, Frank Chandler." She headed off down the path without a backward glance, with Dad and me hurrying to keep up.

As luck would have it, she just about ran head-on into a uniformed park ranger. A uniformed park ranger with wings. A uniformed park ranger with wings who used to date one of my friends. It was Pippin, Trix's ex (?) boyfriend. This was supposed to be a big city, so why was I running into more people I knew in Central Park than I'd expect to in the town's only grocery store back home?

Mom took one look at him, with his pointed ears, slanted eyes, and wings, and screamed bloody murder. He looked almost as shocked, then closed his eyes like he was mentally checking the status of his veiling spell. I ducked behind Dad to make sure Pippin didn't recognize me. The last thing I needed was for him to ask me about Trix. I couldn't begin to explain how I knew a guy with wings who worked in the park.

Dad grabbed Mom's arm again. "Sorry about that, sir," he said with a nod toward Pippin. "She's heard too many stories about muggers in the park."

Pippin looked vastly relieved. "No problem, sir," he said. "But the park's changed a lot in the past twenty years. In daylight, you're as safe here as you are anywhere else in the city." Then he went on about his business, and I let out my pent-up breath in a sigh.

"I didn't think he was a mugger, Frank," Mom protested. "That boy had wings. Was he another one of those alternative lifestyle people, Katie?"

I didn't know how to answer that. No matter what I said, one of my parents would think I was either crazy or a liar. How had I managed a whole year as a magical immune in this city before I had to face the truth, when Mom was getting so close in only one day? I supposed it was because she wasn't even trying to be cool or fit in.

"You know what, Mom?" I said at last. "I learned a long time ago to give up figuring out every little weird thing in this city. It's the only way to stay sane."

Mom came over bright and early Thanksgiving morning to get the turkey in the oven. I was her trusty lieutenant for the cooking. Gemma and Marcia, who weren't so adept in the kitchen, served as foot soldiers, helping clean up so we could keep cooking. Dad, who knew what was good for him, stayed out of the way.

Once the Macy's parade was under way, Mom flitted back and forth from the kitchen to the living room, which wasn't a huge distance. "Frank, can you believe we were just there yesterday?" she kept saying.

"Yes, Lois, we were there," he always replied, with infinite patience.

After one of those bouts, she returned to the kitchen and said to Gemma, "Did Katie tell you what we saw in Times Square yesterday?"

"The naked guy with the guitar?"

"Well, yes, we did see that. But have you seen the people with wings?"

Gemma looked at me over the top of Mom's head and mouthed, "Wings?"

"I think Times Square was a weirdness overdose," I said. "It can be overwhelming."

"There are some very strange people in this city," Mom said.

"Yeah, tell me about it," Gemma agreed. "You wouldn't believe half the weird things I see on a daily basis. And New Yorkers don't even look twice."

The downstairs buzzer sounded and Marcia answered it. She returned to the kitchen and said, "Jeff's here. He's on his way up."

Speaking of weird things, I thought. Jeff was magical, though Marcia didn't know it, and he had a tendency to get magical pranks pulled on him. That was potential disaster around my mother. I managed to be nearest the front door when he got up to our apartment. "Hi, Jeff, good to see you," I greeted him loudly, then whispered, "My mom's an immune, so play it safe, okay?" His eyes widened, but he nodded. I brought him further into the apartment. "Dad, this is Jeff, Marcia's boyfriend. Jeff, this is Frank Chandler, my dad."

Dad stood to shake hands very properly, which took Jeff aback. "Oh, um, hi, good to meet you," he said.

"And it's nice to meet you," Dad said. "Marcia goes way back with us. She's like part of the family." There was a stern warning underlying his friendly words. Jeff wasn't the sharpest knife in the drawer, but he nodded like he got the idea.

Philip came along next, and he was the one I was most worried about, for he really had spent decades as a frog. As a result, he was very old-fashioned and had an unhealthy fascination with flies.

I shouldn't have worried, though. His archaic manners meant he fit right in with my parents, and there were no flies to be seen. He arrived with an armful of flowers—a bouquet each for Gemma and Mom. It didn't take him long to get into Mom's good graces. He handed her the bouquet with a courtly bow. "I must offer you my most sincere thanks for inviting me," he said, then kissed her hand.

"Where did you find him?" Mom whispered to a beaming Gemma.

"Would you believe, in Central Park?"

"We were just there yesterday," Mom said.

I tried to catch Philip's eye and warn him, but he never took his eyes off Gemma. I wasn't quite certain how magical he was other than that he'd been enchanted and didn't seem too shocked about it. He'd managed to hide his origins from Gemma, so he might get through dinner without causing a scene.

We got Thanksgiving dinner on the table with a minimum of disasters, and Jeff and Philip were both intimidated enough by Dad to keep their mouths shut. I got a better sense of why dates in high school had been few and far between for me. Between my dad and my three older brothers, it would have taken a very brave boy to come anywhere near me.

Ethan arrived just in time for dinner. "Sorry I'm late," he said as he came through the door. "I got sidetracked catching up on some work. Good to see you again, Mr. and Mrs. Chandler." I introduced him to Jeff and Philip, and then we gathered around the table to say grace.

Dad made us all hold hands and bow our heads. Jeff looked baffled, but he followed along. I hoped Dad went for a shorter prayer instead of the sermon he could sometimes preach on Thanksgiving. "Oh Lord, thank you for bringing us all together here today," he began. It looked like we were in for the long version. Midway through, there was a yelp from across the circle as apparently Marcia had to keep Jeff from sneaking something from the table. Ethan spent the whole time massaging my hand with his thumb, which felt nice even as I feared it would earn a lightning bolt from heaven. There had to be something wrong with flirting during a prayer. I wasn't sure which I feared most, God or the wrath of my father if he caught us. We all joined in a hearty "Amen!" when Dad finally brought the prayer to a close.

Then it was time to dig in, and we worked our way around the table to fill our plates. As Ethan put a slice of turkey on my plate, he whispered to me, "Is something wrong? You look stressed."

I debated whether I should tell him, but I felt like I needed one sure ally in case things got weird. "I figured out yesterday that my mom's immune to magic. That must be where I got it."

He nodded. "I see. So now you're constantly worried about what she's going to notice."

"Yeah. I almost ran out of explanations yesterday. Please don't say anything about work. I want to get her home to Texas without having to tell her the whole story. You're as immune as I am—as she is. Help me look out for anything I'd need to explain. And please don't tell anyone about this when we go back to the office."

"What are you so worried about?"

"I just—I just want things to be normal. I can handle my job being totally whacked out, that my boss is Merlin, and that I have a fairy in the office next to me. I can even handle the fact that on every date I try to go on things tend to zap in and out of existence, or scary things try to hurt me, or even that people who think they used to be frogs serenade me." I noticed his confused look and said, "Long story. But I need my family to be normal. Not for me, but for them. My life has changed. Theirs doesn't have to. I want them to be able to go home and be happy, understand?"

"I think I see your point," he whispered.

"What are you two lovebirds doing whispering over the turkey?" my mom called out from across the room.

"Of course, with my family, 'normal' is a relative term," I said with a sigh.

Ethan laughed and handed me a glass of Mom's traditional cranberry punch. "I'm not sure any family is truly normal," he said.

There wasn't room for us to sit at the table with all the food on it, so we took our plates to the living room and sat on the floor, the dining chairs, or the sofa. I tried to think of a safe conversation to start, but Mom beat me to the punch.

"I hope you like everything. I'm sure it's different from what y'all eat for Thanksgiving up here, but it's traditional for us back home."

There were mumbles around the room about how good the food was. Food seemed to be a safe topic. "I know a few people were surprised by the corn bread dressing I made last year," I said.

"My mom used to make oyster dressing, before she gave up cooking entirely," Ethan commented. Mom looked like he'd uttered a blasphemy. Okay, so maybe food wasn't such a safe topic. I'd seen from my oldest brother's marriage that what to serve for holidays was a bigger source of marital strife than money or sex. A corn bread dressing person and a sausage stuffing person weren't likely to see eye-to-eye. Oysters in the dressing could be grounds for a holy war. I noticed with great relief that Ethan didn't seem to have any problems eating the dressing we'd made.

Mom had taken on the role of hostess, and she spoke up again to keep the conversation rolling. "Ethan, we ran into a friend of yours the other night," she said. "Or maybe 'friend' isn't the right word. He said some very mean things about you, and I'll have you know I didn't believe a word of it."

Ethan shot an utterly baffled look at me, which I returned, equally baffled. I had no idea what she was talking about. "My friend?" Ethan asked.

"Yes, he was at the restaurant where we had dinner Monday night," she explained. "He came over to talk to Katie—very rude young man. He didn't so much as acknowledge us, though I suppose Katie should have made the introductions."

Only then did I realize what she meant. Oh no, she'd thought Idris was talking about Ethan when he referred to my boyfriend. It was a natural assumption to make, but it was a misunderstanding right out of a bad sitcom, and I couldn't think of a way out of it. I'd been so worried about getting tangled up in magical problems that I hadn't considered the potential for maternal-meddling complications.

Mom continued, oblivious to my discomfort. "Now, I know you do more than walk Katie to and from work. I'm sure you take her to some very nice places. That boy was just being mean."

Realization dawned in Ethan's eyes. I knew he'd figured out exactly who Idris was referring to as my boyfriend. I wished I could play it cool and insist that it was just Idris being a jerk, but I felt my face growing warm. Ethan frowned and nodded slightly, and I was sure he'd noticed. He might not have had magical powers, but I felt like he could see right through me.

A split second later he managed to compose himself. "If it's who I think it was, you can ignore anything he said. I beat him in a tough negotiation once, and he's never forgiven me." Then he abruptly changed the subject. "What do you think of New York so far?" I could have kissed him. Well, I wanted to kiss him anyway, in spite of what he might have thought at that moment, but his coming to my rescue made me want to even more.

"It's interesting," Dad said with a nod. "I'd like to get a better look at the park. You know, I've got this new fertilizer in stock that might help them. I wonder what they're using now."

"Was the city what you expected?" Ethan clarified his question.

"I knew it would be kind of strange," Mom said, then dropped her voice to a stage whisper. "But I wasn't expecting all those alternative lifestyle people."

"Alternative lifestyle people?" Gemma asked. "Katie, you didn't take your parents to the West Village, did you?"

"No, just Times Square," I said, trying not to grit my teeth.

"We saw this woman wearing fairy wings in public," Mom said. "Very odd."

"No, odd would have been a man wearing fairy wings in public," Gemma said with a laugh. "Preferably with pink tights and a tutu."

"Oh, we saw one of those, too," Mom said. "Though not with the tights and tutu. But he had wings."

"There wasn't anything that strange about that woman," Dad said. "Lois just thought she was a street performer and tried to tip her. And the man was a park ranger with a backpack on, not wings."

"Frank, the woman had wings and was flying."

"She was tall. You were imagining things. It wasn't even the oddest sight in that part of town."

"Don't you tell me what I did and didn't see. If you're not going to speak to me with respect, then you don't have to speak to me at all." She crossed her arms over her chest and pointedly turned her back to Dad.

I got up and said, "Anyone for pumpkin pie?" I'd thought my worst problem would be getting Mom home before she clued into the magic. It hadn't crossed my mind that my parents would fight over what Mom did or didn't see. The last thing I needed was for my parents to fall out because of magic.

Later that afternoon while the others watched football, Ethan and I washed dishes. "That wasn't so bad, was it?" he asked softly, his voice masked from the living room by the running water.

"Not quite as bad as the first time my oldest brother brought a girlfriend home for a holiday," I admitted. "But they're still not speaking to each other."

"If they aren't talking, then they can't be comparing stories about what they've seen."

I picked up the pan he'd just rinsed and dried it. "True. But I think this would be easier if both my parents were immune. Then the same story would work on both of them." I chuckled. "Then again, with my dad, he might be immune and we'd never know it because he'd think it was none of his business to comment on someone's obvious physical deformities."

"Think what they'd say if they met Sam."

Ice water ran through my veins. "Oh no, Sam doesn't know that he and his people have to stay out of sight. But I don't want to tell him because I don't want the company knowing about this."

"How often do you see your bodyguards?"

"Almost never."

"Well, then, it's a nonissue, isn't it?" He flicked a bit of suds onto the end of my nose and grinned at me. "You'll be fine."

He was acting like nothing had happened, but I still felt the need to clear the air. "About what my mom was saying earlier . . . that was just Idris playing his usual games."

"I figured as much."

"I don't even know what he wanted, approaching me like that."

"He wanted to make you nervous."

"It worked. But you know, he can't be too bright if he can't figure out who my boyfriend really is."

"Don't worry about it. It didn't mean anything." He didn't look at me as he answered, and I wasn't sure if it was because he was busy rinsing a glass or because there was something else going on.

I heard my mother's voice from the living room. "I still say there was one of those garden gnomes working in the park. I know what I saw." She was probably the most vocal person around when it came to not speaking to someone.

I moaned. "I need a drink." Ethan took the glass he'd just rinsed, filled it with water from the tap, and handed it to me. This was going to be the longest weekend in my life.

Mom and Dad still weren't happy with each other the next morning, so Mom declared that she wanted to go shopping and spend Dad's money. Bright and early, we headed uptown to window-shop on Fifth Avenue and Madison Avenue. I barely had a chance to look in the store windows; I was too busy keeping an eye out for weirdness I might have to explain to Mom. Fortunately, I didn't see anything particularly odd. The magical world must have been smart enough to stay home on the biggest retail day of the year. That should have been enough to relax me, but I still had to deal with Mom, which was seldom relaxing.

She made me take her picture in front of Tiffany's, then I led her a few blocks over to Bloomingdale's. She sighed in wonder as we reached the women's clothing department. "Just look at all this. It beats the heck out of the Wal-Mart in the next town over."

"Yeah, it is something."

"I want to buy you a nice new outfit. You need to look more so-phisticated."

"Mom!" I protested, but I had to admit she had a point. In spite of all Gemma's efforts to teach me fashion sense, I still tended to err on the side of practicality, from my sensible business pumps to my mix-and-match wardrobe of skirts, blouses, and sweaters.

"We can call it your Christmas present in advance. You need something nice to wear on a date with Ethan. I really like him."

"So do I."

"I should hope so. A lawyer who drives a Mercedes and who's nice enough to pick your parents up from the airport *and* do the dishes—well, hang onto him, honey."

She pulled a smart little suit off a rack. "How about this?"

"I don't really need a suit. I don't wear them for work, and I wouldn't wear one on a date."

"Hmm." She wove her way around clothing racks. "This would look pretty on you." She held up a slinky black velvet dress. "You'll need something for New Year's, now that you've got an almost guaranteed date. You could also wear it to a fancy office party."

I did like the dress, but I didn't know that velvet fit so well into my lifestyle. "I can't guarantee I'll have a date for New Year's, or that we'd do anything I could wear velvet for."

"You should have it, just in case. Now go try it on. Shoo!"

She followed me to the fitting room, then waited outside when it came my turn to go inside. The dress fit beautifully, clinging to my waist, skimming over my hips, and then flowing almost to my knees, and I could already imagine wowing Ethan with it on a date. As guilty as I felt about letting my mom buy me things, I couldn't let this go. "Come on out, honey, I want to see you in it," she called from outside the fitting room.

I came out and gave her a catwalk turn. She nodded. "Yep, we're getting it, and your dad can lump it. Tells me I'm seeing things, ha!"

After she paid for the dress, I got a burst of inspiration. "Come on, there's something I want to show you," I said, leading her to the escalators. This was a sight she'd appreciate more than almost any tourist attraction in the city: the designer shoe department. I didn't expect the worship Gemma gave the place, but Mom would be suitably impressed, I was sure.

"This is the designer department," I said in a hushed voice as we stepped off the escalator and walked past all the high-end boutiques.

"Your Aunt Sally would think she'd died and gone right to heaven if she saw this," she said in an equally hushed voice.

"And here are the shoes. Some of these are amazing."

She didn't hold any to her breast in rapture like Gemma did, but she did gawk. I'd been right about her considering this as good as visiting a museum.

I squeezed her hand. "There's one pair of shoes I really want you to see. Gemma and I found these a couple of weeks ago." I led her to the boutique where the red stiletto pump was on display.

The moment I saw it again, I knew those shoes were meant to be mine.

ten

"I'm going to get those," I said softly, more to myself than to Mom. "Aren't they gorgeous?"

"They're beautiful," she agreed. "But aren't they a little flashy for you?"

"You were just saying I needed to be more sophisticated and glamorous."

A salesman approached and said, "May I help you?"

I picked up the red shoe. "I'd like to try this in a seven medium, please."

"One moment, miss."

Mom took the sample shoe away from me and turned it over to look at the price tag. Then she gasped. "Katie Beth, did you see how expensive these are? You could buy a whole outfit for that much."

"I just want to try them on," I said, flopping into a nearby chair and slipping out of my loafers. "And they're not that expensive for good shoes. They're half the price of a pair of Manolos or Jimmy Choos."

The salesman returned with a box, then knelt at my feet. As he slid the shiny red pump onto my foot, I knew exactly how Cinderella must have felt. I felt a surge of power, like I could take on the world and have any man I wanted. "Wow," I breathed, more sigh than actual speech.

"How do those feel?" the salesman asked, sitting back on his heels. I thought I saw a flicker of desire in his eyes. Maybe he had a foot fetish and had found his dream job of putting gorgeous shoes on women's feet all day.

I gingerly stood up, wobbling for a second in the unfamiliar high, narrow heels. Once I got my balance, I took a few tentative steps that flowed into a supermodel strut. I felt like every head in the entire department had turned to watch me, and I loved the feeling. I'd never felt more alluring.

"I am definitely getting these," I said, when I returned to Mom and the salesman.

"But what would you wear them with?" Mom asked. "You couldn't wear red with them because it would either clash or be too much."

"These shoes would be the outfit. I'd wear something basic and simple as a backdrop," I argued, using Gemma's reasoning. Now I understood what Gemma had meant. I should have listened to her and bought these shoes the first time I saw them. Everything would have worked out so much better if I had, I was sure.

Mom picked up the same style of pump, but in basic black. "If you want to get those shoes, why not these? They're more versatile. You could wear these with everything, but without drawing so much attention. You don't want people saying, 'Oh, here comes Katie in her red shoes again.'"

"Why not?" I challenged. "They could be my signature item."

She shook her head. "But they're not you. You'd be wearing someone else's signature."

I put my hands on my hips. "Why aren't they me? They might be me, but you don't know me anymore. Or I could grow into them." I whirled to look at the salesman, who'd shrunk back and was pretending to mind his own business. I had a feeling this wasn't the first shoe department dispute he'd ever heard.

"They do look lovely on you," he said, "and those shoes are very popular. I can show you a pair in another color, if you like."

"No thank you," I said. "I want these." I walked over to a mirror and admired myself. I'd wear these shoes on my next date with Ethan. He wouldn't be able to resist me. I could already see how the date would go: everything would be perfect, with absolutely no weirdness; we'd go back to his place, drink that bottle of wine, and then I might have the first sex I'd had in longer than I cared to think—since my last serious college boyfriend.

But I couldn't use that reasoning on Mom, who still thought her little girl was a virgin. I might as well have been, considering I'd been with only one guy a couple of times more than five years ago. It was almost embarrassing how inexperienced I was for someone my age. Part of it was that I couldn't bring myself to treat sex as casually as most people my age seemed to. Part of it was that most men acted as though they thought touching me would be like defiling their baby sister.

That was all going to change. I was ready, and it was high time, too. I sat down and reluctantly slid my feet out of the shoes, then put my old loafers on again. "You're really going to buy those?" Mom asked, her voice heavy with disapproval.

"Yep, and it's my money, so I can get them if I want to. They'll go great with that black velvet dress." Before she could stop me, and before I could change my mind, I handed my credit card over to the salesman. If I didn't eat out for a month and stayed away from the bookstore, I could probably pay the shoes off in a couple of months. By then, I was sure I'd have worn them several times and my life would have changed completely.

Once I'd signed the credit card slip and had the shoes packed carefully into a big shopping bag, I had to resist the temptation to peek in the bag repeatedly on the way down the escalators and out of the store.

"I don't know what's gotten into you, Katie," Mom said. "You were always so practical."

"But Mom, practical is boring. I want to do something different. It'll be good for me to get a little wild and crazy. I'm only twenty-six, and I act and dress like a middle-aged woman. This is my chance to get out of my rut and shake things up."

She looked at me with wry amusement. "And you think those shoes are the key?"

"I think it's the attitude the shoes give me. They're like Dorothy's ruby slippers, only they get me away from home instead of taking me home."

"I'm sure you know what's best for you."

I thought I did. But then I was hit by a wave of buyer's remorse. I looked into the bag again, wondering if I should turn around and return the shoes. Who was I kidding? They were totally impractical, and me wearing those shoes would be like a Halloween costume. Nobody would believe it. They'd just think it was sweet little Katie, trying to act all grown-up and sexy. They'd laugh at me instead of being impressed.

"Maybe you're right," I said with a deep sigh. "Where am I going to wear these, anyway?"

"Thank goodness. I knew you'd see reason eventually."

We turned around to head back to Bloomingdale's, but we must have caught the surveillance detail off-guard, for they didn't have time to get out of sight—and since I doubted they yet knew about Mom's immunity, they probably weren't concerned about staying out of sight. We nearly came face-to-face with a hovering gargoyle.

I grabbed Mom's shoulder and spun her around to walk in the opposite direction. "On second thought, they'll think I'm crazy if I go right back. Let's window-shop a while longer and then we can return the shoes."

As we walked away, I glanced back over my shoulder, trying silently to signal the gargoyle that it had to stay well out of sight, but it was gone.

"Did you see that?" Mom asked, also looking over her shoulder.

I tried to keep her moving forward. "See what?"

"There was this thing, flying right at us."

"I think a little kid had a helium balloon. The street vendors are really out today. Want to buy a designer knockoff purse?"

She glanced over her shoulder again. "No, I don't think it's on a string."

I looked behind us, but the gargoyle must have finally caught a clue and ducked out of sight. I'd have to have a word with Sam about his people. This one seemed a bit slow. "Well, there's nothing there now," I said, steering Mom around the corner.

"Why don't you return the shoes now, and then we won't have to worry about coming back."

I peered into my shopping bag and even opened the shoe box lid a crack so I could admire the red stilettos. "On second thought, I've changed my mind. I want to keep them. They're the most beautiful shoes I've ever owned."

She shook her head wearily. "Well, if you say so. But I'm not letting you spend anymore money today."

"There's nothing more I want to buy."

"Then we can get lunch. I want to go to a deli, like in the movies."

This part of town wasn't my usual stomping grounds, but you can't swing a dead cat in Manhattan without hitting a deli, so finding a place for lunch wasn't too difficult. I doubted that the fact that there was an available table at the first deli we found on a day like today was a good sign of quality food, but I didn't feel like looking for anything else, so we settled in for lunch. It's pretty hard to mess up a corned-beef sandwich. I pondered trying on my new shoes again while Mom studied the menu.

"I guess I'll just get a sandwich at these prices," she said. "But will that be enough?"

"It should be more than enough. We could probably even share one sandwich. They make really big sandwiches around here."

"Hmm. Or maybe I could try matzo ball soup. I've never had that before. What's it like?"

"It's like chicken soup with big, round dumplings in it."

"Oh." She frowned at the menu some more, then looked up and blinked. "Isn't that your friend over there?"

I turned to see where she was pointing. "Over where?"

"Leaning against that wall."

The entrance to the deli was crowded enough that it was difficult to make out if anyone leaning against the wall was someone I ought to know, but then a tall, thin man emerged from the crowd and walked toward us, a smug smirk on his face—I mean, even more smug than normal, which was pretty smug. "Oh, that friend," I said. "And he's not really a friend."

It appeared that Owen had been wrong about one thing—which might have been a first. Idris wasn't after him. He appeared to be focusing on me. If Idris had been targeting Owen, he'd be up in some village on the Hudson, disrupting Owen's weekend with his foster parents. And from what little Owen had said about his foster family, I got the distinct impression that he'd welcome the distraction. I, however, would have preferred to skip the intrusion.

My glower didn't appear to bother Idris in the least, though. He walked up to our table, pulled out a chair, and plunked himself into it. "Mind if I join you?" he asked rhetorically. "It could take forever before I get a seat on my own."

It was a situation Emily Post didn't cover: What do you do if your sworn enemy invites himself to join you and your mother for lunch, and you don't want your mother to know you even have sworn enemies? The only answer I could think of was to act like it was no big deal. That would probably drive him crazier than anything else I could do. And it wasn't as if he could use magic to harm either of us or do anything else to us in that crowd.

"Please, join us," I said with a cyanide-laced saccharine smile. "Mom, this is Phelan Idris. You probably remember him from the other night, when he left before I could introduce you. I know him from work." Which was true enough. "Mr. Idris, this is my mother, Mrs. Chandler."

I had to fight back any signs of triumph at how intensely uncomfortable he looked with formal manners. "Um, hi," he said, fidgeting in his seat. I wished now that we'd gone to some froufrou ladies-who-lunch restaurant where he'd have been even more out of place. Mom narrowed her eyes at him. Clearly, she thought he couldn't come from good people to be so lacking in manners.

I continued acting like I was hosting a tea party. I might not be able to zap him the way Owen did, but I could Southern-belle him to death. "What brings you out today? Getting a start on your Christmas shopping?" I asked with fake cheer.

He fidgeted some more, looking like a six-year-old his first time at the grown-up table. "Um, well, uh," he said, quite eloquently. It was hard to believe that this was the guy who had all of MSI up in arms, the reason Merlin had been brought back to lead the company. He was nothing more than a geek with delusions of grandeur.

The waitress came to take our orders. After Mom and I ordered lunch, and Idris ordered a coffee, I said, "That will be on one check." Then I turned to Idris and said with my sweetest, most honeyed drawl, "It's so nice of you to treat us to lunch like this. I guess you're doing great now that you have corporate clients like that winery." His mouth opened and closed, but the waitress was gone before he could say anything. The absolutely gobsmacked look on his face told me that I'd been right about the source of that spell the winery had been using. I had no illusions of him actually paying our check, but his reaction was funny, and Mom would be even more unimpressed with him when he bailed and left us paying for his coffee. He might be the one man she met while in New York whom she didn't try to set me up with.

He must have regained his footing by the time the waitress brought him his coffee, for he traded his deer-in-the-headlights expression for his more typical sneer. "So, you're brave enough to go out shopping without your boyfriend," he said.

I didn't have to respond to that one. Mom jumped in faster than I could. "Don't be silly," she said, even more syrupy Southern than I was being. "She wouldn't drag her boyfriend out shopping. This is a girls' day out."

Go, Mom! I thought. That apparently wasn't the reaction Idris was expecting. To be perfectly frank, I wasn't sure what he was after. This seemed to be merely a nuisance call, something intended to keep me off-balance. Well, I wasn't going to let it work. "Yeah, I needed a day out. Things are getting so busy and hectic at work," I said, then waited to see how he'd respond.

"Yes, I imagine they are. And things will probably get busier very, very soon, so I hope you're up to the task—in every possible way." He emphasized every other word or so, like he was embedding extra meaning into his simple statement. He might as well have swirled his cape and said, "Mwa ha ha!" That would have been more effective as a threat. As it was, I had no idea what he was talking about, but I suspected that my theory about him just wanting to throw us into chaos was proving accurate.

"You can bet Katie will be up to any task," Mom said. "She's our little go-getter." I turned to stare at her in shock. Did it take being forced to sit with the bad guy for her to praise me without qualifiers? I almost felt like I owed Idris a favor.

The waitress brought my sandwich and Mom's bowl of matzo ball soup. Mom picked up her spoon, then shrieked and shoved the bowl away. "Mom, what is it?" I asked, trying to see what was wrong but distracted by the way Idris was smirking.

She was beyond words, which is really saying something when it comes to my mother. All she could do was point with her spoon at the soup bowl. I couldn't find anything wrong with her soup. "Those are just matzo balls," I explained. "I guess I didn't describe them right. They're not the kind of dumplings we make back home."

"Are they supposed to blink?" she asked.

Idris giggled, and I turned to glare at him. As I did so, I noticed out of the corner of my eye that the matzo balls were, in fact, blinking. They weren't matzo balls at all. They were eyeballs. I screamed almost as loud as Mom had. The really gross thing was that if Mom and I saw the eyeballs, it wasn't just an illusion. There really were eyeballs floating in the soup bowl. Ewwww. I'd never be able to eat matzo ball soup again.

The waitress came over, probably drawn by the screams. "How is everything?" she asked. Then again, maybe not. Either she hadn't heard the screams, she was tuning them out like a good New Yorker, or Idris was blocking out the fun at our table from the rest of the deli. In the latter case, I was grateful to him, but the good deed was more than mitigated by the trick he'd played on Mom.

"I don't think the soup was quite what she expected," I told the waitress, handing her the bowl with my eyes averted so I wouldn't accidentally make eye contact with the soup. You never want to make eye contact with your soup. "Could we maybe get some plain old chicken noodle?"

The waitress studied the soup bowl like she couldn't see anything wrong with it. Now that she was holding it, I couldn't see anything wrong, either, but I suspected Mom had lost her appetite for matzo balls, judging by the sickly green shade of her face.

Idris was still giggling. I'd have loved to read him the riot act about playing magical practical jokes, but I couldn't do that without spilling the beans to Mom. Fortunately, Mom could more than take care of herself. "Young man, it's rude to laugh at other people's discomfort," she scolded. "Do they not teach manners up here? Really, Katie, I question your choice of friends."

"I never said he was my friend," I muttered while trying to get my leg into a position where I could kick him in the ankle under the table without stubbing my toe on the metal post supporting the table. Then I pushed my sandwich over to Mom. "Here, why don't you eat this? I guess the soup was a little too exotic for you."

Mom didn't even argue, which told me how upset she was. Normally, she'd play the suffering martyr role to the hilt, gladly (and noisily) starving. I had no doubt that she fully believed matzo balls were really eyeballs, and she'd be telling everyone back home all about it.

She took a tentative bite of the corned-beef sandwich—like she expected it to moo at her. I held my breath, not sure what to expect, but I soon realized that his next prank had nothing to do with food. One by one, the other patrons in the deli stood and formed a chorus line. With precision to rival the Rockettes, they launched into a synchronized dance number. All I could do was stare openmouthed as elderly women, paunchy middle-aged men, teenaged girls, and every other type you might find in a Midtown deli at lunchtime tapped and shuffled their way across the floor like it was the most normal thing in the world.

I chanced a nervous glance at Mom, sure this would be enough to send her straight over the edge (not that she was all that far from the edge to begin with), but she was staring at the impromptu chorus line in delight, her eyes shining. I looked back at the dancers, dreading the high kicks that were sure to come at the end of the number. Most of these people looked like they'd need traction if they tried something like that.

The funny thing was, although I couldn't hear any music, I felt like I was listening to the same catchy tune all the deli patrons were dancing to. I couldn't help but tap my feet under the table. I forced myself to stop, stubbornly wrapping my ankles around the chair legs so I could resist the urge to join the chorus line.

I had no doubt that Idris was behind this. It looked a lot like the results of that control spell he'd been selling earlier, the one I saw Owen and Jake testing and that had been used during the wine dinner. I forced my eyes away from the dancers, who were moving into a Busby Berkeley formation that probably looked stunning from the ceiling, and turned toward Idris. He was pale, and sweat ran down his face, but he looked more caught up in the happenings than Mom was. He moved his fingers and the formation changed. All we needed now was a fountain rising from the middle of the deli, or maybe a giant staircase for showgirls to float down.

The waitress came out of the kitchen, carrying a tray loaded with food, then froze in shock. Idris caught my eye and grinned—a non-sneering, nonthreatening grin, for a change. "Watch this!" he said. A moment later, the waitress's tray turned into a feathered fan, and she began darting in and out of the line of dancers with surprising grace, waving her fan in front of her.

Idris laughed in delight. "Ooh, and how about this?" he said, still grinning. Soon the sounds of cookware being banged in rhythm with the dance came from the kitchen. "Good one, huh?" he asked. He looked like a little kid with a new toy. "Maybe they should dance, too."

One by one, the cooks came out of the kitchen, still banging pots and pans, to join in.

Idris must have improved the spell, for it seemed to work better than the earlier versions had. I waited for him to spring the big surprise on Mom and confront her with the evidence of magic, or maybe to blackmail me into quitting MSI, but all he did was add more and more details to his extravaganza.

Then it hit me: our evil archvillain had a raging case of ADD. He had the attention span of a toddler on a sugar high. He couldn't maintain a good threat long enough to do any real damage before he got sidetracked by something shiny. The real danger wasn't that he would take over the world. It was the chaos he could stir up while entertaining himself. He was more Dr. Evil than Dr. No.

Finally, he let out a gasp, then slumped onto the table, drenched in sweat. Around the deli, the patrons stopped dancing, returned to their seats, and collapsed, rubbing their temples. The waitress's fan became a tray once more, but she didn't get it settled before the soup hit the floor. She sank into the nearest chair, looking weary. The cooks joined her. I remembered the headache Owen had after a spell much like this one had been tested on him, and he'd only been under the influence for a few seconds. I could only imagine how these people must feel.

I was trying desperately to come up with a way of explaining what had happened when Mom rose from her seat, applauding. "Bravo!" she shouted. "That was wonderful. Thank you so much." They all looked at her like she was crazy, then returned to rubbing their heads. Mom sat down, still beaming. "It's just like in the movies," she gushed.

I blinked at her in disbelief. She didn't see anything weird about an entire deli breaking into a spontaneous dance number? Then again, her view of New York was largely shaped by television and movies, and she did have a fondness for old musicals, so people doing dance routines in public might not have been all that shocking to her.

"I guess they have to come up with some way to keep all those Broadway dancers employed," she went on. "Entertainment at restaurants is a wonderful idea." That was a relief. I'd have hated to think my mom was so clueless she thought people in New York really did do spontaneous dance routines. There certainly were restaurants with singing, dancing waiters, and she didn't have to know that this wasn't really one of them.

Before Idris got any other bright ideas, like reenacting the infamous deli scene from *When Harry Met Sally* (something I did not want to see with my mother around), I picked up my purse and shopping bags, threw enough bills to cover our uneaten lunches and Idris's coffee onto the table, along with a nice tip for the waitress, who'd been a really good dancer, then grabbed Mom's arm. "Let's get out of here," I suggested. "The floor show's over, and the food isn't all that good."

"What about your friend?" Mom asked, glancing to where Idris was looking decidedly ill.

"He's not my friend, and he's not my problem." If he wanted to do draining, badly designed (according to Owen) spells as a prank, and overreach himself by making the spell a little too elaborate, he could live with the consequences on his own. I wanted to get away from him before he recovered enough to do something more serious to us.

"There was something odd about that boy," Mom said in a conspiratorial manner when we were safely outside the deli. "I think maybe he was hitting the sauce a little too early in the day." She made drinking motions with her hand, as though she felt I wouldn't get what she meant. "Mavis Alton used to show up to UMW luncheons at the church acting like that, and we all knew she'd been sipping the cough syrup, if you know what I mean. Maybe he has a problem. Mavis sure did. She had to spend a month at a 'spa' to get over it."

"Oh, he's got problems, all right," I said. I wondered if a Ritalin prescription would help or hinder our cause.

When we got back to my apartment late that afternoon, Dad was there having coffee with Gemma, Marcia, Jeff, and Philip. Dad was laughing at something as we came through the doorway, and I hoped Gemma and Marcia had enough sense to edit whatever they told him for parental consumption. Not that I'd done much of anything worth editing, but that was about to change.

"I've finished our Christmas shopping," Mom declared as she dropped her armload of shopping bags on the floor. "We have presents for the boys, their wives, the grandkids, and my sisters. You're on your own for your side of the family."

Dad took a sip of coffee, savored it, swallowed it, and said, "I take it you're speaking to me again."

"Spending your money was rather therapeutic, and we had a good time at lunch." I wouldn't have called it "good," but if she wanted to think of it that way, who was I to stop her?

"Did you get anything, Katie?" Gemma asked.

"As a matter of fact, I did." I opened the Bloomingdale's bag and pulled out the shoe box with a flourish.

"Those aren't—"

"Yes, they are." I slid the lid aside to show her.

"Oh my God!" she squealed. "I'm so glad you got those!"

Marcia leaned over. "Let me see."

I took one shoe out of the box and held it up for inspection. "Gorgeous, huh?"

"Oooh," Marcia breathed. "Put them on and let us see."

Mom rolled her eyes as she took off her coat and draped it over the sofa arm. "Honestly, you girls and your shoes. Katie, honey, if you're going to show the shoes off, show them with your new dress while you're at it." She addressed Dad. "I bought Katie her Christmas present early."

Gemma made shooing motions at me, moving me toward the bedroom. "Go on, show us the whole outfit."

I went into the bedroom, shut the door behind me, and took off my clothes before putting on the dress. As a finishing touch, I slid into the shoes. I felt that same burst of power I'd noticed when I first tried them on, and I was glad I hadn't let my practical side win.

Before I went back into the living room, I admired myself in the full-length mirror on the back of the bedroom door. I didn't even look like myself. I looked older, more sophisticated. Yes, even sexy, and that wasn't a word that applied to me very often. Then, with a deep breath, I opened the door.

Jeff let out a low wolf whistle. Philip rose slowly from his seat, a look of awe in his eyes. I couldn't remember ever getting that look from any man. Gemma applauded and Marcia shook her head slowly in admiration. Dad swallowed hard, then said roughly, "You look real nice, baby."

Only Mom seemed relatively unaffected. She eyed me critically, then said, "Well, I guess you're right. Those shoes do go with that dress. It makes a nice outfit. But I still say if you were going to spend that much money on a pair of shoes, they should be shoes you could wear every day."

"They wouldn't be special if you wore them every day, Mrs. Chandler," Gemma said. She turned, saw Philip still gazing at me, and elbowed him in the ribs. He blinked and sat down.

"I hope Ethan has something good planned for New Year's Eve," Marcia said. "If he doesn't, he doesn't deserve to see you looking like that."

"I was hoping for something a little sooner than New Year's," I said. "Maybe not the full outfit, but I have to wear the shoes on our next date."

Gemma gave me an assessing nod. "Yeah, I think with a little black dress, or maybe a black skirt and white blouse. It depends on where he's taking you."

"Like he'd tell her where he's taking her," Marcia said with a snort.

"He does seem to like the top-secret dates," I admitted. "I think he enjoys surprising me."

"Well, he can surprise you with someplace very, very nice," Gemma said.

Jeff, staring at me like he used to when he was under the enchantment that made him obsessed with me, said, "Even if he isn't planning that, he'll change his plans once he sees her. A girl looks like that, she's going to be taken someplace special."

"I would have to agree," Philip said softly. "When a lady has made that obvious an effort with her appearance, she deserves a certain level of treatment."

I shot my mom a triumphant look. It was nice to have validation from actual men. Maybe that's what I'd been doing wrong all along. I'd been so worried about being practical that I'd forgotten about making myself special. If I didn't think I was special, why should anyone else?

And I was special, I reminded myself. I was immune to magic, a trait that was extremely rare. I had an important job because of that. I might as well dress like it.

Mom sighed and shook her head. "A lady should be a lady no matter how fancy she's dressed," she said. She went to the kitchen, opened the refrigerator, and took out a can of soda.

"I think that a lady who attires herself well is complimenting the gentleman she's with, showing him that she values his company," Philip argued. That totally stunned me. He seldom said much of anything. I halfway suspected he'd spent too much time as a frog and had forgotten how to communicate as a human. Gemma never seemed to notice or mind.

"He's right," Dad said. "You hush, Lois. Don't bring the girl down. She looks nice. She is all grown-up, you know, and if you ever want to throw that wedding you've been daydreaming about, she's going to have to dress herself up to land a man."

I was glad he was on my side, but I wasn't sure I liked the implication that I had to dress up to get a man. Then again, I hadn't had dramatic success up to that point, other than with Ethan.

"Well, fashion show's over. Time for me to turn back into Cinderella," I said, then went into the bedroom and shut the door. I admired myself in the mirror one last time. "Mirror, mirror on the wall, who's the hottest of them all?" I said softly. Then I took the dress off and hung it up. I put my sweater back on before I finally forced myself to take off the red shoes and put on my jeans. I carefully wrapped the shoes in tissue and replaced them in their box, then stashed the box on a shelf in the closet. Fortunately, neither Gemma nor Marcia wore the same size shoes as I did. We could share tops and sometimes even skirts, but they were taller than I was and wore bigger shoes. Before, I'd always regretted that because Gemma had a fantastic shoe wardrobe. Now, though, I was glad because it meant those shoes were all mine.

I went back out into the living room and asked, "Is there any pumpkin pie left?"

"I made an extra just for leftovers," Mom said.

"Anyone else want some?" I offered. They all nodded or raised their hands. I went into the kitchen and poured myself a glass of water before I got out the pie and cut slices for everyone, then topped them with whipped cream and passed them out.

I stood at the kitchen counter, eating pie and sipping water, while I listened to the hum of conversation. I'd dreaded my parents coming to visit, but I was glad they had. It was good having them around again.

"So, Katie, what are you going to show us tomorrow?" Mom asked, startling me out of my thoughts when she brought her plate to the kitchen.

"Is there anything you'd like to see?"

"We were hoping we could see where you work." She held up her hand to quiet my protest before I could get a word out. "I know we won't be able to go inside, especially not on a Saturday, but I want to see the building. That way, when you talk about going to work, I'll be able to picture it."

"That's a great idea," Marcia said. "You work near City Hall, don't you, Katie?"

"Yeah, and near the Woolworth Building."

"Okay, then," Gemma said, "tomorrow it's downtown. We'll come along, too. Katie hasn't shown us her office, either."

"It should be relatively quiet down there on a Saturday," Marcia added. "We can show you Wall Street, the Stock Exchange, and Battery Park, too."

It felt nothing short of inevitable. I had no good reason why we shouldn't go downtown and see where I worked—at least, no good reason I could share with the others. I had plenty of reasons I had to keep to myself. For one thing, the office building was on a street that didn't appear on any maps, and it tended to be the kind of place you didn't notice unless you were looking for it. It also didn't fit in at all. It looked like a medieval castle transplanted into Lower Manhattan. Those alone were reasons I didn't particularly want to parade my friends and family by my office. Then there was the fact that the security guard was a talking gargoyle. I crossed my fingers and hoped Sam would be off moonlighting at a church over the weekend. He could probably pick up some extra cash filling in for a gargoyle at St. Patrick's.

"Downtown it is, then," I said, trying to force more enthusiasm than I felt into my voice. If I sounded like I was trying to hide something, the folks would get suspicious, and there were enough reasons for suspicion without me adding to them. I sincerely hoped Idris had something better to do on a Saturday than keep stalking me.

The next morning, Gemma, Marcia, and I guided my parents onto a city bus. Gemma insisted on the bus instead of the subway because it was the best way to see the changing neighborhoods of the city. We got off in front of the Woolworth Building, where we peered through the front doors into the ornate lobby.

"Now do we see your office?" Mom asked. "Didn't you say it was near here?"

Actually, you could see it from there, if you knew what to look for, but I preferred to prolong the inevitable. "Why don't we come back by there after we've seen everything else?" I suggested.

I let Marcia lead the way once we entered the financial district, since that was more her domain than mine. While she rattled off facts and figures about the buildings we passed, I kept my eyes open for potential magical strangeness. In the days before I learned about magic, I frequently saw odd sights in this part of town, probably because of the proximity to MSI headquarters, where a large portion of the magical community was employed. They all seemed to have stayed away during the holiday weekend, much to my relief. I saw nothing with wings, nothing moving that wasn't supposed to, nobody making anything disappear or appear out of thin air. This was probably the most normal I'd seen New York since I'd moved here.

We made a side trip by the Ground Zero site, then went all the way down to Battery Park, where we looked out across the water to the Statue of Liberty. Marcia led us down Wall Street, and we paused to take pictures in front of the Stock Exchange. By the time we reached the South Street Seaport, we were ready for lunch.

All that walking had left everyone tired, so conversation was muted. I hoped that meant they would all be too tired to ask many questions once we reached my bizarro office building. With luck, they'd be so tired they'd just want to hit the subway station and go home.

I took the lead when we finished lunch and headed up the hill. I couldn't help but hold my breath as the MSI building's turrets came into view. I could see them, and that meant Mom could, too, but I wasn't sure what anyone else might see. I didn't want another fight between my parents about whether or not Mom was seeing things.

"Now, that's an interesting building," Dad said.

"Which one?" I asked, probably a little too casually as I tried to hide my anxiety.

"That one, the one that looks like a castle."

"Oh. Well, that's my office building, believe it or not."

"I didn't even know this was here," Marcia said, frowning. "I've been by here hundreds—thousands—of times, and I've never noticed it."

"It's amazing what commuter tunnel vision will do to you," I said. "I'd never noticed it, either, until I went for the interview."

We drew nearer, so the rest of the castle-like building was visible. Fortunately, Sam was off-duty. There was nothing unlikely perched on the awning over the main entrance.

"I can't believe I've never seen this," Marcia said, still frowning and shaking her head.

Gemma pulled her guidebook out of her bag. "It's got to be in the guide, since it's so unusual. Maybe it's Victorian-era Gothic Revival."

I knew she could flip through the guidebook all day long and never find that building, but I didn't say so.

I tried to keep my pace steady so they'd be less inclined to slow down and look too closely as we passed. "So, anyway, this is where I work," I said. "There's a subway station on the other side of the park."

They didn't take the hint. They all came to a stop to stare at the company logo on the shield by the door. "What does MSI stand for?" Dad asked.

I shrugged. "I'm not sure it stands for anything, or if it ever did, it doesn't anymore. It's like IBM—does anyone really know what that stands for?"

"International Business Machines," Dad said without missing a beat.

"Oh. Well, they left that part out of the company orientation, so I guess they just consider it a name these days. I suspect that it's maybe the names of the founders, or something like that." That was a pretty good fib, if I said so myself. I mentally filed it away for future use.

"What did you say they do?" Dad asked.

I hadn't, actually. "It's kind of like software. To be honest, I don't understand a lot of it. I just do administrative work." Which was true, sort of. Spells were like the software of the magical world, I didn't understand how it all worked, and I did do administrative work. I started walking again, hoping they'd follow me. "There's a subway station across the park. We can get home and have some more pie." The mention of pie did the trick. Gemma and Marcia were soon right behind me, and my parents had no choice but to follow.

We reached Park Row and crossed the street to the park, where we all paused to flip coins into the fountain. "See the gaslights," I pointed out, relieved to be showing off normal touristy stuff once more. Now that my parents had seen my office building and hadn't had a complete freak-out, it looked like the worst was truly over.

As we approached the subway station, a handsome man in his early thirties crossed the street toward us. Gemma and Marcia's heads turned in unison to watch him, and I couldn't help but take a gander myself. He really was gorgeous, in a slightly dangerous bad-boy way.

He wasn't the sort of man I usually went for, but he looked like he might be fun for a fling. He also looked vaguely familiar, though I couldn't place him. You'd think that if I'd met him before, I'd have remembered. I glanced at Mom, who didn't look quite as impressed. She was probably afraid of the bad-boy thing. He wasn't the kind of man she'd choose for her little girl. It was just as well that Mom would be gone in a couple of days.

He flashed us all a big smile as he approached. I twirled my hair with one finger and smiled back at him. Gemma stepped up to my side, gave him a come-hither look, and elbowed me in the ribs. "Hey, isn't that the guy who recruited you for your job?" she hissed. "You did say you weren't interested, right?"

Before I could remind her that she had a boyfriend, so she could get out of my way, he directed a grin right at me and said, "Hi, Katie, what brings you down here on a Saturday?"

I froze. It was Rod's voice. And then I remembered where I'd seen him before. It was Rod's illusion, the face he showed to the rest of the world. I'd seen it only once, reflected in an image checker mirror. Otherwise, I couldn't see what others saw because an illusion was a spell cast on other people to make them see what the caster wanted to see. That meant it didn't work on me, and I always saw the real thing.

But I was seeing the illusion now. That could mean only one thing.

I'd lost my magical immunity.

eleven

In that moment, I felt my world turn upside down. If I was no longer immune, that meant I couldn't count on anything my senses showed me. I didn't know how it could have happened or why, and I could only begin to wonder how long it had been going on. I tried to think of the last magical thing I'd seen. I'd seen the gargoyle briefly the day before, but it had been appearing and disappearing. I hadn't been affected by Idris's spell in the deli, but it had made my toes tap, now that I thought about it. Since then, I couldn't recall a thing. All that time I'd been relieved not to see anything weird I'd need to explain to Mom, and maybe I'd really been no longer capable of seeing anything weird. There was no telling what she might have seen that I didn't.

But I didn't have time to process it all at the moment. I was there with my parents and roommates, and I had to respond to Rod. "Hi!" I greeted him, hoping that only a second or two had passed instead of the hours it felt like. "I was showing my parents where I work." I turned to my parents. "Mom, Dad, this is Rod Gwaltney. He's the one who recruited me for my new job. Rod, these are my parents, Lois and Frank Chandler. And you remember Gemma and Marcia, of course."

"Hi, Rod," Gemma and Marcia chorused in unison, a lustful sigh in their voices. Hey, didn't they have boyfriends? What were they doing coming on to him like that? I flipped my hair back over my shoulder and fluttered my eyelashes at him, then remembered that I had a boyfriend, too. Oops.

Rod shook my parents' hands. "Nice to meet you," he said. "Katie's been such an asset to the company."

Mom looked at him, glanced at Gemma, Marcia, and me, then frowned and looked back at him, like she was trying to figure out what all the goo-goo eyes were about. Only then did I remember that it was an illusion and that he must have been using one of those mild attraction spells he'd talked about. I didn't realize he used it constantly. That explained his spectacularly successful social life.

I forced myself to stay aware of the illusion and the attraction spell. I was not going to become yet another notch on his bedpost. I'd hate to lose my status as one of the few women in the company who hadn't gone out with him. To keep myself focused, I tried making a mental list of the women I knew had gone out with him, which was essentially the female side of the company roster and a good portion of the Manhattan residential white pages.

Before Gemma and Marcia reached the point of throwing themselves at him, I decided it would be best to get away. That would make it easier for me to have him all to myself later. *No!* I shook my head to clear it and conjured up an image of the female staff members of the accounting department—numbers twenty-four, twenty-five, and twenty-six on my mental list of Rod's former flings. "It was great running into you," I said, "but we've got to get back home. I'll see you Monday!"

"Yeah, see you Monday. And it was nice meeting you all," he said.

I practically had to drag Gemma and Marcia to keep them from following him, and it was only my worry about getting them away, along with the thought of an anonymous blond woman in a coffee shop who was the twenty-seventh person I was aware of who'd gone out with Rod in the short time I'd known him, that kept me from wanting to follow him. Besides, I reasoned, I'd have him to myself Monday. Realizing where my thoughts were going, I reminded myself of the two girls in the lab down the hall from Owen's office who, according to Ari, had been in tears after finding out they'd both gone out with Rod in the same weekend. No. I was not going to fall for that.

"Well, he was certainly interesting," Mom said once we were on the subway platform, waiting for a train. "I wish I'd brought some samples with me. I could do a lot to improve his skin."

Dad, Gemma, and Marcia all turned to look at her like she was crazy. I finally understood why people reacted to Rod the way they did. Usually, I was the only one wondering what all the fuss was about and wishing I could do a makeover on him to help him make the most of his natural assets so he could quit hiding behind that illusion.

Then Mom let out a bloodcurdling scream, and we all whirled to see her swinging at thin air with her handbag. "Get away from me, you ugly, nasty thing!" she shrieked, punctuating her words with blows of her huge carryall purse. "There now, you go! That's it! And stay away!" she shouted defiantly down the subway tunnel.

Dad looked at the rest of us, concern in his eyes. "Lois, there wasn't anything there," he said.

"There isn't now. That's because it flew away. I guess I scared it off."

"It was probably a bat that lives down in the tunnels," I suggested, feeling bad for Mom. I knew she probably really was seeing something the rest of us didn't. That was a switch for me. I was usually the one seeing things. I felt like I'd lost one of my senses.

"Biggest bat I ever saw, and hard as a rock, too. I hope I didn't tear up my purse."

"Do they have bats in the subway tunnels?" Gemma asked Marcia quietly, while Dad looked like he was wondering if he should put Mom in a rest home.

A nearly empty train stopped at the station, saving us from further discussion, and we all boarded. As we rode uptown, I tried to reassure myself. It was probably nothing more than a glitch. Maybe we'd been in a weird zone that reversed the polarity of power, or something like that. I knew that the office building was enhanced with extra power to draw upon. Maybe that had effects in the areas surrounding the building. Come to think of it, I'd never seen anything magical in that particular spot before.

Or it might be temporary. I'd noticed the gargoyle guarding me the day before, so this hadn't been going on for long. It might even be a good educational experience. I'd often wondered what other people saw, so spending some time susceptible to illusion would give me a basis for comparison that would help me do a better job.

Only when we left the train at Union Square did I have another realization that sent shivers down my spine. It wasn't just illusion that worked on me now. Other magic would affect me as well. If Mr. Bones or his ilk tried to attack me again, those magic fireballs would probably work, and I wouldn't even see it coming. I was a sitting duck for all of Idris's minions. I became eager to reach my magically warded home, where I should be safe. I didn't even want to think about what would happen when I had to go to work Monday morning.

Sunday passed in blissful peace. If any magical folk were about, they must have stayed out of sight, for Mom didn't comment on anything odd—or maybe she'd learned not to say anything when she thought she saw something. Although my stress levels were sure to drop considerably once they were gone, my heart was heavy when I stopped by my parents' hotel Monday morning to say good-bye.

"I'm so glad you came," I said, hugging them one last time. And I was, I realized. As much as I'd dreaded their visit, I dreaded seeing them go.

"We had a real nice time," Mom said, blinking back her own tears. "I can see why you like it here."

"So you're not going to drag me home?"

"Is that what you thought?" Dad asked with a chuckle.

"I knew you weren't happy about me coming here."

"You had to do what was right for you," Mom said. "And now we know it was coming here. You've grown up so much."

"And now that we've seen it," Dad added, "it doesn't seem like such a bad place. You know how to take care of yourself."

"It is really weird, though," Mom said. "No one's going to believe the things I've seen."

"*I* don't believe the things you've seen," Dad muttered. Mom punched him playfully in the shoulder.

"I have to get to work," I said, cutting in before they could start fighting. "Are you sure you're okay getting to the airport on your own?"

"We'll be fine," Dad said. "We made a shuttle reservation at the front desk."

I nodded with approval. "Good. They'll get you there on time. Give me a call and let me know when you get in, okay?"

I waved over my shoulder as I turned and headed down the sidewalk toward Union Square. The hotel was past my apartment, so I hoped Owen wasn't waiting for me in front of my building like he usually was. It turned out I shouldn't have worried. He was waiting at the next street corner, as if he'd read my mind or already knew where I'd be. Then again, this was Owen I was dealing with, so he probably did know.

"Did you have a good visit with your parents?" he asked. "It doesn't look like they're forcing you to go home."

"It did go well. Now that they know the city isn't quite the crazy place they thought it was, and now that they've seen how I can cope with it, they feel better about me living here." With my parents on their way out of town, I felt it was probably safe to spill the beans about my mom's immunity, and if I could trust anyone, I could trust Owen. I was curious to find out what he thought about it. I glanced around to make sure no one was in eavesdropping range, then said, "One crazy thing, though—my mom's an immune. I had to do some fast talking to explain what she saw, and now she believes there are some truly strange people living here."

I expected surprise or shock, but he simply nodded. "That makes sense. It's an inherited trait, so chances are you got it from at least one of your parents, and living in a place like Texas with such a low level of magical activity, she could have gone through her entire life without seeing anything magical."

"And the way my mom is, even if she did see something, my dad would have just thought she was being loopy, as usual. Come to think of it, this explains a lot about my family. But please don't tell anyone at the company. I don't want to see her shanghaied into working for us."

He laughed. "Is that what you were afraid of? Don't worry, we generally don't recruit anyone that age. If she's lived her entire life ignorant of magic, breaking the news at this point may be too traumatic."

"That's a relief. I know how desperately you're always trying to recruit immunes."

"As desperate as we are, we're still very selective about who gets let in on the secret." He suddenly looked worried. "She didn't figure anything out, did she?"

"No. She just thinks there are more strange alternative lifestyles in New York than she'd realized. My dad may think she's a bit crazy, but he's always thought that. Oh, and she thinks Idris is a drunk."

"That would explain a lot," he replied with a grin. Then he suddenly looked concerned. "Idris was bothering your parents?"

"Just a little mustache twirling. He didn't actually do much of anything other than play pranks. And who knew he was such a big fan of old-time musicals?"

His eyebrows shot up. "Musicals?"

"Long story."

We reached an intersection just as the pedestrian signal switched to WALK. I started to step off the curb, but he put his arm out in front of me, holding me back. The first thought to cross my mind was that we were under magical attack, and I hadn't spotted it in time. I frantically looked for a walking skeleton, a harpy, or even a deranged wizard geek, but didn't see anything. A split second later a delivery van screeched through the intersection, running the red light. My heart pounded in my chest as I turned to look at Owen. He'd gone white as a sheet. "Thanks," I managed to gasp. I wasn't sure what relieved me most, the fact that I hadn't been hit by a van or the fact that it was something as ordinary as a van instead of all the other things I'd feared.

"Don't mention it," he replied, his voice sounding a little shaky. Both of us looked carefully before we ventured into the crosswalk. Once we reached the other side safely, he let out a long breath and said with a weak smile, "Sometimes that particular gift really has its moments."

It was a harsh reminder of what I'd lost. My gift—which was the complete lack of magical gifts—might not be as dramatic as his, but I'd learned to rely on it, just as he used his gifts. I opened my mouth to tell him what had happened, then shut it again. I didn't know what was going on yet. I wasn't even sure the immunity was still gone. I needed to wait until I knew the score before I said anything. My job was based on me being immune to magic. Without that quality, I'd be just another secretary. I didn't think I'd be fired outright, but I couldn't be sure. They'd recruited me because I was magically immune. Would they keep me if I wasn't?

"So how did your holiday go?" I asked Owen, hoping to distract myself from that line of thought.

"It was good. Better than I expected, actually. Possibly the best Thanksgiving I can recall."

"Really? How so?"

He shrugged casually, but I could see that his eyes sparkled as he talked. This clearly meant more to him than he was willing to let on. "I don't know. It wasn't ever like we didn't get along, but we really got along this time. We actually seemed to have a real relationship, for the first time in my life. It's still not what I'd consider a typical parent–child relationship, but it seemed to me that they did care for me, in their own way."

"Maybe they see you as a grown-up now, someone they can relate to as a peer. There are people who don't know how to deal with children, but now that you're an adult, they can get along with you."

"That could be the case. They never had any children of their own, and I don't think they knew quite what to do with a small child.

Whatever the cause, it was a nice change of pace. I still feel like a guest in their home instead of a family member, but now I feel like a welcome guest." He grinned. "I'm even thinking about going there for Christmas, and that's something I usually avoid. I haven't been invited yet, but I wouldn't be surprised if I am."

"That's wonderful. I'm happy for you." I couldn't help but feel a pang of homesickness as I realized that I'd be away from home for Christmas. I'd managed it the year before, but I was so new to New York then. Having my parents around for Thanksgiving made me remember what a Christmas at home was like.

He gave me a sidelong glance, then looked down at the ground and said, "Could you do me a favor?"

"Sure. What?"

A faint stain of pink spread across his cheekbones. "I'd like to get them something special for Christmas, and I'm pretty much helpless when it comes to shopping. Do you think you could help me? Maybe we could go someday after work, or a Saturday afternoon."

"Too bad you didn't catch me while my mom was still here. She's the shopping pro. But I'd love to help, if I can."

"You've got to be better than I am."

It was nice to know there was one thing I could still do to help, even without my magical immunity intact. I wasn't totally useless to the entire magical community, although I doubted I could make a living as a personal shopping assistant to socially awkward wizards.

When we reached our stop and came aboveground, my heart began beating faster. This would be the moment of truth, where I learned whether or not I still had any abilities. There hadn't yet been a morning when at least one gargoyle hadn't stood guard on the awning over the building entrance. If I didn't see one, it meant I'd really lost my immunity.

To my immense relief, Sam was in his usual spot on the awning. I felt like hugging Owen—well, I often felt like hugging Owen, but this had nothing to do with how cute he was. "Good morning, Sam!" I said cheerfully. Then I noticed that he had what looked like a black eye.

"What happened to you?" Owen asked.

"Katie's ma has a strong right hook. We may not recruit her as a verifier, but I could probably use her on my security team."

I cringed. So that's what my mom had been attacking. "Sorry about that," I said. Still, as bad as I felt, it didn't negate the fact that I could see Sam, which was a cause for celebration.

"Don't mention it. It's my own fault for letting her see me, immune or not. I'm supposed to be stealthier than that."

As we entered the building, I felt like I had Ari's wings. It had just been a glitch. My career wasn't over. I was still safely immune to magic.

"You're awfully perky for a Monday morning," Trix remarked when I reached Merlin's office suite. She had wings and slightly pointed ears, and she hovered over her desk chair, like she always did.

"I survived my week with the parents," I said. "It's good to be back to work—and back to normal." Back to normal in more ways than one. Or was I? Halfway to my office I paused and turned back. "I'm curious about something. I was thinking about this while I was showing my parents around. How does that veiling thing y'all do to hide yourselves from the rest of the world work? Do you cast a spell on everyone in general to make them see what you want them to see, or is it more specific? Like, do magical people see you as you really are, or does the illusion also work on magical people when you're out in public?"

"It depends on how you cast the illusion and which spell you use. Most of the magical creatures generally just set the veiling illusion so it affects nonmagical people. Magical people see us as we really are, while normal people see our human illusions. It takes more energy to affect magical people, so most of us usually don't amp up the illusion that high. But we could go totally incognito, except with people like you who don't see illusion. And if you want to get fancy, you can filter it to affect only specific people. The more selective spells are a lot more expensive, of course."

I nodded. "I see. So like with Rod, his illusion is pretty universal, working on everyone who isn't immune. What about Sam? Do all magical people see him sitting out front, or just some?"

"He only shows himself to employees and expected guests when he's on guard out front. Otherwise, no matter how powerful a wizard you are, you aren't going to see him when you walk by. His spell is automatically updated when someone new joins the firm so the new people can see him. You're probably in there, too, even though you're immune. I think they feed the whole company roster into the spell. Most of us, except for Rod, the big loser, drop the illusion entirely when we're not out in public. It's a real energy drain."

I tried to keep my face from falling completely. Maybe I wasn't better. I needed more information to be sure. "Thanks. That's really helpful," I said, fighting for a casual, chipper tone.

"No problem. Any reason in particular you were curious?"

"It turns out my mom is immune, too. I had an interesting time during the holiday explaining the things she saw that my dad didn't see. And that made me wonder how it all worked."

"Wow, your mom is immune and you never knew?"

"I didn't know I was until a little while ago. There's not much magic where I come from."

Before I could head to my office, Merlin emerged from his office. "Good, you're here," he said, even though I was pretty sure he already knew I was there. He always seemed to know. "When you get settled, I need to speak with you."

"Give me a sec," I said brightly. Inside, I felt like a kid who'd been called to the principal's office at school. As I went into my office and put away my purse and tote bag and skimmed over my e-mail in-box, I wondered what it was about. Was it the business-world equivalent of getting an award, or was I in trouble? A shiver of fear shot through me as I realized that with his uncanny ways, Merlin probably already knew I'd lost my immunity. I should tell him, I supposed, but I wasn't exactly sure what to say yet. Based on what Trix told me, seeing Sam didn't prove anything.

I gathered a notepad and pen and went to Merlin's office, silently praying that he just wanted me to take a memo. "Please, have a seat," he said as I entered. He seemed friendly enough. I'd seen him angry, and this wasn't it.

He brought over two cups of tea, handed one to me, then joined me on his sofa. "How was your visit with your parents?" he asked, his tone entirely conversational.

"Great. I was just telling Trix that it turns out I get my immunity from my mom, which made things interesting."

"But they feel better now about you living here?" He sounded concerned.

"Yes, sir, they really seem to. I think they may have liked it here. They didn't even try to make me go home with them."

"Good. Good. Now I would like an update on the status of your investigation."

With a deep sigh, I said, "There isn't much status to speak of, unfortunately. I don't think I've ruled anyone out entirely as a suspect. I have a few new things to check out." Such as what Hertwick the sales gnome was doing in Central Park on a weekday afternoon, but I wasn't going to rat him out until I'd talked to him. "And Idris has started stalking me, which may or may not mean anything. To be honest, I'm kind of hoping our spy makes another move this week. Otherwise, I don't have a lot to go on. I'm more convinced that the intent is to keep us all from trusting each other. Gathering information may not be the primary goal. I even get the impression that Idris is trying to shake me up more than he's trying to harm me or get me out of the way."

He nodded. "That may be a wise assumption. It was through rumor and innuendo that Mordred divided Camelot. I wasn't there to stop it, and I cannot allow that to happen here."

"I'm sorry I don't have more to report." I might not lose my job because of losing my magical immunity, I realized. My complete lack of results was more than enough grounds for firing or demotion. Desperately I struggled for an idea, any idea that might make things better. Finally something struck me. "We'll still want to catch our mole, of course, but if their goal is to divide us, maybe we can fight back by finding ways to pull the company together."

His face lit up, and for a moment he looked centuries younger. "Excellent idea! I've been reading about morale boosting and productivity. There was one particular book about a fun workplace." He got up and went over to his desk, then began rummaging around in the books and papers. "Now, where was it?" He returned with an armful of the latest management fad books. Someone needed to cut off his access to the Barnes & Noble online catalog.

"Let's see, this one was about how to improve productivity by creating a fun working environment." He handed a book to me. "This one was about team building." He handed me another. Soon I had an armload of books. "Do you have time to put together some activities and events?" he asked.

Quite frankly, I was swamped, but planning team-building and employee morale events was important and probably our best way of undermining the mole, so I agreed. "No problem," I said. "It'll be fun. With the holidays here, there are all kinds of things we can do." Then I had a brainstorm. I needed to be absolutely sure what was going on with my immunity, and since I'd seen Rod's illusion the other day and knew it was supposed to work on everyone, a visit to him now would confirm whether or not my immunity really was gone. On top of that, he had access to everyone's employee records, so he might be able to help in the investigation. "I probably ought to work with Rod on this, as it should fall under Personnel," I added.

He nodded. "Good thought. Thank you for your time, Katie."

I took the dismissal hint. As I returned to my office with an armload of business books, I tried to think of things that might work to help us all overcome our distrust of each other. We simply had to encourage people to be willing to work together. Once that got going, the mole might become obvious as the person who wasn't cooperating. Or maybe we could set a trap within the fun activities.

I called down to Isabel and got on Rod's calendar for the afternoon. Having an important role to play in the current crisis would be good for him. He'd finally feel like he was being noticed in the upper echelons of power, and I could pick his brain.

Flipping through the business books for ideas, I came to the conclusion that little of the advice would work in a magical corporation. It was nice that Merlin was trying to acclimate himself to the twenty-first-century business world, but I wasn't sure if the Pike Place Market in Seattle would resonate with him as a metaphor for adding fun to the workplace.

I glanced at my phone and noticed that the voice-mail light was blinking. Someone must have left me a message while I met with Merlin. I picked up the phone, dialed into the voice-mail system, and found one new message. It was from Ethan.

"Hey," he said. "Just checking in to see how the rest of the weekend with the folks went. Thanks again for inviting me for Thanksgiving, and be sure to pass my thanks on to your mom. I was also hoping that you'd be free for lunch tomorrow. Give me a call when you get a chance."

All at once, the memory of buying the red shoes and the thoughts about Ethan that had gone through my mind at the time rushed over me. A shiver went up and down my spine—this time a pleasant shiver. I'd be glad to see him, the sooner the better, even though lunch wouldn't be prime time for what I had in mind.

With a smile on my lips, I called his office. "Hey, yourself," I said when he answered.

"Katie! So you got your parents off on their way home?"

"Yep. They left this morning."

"And everything went well the rest of the weekend?"

"Just a few minor glitches, but nothing I wasn't able to smooth over. My parents even started speaking to each other again."

"I'm glad to hear it. So, lunch tomorrow?"

"I don't have anything on my calendar."

"Okay, how about I pick you up at noon? I'll come up to your office. I have some things I need to drop off for the boss while I'm at it."

That wasn't the most romantic lunch invitation I'd ever heard, but I wasn't going to quibble about it. "Sounds good. I'll see you then."

As I hung up the phone, I wondered if the red shoes would be overkill for wearing to the office. Probably, I decided. Besides, I wanted to save them for a special night out. It would be a shame to waste them on a lunch when he wouldn't have time to ravish me properly. However, that didn't mean I couldn't wear something cute and alluring. I'd have to get Gemma to help me pull an outfit together that would whet his appetite for the weekend.

Forcing my mind back to my work, I gathered the notes I'd made from Merlin's books and headed down to Rod's office to discuss Operation Morale. Isabel gave me her usual enthusiastic greeting.

"Hi, sweetie! Good Thanksgiving?" she boomed.

"Wonderful Thanksgiving. How about you?"

"Nothing special. I helped with one of the balloons in the parade. I make a pretty good anchor, if I say so myself."

"That must have been fun."

"It was. Let me tell him you're here." She waved a hand over the crystal ball thingy that served as a magical intercom, then said, "Go on in."

I opened Rod's office door and knew right away that whatever it was, it hadn't been a glitch. Instead of the Rod I knew, the same gorgeous and slightly dangerous-looking man I'd seen on Saturday sat behind his desk.

I was in huge trouble.

twelve

Not only was I finally certain that I really had lost my magical immunity, I was also susceptible to Rod's attraction spell. While part of me wanted to throw myself at him, the other part had to forcefully remind me about Ethan, the guy I'd just made lunch plans with, the guy I hoped would have his wicked way with me that weekend. Then again, I was sure the red shoes would work on anyone. Even if I wasn't with Ethan, I could wear those shoes and make Rod want me as much as I wanted him.

I went back to my mental list of Rod's recent dates to snap myself out of the spell. Did he never turn that off, even at the office? What kind of raging insecurity would lead a man to artificially enhance his appeal that way? And what depths might he stoop to in order to get attention? I mentally reevaluated his status on my list of suspects.

"Hi, Katie," he said, giving me an innocuous look, though I felt like his eyes were searching my face closely. "What did you want to see me about?"

"My latest wacky save-the-world plan," I said, taking a seat in the chair in front of his desk. I automatically crossed my legs and let my skirt rise above my knees, then realized what I was doing and yanked it back down again.

"And I'm a part of this plan?" His eyes shifted away, and then he seemed to force himself to look at me again.

"This one falls squarely in your domain." I licked my lips and wondered if I had lipstick on my teeth. I should have put on some lip gloss before heading off for the meeting. Had I put on perfume? *No,* I reminded myself. *Work.* "You see, I have this theory that the real intent of our mole isn't so much to spy as it is to disrupt the company. If we're all suspecting each other, we're not working together, and that will make us less prepared to face whatever Idris is up to."

"So your plan is to work on morale to undercut those efforts? Good idea. What did you have in mind?"

"Some of these are going to sound really silly," I warned. "For starters, I think we need a secret Santa program."

"What's that?"

Was there really a corporation in America that didn't put its employees through that torturous ritual, whatever politically correct name they gave it? I'd been stuck playing Santa to my evil former boss, Mimi, the year before, and it had taken every ounce of self-control I had to do nice things for her instead of lacing homemade fudge with rat poison.

"It's like a secret pal program. Everyone draws names, and then they do little surprises for the person whose name they drew. In some places, they just do one gift exchange. In others, they spend the entire month of December leaving fun little clues and presents, leading up to a more major gift exchange where the secret Santas are revealed. I was thinking that could work in two ways for us. If people have to focus on being nice to a particular person, that means they'll have to pay attention to that person to figure out what to do and what their routine is so they can surprise them."

"And that means you're actually putting together a one-on-one surveillance program," he concluded. "I like it."

"But it's also going to make people feel good once they start getting surprises, and since they won't know who's giving them treats, they might be motivated to be a little nicer to everyone."

He made a note on the pad by his computer. "Isabel and I will take care of matching up names and getting the instructions out there. I take it you want to do this throughout the month?"

"Yeah. And then is there a big company holiday party?"

"Yes. It's quite the to-do. We haven't exchanged gifts before, but we could do a gift exchange where the identities of the secret Santas are revealed. That would even work as an icebreaker." He made another note, then gave me a wicked grin that nearly made me swoon. I forced myself to imagine his bedpost, riddled with notches from women who'd fallen under his spell—literally—and to remember his status on my suspect list. "We don't have to assign people truly randomly, do we? We can act like it's random, but we can match up people who need to get over some personal issues."

"I wouldn't go so far as to match up sworn enemies," I cautioned. "Then it can get ugly. It works best with people who don't know each other all that well. It forces them to get to know each other."

"Good thinking. Any other ideas?"

"That's my most immediate one, and the one I think that'll be easiest to implement. We should probably also do some team-building activities, something that brings a group of people together from various departments to solve problems."

He smiled, and my heart rate increased. "This is taking me back to my days in business school when I was studying human resources. I never thought I'd implement any of that at a company like this. Give me a chance to see what I can come up with, okay?" There was a fresh gleam in his eye. It might have been part of the illusion, but I suspected it had more to do with him finally feeling useful and relevant in the grand scheme of things.

He should feel grateful for that, I thought. So grateful, maybe, that he'd feel the need to thank me in very interesting ways. I had a few suggestions, in case he couldn't think of anything. I cleared my throat to drop a hint, then caught myself. I didn't want to get involved with anyone who could date twenty different women in a month. "So, I guess that's everything we needed to talk about," I said, the words spilling out of me in a rush as I pushed myself out of my chair. "E-mail me when you get some ideas." I fled his office before he could say anything else.

My mental to-do list was growing longer by the minute. I needed to figure out why I wasn't immune anymore and how to reverse it, if such a thing was possible. I needed to find our spy. I needed to find out why Hertwick had been in Central Park the other day during business hours and if it had anything to do with the things I was investigating.

I passed a man banging furiously on a shut door. "I'm supposed to be in that meeting, damn it!" he shouted as he rattled the doorknob. "Open the door or I'll blow a hole in the wall. I'm not a spy!"

Oh yeah, and I had to help ratchet down the paranoia level in the company. That would have been a lot easier if I didn't have very good reason to be paranoid myself. It was hard not to feel hunted when Idris and his henchmen kept showing up and my immunity was on the fritz.

Suddenly a horrible idea came to me. The way Rod had looked at me—had he known my secret? I hadn't ruled him out as the spy, but what if he was also the one who'd found a way to remove my immunity? After all, he'd been there when I realized for the first time that my immunity was gone. Come to think of it, what was he doing heading to the office on a Saturday afternoon during a holiday weekend? If he'd tampered with my immunity somehow, he'd be able to influence me and distract me from my mission. I made a mental note to look into this and see what the chances were that he'd had anything to do with the break-in. But first, I had another errand to take care of while I was out and about.

I made a detour to the sales department and found Hertwick in his office. As soon as I appeared in the doorway, he became uncharacteristically bashful. "You want to know why I was in the park, right?" he said gruffly, looking like a schoolboy being called on the carpet for dropping cherry bombs in the toilets. "I bet that looked pretty suspicious to you, huh?"

"Yeah, it did. But these days, everything looks suspicious."

"I was taking a break."

"A break?"

"If you had a meeting out of the office, and nothing pressing waiting for you, you'd maybe stop off at Starbucks for a latte on the way back, wouldn't you? You know, give yourself a break, something to boost you through the next couple of hours, right?"

I probably wouldn't, because I was too frugal to buy designer coffee, but I knew what he meant. "Yeah."

"So, for my people, digging in the dirt is like a double latte with that chocolate stuff sprinkled on top. We weren't made for working in offices."

"Why do you?" I couldn't help but ask.

He reddened, and for a brief moment he looked more cute than gruff. "Because I'm probably the one gnome in all creation with a brown thumb. I love digging in the dirt, but everything I touch dies."

I bit my tongue to keep myself from laughing. He probably didn't think it was all that funny. "Okay, sounds reasonable," I said.

"So you don't suspect me of spying?"

"Not unless you give me any other reason to think you're a spy." I couldn't help but believe him. I doubted he'd admit to something so embarrassing if it weren't true. If he'd been lying, he would have come up with a better story.

That was one item checked off my list. Only three major things to go. Then I remembered one more item to add: knock Ethan's socks off at lunch the next day so I could look forward to a truly hot weekend.

I got up early the next morning to get ready for work in the sexy but still-business-appropriate outfit Gemma and Marcia helped me plan. As I finished dressing, I gave my new shoe box a quick pat for luck. I might not be wearing the red shoes to work, but I hoped I could carry their aura with me into the day.

As soon as I entered the office suite, Trix gave a low whistle. "My, don't you look hot!" she said, fanning herself. "You wouldn't happen to be meeting a certain lawyer for lunch, would you?"

"Maybe." I tried for an enigmatic expression, but failed utterly, breaking out into a grin. "Actually, he's supposed to come by here at noon to pick me up."

"Lucky girl." She sighed mournfully.

"What's wrong? You and Pippin haven't worked things out?"

"It may not happen at all. He got mad because I wasn't returning his calls, and now I'm the one calling him and begging him to forgive me. I should have known better than to play games. And I really should have known better than to take relationship advice from someone who can't manage to stay in one. Next time I listen to Ari, slap me, okay?"

"If you insist. But he'll probably come around once his bruised male ego heals."

I got to my office to find that Rod already had the secret Santa memo out. I'd been assigned as Owen's Santa. I suspected Isabel was responsible for that. She occasionally teased me about Owen's attention to me. I wasn't quite sure how I felt about being Owen's Santa. Once I might have been thrilled at the chance. Now I was apprehensive. On one hand, I was gradually getting to know him, to the point that I probably knew him better than I knew anyone else at the company. I might even have considered him my best friend at the company. But on the other hand, me sneaking into R&D to leave him treats would certainly ratchet up the company gossip.

"So, who'd you get?" I looked up to see Trix hovering in my doorway.

"It's supposed to be a secret. You know, as in secret Santa," I said, trying to look enigmatic.

"Good point. Tell one person around here, and within an hour the entire company will know. Sometimes I think the walls have ears."

"Around here, that's not so far-fetched."

She glanced over her shoulder, like she was making sure nobody was eavesdropping, then said softly, "Well, can you at least tell me if you got someone good? I mean, will it be fun to do stuff for them, or are you going to have to grit your teeth and force yourself not to be a teensy bit mean?"

I couldn't help but smile. "I got someone good. Challenging, maybe, but being nice won't be hard. What about you?"

She sighed and rolled her eyes. "Mine won't be hard, but it won't be much fun, either." Her phone rang in the outer office, and she said, "Oops, gotta go!" then fluttered away.

That brought up an important question: who had been assigned to me? And what would they do? At a magical company, they could easily wave some treat into existence in my office. I was at a distinct disadvantage because I'd have to sneak around and get into a highly secured department. To make matters worse, my primary excuse for getting into that department was the person I'd be trying to surprise. It looked like I'd be hanging out with Ari more often to give me an excuse to go down there.

In the meantime, I had a date to worry about. I had to force myself to concentrate on work all morning instead of looking at my watch every five minutes and daydreaming about how lunch would go. I laughed at how silly I was being once I became aware of what I was doing. I hadn't put that much importance on our first date, when the fate of the magical world had hinged on the outcome. But that was the world. This was about my own fate.

When noon rolled around and I heard Ethan's voice outside in the reception area, I restrained myself from rushing out there, waiting instead for Trix to call me and tell me my visitor had arrived. He surprised me by coming himself, tapping on my door, sticking his head inside, and saying, "Ready to go?"

"Just a moment." I made a show of closing out the document I was working on, even though my hands shook. Then I got my purse out of a desk drawer, stood up, and took my coat off the hook on the back of the door. "Now I'm ready," I said, with what I hoped was an enticing smile. Trix winked and gave me a thumbs-up as we headed toward the escalator.

He took me to a nearby restaurant that seemed designed for business lunches. The tables were all set in booths with backs high enough to keep sound from traveling to other tables. You could sit in there and talk business without worrying about your competitor eavesdropping from the next table. It said a lot about what I'd been dealing with at work that this was my first assumption when I saw the restaurant. It was also possible that the low lighting and high-backed booths meant it was a prime location for illicit trysts. I wasn't sure what Ethan's motive for taking me there was. Maybe they simply had good food.

"So, your parents got home okay?" Ethan said once we'd been seated and the waiter had taken our drink orders.

"Yeah, and Mom remains blissfully unaware of the existence of magic, so all's right with the world."

He chuckled. "That was certainly an interesting Thanksgiving dinner."

"Oh, please," I said, rolling my eyes. "Parents have a talent for embarrassing their offspring. I'm sure if I'd been with your family, something equally wacky would have been going on."

"You're probably right."

I cast him what I hoped was a properly flirtatious glance. "You did make quite an impression on my parents. Picking them up at the airport, being such a perfect gentleman at dinner—it all added up to high parental brownie points." I attempted an eyelash flutter, making use of that second coat of mascara I'd put on. "And I don't think you're so bad, either."

It might have been the dim lighting, but I was pretty sure he blushed. It wasn't quite as cute on him as it was on Owen, and I thought he almost looked uncomfortable. He picked up his menu and said, "I guess we'd better figure out what we want to order. I come here with clients a lot, and everything I've had is good. They're also pretty quick, so we can get back to work."

I gave him a mock pout. "So you're not whisking me away after lunch to have your wicked way with me?"

"Alas, duty calls. My clients might object, and your boss certainly would. I think I'll have the pork medallions."

There was something wrong about that, or was I being paranoid?

While I knew we both had to go back to work, would it have killed him to give me a little hope? He could have expressed true regret or taken a rain check. It was the perfect opportunity for him to ask me out for the weekend. I took a flat bread from the basket on the table and snapped it in two. "The chicken breast looks good," I said, trying not to sound as sullen as I felt. Maybe it was me. I needed more remedial flirting lessons if I couldn't get across the message that I'd be available for amorous activity, if he so desired.

The waiter returned with our drinks, and I suddenly wished I'd ordered something other than iced tea, even if I did have to go back to work. Ethan ordered for both of us, then took a bread stick from the basket and nibbled on it. I scraped the seeds off my flat bread with my thumbnail onto my bread plate, not because I didn't like seeds but because I needed some way to expend nervous energy.

I'd been on some spectacularly weird dates in my lifetime—most of them in the past couple of months—but none of them had been quite this weird in quite this way. The mixed messages were enough to make my head explode. He'd invited me out for lunch by making plans ahead of time, he'd made a reservation, and he'd brought me to a fairly nice place that certainly wasn't cheap. That all made it a real date instead of a casual "hey, let's go grab some lunch" thing.

But he didn't act like he was on a date. He was nowhere near as affectionate or enthusiastic as he'd been any other time he'd been around me. I realized he hadn't kissed me at all, not even after we left the office building. And he hadn't responded to my feeble attempts to flirt. I might as well have been one of his clients. It was like at any moment he was going to pull out some documents for me to read and sign. Maybe that was it. He was in lawyer mode and having a hard time breaking out of it.

I might be able to do something about that. I slid my foot up the inside of his leg, from ankle to knee. His eyes widened and he jumped. Then he looked relieved. "Whew. That was you. There's not a lot of legroom under these tables, is there?"

What red-blooded American male would react that way to a woman playing footsie under the table? With all the cat-and-mouse games I was dealing with at work, I didn't have the mental or emotional energy to play games in my social life. "Is something wrong?" I asked.

With the impeccable timing that had to be bred into waiters (the same timing that enabled them to always show up and ask how everything was the moment you put a bite of food in your mouth), the waiter arrived then with our lunches. "See, I told you they were quick," Ethan said, entirely ignoring my question as he began eating.

There was definitely something wrong, then, and he wanted to avoid dealing with it until after he'd eaten. If he'd been so eager to see me after not having a real date over the weekend that he couldn't wait until the next weekend, the conversation would have gone totally differently. He'd shown no signs of bashfulness or hesitation when it came to asking me out, so I couldn't imagine that his behavior came from nervousness about inviting me to go to his place for an evening (and maybe morning) in that weekend. His jumpiness was more appropriate for someone gearing up to propose, and we were nowhere near that point in our relationship.

I remembered something Gemma had once said about how men always seem to break up with you in restaurants. I'd argued that maybe it was a classy maneuver, better than doing it over the phone. Marcia thought it was because they wanted to avoid a big scene with crying and hurling of breakables. In a public place, a woman would feel compelled to react quietly and swallow her tears. She might fall apart later, but he wouldn't have to watch it.

"This is good," I commented after taking a bite of chicken. I was glad it had come with mashed potatoes. I suspected I'd need the starchy comfort food.

"Yeah, that's why I like this place. Good, simple food that nearly everyone seems to enjoy."

Wow, was this conversation scintillating, or what? I tried to decide what the breakup risk was on a midweek lunch date. I'd hate to think he'd be cruel enough to do anything at lunch that would make it difficult for me to go back to work. The midweek part, though, seemed like he wanted to clear the way in time for him to have moved on before the weekend.

My appetite totally gone, I shoved my plate away and asked again, "Is there something wrong?"

He looked across the table at me, but didn't quite meet my eyes. "Wrong?" he asked.

Yeah, there was definitely something going on, and I didn't need magical immunity to see through his illusion. "You're acting weird," I said.

"Weird how?"

"Well, you're not talking to me. You're not even looking at me. And you've sidestepped every effort I've made to flirt with you. You have to admit that's a very weird way to act when you invite someone to lunch. I could see it if I roped you into it or invited myself along, but you called me. Is there something wrong at work that's distracting you? Because if there is, you should know I wouldn't have minded if you'd canceled or postponed our lunch." I made one last attempt at flirting. "That is, as long as you made it up to me later."

That attempt, like all the others, sailed right over his head. "No, nothing wrong at work," he said, sounding vague and distant.

"Then do you have a problem at MSI that you want my help with?" I felt like I was grasping at straws, eliminating all the best-case scenarios until only the one reason I hoped to avoid was left.

"No, no problems there. In fact, I'm having fun with work, and it's generally easy to get on people's calendars."

I leaned back in the booth and crossed my arms over my chest. "Okay, then, what is it? I have to be back at work in about twenty minutes, so I don't have time for guessing games." I was surprised by how firm and assertive my voice sounded.

He finished clearing his plate, then shoved it aside. "I wanted to talk to you about something," he said.

"Yes?"

"You sometimes seem a little unnerved about the magic stuff."

"Do I? I don't think so, not at work. I'll admit that I don't really like it affecting my personal life, especially where my friends and my parents are concerned. It's not like I'm an anti-magic bigot."

He shook his head. "No, that's not what I meant. But yeah, I have noticed that you don't seem to like it in your personal life that much."

"If you'd seen the way it's affected my personal life, you'd understand. Wait until you have someone under the influence of a spell show up while you're on a date with someone else and sing arias to you—off-key."

He laughed. "Really? That must have been hysterical."

"In retrospect, maybe, but at the time it wasn't funny at all. My date didn't think so, either. I never heard from him again."

"Then you didn't belong together."

I frowned at him. "What would you think if that happened to someone you were out with?"

"I'd probably figure that it had something to do with a spell."

"But you know about magic. That poor guy didn't."

"The thing is, though, you and I both know about it. We don't have to keep the secret from each other, so it should be fun."

What little food I'd managed to eat threatened to come back up. I had a feeling I knew exactly what he was going to say next.

And I was right. "Katie, I don't really know how to say this, so I guess I'd better be direct. I think you're a great girl, but I don't think we're going to work out together."

This would have been the perfect time for a witty comeback, but all I could do was stare at him in shock. "Not work out together?" I repeated.

He looked intensely uncomfortable, which I couldn't help but enjoy. The more he had to squirm, the better. "I guess this is when I should say it's not you, it's me, but the thing is, it is you, and it is me."

"Do you think you could diagram that sentence for me? I don't quite follow it."

"Okay, then, like we were just saying, you want things to be as normal as possible. I don't, really. I've discovered this whole other world and I want to explore it as fully as possible, take every advantage of it. But you don't want magic intruding on your regular life. That means ultimately we'd be incompatible. I'd enjoy something that was your idea of a disastrous date."

"So you like being ambushed by the minions of evil on our way to a party?"

"We got away okay, didn't we?"

"That time, yeah. But it still wasn't my idea of a good time. I don't even really have anything against magic or magical people. If I were dating a wizard or a sprite, elf, or gnome, I'd still want it to be a regularly normal date. They're just people with different abilities, you know. They're not a freak show for your amusement."

He groaned and shook his head. "No, that's not what I meant. It's just that I want to explore the differences right now, and you don't strike me as wanting that."

"So I'm too normal for you?" It was the story of my life.

"Like I said, you're a great girl, and if I'd never learned about the whole magic thing, then I probably would have been very happy with you. But the more I learn about other things, the more I want to learn about them."

"You want to try going out with chicks with wings," I clarified.

"No!" He shook his head, but the redness rising from his collar was a pretty good sign I'd hit close to the mark. "Well, maybe, but it's not only that." He looked down at the table and fiddled with his silverware. "I have a feeling I'm not really what you're looking for, either. And I'm fairly certain I'm not your first choice."

There wasn't much I could say to that, since I'd just been thinking about telling him he'd been my second choice, anyway, and I'd only gone out with him because I'd convinced myself that I could never have the man I really wanted. But although I knew that was true, I couldn't bring myself to admit it now. "Wait a second, are you taking what Idris said seriously? You know that's one of his things, where he tries to get under Owen's skin by saying I'm his girlfriend. My mom misunderstood. It's not like I've been two-timing you."

He looked across the table at me, and I had the uncomfortable feeling that he could see right through me. "Be honest, Katie," he said softly. "If not with me, then with yourself. If you want something, you have to believe you deserve it. I like you enough that I can't deal with the idea of you being with me only because you don't think you deserve anything better."

"So now this is for my own good?"

"It's for both of us. I'd rather end this before it gets deep enough that we get hurt. At least this way we haven't crossed too many lines that could keep us from ever being friends again."

If I could put aside my hurt and disappointment long enough, I knew I'd be grateful for the timing. I'd have been utterly desolate if he'd broken up with me after we'd slept together, which is what would have likely happened soon enough if things had gone according to my plans. Then my throat started to ache in the way that meant tears were imminent. I couldn't let him see me cry.

"Well, thanks for lunch," I said, fighting for control. My hand shook as I took my napkin off my lap and threw it on the table. "I have to get back to work now. Oh, and the lunch idea was quite the stroke of genius. No time for prolonged conversation or fighting. But for the future, have some mercy and remember that the poor girl has to face her office again after you've dumped her. At least do it at the end of the day so she can go straight home and eat ice cream instead of having to pretend to work." I slid off the booth seat, adjusted my skirt, collected my coat, and turned to go.

"Katie!" he called after me. "I'm sorry. I didn't think about that."

I couldn't turn back. The tears had already started to fall and I didn't want him to see them. Instead, I ignored him and kept on walking. I wasn't even sure why I was crying. It wasn't like I'd really fallen in love with him. Deep down inside, I had to admit to myself that he was right, in a way. I did want normal, as much as I'd hated being so utterly ordinary before I joined MSI. I didn't see how normal and the magical world were necessarily mutually exclusive. The time I'd had dinner with Owen flashed into my brain. That had been such a delightfully normal, ordinary evening, even though Owen was about as magical as you could get. And Ethan was also right about where my heart really was. That didn't make me feel any less heartbroken. Not only did I not have Owen as anything more than a friend, but I didn't have Ethan, either.

I paused on the sidewalk to find a tissue in my purse so I could wipe away the tears, and that's when I felt the tingle. I might not have been able to see anything veiled by magic, but I'd learned to recognize the sensation of magic in use. And magic was in use very close by me, but without my magical immunity I had no idea what was happening. I was as good as blind, and more vulnerable than I'd ever been.

thirteen

Unfortunately, the magical tingle wasn't a directional thing. I got the same sense of the little hairs at the back of my neck standing on end no matter where the magic came from. The best I could manage was to play "hot or cold" and see if the tingle got stronger in a particular direction. But I was not up to playing games at that moment. Instead, I stood my ground, facing straight ahead the way I would have even if I could have seen what magical mischief was afoot. "Look, I don't know what you're up to, but this really is *not* the time," I said to no one in particular. "I'm tired and I'm pissed off, so get the hell out of my way and leave me alone."

Even a magical creature must have known better than to mess with a woman who'd just been dumped, for the tingle quickly faded. Not wanting to take any chances, I hurried forward to get to the safety of the office before my invisible stalker had second thoughts about letting me go.

I paused before I turned the corner to approach the MSI building and found a clean tissue in my purse. Then I dabbed at my eyes, blew my nose, and checked my reflection in my compact mirror. I didn't look great, but there was no mascara running down my face, and any redness around my eyes could have come from being out in the cold. With a deep breath, I forced myself to hold my head high and walk toward the entrance with my most confident stride.

I gave a passing nod to the guardian gargoyle—not one I knew, thank goodness—then hurried up to my office. The reigning paranoia meant I didn't have to worry about anyone trying to strike up a conversation with me along the way. I didn't even have to worry about anyone making eye contact. I managed to hold myself together until I got to Merlin's office suite, where Trix cheerfully asked, "So, how was the hot lunch date?" without looking up from her computer.

Then I lost it utterly. The tears came once more, and I couldn't shut them off. "He broke up with me," I sobbed.

She immediately jumped up, flew over the top of her desk, and grabbed me by the shoulders. "You poor thing," she said as she hustled me into my office, where she shut the door behind us and pushed me into my desk chair. Then she conjured up a cup of tea, a box of tissues, and a tray of chocolates. "Now, tell me all about it," she said, sitting in the chair next to my desk. "Why did he break up with you? Things seemed to be going so well, even when he picked you up today."

I tried to shrug, but it was difficult because my shoulders were shaking so badly. "Because I'm boring." I grabbed a tissue out of the box and blew my nose loudly.

"Did he actually say that?"

"Well, he did say I was too 'normal,' but he meant boring." I adopted a mocking tone. "Apparently, he wants to explore and experience this new world he's discovered, and he thinks I want things to be too normal, so we have totally opposite ideas of a good time." I bit a chocolate in two, then licked the caramel filling off my lips.

The light on my phone indicating a call coming in to Trix's line flashed. "Hold that thought," Trix said, leaning over my desk to grab the phone. "Mr. Mervyn's office," she said briskly, then after a pause said, "One moment, please. Let me connect you." She pushed a few buttons, hung up the phone, then picked it up again and pushed more buttons. "Ari, emergency summit meeting, Katie's office, now. Get Isabel."

When she hung up and returned to her chair, I asked, "Are you sure that's a good idea?"

She waved a hand, dismissing my concern. "I wouldn't take her romantic advice, but there's no one better for venting when you're mad at a guy. Once we get past that, then we can strategize about what to do next. It should be easy enough to convince him that you're not too normal for him."

"But he's right. I do like things normal. Don't get me wrong, I like magical people, but for fun I like to do normal stuff. When magic intrudes on my personal life, everything always goes horribly wrong."

"If he's looking for magical excitement, he's going to be unpleasantly surprised. Most of us aren't usually off doing wild and crazy magical things. Magic is a convenience, not a lifestyle, except among certain fringe groups." She giggled, a sound like tinkling bells. "And I can't picture him in any of those groups. They'd kick him out for being too normal."

I couldn't help but laugh at that. "Talk about irony!"

There was a knock at my door and Trix called out, "Come in." The door opened and Isabel and Ari spilled into my office.

"What's up?" Ari asked, then she got a good look at me. "Don't tell me, he ditched you already?"

I nodded sadly while Trix got them up to speed. "If you can believe it, he made a lunch date with her, took her out, then dumped her at the restaurant. He said she wanted things too normal while he wanted to really get into the whole magical world."

Ari licked her lips slyly. "So, what exactly did he want that you thought was too out there?"

Isabel smacked her lightly on the shoulder, which sent her reeling. "Really, Ari. Please!"

"It wasn't like that," I explained wearily. "I don't like it when weird, magical stuff gets in the way of my personal life, and he finds that exciting."

"Too bad you didn't find that out earlier," Ari said. "You could have used that as a great seduction technique."

"That was kind of the plan for this weekend," I admitted. "But not the using-magic-to-get-him-excited part. I had this really hot pair of red shoes."

Trix clapped her hands delightedly. "You bought them!"

Isabel put her arm around my shoulders and gave me a squeeze, nearly suffocating me in the process. "Oh, honey, no wonder you were so disappointed. I hate it when guys do that. Why is it that just when you're ready to take things to the next level, they decide they want out?"

"Though normally they back out right after that particular next level, rather than before it," Ari put in. "So, what do we have planned for revenge?"

I shook my head. "I don't need revenge. This is a situation where we can let the universe handle it."

"Yeah, he'll get himself ditched by some magical girl for being too normal," Trix said. "And in the meantime, Katie will find herself someone fabulous."

I got another tissue and wiped my eyes and nose. I was already feeling much better. "You know what's funny?" I asked. "I wasn't that incredibly into him to begin with. I only asked him out in the first place because we needed an intellectual property attorney. I thought he was okay, but it was definitely not love at first sight. And then when he kept asking me out after that, I thought I might as well go out with him. I mean, he seemed nice, he's cute, and he'd be a good catch."

"He's good on paper," Trix agreed with a world-weary sigh. "But he can be the perfect catch and not be right for you if there's no chemistry."

"I thought there was chemistry," I said. "But maybe I was only trying to convince myself." I knew better than to share the real reason why I'd tried to talk myself into falling for Ethan with this bunch. That would be asking to become the center of office gossip and dragging Owen with me. "I think I just wanted somebody, and he was better than my other options at the time."

"That doesn't get him off the hook," Ari insisted. "He dumped you at lunch in a restaurant, for crying out loud."

"But at least he told me," I argued. "Most guys would have just fallen off the face of the earth. They'd have stopped calling me and left me to figure it out for myself when I didn't hear from them for a few weeks."

"She does have a point," Isabel said with a sigh.

"Still," Ari said, "lunchtime! So she had to go back to work and face the rest of the day. What, he couldn't spring for dinner for his breakup meal? Or did he already have something lined up for the evening?"

"I'll be fine," I said with only the tiniest of sniffles.

"Want to go out for drinks after work?" Isabel offered.

I shook my head. "No, I want to go home and eat ice cream. My roommates will look out for me." That was, if they weren't out with their boyfriends. I was the lone single girl once more.

"Girls' night out Friday," Trix declared. "I think we can all use the break."

I wasn't so sure. The first time I'd gone out with all of them, we'd wound up kissing frogs in Central Park, which was how both Philip and Jeff had come into my life. But since then, we'd had a few perfectly normal (there was that word again) outings where the only things that were magical or odd were Trix's and Ari's wings.

"You could even wear those hot red shoes and let other men get the benefit," Ari suggested.

"Can I get back to you later in the week?" I asked. "Let's see how I'm feeling then. Right now, I just want to hibernate for a while."

Ari and Isabel soon left, then Trix said, "Why don't you go on home? I'll cover for you."

"No, I can't abandon you like that, not after taking the day off before Thanksgiving."

She snorted. "Yeah, like that was a busy day. I gave myself a manicure and pedicure. And I missed a whole day of work from my breakup."

"But I have work to do."

"And how effective will you be? Will you get anything done at all, or will you stare into space and think about what you should have said?"

I sighed deeply. "Maybe you're right. But if I go home early, won't he know he got to me?"

She winked. "How will he know you went home early? As far as he'll know—if he even checks—you're in important meetings all afternoon. Go home or go shopping or make something for your holiday buddy. That'll count as work, sort of. This program was your idea, so you have to set an example and do it right."

"Okay, you don't have to twist my arm. I'll go." As much as I felt like a slacker and a wimp, I didn't want to be in the office. I'd never before taken time off because a boyfriend had broken up with me, but that could be because I hadn't had much of anything resembling a boyfriend since I'd been working. I'd had dates since moving to New York, but nobody around long enough to be called a boyfriend, and while I was working at my parents' store after graduating from college, there had been nobody. No wonder I'd let myself fall for Ethan in spite of my doubts. I'd been lonely, pathetic, and desperate.

On my way home, I stopped at a neighborhood grocery store to pick up ingredients for my favorite Christmas cookies. As I approached the entrance to my apartment building, I saw Mrs. Jacobs with her little rat-like dog (actually, I kind of suspected she'd put a leash on a real rat) going through the door. There was no point in picking up my pace and asking her to hold the door for me, even though it would have helped if I didn't have to juggle my grocery bags while unlocking the front door. She'd let the door slam in my face, smugly citing the rule that we weren't supposed to let anyone follow us into the building.

But she did hold the door for me. I'd have to call the *Times* when I got upstairs. She even greeted me with a smile. "You're home from work early today. Is everything okay?" The *Times* story moved to the front page. I had proof of alien invasion. The body snatchers had definitely landed.

"Just taking a little time off," I said as I stepped through the door and allowed her to close it. "Thanks for holding the door."

"You had your arms full," she said. "Come on, Winkie." She tugged on her rat's leash and headed up the stairs.

I watched her in shock until she was inside her apartment, then climbed the stairs to my own place. Of all days, I needed her to be nice to me today. If she'd been her usual self, I'd have burst into tears.

Inside my apartment, I put away the eggs and butter, then tried to decide what I should do. Now that I was home, being alone in the empty apartment didn't seem like such a good idea. At work I'd have had something to distract me. If I sat on my bed and cried my eyes out, I could get it out of my system enough so I could act like I was fine when my roommates came home. I didn't want them pitying me.

That decided, I went into the bedroom and changed out of my work clothes. After I'd put on jeans and a sweatshirt, I paused to touch the shoe box. I couldn't even bring myself to look at the red shoes now that I knew they weren't going to get me what I wanted.

That was when the tears returned. It was so unfair. I was doomed to be alone the rest of my life because I was too boring and ordinary for anyone to want me. I'd never have a chance to wear the wonderful red shoes because I'd never have another date again.

Finally the sobs subsided and I began laughing instead. I was being an utter idiot. So what if I was having the suckiest week ever, from losing the magical immunity that was the main reason I had my job to losing my boyfriend. I still had a lot going for me. I couldn't think of much at the moment, but I was sure there was something.

I went into the bathroom to wash my face. On the way back into the living room, I noticed the light on the answering machine blinking. I hit the message PLAY button and heard my mother's voice. "Um, this message is for Katie. This is your mother. I wanted to let you know I got the information on that place where Mavis went to dry out. I put a brochure in the mail to you. Maybe you could give it to that friend of yours next time he bothers you." That was the final thing I needed for my cure, the mental image of doing an intervention on Phelan Idris and sending him off to the Betty Ford Center.

When I finished laughing, I turned on the radio to a station that was already playing Christmas music and went to work on my cookies. Baking always made me feel better about life. The kitchen was a mess and I was covered in flour when my roommates got home, but at least I was no longer weeping. I was able to give them a reasonably cheerful greeting, and when Gemma asked, "How did your date go? I want details," I managed to roll my eyes instead of crying.

"Would you believe, it wasn't a date at all? He planned the whole thing just to break up with me."

"You're kidding!"

"I told you he was an ass," Marcia muttered. "Can I have a cookie, or are these for something?"

"Take one of those over there that aren't shaped right," I said, pointing with an icing-covered spatula. "And he wasn't quite an ass. He simply didn't want to go any further with me, so he told me about it. It's not like I can blame him for having an opinion that differs from mine."

"On the first day of a breakup?" Gemma asked, picking up a cookie. "You can blame him for anything you want to. It's only a day or so later that you have to start being reasonable."

I went back to stirring icing. "Well, it's not like I'd want him to keep going out with me if he wasn't really interested, and I definitely wouldn't want him sleeping with me if he wasn't interested. I'd be even more pissed off if he hadn't told me at all and had left me hanging with no explanation and a lot of 'I've been busy' excuses."

"Girl, you are way too reasonable," Marcia said. "I'd still be calling for his balls."

"He did break up with you at lunch, therefore ruining your whole day," Gemma added. "It looks like you came home early, based on your cookie output."

"My coworker said she'd cover for me," I explained. "And besides, we've started this secret Santa thing around the company, so I had to come up with some treats for my secret pal."

She eyed the stacks of gingerbread on the table. "You must really like your secret pal. Wait, are those pieces for a gingerbread house?"

I couldn't look her in the eye. Maybe I had gone a little overboard. "The house may not be for him. It may be a little something for us, since, if we put up a tree, we'd have to charge it rent."

"Oh, a him, is it?" Marcia said around a mouthful of cookie. "The plot thickens. Do we have any milk?"

While she rummaged in the refrigerator, Gemma picked up the inquisition. "This wouldn't happen to be that cute guy you've mentioned, now, would it?"

"Maybe," I hedged.

"Now, that's an interesting color of pink," she teased. "Marce, get a load of that blush. I do believe our girl has already moved on to greener pastures."

"He's just a friend," I insisted. "He's shown no signs whatsoever of being interested in me as anything other than a friend."

"Then why are you turning into Betty Crocker here?"

"Because I kind of feel sorry for him."

Marcia finished pouring milk for all of us and put the bottle back in the refrigerator. "We still don't have any water," she said.

"Because it's your turn to buy it," Gemma shot back. "And don't change the subject. We're dissecting Katie's love life. Now, why would you feel sorry for Mr. Cutie?"

"I think he's lonely. He's an orphan, and it sounds like the people who brought him up kept him at a distance emotionally. I thought some homemade treats would help give him a nicer holiday."

Marcia played a dramatic air violin solo while Gemma dabbed away imaginary tears. "It's like something out of Dickens," she said with an audible sigh. "You know how else you could ease his loneliness?"

"Ask him out!" Marcia answered. "That's the only way to find out if he's interested in you or just shy."

I snorted and returned to my icing, which had started to harden while I was chatting. "I'd have to get recertified in CPR before I could ask him out," I said, stirring vigorously. "He'd keel over and die. Besides, I don't want to do something like that on the rebound. When the time's right, I'll know."

They looked at each other. "Is there any wonder she hasn't been laid in five years?" Marcia asked.

I discovered the next morning that baking the cookies or even sneaking them into the highly secured department wasn't going to be my biggest secret Santa challenge. First, I had to get my treats to work without cluing Owen in. That was difficult, given that he waited for me outside my building every morning and escorted me to work.

I came to the conclusion that me carrying something unusual wouldn't raise any suspicions, since everyone had a secret Santa assignment, and I'd be expected to carry something for someone. The trick would be to make what I was carrying look very different from what I actually left for Owen, once I figured out how to get it to him. I arranged the gingerbread on a plastic Christmas plate, covered it with colored plastic wrap tied with a bow, then put that in a bakery box and wrapped a bow around that. With luck, he'd think the bakery box was my treat and wouldn't suspect anything when he saw my gift.

I was glad I'd taken the precautions, for he definitely noticed that I was carrying something. He was still playing guessing games about my bakery box when we approached the office building. "You can trust me. I won't tell anyone else," he insisted.

"No offense, but the way news spreads, I'm not trusting anybody with my secrets."

"Maybe you might have some leftovers you could share with other people?"

If the "leftovers" were the same as the treat I'd already given him, he'd definitely figure out who his secret Santa was. But he looked so eager that he was too cute to resist. I decided to bake something entirely different to give him as "leftovers" to throw him off the trail. "Maybe tomorrow," I said.

His whole face lit up, so that he looked like a small child seeing his first decorated Christmas tree. If I hadn't had my arms full with the bakery box, I might not have been able to resist hugging him. It was almost enough to make me forget about Ethan breaking my heart the day before.

The building doors swung open for us, and a man even more handsome than Owen greeted us. It took me a couple of seconds to remember that this was Rod with his illusion in place. "Oh good, I'm glad you're here," he said.

Owen and I exchanged a look. "You are?" Owen asked suspiciously.

After I took a glance around the lobby, I could see why. It had been transformed into one of those rope-climbing courses, with the ropes hanging suspended in midair. "You two can be the first to try it out," Rod said.

It looked like the team-building effort for MSI had begun. Maybe paranoia and distrust weren't so bad after all, I thought as I looked at the rope-filled maze.

fourteen

"Don't even think about it," Owen said, and I was glad he declined before I had to.

Rod's face fell, and for a moment I thought I could see some of his true self that lay behind the illusion. "Why not?"

"Bad shoulder, remember? I'm still not completely healed. Wouldn't want to risk it."

"I'm wearing a skirt today, so it probably wouldn't be a good idea," I hurried to add. "And maybe we ought to start smaller? I'm not sure having that many ropes around when people are already at each other's throats is such a good idea."

Rod winced. "You may be right. But don't worry, I have other ideas." He waved a hand and the rope course disappeared. Owen looked visibly relieved. I was glad to get out of anything that gave me unpleasant high school PE flashbacks, not to mention the fact that I didn't really want to get tangled up in ropes set up by someone I still had on my list of suspects. Before Rod could come up with anything else he wanted to test on us, both Owen and I made excuses about busy days and hurried out of there.

My office turned out to be even more disconcerting than the lobby had been. It had been thoroughly decorated overnight. There was a small Christmas tree in one corner with snow delicately drifting down onto it, only to vanish before it hit the ground. Twinkling stars were suspended beneath the ceiling, with no visible cords attached.

As I stood in the doorway admiring the view, Trix came up behind me. "Do you like it?" she asked.

"Yeah. Who did it?"

She winked. "It's a secret. How are you doing?"

"Better. In fact, I think I'm almost fully recovered."

"Good to hear it. He's not worth wasting tears over if he can't appreciate you for who you are. So does that mean you'll be joining us for girls' night out Friday?"

"I think I will."

"Then bring those sexy red shoes and we'll take 'em out on the town for a good time."

I was sure I had work to do, but first I needed to find a way to get my cookies to Owen without anyone catching on. I checked Merlin's calendar and saw that he had a meeting with Owen that afternoon. Quite often, I was invited to those meetings, but I hadn't been invited to this one, much to my relief. If I were there, I'd be there in my capacity as a verifier, and that was something I couldn't do without magical immunity. But while Owen was in the meeting, I could drop the cookies off at his office.

I wasn't entirely off the hook when it came to verification, though. Midmorning, Merlin called me to his office. "I'm afraid this is short notice," he said, "but I have a meeting with Corporate Sales and a new potential corporate customer in a few minutes. We're not putting together a contract yet, but I'd like to have you there, just in case. I'd insult them if I brought in a regular verifier, but having you there as my assistant and letting it be known you're an immune might intimidate them into good behavior."

I thought the lump that grew in my throat would choke me to

death. Could I bluff my way through a meeting, even if I wasn't called upon for official verification? "No problem," I said, hoping I sounded perky instead of nervously shrill.

When the visitors arrived, I thought they didn't seem particularly unusual, but then again, would I know? The potential customer could have been Satan incarnate, complete with horns, cloven hooves, and pointy tail, and if he wanted us to think he looked normal, he'd look normal to me. But he didn't act like someone who was pulling one over on us. I'd noticed that there was a smugness about people who were doing something they thought others wouldn't see. It was like that old T-shirt slogan: SMILE! MAKE OTHERS WONDER WHAT YOU'RE UP TO.

The Corporate Sales guy, whom I remembered was named Ryker, introduced the customer to Merlin, then Merlin introduced me. "Miss Chandler will be observing the meeting and taking notes," he said. He put special emphasis on the word "observing," which I supposed implied that I'd be looking at the meeting with my supposedly unique perspective. I felt a surge of guilt. I ought to have told Merlin. It wasn't fair to let him think he had a magically immune assistant when he didn't.

But the customer didn't even blink. He just took his seat. The others followed his lead. I sat behind Merlin and kept my eyes peeled so hard that I thought they'd come out of their sockets. Instead of listening to the words being said, I strained to hear the meaning behind them in tone and inflection. I tuned into every nuance of body language that would tell me that someone was lying or cheating. By the end of the meeting, I had a splitting headache. I was pretty sure nothing untoward had happened, but I couldn't be absolutely certain.

Merlin escorted his guests out, then returned to where I was gathering my notes. "I assume there was no skulduggery at work?" he said.

"None that I could see," I said. On the surface, that wasn't a lie. The lie came in not admitting how little I could actually see.

He nodded. "Good. I didn't sense any magic use. Your mere presence may have been enough to deter it. Or we could have been dealing with a rare honest businessman."

"Then we should probably capture him and put him in a museum," I quipped.

"Thank you for your assistance. And your secret Santa program appears to be working already. Spirits seem to have lifted, and I've noticed employees actually speaking to each other again instead of eyeing each other with suspicion."

"Great. I'm still trying to come up with other ideas."

"We should form a task force!" He said it with great enthusiasm, and I knew he'd been reading business books again.

"Maybe," I hedged. I hadn't seen too many task forces accomplish much of anything other than generating a lot of memos and a few binders full of presentation slides. I said a silent prayer that Merlin wouldn't discover PowerPoint anytime soon.

That afternoon I waited until about five minutes after Owen's meeting with Merlin was supposed to have begun, then called Ari's lab in practical magic. "Hi, it's Katie," I said when she answered. "I need to drop something off down there. Can you let me in?"

"Ooh, I bet you've got a secret pal," she cooed. "But why not have your usual buddy let you in? I'm sure he'd be glad of an excuse to see you."

I didn't have to ask who she meant. "He's in a meeting up here."

"Okay, I'll meet you at the department door in a couple of minutes."

"Thank you! I owe you one." After hanging up, I put my bakery box in a shopping bag I found in a desk drawer and headed out. "I have to drop something off. I'll be back in a sec," I explained to Trix as I passed her desk.

As I rounded the corner onto the corridor that led to R&D, I nearly ran into Gregor, who appeared to be heading in the same direction, carrying a gift bag with a reindeer printed on it. He glowered at me, which was his usual expression. "I understand you're responsible for this," he growled.

For a change, I was grateful for having lost my immunity. That meant I couldn't see if he'd turned into an ogre. "Yes, and isn't it fun?" I said brightly. His face darkened, and I imagined it was actually turning green and sprouting horns and fangs.

When I didn't react, his face returned to its usual ruddy color. "Hmmph," he snorted.

True to her word, Ari was waiting for me at the entrance to R&D. Gregor glanced at the doorway, then kept walking. "Just what I thought," Ari said. "You've got a secret pal down here. I wonder who it could be."

"This is the biggest department in the company. There are a lot of people it could be. Now go back to your lab, and no fair peeking."

She fluttered alongside me until we got to her lab entrance. "Can't you at least tell me what it is?"

"Nope. Do you not understand the concept of secret?"

She veered off to head into her lab. "I'm actually quite good at secrets," she tossed over her shoulder. "You might be surprised at some of the secrets I'm keeping."

I shook my head in amusement as I continued down the corridor to theoretical magic. Ari sucked at secrets. The moment she heard one, she felt compelled to share it.

Owen's lab was empty, which made my job easier. Otherwise, I might have had to bribe Jake to secrecy. All I had to do was get into Owen's office, pull the plate of cookies out of my box, place it on Owen's desk, then leave with my shopping bag and box so no one would know what it was I'd left, or where.

With one last glance over my shoulder, I stepped through Owen's doorway and barely kept my balance as an invisible force threw me backward. Only then did I remember that he'd warded his office so no one else could get in. The wards hadn't worked on me before when I was immune to magic, but now with my immunity missing, I was kept out along with everyone else.

Instead, I left the cookies on a table in the lab, with the card with his name on it clearly visible. Now that I thought about it, that was probably a better option, anyway. If cookies appeared in his office, they would have had to come from an immune. I suspected the wards would have kept out even a magical spell to conjure up something in there.

My mission completed, I started to head out of the department, but I paused before I left the lab. If there was anyplace in this company that held the answer to what had happened with my magical immunity, it was Owen's lab. I couldn't get into his office where the really good books were, but there were plenty of books in the lab outside his office.

Unfortunately, as neat and precise as Owen could be, he was also wildly disorganized. I suspected he had a system that made total sense to him and he could find anything he needed within seconds, but to me it all looked like a random jumble. Acutely conscious that I had a limited amount of time, I hurried to skim the spines on the lab bookcase. I could rule out any book that didn't appear to be in English; even if it contained the information I needed, it wouldn't do me a lot of good if I couldn't read it.

There was a fairly modern-looking volume that seemed to be about magical maladies. I pulled it off the shelf and opened it to the table of contents. Much to my surprise, it contained a chapter on magical immunity. Even more to my surprise, there was a Post-it note stuck on the first page of that chapter, not quite sticking out like a bookmark, but still there. Was Owen researching me—or was someone else?

Feeling more and more rushed, as I knew Merlin's meeting was likely winding to a close, I glanced through the section headings in the chapter. Most of it was information I already knew, only written using much larger words. Finally, there was a section on the disruption of magical immunity. It was long—pages and pages' worth—and full of even bigger words, with magical terms I didn't know. I'd need a reference book to be able to read this book. I glanced at my watch. Merlin's meeting with Owen would be ending at any minute. I pondered "borrowing" the book, but as paranoid as Owen was lately, he'd probably know as soon as he walked in the room that something was gone. Reluctantly, I put it back on the shelf. I'd know where it was in the future, and the relevant chapter was already marked. Maybe I could even come up with an excuse for borrowing it later.

Before I could safely sneak out of the department, Ari caught me in the hallway outside her lab. "Did you leave anything, or what?" she asked, eyeing my shopping bag and bakery box.

"Nope. I was just down here spying," I quipped. "Thanks for letting me into the secured area."

"Nice try, Katie, but I know you aren't our spy."

"And how would you know that?"

"You're too nice. And I doubt you could keep the secret for too long. The strain would show."

I edged past her and kept walking. "Maybe that's part of my cover," I shot over my shoulder as I left. It remained to be seen how right she was about my ability to keep a secret. So far, I wasn't doing too badly at keeping everyone in the dark about my loss of magical immunity. In fact, it came as something of a surprise to me how seldom my abilities were really called upon. That made it that much easier to keep the secret, and it made me a little less afraid that I'd lose my job if anyone knew.

Then again, one more day meant it was one day closer to being permanent. A temporary effect should have passed, or so I would have hoped. Had I transferred my lack of powers to my mother instead of inheriting them from her? I needed to get back into Owen's lab and get another look at that book.

Inspired by the decorating job done on my office, I took advantage of the fact that Owen wasn't on the train with me on the way home to pick up some Christmas décor. Hauling shoes and clothes to change into for the girls' night out on Friday would give me the perfect cover for bringing in the decorations right under his nose. I just had to find a good time to sneak in and put them up in his lab. The ones I'd bought were cheesy enough that it might possibly look like a magical person had gone mundane on purpose.

Ari invited me down to her lab for lunch on Friday, which gave me the perfect opportunity to sneak in with the Christmas decorations. "Let me guess," she said when she saw my bag. "More secret Santa stuff."

"It was my idea, so I have to do a good job."

"You know, if you'd tell me who your secret pal is, I could help you."

"Then it wouldn't be so secret anymore, would it?"

When she got a phone call after lunch, I took that as a good time to dash out of her lab and hurry down the hall to Owen's lab. I nearly ran into Jake on his way out. "You just missed him," he said. "He had to go to a meeting."

"That's okay. I'm only dropping some paperwork off in his office."

"Cool." He was already off down the hall, grooving to whatever was on his iPod, before he could think to ask why paperwork required a shopping bag. I spread out the cheesy plastic Santas and silvery tinsel on the big table in the middle of the lab so it would look like I was in the middle of decorating, then found that book again and flipped to the conveniently placed Post-it.

It was like looking for information on what to do about the common cold in a medical journal. I imagined I'd need years of study to properly understand what I was reading, but it did appear that there were ways of making a magical immune susceptible to magic. There was a whole list of chemical names, and none of them sounded familiar. It looked like once the drug was in the person's system, they could then have spells done on them to really solidify the loss of immunity.

Well, that was great, but I wasn't taking any drugs, not even the occasional aspirin. I hadn't changed my routine or eaten or drunk anything new—not that I was aware of. The loss of immunity had hit before the secret Santa game started, so it couldn't have been caused by any treat that had been left for me. Short of closing myself in a plastic bubble, there wasn't much I could do until I figured out what was being done to me.

I put the book back on the shelf, then put up the decorations around the lab as quickly as I could. I stuck an anonymous secret Santa greeting note on Owen's office door before hurrying out. Ari was still on the phone as I passed and didn't seem to see me.

I was out of breath when I returned to my office. I didn't see how our spy could stand the stress. The sneaking around for a good reason, with no consequences other than maybe embarrassment and a good laugh, was difficult enough. I'd nearly had heart failure from sneaking a peek at a book that Owen probably would have loaned me willingly, even if he would have asked me why I wanted it.

I rewarded myself for a successful mission by slipping out of my sensible business shoes, taking the red shoes out of their box, and putting them on. I felt the usual surge of power, like I could rule the world if I really wanted to. I'd always laughed at Gemma when she said it, but I was starting to believe that the right pair of shoes actually could change your life.

I kept them on for the rest of the day, and as a result, all I had to do to get ready for going out was touch up my makeup, add a little sparkle, and change my blouse. I got down to Isabel's office, where we'd agreed to meet, and found it empty. Rod then appeared in his doorway, and I realized I must have become accustomed to his illusion when I didn't have to pause and remember who he was.

He gave me a low whistle and said, "You look great. You shouldn't have any trouble attracting attention tonight." A warm glow spread through me at his praise. Maybe I wouldn't have to go out to get attention. All the attention I could want was right there in front of me. Then he looked more somber, jolting me out of what had to have been the effects of his attraction spell. "Can I speak to you for a moment?"

I forced myself to focus. "Sure."

He gestured me into his office and said, "Have a seat, please." He perched on the edge of his desk, and I sat in the guest chair, crossing my legs like I was modeling panty hose. His eyes were serious enough to snap me out of it once more. It would have helped if he'd turn that spell off even for a second, but I guessed he didn't realize it was affecting me—unless he was deliberately affecting me. "This is probably none of my business, and I'm sure I'm totally out of line. I also want to make sure you know I'm not saying this in any official capacity, but rather as a friend. I'd like to think that you're my friend, and Owen has been my best friend for a very long time. But be careful, please."

Goose bumps grew on my arms, and I momentarily forgot all about the effect Rod had on me. "Careful of what?"

"I know you and Owen have been spending a lot of time together lately."

"We come to work together in the morning, and we've gone to dinner together once. That's not exactly a lot."

"For Owen, it is. It's enough that I feel like I ought to warn you. Owen's a great guy. But he's also dangerous. I don't think he'd do any-thing deliberately to hurt anyone, but he could easily do it without meaning to. He's also, well, he doesn't have much experience outside his lab. I don't want you getting hurt, but I'm more worried about him getting hurt, and what might happen if he did."

I thought I understood where he was going with this. "You mean, you don't want me to break his heart so that he then goes insane with grief and blows up the island without realizing that's what he's doing?"

He nodded. "Yes, something like that." I'd been joking, sort of, but he wasn't smiling at all. "I'm glad you understand me."

I might not have had a lot of romantic experience, having had only a handful of real boyfriends, but I'd grown up with brothers and all their friends, so I knew a thing or two about men. My experience had taught me that when a man warned a woman away from another man, it usually had more to do with jealousy than with real worry about that other man, whether or not the guy actually realized it. While I didn't doubt that Rod was worried to some degree about Owen, I had the strongest sense that he was actually jealous.

That didn't mean he was really interested in me himself. But if he went to the effort it took to mask his appearance with an illusion, and with his best friend being a total knockout naturally, it wasn't far-fetched to think he might have issues about me seeing him as he really was and comparing him with Owen. Could that have been his motive for spying on Owen and tinkering with my immunity, if he was the one who'd done it?

Regardless of whether or not he was the culprit, I knew enough about men not to accuse him of jealousy to his face. Instead, I said, "I don't think you have anything to worry about."

"I don't?"

"Think about it. You've known Owen a long time, right?"

"Since we were kids."

"So you've seen him around someone he was interested in. And if I read him the right way, I'd guess that when he's interested in someone, he freezes entirely and can't speak to her."

"That's pretty much it," he agreed.

"Well, he talks to me. Often, and quite comfortably, at that. I'd say that's a pretty good sign he's got me filed in the 'friend' category. Or, given the way he seems to organize things, I'm somewhere in the middle of the 'friend' pile."

He brightened considerably at that, even as my heart sank when I recognized the truth in my own words. My "like a sister" curse had struck again. "You're probably right. I guess I overreacted," he said.

"No problem," I said with a shrug. Then I realized this was my chance to probe him a little bit about his involvement. "While I've got you here," I said as casually as I could manage, "I just need to take care of a few details in my investigation. Formalities, you know. First, how often do you come to the office on weekends?"

He frowned. "Are you talking about when you saw me nearby last Saturday?" It wasn't much of a reaction. He didn't seem surprised by my question, and he didn't go overboard to act like he was shocked that I'd dare ask such a thing. In fact, he acted the way you'd expect an innocent person to when asked a question like that.

"Yeah. Since I did see you here on a weekend, and since that one break-in we know of happened over the weekend, I really want to tie off that potential thread."

"Of course," he said with a nod. "I usually don't come to the office on weekends. I have a lot of other things going on." His eyes sparkled a little bit, and I got the feeling I knew what else he had going on. "But that weekend, I'd written the phone number of the girl I was going out with that night on something that I left at the office, and I didn't realize that until I needed to call her to finalize plans, so I had to come to the office to get it."

It was an entirely plausible excuse, given what I knew of Rod's social life. I wasn't sure I could write him off entirely as a suspect, but he certainly wasn't acting suspicious. "Okay, thanks," I said, surprised at the surge of jealousy that hit me when I thought about him going on a date. "So, on the weekend of the break-in, you weren't here?"

"No, I have an iron-clad alibi for that weekend. I was babysitting Owen."

"Babysitting?"

"He was supposed to be resting, and you know him when he has a puzzle he wants to solve. I picked that weekend to have my cable go out, which meant I spent the weekend watching football at his place so he had no choice but to be a couch potato, too."

That was a huge relief. I didn't want Rod to be the bad guy. He had issues, but he was still my friend. Or could he be more? I wondered how much longer Isabel might be. Even if I knew it was an illusion and an attraction spell at work, Rod was awfully tempting, and he was looking at me with definite appreciation. I licked my lips—because they were dry, of course. Not for any other reason. He took a step toward me, his eyes darkening.

But before either of us could make more of a move than that, Isabel came back, booming, "Now I'm ready to hit the town!" She was dressed neck-to-knee in sequins, which made her look like a walking Times Square billboard.

With a great sense of relief, I got out of my chair and moved from Rod's office into Isabel's outer office. "You look really, um, striking," I said.

She did a pirouette that was surprisingly graceful for someone twice my size and nearly a foot taller. "Fun, isn't it? I've been looking for an occasion to wear this." She then saw my shoes and gasped. "Oh my! Those are amazing!"

Ari and Trix joined us, dressed in outfits so skimpy it would have taken all the material in both their dresses to make my skirt. I suddenly felt frumpy in comparison and wished I'd done more to dress up than put on a silk blouse with my black work skirt and red shoes. Their reactions, though, made me feel better. "Fab shoes, Katie," Ari said.

Trix fluttered over to me. "Yeah, look at you! I bet you'll find someone to replace Ethan by the end of the night."

"You can count on that," Ari added with a firm nod.

Isabel picked up some papers from her desk. "I've done a little online research, so I think I have a plan for the evening. Happy hour at one of those beautiful-people bars in SoHo—since we are definitely beautiful people tonight. Then dinner in the Village."

"And then there's this club I heard about," Ari said. "Very hot, very now. I'm sure we can find a way to get in."

Trix posed saucily. "We'll have to cast a spell on them—whatever kind of spell it might take."

I felt almost like a character on *Sex and the City* as we left the office building, going out for a glamorous night in New York with a group of girlfriends. Then I got a good look at Ari and Trix and nearly tripped over my own red shoes. They must have turned on their magical veiling spells when they left the building. I'd never seen them away from work without my magical immunity, so I'd never seen the illusions they wore to hide their status as fairies from the rest of the world. I still recognized them, but it was disconcerting to see them as wholly human. Without her slightly pointed ears and her gauzy wings, Ari's halo of short blond curls made an even more striking contrast with her goth girl makeup and her edgy clothes. Trix, with her straight strawberry-blond pixie cut, looked like an incredibly cute, pert young woman. Isabel's appearance hadn't changed at all, so I presumed that meant she didn't bother magically hiding her giant size in public.

Isabel put that size to good use and hailed a cab for us by blocking the street with her body. "We can't be expected to deal with public transportation when we look this fabulous," she explained.

The cab dropped us at a neon-trimmed bar in SoHo. Half the people in the place looked like models. Some of them were almost as tall as Isabel, but they nearly disappeared when they turned sideways. Isabel had no trouble shoving her way through the crowd and securing a table for us. All the other patrons were too frail to stand up to her.

We ordered drinks—tiny bottles of champagne with straws in them, like all the models were drinking—and watched the crowd. "We don't stand a chance of getting anyone's attention with all these models here," I muttered dejectedly.

"You'd be surprised," Ari said, a wicked gleam in her eyes. "We have our own ways."

"Yeah, but where does that leave me?"

Trix patted me on the arm. "Don't worry. Leave it to us."

They must have worked quickly, for moments later, there was a rather attractive man at my side. "Hi there," he said. "I haven't seen you here before." I glanced around me to make sure he wasn't talking to someone else. "Yes, you," he said with a grin. "You're the cutest thing I've seen in a long time."

I almost fell off my bar stool. "Me?"

"See? You're so cute! Most of these models know they're gorgeous and expect you to worship them. But you're utterly irresistible."

I looked over to Ari, sure she was putting the mojo on this poor guy, but she gave me an innocent shrug. "That's really sweet of you to say so," I replied, not sure he was entirely sane.

"I love your accent. Where are you from?"

"Texas."

"Of course. That would explain why you're so charming and genuine." He held his hand out to me. "I'm Matt."

Feeling bolder from his attention, I shook his hand. "Hi, Matt. I'm Katie."

He leaned one elbow on the table in front of me, then placed his other hand on my knee. "Tell me, Katie, how long have you lived in New York?"

"A little more than a year." I looked over to my friends, who were all watching me. None of them had men around, so I felt bad for abandoning them. "It's very nice to meet you, Matt, but I'm here with my friends, and I don't want to be rude to them."

He grinned. "See, that's what I like about you. You're a good person." He pulled a card out of his back pocket. "You can give me a call and we can get together sometime when you don't have your friends with you."

"I'll have to do that," I said, taking the card from him and tucking it into my purse.

He gave my knee a squeeze and said, "Don't ever change," before disappearing into the crowd.

I turned back to my friends. "What did you do that for?" Ari asked.

"Do what?"

"Ditch the cute guy. You had him right where you wanted him. You might have even had a little fun tonight."

"But I was with y'all. I didn't want to ignore you because some guy was talking to me. I did get his phone number, though."

"You have to promise to call it," Trix said.

Isabel draped an arm around my shoulders. "I think it's great that she didn't ditch her friends. This is a girls' night out, after all."

Ari snorted. "Yeah, well, if someone who looks like that is all over me, don't count on me joining you for dinner."

A waitress came to our table and handed out another round of drinks. "These are from Matt," she said. I looked up to see him raise a glass to me from across the room. The only other times a near stranger had bought me drinks, magic had been involved. As far as I could tell, this was the one time in my life when a man had bought my friends and me a drink just because he really liked me. I could get used to that, I thought.

The first little bottle of champagne went straight to my head. The second, along with the giddy feeling of having enticed an attractive man, made me unsteady. I didn't see how I'd make it through the rest of the night, when Ari declared, "How about dinner now? This place is dead, except for Katie's admirer, and I'm starved."

I was proud that I only staggered a little bit when I slid off my stool. I caught Matt's eye as I made my way out of the bar and gave him a wink and a smile. *Take that, Ethan,* I thought.

The cold air outside was almost refreshing after all the body heat in the bar, though I knew it wouldn't be long before I was freezing. Isabel set out to find us a cab while Ari, Trix, and I stayed close to the building. Ari whipped out a cell phone and began chatting with someone about our evening's activities so far. I'd just started shivering when Isabel called out, "Hey, I think I've got one!"

We all dashed over to her. I suspected Trix and Ari were using their wings, even though I couldn't see them, because they easily outran me. Or maybe I wasn't used to wearing such high, pointy heels. Before they got to Isabel, though, they came to a sudden stop. I picked up my pace, taking advantage of the opportunity to catch up with them. But then something hit me in the middle of my back, and quite suddenly I wasn't cold anymore.

fifteen

I fell forward, but Trix got to me in time to catch me before I hit the ground. She held tightly to me as Isabel joined us, looking like a sequined vengeful Valkyrie. I could feel the charge in the air from the magic that must have been flying fast and furious around us, but I couldn't see a thing. Normally in a fight like this, I was the one who could tell what was going on, and I was usually able to pitch in by at least throwing a rock at something nobody else could see, but this time I was utterly helpless. At one point, Trix grabbed me tighter, like she was afraid of something. I kicked out blindly, hoping I hit someone where it would really hurt with my pointy heel.

Then the fight must have ended, for Trix, Ari, and Isabel were wiping sweat from their brows and heaving huge sighs. Isabel paused and looked like she was talking to someone I couldn't see. "You okay?" Trix asked me, releasing her hold.

I checked my body as best I could for signs of damage. My back was sore from whatever had hit me, but otherwise I seemed to be un-scathed. My shoes weren't even scuffed. Trix must have shielded me before any real damage was done. "Yeah, I think I'm fine. Just a little shaky."

"We'd better get a cab while Sam and his people wrap things up," Isabel said, returning to the curb to flag one down. She must have let the last one go when she came to my rescue.

"What did you see? Were those the same people who ambushed you at the party?" Trix asked me.

I had no idea, given that I hadn't seen anything at all, but it was a good bet. The burst of heat I'd felt on my back could have been from one of those fireball things that skeleton guy had tried to hurl at me. "Yeah, I think it's the same guys, but I didn't get a good look." That was putting it mildly. I wondered if the fight was still going on right in front of me.

"Are you sure?" Ari asked.

"Not a hundred percent, obviously. I mean, most skeleton crea-tures look alike to me," I said, trying to turn it into a joke. It was going to be more and more difficult to bluff this out, especially if I was going to be in physical danger.

Isabel got a cab, and Trix hustled me over to it, then helped me into the backseat. "Do you want to go home?" Isabel asked me.

I shook my head. "No, not really. It would probably be better if I got a chance to wind down after that."

"You need a drink or three," Ari declared, her jaw set and stub-born. "And then maybe a really hot guy to make it all better."

"Dinner it is," Isabel said, then turned to the driver and gave him an address.

"You must really be closing in on that spy if they're attacking you like that," Trix said, patting my shoulder maternally.

I gave a shaky laugh. "How little they know. I have no clue what-soever."

"Really?" Ari asked. "I thought you'd be closer than that."

"Nope. I have some ideas, but that's it."

"And you've come up with some pretty good countermeasures," Ari added reassuringly. "Or maybe whether you realize it or not, you've gotten too close for comfort."

We stopped on a narrow street somewhere in Greenwich Village and went into a nearby restaurant. As soon as we were seated, Isabel ordered a cup of tea for me. "We'll get you a drink later, but you need strong, sweet tea after a shock like that," she said.

I didn't like feeling so helpless, as though everyone else had to look out for me, but I knew I pretty much *was* helpless, so I gave in and let them look after me.

Once they had drinks and Isabel had made me drink tea sweet enough even to please my sweet-toothed Southern grandmother, Ari made an obvious effort to change the subject to lighter things. "So now that Katie and Trix are both single once more, it's time to come up with a strategy," she said.

"Leave me out of it," Trix muttered. "I'm not ready to give up yet."

"And I don't think I'm ready to bounce into another relationship," I added. Especially not while I was still so disconcerted from having lost my magical immunity. What if the guy I hooked up with turned out to be like Rod, hiding behind spells?

"What are you talking about?" Ari teased. "You've already got one phone number, and it's not like you two were together long enough for it to count as a real breakup. You need to show him by getting out there again and snagging a man right away. Make him know what he's missing."

"It took me a year in New York to find him. I doubt I'll have anyone else within the next couple of weeks," I said with a sigh. I had to blink back tears at the thought. The champagne earlier, then the shock of that attack, and now all the sympathy were combining to make me especially emotional.

"What about Owen?" Isabel asked. "He seems to really like you."

"Yeah, you do spend a lot of time together," Ari said. "What's the deal with you two?"

"We're just friends."

"But he talks to you," Ari said. "I've been trying for years, and I haven't managed to get him to say two words to me that weren't about work."

"Most of what we talk about is work," I insisted. "We only commute together because he has bodyguard duty. We've had maybe a couple of conversations that were even remotely personal."

"That's two more than anyone else in the company has had," Ari muttered, rolling her eyes. "I swear, that boy's hopeless. Cute, rich, and powerful, but utterly hopeless."

"I don't think it's that big a deal," I said with a shrug. "I've been told I'm easy to talk to, so I probably make him comfortable. Trust me, that's not generally a good thing with a guy. It usually leads to the 'you're such a good friend, like a sister' speech."

Isabel took the garnish off the rim of her glass and chewed on it, then said, "Well, if you don't think Owen's interested, I know someone else who might very well be."

The others giggled, and I felt like they could use my face to direct ships in the harbor. We needed to move the topic of conversation over to someone else's love life, pronto.

"Who might that be?" Ari mused.

"I think Rod has a teeny little crush on you himself," Isabel told me.

"You have got to be kidding." I wasn't the sort of woman men had crushes on. The only way I ever met guys was by being set up on blind dates. It was inconceivable that I would have two men showing enough interest in me to stir up office gossip. Though, come to think of it, Rod had been eyeing me in his office earlier, and he had warned me off Owen, which was a possible sign of jealousy.

"He wears an illusion, doesn't he?" Ari asked. "You see something totally different than we do when you look at him."

"Ooh, what does he really look like?" Isabel asked, leaning forward across the table. Trix leaned closer, too.

Now that I knew the full impact of the difference between Rod's reality and his illusion, I better understood their curiosity. Even though the illusion was undeniably attractive, I preferred the reality, simply because it was real. He didn't look like Rod to me when I could see the illusion. "He's not that bad, really," I said, feeling mean for talking about him behind his back. "He's not particularly handsome, but he has the kind of face that's really affected by his personality, so he can be pretty cute when he smiles. He'd be better off if he quit hiding behind that illusion and made some effort to work with what he's got." I shrugged. "I don't like artifice that much." Alarmed at the looks on their faces, I hurried to add, "And don't you dare tell him I said so."

"But maybe you should tell him," Trix said. "For his own good."

"Maybe when I get to know him better."

Isabel shook her head. "He'll never drop that illusion. From what I hear, he's been doing that ever since his teens. I guess he was competing with Owen, but it's not as though Owen was any competition. Rod always gets the girls."

"That's because you have to ask them in the first place to get them," Ari said. "Owen doesn't even manage to catch the ones that throw themselves at him."

"Someone sounds bitter," Isabel said, raising an eyebrow.

Ari appeared flustered, for perhaps the first time since I'd met her. She recovered quickly. "Hey, can you blame me for trying? I mean, look at him. At least I can say I tried, unlike everyone else in the company." She cast a sly, sidelong glance at me. "Well, except maybe for Katie. We'll have to see how that sweet, innocent, 'let's-just-be-friends' strategy works."

"It's not a strategy," I insisted. To change the subject, I grabbed the dessert menu from the middle of the table. "So does anyone else need chocolate?"

I was ready to go home after dessert, but Ari insisted we had to go to this new club. She led us to what looked to me like a warehouse in the middle of nowhere. There wasn't even a sign, which she said meant it was truly hot. You had to be in the know to even be aware that it was a club. It looked like a lot of people were in the know, for a line snaked around the building. As we passed the head of the line, I noticed that for every person the imposing man at the door let in, he turned at least three away. Ari and Trix might get in on the force of cuteness. Isabel could work some mojo on him. I, however, didn't stand a chance. I didn't look forward to waiting in line, only to be humiliated.

The line moved quickly—probably because the doorman was able to dismiss most of them with a glance—so we didn't have to wait long in the cold before it was our turn. I hid in the back of the group, behind Isabel, hoping I wouldn't hurt my friends' chances of getting in. Hip New York nightclubs weren't known for their fondness for the ordinary.

I was almost relieved when the doorman shook his head at Trix and Ari. That meant I hadn't been singled out for my lack of cool, and maybe we could find somewhere else to go. I stepped out from behind Isabel to join the others. The doorman looked at me, did a double take, and then offered me what might pass for a warm smile in big, burly bouncer world. He asked, "Are these people with you?"

I looked behind me to make sure he wasn't talking to somebody else, then turned back to him and said, "We're all together. Why?"

With a gallant flourish he unclipped the velvet rope and waved us forward, giving me a wink as I passed by. Once we were safely inside the club, Trix whooped and clapped me on the back. "Way to go, Katie!"

"What did I do?"

"I don't know how you did it, honey," Isabel said, "but he let us in because we were with you."

"Maybe having a plain Jane in here will make everyone else look cooler by comparison," I mused as we found seats on a big sofa overlooking the dance floor. It was still pretty early in the evening for New York club life, but the place was already packed with people who looked a lot like those who'd been in the bar in SoHo.

I'd barely seated myself and carefully crossed my legs—the sofa was low enough to make sitting in a short skirt a dangerous prospect—when a good-looking guy dressed in black slacks and a white shirt perched on the arm of the sofa near my left elbow. "Hi there," he said.

Again I looked around to make sure he was talking to me, then I gave him a cautious smile. "Hi," I said, in what I was sure would go down in history as a brilliant conversational opener. The guy reminded me of Rod's illusion, except Rod would have had better taste than to unbutton his shirt that far down. Even in the crowded club, I could smell his cologne from where I sat.

"Come here often?" he asked, going for his own gold medal in competitive conversation.

"It's my first time," I said.

He nodded. "Can I buy you a drink?"

"No thanks. I'm not that thirsty."

He nodded again, got up, and moved on to presumably greener pastures. Ari elbowed me in the ribs. "What was that about?"

"What?"

" 'I'm not thirsty'? Please! A guy offers to buy you a drink a minute after you walk in the door, and you turn him away?"

"I was choking on his cologne."

Trix leaned forward to talk to me around Ari. "Don't listen to her, Katie. If you had one within minutes, someone better is likely to come along."

And, oddly enough, she was right. An even more gorgeous man who looked like he'd stepped out of a Gap ad—the edgy side of the boy next door—soon took the perch on the sofa arm. "I know I haven't seen you here before, or I'd already be married," he said.

I glanced over at my friends. "Okay, be honest," I said. "You set this up, didn't you? I appreciate it, but my ego doesn't need this kind of help." They all looked blank, so I turned back to Mr. Gap Ad and smiled. "It's my first time here." I had a burst of boldness and added, "You wouldn't happen to know what the best drink in the house is, would you?"

You'd have thought I'd tied my scarf around his lance so he could go into combat in my honor. "I'll bring you one, right away."

When he'd gone, I turned back to my friends. "Really, you can tell me if this is a joke. I'll laugh."

"Don't sell yourself short," Trix said. "Have you ever considered that they might actually find you irresistible?"

I snorted. "Yeah, right. Seemingly overnight, I've gone from invisible to hottest thing in town. Maybe it's one of those contests to see who can snag the most boring or ordinary girl."

"Or maybe he has an unhealthy girl-next-door fetish and is already dreaming about defiling you," Ari suggested.

Instead of taking her bait, I smiled and said, "That could be a lot of fun."

My suitor then returned with a bright pink drink in an unusually shaped glass that made me dizzy if I looked at it too long. "Oh, thank you," I said with my sweetest smile. I couldn't help but enjoy the expression of delight that spread over his face at my approval.

He seated himself once more on the arm of the sofa. "By the way, I'm Rick."

"And I'm Katie. Nice to meet you, Rick."

"Has anyone ever told you that you make him want to settle down and have babies?"

"Um, no, not that I can think of." I couldn't decide if he was being nice or creepy. While normally I'd like the idea of a guy thinking of me as someone to settle down with, it was more than a little weird for him to use that as an opening line. "Actually, I'd rather wait a few years to have children," I added, just in case.

"You look like you belong behind a picket fence."

And you sound like you belong in a padded cell, I thought, but I merely smiled at him before casting a *Help!* look at my friends.

Help arrived, but from an unexpected quarter. Another guy appeared in front of me. This one looked more like a guy in a cologne ad, with perfect bone structure and mysterious eyes. "Is he bothering you?" he asked, indicating Rick.

"We were just discussing family planning," I said, not sure whether to be worried or relieved. I wasn't yet sure if Mr. Cologne was going to be an improvement. The bar wasn't set all that high. As long as he didn't immediately get into how he wanted to see me barefoot and pregnant, he'd be a better conversational partner.

Rick slunk off, and Mr. Cologne extended a hand to me. "Dance," was all he said.

Normally I wasn't big on dancing, but if I was on the dance floor with a man it would be hard for anyone else to hit on me. Besides, it looked like it could be fun. I wordlessly handed my pink drink to Ari and took Mr. Cologne's hand.

He didn't speak as he led me to the floor, then folded me into his arms. I decided that was definitely an improvement as we swayed together to the trance-like music. It felt good to be held like that, to be wanted. That feeling almost made the last of my worry about the attack earlier in the evening go away.

As that song faded into another song, another man came up, tapped Mr. Cologne on the shoulder, and held a hand to me. I took it. This was already the most dancing I'd done in one night in as long as I could remember, and definitely the most men I'd danced with in one night.

It went on like that for what felt like hours, with man after man asking me to dance. I was the belle of the ball, and with each new dance partner I felt a surge of power and confidence. That confidence only appeared to increase my appeal, so it was the best-looking men in the place who were waiting in line to dance with me, while a row of miffed blond beauties stood at the edge of the dance floor, glaring at me.

The latest suitor was possibly the most handsome of the evening. He looked like a taller, older version of Owen, with dark hair, blue eyes, and an amazing body. I could tell from the way he held me so tightly against him that he found me rather attractive, too. Normally, I'd have been a little freaked out by learning that kind of intimate detail about a total stranger, but I found it pleasantly arousing. I wasn't a one-night-stand kind of girl, but maybe just this once . . .

I let myself melt against him. He tightened his hold on me, then leaned down to whisper in my ear, "My, my, does your boyfriend know what you're up to tonight, Katie?"

I tried to pull away from him, but he tightened his hold on me. I looked up to see an all-too-familiar smile on the otherwise unfamiliar face, and once I knew it had to be there, I felt magic in use. The throbbing music and my alcohol consumption must have kept me from noticing that telltale tingle sooner. Not that I would have expected Phelan Idris to be disguising himself on the dance floor to attempt to seduce me.

"This is getting old," I said, trying to sound totally cool even as fear chilled my guts. Where were my magical friends who could help protect me from him? "What do you want from me, anyway?"

He pulled me even closer against him. "I think that should be pretty obvious," he said.

Ewwww. "Fat chance," I replied. "And if that's what you really want, you're going about it the wrong way. Try reading a romance novel. They're full of seduction techniques that are a lot more effective than this. So, come on, what are you trying to accomplish other than annoying me to death?"

"There's a quick and easy way to get me totally out of your life."

"Please, tell me more."

"Quit your job. You'll never see me again."

Although I was still scared because a powerful wizard had me in his grasp and I was susceptible to his power—and he obviously knew that—I couldn't help but laugh. "You've got to be kidding. You're worried about a secretary? Get rid of me, and there are a number of other immunes who'd fight each other over the job."

It was his turn to laugh. "And you're supposed to be so smart. Maybe it's not about you."

Now I was nervous. There was something in his tone that went beyond his usual teasing banter. I'd never taken him all too seriously as a threat because he was so very ridiculous, but I sensed real menace. Whatever it was he was up to, me being at MSI was getting in his way. Or maybe me being away from MSI would make it easier. Either way, this went beyond taunting me or just stirring up trouble.

As if I were dealing with an angry dog, I tried to stifle my fear. If he sensed it, he'd jump at the weakness. "I can't afford to quit my job without having something else lined up," I said. "Do you have any leads?"

That took him aback. He clearly hadn't thought this through.

Come on, this was Manhattan, home of some of the highest rents in the nation. How could he expect me to just up and quit my job?

"Maybe you won't have to quit," he said when he'd recovered. "Maybe you'll get fired when they find out about you."

"Find out what?" I asked, projecting all the innocence I could muster. His mouth hung open. I had him, and he knew it. Anyone who reported my lack of immunity would be revealing that they knew about it, and at this point anyone who knew about it was probably responsible.

While he processed that, I took advantage of his distraction to slip out of his arms. He grabbed my arm before I could get away, and I stepped back toward him, letting my stiletto heel sink into his foot, right above his toes—and Mom said those shoes weren't practical. As he hopped up and down on one foot, I broke away and ran for my friends.

Isabel was sitting alone on the sofa. "I guess Ari and Trix are dancing," I said. I couldn't spot them on the dance floor, then I remembered that I wouldn't see their wings, which was how I usually found them in a crowd.

"I'm not sure Ari's dancing, if you know what I mean. Trix went to get another drink."

"If you're ready to head out, I'd go with you," I said. "I don't think I can take much more of this." The truth was, I was totally wigged out and felt like I needed a shower to wash Idris's touch off me. I supposed I was lucky that he'd been too arrogant not to make sure I knew what he was doing. The thought of what might have happened if he hadn't said anything was too horrific to even consider. I fought off a shudder. I started to tell Isabel what happened, then realized I'd have to admit that I'd fallen for Idris's scheme. In my normal state, I wouldn't have let him get within ten feet of me on the dance floor, let alone get close enough to me to freak me out that much.

I must have looked bad enough not to have to explain, for Isabel said, "When Trix comes back we can tell her, and she can tell Ari. I don't have the stamina to keep up with this pace."

"Neither do I."

"But you were very popular tonight. You must have been having a good time."

Since the other two were gone, I felt like I could get a more honest answer, so I asked once more, "You really didn't set this up? I'm not going to see a bunch of men pocketing five-dollar bills as I leave, am I?"

She shook her head. "As far as I can tell, you're doing it honestly. You're a lot cuter than you give yourself credit for."

I looked around the room at all the glamorous model types and exotic-looking girls showing great expanses of skin, then considered myself. There was no comparison. "Okay, I may be cute, but cute doesn't seem to be what cuts it in a place like this."

"Or maybe it does. You were cutting it very well. You're different, and they might find that refreshing."

I was still pondering that possibility when Trix returned with a pink drink like the one Rick had bought me. "I think I'm going to head out now and make sure Katie gets home okay," Isabel told her.

"You're leaving already? But Katie, I thought you were having a good time. You had all those men after you."

"I was having a good time," I said, "but my feet are killing me, and I think the whole evening has suddenly caught up with me." Not to mention my enemy—who had apparently tampered with my magical immunity and who thought I somehow figured into whatever his grand scheme was.

I kept my adventures to myself all weekend, spending more time pondering my unlikely appeal and Idris's behavior than I did the possible reasons behind that strange attack earlier Friday evening. As a result, it took me a second or two to respond when Owen greeted me Monday morning with a worried, "Are you okay?"

"Huh? Oh yeah, yeah, I'm fine. I guess Sam must have told you. I'm not sure it was anything serious. They gave up pretty quickly."

"You must be close to something to get them to respond like that."

I thought about telling him about my immunity being gone. If I was going to be attacked on the streets by people I couldn't see, that was probably something the people watching me needed to know. Come to think of it, it was strange that nobody had figured it out yet. Magical people often talked about how ordinary people missed so much of what was going on all around them because they saw what they expected to see, but this experience proved that magical people were just as bad. I hadn't even had to lie all that much, and they still assumed I was seeing through illusions because that was what they expected of me.

I needed to tell somebody before I got hit by another attack like that. But not yet. I needed to think about it. I wanted to be able to offer a compromise or solution before I dropped that news. I needed to have some sense of what I'd do next, and right now I had no idea.

Owen interrupted my frightened musings, asking, "You know how I asked you to help me shop for my foster parents?"

"Yes, of course." I was relieved to have something else to think about.

"Well, I was wondering if you had time this evening. Nothing major—maybe hit a few stores in our neighborhood. We could also grab dinner."

"Sure. That sounds great," I said. It would even give me a good nonthreatening environment for me to talk to him about my little problem.

"Shall we meet in the lobby after work? I'll give you a call if I'm going to be late."

"That'll be fine."

He gave me a businesslike nod. "Okay then. I'll see you after work."

I'd only been waiting a few minutes that evening when he came barreling down the main stairs, out of breath, his necktie askew and his overcoat still over his arm. "Sorry I'm late," he said when he came to a stop next to me and struggled into his coat.

"I haven't been here that long," I told him, as I helped him untangle a sleeve. "Relax. So, any particular destination in mind?"

"That's what I hoped you could help me with," he said as we headed out of the building together. "I don't shop all that much, so I wouldn't begin to know where to look."

"Well, maybe we should start with what you have in mind to buy for them."

He looked utterly terrified. "I don't have anything in mind."

"What have you bought them in the past?"

"For a while, I ordered gift baskets from a catalog, and then when they told me I didn't have to get them anything, I started making contributions to their favorite charities in their honor. I thought I'd go with something a little more personal this year."

"You do realize that being a girl doesn't make me an expert shopper, don't you? Maybe I should have made an appointment for you with my roommate, Gemma."

"Sorry. I guess this was a bad idea."

"No, I'm glad to help. But don't expect miracles. Why don't you tell me a little about them, and that might help me decide?"

We entered the subway station, where we were blessedly out of the cold wind. "Well, let's see, they're both fairly old, in their eighties, at least. Very traditional, highly educated, quite independent. Gloria is elegant—I've never seen her when she wasn't fully dressed and put together, even first thing in the morning. James is like a lifelong student. Even now, he's constantly reading. Does that give you enough to go on?"

"I have some ideas." A train approached, and as we boarded I said, "We should get off in SoHo. I'm thinking some nice jewelry for Gloria, then a book on a fascinating subject for James."

"You are good," he said, with a smile that did funny things to my insides.

"And you really must be a lousy shopper if you couldn't come up with that on your own." That surprised me, given that he always wore perfectly tailored suits. Either he conjured them up or he had a personal tailor, more for convenience than fashion.

We left the train at Prince Street. "I seem to recall that there's an interesting little store a couple of blocks over in Nolita—not that I've actually ever bought any jewelry, mind you," I said.

"Lead the way. And how do you know all this?"

"I have a roommate who works in fashion. She sometimes makes me come with her on her research expeditions."

"See, I came to the right person."

The jewelry store was where I'd remembered it, and it was still open. The saleslady greeted us with a friendly smile. "Hi! Can I help you find something?" she asked. "Let me guess, you'd like to see our selection of engagement rings."

Owen clammed up, looked at the floor, and left everything to me. I decided where he really needed my help was in communicating with the salespeople, not in deciding what to buy. In this case, though, even I was embarrassed. I tried to pin the saleslady with a steely glare as I said, "Actually, we're here to look for a gift for his mother. Maybe a brooch?"

It was her turn to blush. "Oops, sorry about that. Didn't mean to embarrass you. Right over here we have a nice selection of brooches. We carry the works of some of the freshest designers around." She led us over to a display case. "Let me know if you want to get a closer look at something."

Only after she'd gone to greet some other new customers did I dare glance over at Owen. His eyes were firmly locked on the display case, but his cheeks were still a bright red that had nothing to do with the cold wind outside. My own face felt a little too warm for comfort. There weren't too many situations more awkward than being mistaken for an engaged couple when you were just friends, especially if there was even the slightest undercurrent of more than just friends from either side. I felt like she'd pulled my deepest, most hidden feelings out for public display.

"See anything you like?" I asked.

He pointed toward a delicate brooch that looked almost like someone had taken a feather and dipped it in gold. "That's it. It's her."

"Wow, that was easy," I said, turning to get the saleslady's attention. She was with another customer, and the moment I saw who that customer was, I ducked behind Owen.

"What is it?" he asked.

"That other customer—no, don't look!—is my former boss. She's evil. She's worse than Gregor in ogre mode, except she doesn't actually turn green and grow horns."

In spite of my warning, he turned to look. "She doesn't seem so bad."

"That's what's so evil about her. She seems perfectly nice, totally rational. And then in the blink of an eye she turns into this monster. You never know what might set her off. With any luck, she'll get out of here before she recognizes me."

Of course, that pretty much jinxed me right away. It was as good as saying a magic spell to make her notice me. "Katie, is that you?" Mimi said, crossing the store to give me an insincere air kiss.

"Yeah, it's me," I said.

"And how are you doing in your new job?"

"Great."

She raised a thin, overplucked eyebrow. "Really? I find that surprising, given your skill level. I would have thought you'd find it a real challenge to take on a new job." Even though the words were venomous, she maintained a pleasant tone and expression.

I felt like I was right back in my old position, when she could make me feel so helpless I wanted to burst into tears. I'd only managed to stand up to her when I already had the new job lined up. Otherwise, I'd spent my time trying not to set her off.

"It must have something to do with the quality of the management, then, because Katie's already been given a big promotion," Owen said in the kind of smooth, calm tone he tended to use in business meetings when he was intimidating people. It was as good as a knight in shining armor coming to my rescue.

Mimi glanced at him, got the appreciative look in her eye that women tended to get when they saw him, then turned to me and sniffed disdainfully. "You would have needed a lot more training and experience before you were ready to move ahead in our organization."

Bolstered by having Owen staunchly at my side, I tried to match her saccharine smile and tone. "And that's why I looked for opportunities elsewhere."

She pulled the tall, silver-haired gentleman she was with closer to her. "You've met Werner, haven't you? We're here looking at engagement rings."

"It's good to see you again, Werner. Congratulations. And this is Owen Palmer. We work together. Owen, Mimi used to be my boss."

With the kind of almost evil smile I wouldn't have thought him capable of, Owen said smoothly, "I must thank you for making it so easy for us to recruit Katie. She's been invaluable to us."

Mimi blinked like she had to mentally diagram the sentence in order to figure out what he'd said and how she should react to it. The moment her nostrils began to flare, Werner took her arm and said, "It was nice seeing you again, Katie. A pleasure to meet you, Owen." Then he dragged her back to the engagement ring display.

"I see what you mean," Owen said softly, raising one eyebrow. "Rod could have probably come in lower on the salary offer and still lured you away from that."

The saleslady returned to us. "Is there a piece you'd like to see?"

Owen maintained his business cool long enough to point to the feather brooch and say, "That one, please."

"Excellent choice, sir. I love that one." She slipped the key chain from around her wrist and unlocked the case, then took out the feather brooch and laid it on a black velvet cloth for inspection.

"I'll take it. And can you gift-wrap it?"

"Of course, sir."

He handed over a credit card without even looking at or asking the price. I caught a glimpse of the price tag and almost choked. I'd driven cars that didn't cost that much. I knew he had to be pretty well off, given that he lived in a neighborhood where a million might buy a modest place, but I hadn't actually given much thought to how rich he might be. I guessed he was making up for years of gift baskets.

While he finalized the transaction, I spied on Mimi and Werner, who were studying rings. Getting away from her had been the best part of being offered the job at MSI. Seeing her again reminded me why I was keeping quiet about my loss of immunity until I had a better sense of what to do. I couldn't face going back to that life. While I knew that most bosses weren't like her, I also knew that without having any particular qualifications that I didn't already share with half the young career women in Manhattan, I wasn't likely to be treated like anything other than a disposable commodity. At MSI, I at least had one quality they desperately needed. Or I'd had it once. I didn't know what I'd do if it didn't come back.

Owen tucked the small, gift-wrapped box in the breast pocket of his suit coat and said, "What next?"

"For books, I'm thinking the Strand. Maybe something rare and interesting like a first edition?"

"Good idea. Think you can walk from here?"

"Of course." I figured we'd already wrapped up our encounter with Mimi, so I didn't feel the need to say anything as we left. We headed back over to Broadway, then uptown. "Do you have any ideas for books that would be good?" I asked.

"I'll have to see what they have, but I got a look in his library at Thanksgiving, so I know what he already has."

"I wish it were that easy to shop for my dad. I can't keep up with what he has in things like books from this far away, and he never seems to ask for anything other than socks and gloves."

"Socks and gloves? Really?"

"You'd have to know my dad. For him, that's extravagant. What do you usually ask for?"

"I don't. There's not much of anyone for me to ask." I mentally kicked myself for asking without thinking. Given what he'd told me about his home life, I should have known better.

We reached Grace Church, where Sam's occasional appearances used to make me uneasy before I learned about magic. I tried to keep from looking at the church as we passed, instead keeping my pace brisk. I didn't like the reminder of what I'd lost. Owen slowed down, though. He paused, and then he seemed frozen in time. If I hadn't known that something was likely going on, I wouldn't have noticed it at all. So that was what the rest of the world saw when one of us paused to chat with a gargoyle. The frozen image must have masked the conversation. Losing my immunity might have been a pain at times, but it was certainly educational. I was more than eager, however, to end the lessons and get back to what passed for normal in my life.

Owen unfroze and resumed walking with me. "Odd," he mused out loud. "Sam usually takes that shift."

I tried to pretend I had the slightest clue what he was talking about. "He did say he'd worked a lot over the holiday. Maybe he traded off with somebody else."

"That's probably it." I was surprised that he didn't even question me about not participating in the conversation.

We reached the bookstore, and he headed straight for the rare-book collection in the adjacent building. Apparently, he'd done this sort of thing before, which shouldn't have surprised me, considering the stacks of old books in his office. He probably knew every rare-book dealer in town. We went up in the elevator, then entered the rare-book room. The bookseller on duty there recognized Owen, and Owen seemed to know him, which was good because I doubted I could have handled this transaction if Owen had gone mute on me again.

Owen walked past shelves and tables full of books. He stopped in front of one bookcase, frowned, then ran his hand about an inch behind the spines. At one book halfway down the shelf he grinned and pulled the book out. "Look at this," he whispered. "It looks like a fairly early printing of a Dickens, which would be valuable enough, but what do you see?"

He was asking me for my opinion as a magically immune verifier, and I couldn't see anything.

sixteen

"I don't know anything about rare books," I managed to stammer even as I fought back a flood of panic. *I should tell him now,* I thought, but the encounter with Mimi was still too fresh in my mind. I couldn't risk losing my job because I'd lost the ability that made them want me.

"I do know you were once able to tell the difference between a Tom Clancy and a rare codex."

"Yeah, but that difference was obvious—new book as opposed to really old book. All old books pretty much look alike to me."

He glanced over his shoulder to make sure the bookseller wasn't watching too carefully, then held his hand over the book. It shimmered, then an even older, more ornate book appeared. "Ah, just what I thought," he said. "This is very rare. James will love it." He took the book over to the bookseller and asked, "How much do you want for this one?"

The bookseller's eyes grew huge. "I didn't realize we had that. Let me check for you."

"If you want to have it appraised, I can come back and pick it up later," Owen offered. The bookseller took his contact info and promised to call when he had an answer.

As we left the store I asked, "How did you know that was there?"

He shrugged. "I felt the magic. You sometimes find things like that, truly rare items veiled as moderately rare things. It's a way of hiding valuables in plain sight. And then when an estate has to be sold off, the heirs may not even know what they have. Sometimes books can go for generations hidden like that."

"You could have reveiled it and paid only for the Dickens, you know."

"But that would have been cheating."

"I think I've finally found someone who's more of a goody-goody than I am," I said with a laugh. Not that I was too much of a goody-goody, considering how much I seemed to be lying lately. "And I don't think you needed me all that much, after all."

"I wouldn't have found the brooch without you, and a book was your idea. Now, dinner? There's a restaurant I know a couple of blocks from here. It's run by magical people, although I doubt most of their customers have figured that out. We won't have to be so careful about our conversation there."

That left me with quite the dilemma—I wanted to spend more time with him, but there was no way I could keep my secret at a magical restaurant. In fact, the more time I spent around him, the harder it was to keep my secret.

I must have hesitated longer than I realized, for he frowned at me and asked, "Katie? Is something wrong?"

"To be honest, I'm not sure I'm up for dinner right now," I said, and it wasn't a lie at all. My stomach had tied itself in knots and I felt queasy. "Do you mind if I call it a night?"

If he was disappointed, he hid it well. "Not at all. I'll make it up to you some other time."

"I think I'm the one who would have to make it up to you," I said as we resumed walking up Broadway.

"You were the one doing me a favor," he argued.

"I made a couple of gift suggestions. That's not worth a dinner."

He didn't say anything after that, and I feared I'd pushed back too hard. While I didn't want him to know how big a crush I had on him, I also didn't want him to think I didn't like him at all. Though really, the crush had faded somewhat with time, which was what I'd hoped would happen. He was less of an ideal and more of a real person, even if his smiles did make my legs turn to jelly.

He walked me to my front door, then said, "Thanks again for the help."

"No problem. You'll have to tell me what they think."

"See you tomorrow."

"Yeah." I looked over my shoulder after unlocking the door, and he'd already disappeared.

Owen was uncharacteristically quiet the next morning. Not that he was usually all that talkative, but there was a subdued quality to his quiet that was new. I hoped I hadn't hurt his feelings. Maybe he was just lost in thought.

The quiet commute was a sharp contrast to the building lobby when we got to work. It seemed like almost the entire MSI workforce was gathered there, and judging from the bits of muttered conversations I overheard, I got the impression that no one else had any more of a clue about what was going on than I did. Owen edged closer to me. He looked distinctly uncomfortable in the crowd.

Hughes, the lobby doorman, approached us, ticked something off the clipboard he carried, then murmured a few words under his breath. Two baseball caps with the MSI logo on them appeared in his hand. "Here you are, sir, Miss Chandler," he said, handing one to each of us. "You'll find an envelope inside your cap. Please keep it sealed until you're instructed to open it." Before we had a chance to ask questions, he moved on to greet the latest arrivals.

Owen studied his ball cap like he thought it was going to bite him. "What's going on?" he asked.

I spotted Rod moving through the lobby toward us. He looked

more energized and excited than I'd ever seen him, and I wished I could see what that lively expression would have done to his true face. He'd probably be almost as irresistible as he was with all his spells. Speaking of spells, I felt his magnetism hit when he got within about five feet of me. While I was still moderately in control of myself, I took a step backward and sighed in relief when that eased the urge to throw myself into his arms.

"Great! You two are here," Rod said.

"For what?" Owen asked.

Rod grinned and took a step forward. I shifted sideways and back half a step. "It was one of Katie's ideas. We're boosting morale and teamwork. Don't worry, this'll be fun." He turned to me. "Can I take your coat and your other things? I can get them up to your office." In order to hand him my coat and bag, I had to step within his sphere of influence. I could feel the waves of desire wash over me, and I forced myself to keep my eyes on Owen. Surely his very real charms—his strong jaw, sculpted cheekbones, and blue eyes full of intelligence, kindness, and a hint of sadness—would be enough to counteract any other man's attraction spell.

It must have worked, for I was startled when Rod said, "Oh, gotta run. I need to brief the boss. Katie, your things will be in your office." Only then did I notice that he no longer held my coat, purse, or tote bag.

Once he was gone, Owen turned to me with a look that almost made me feel like I'd stabbed him in the back. "This wasn't my idea," I insisted. "I may have suggested that boosting morale and teamwork might counteract the effects of the mole, but I didn't suggest anything like this. I'm afraid I may have created a monster."

"And what, exactly, do you think this is?"

I looked around at the ball caps and at the posters I now saw hanging from the balcony railing above. "I suspect we're in for a company pep rally and a team-building exercise. There will probably be sharing and hugging, that kind of thing."

"Oh." He looked like he'd rather be wrestling a dragon, or maybe having dinner with Idris. I turned to watch Rod with Merlin. Merlin looked utterly fascinated by the goings-on. He was even wearing his ball cap proudly.

I turned back to reassure Owen that I'd try to do what I could to get him out of stuff like this, but he was gone. I had a feeling that if my magical immunity had been in place, I would have been able to see him sneaking around the periphery of the lobby and then up the stairs to the relative safety of his lab. It was no fair. Why couldn't I veil myself with invisibility?

A trumpet sounded a flourish, and the whole crowd turned to face the stairs. The playerless trumpet that hung over the stairs near Merlin disappeared. "Thank you all for being here this morning," Merlin said, his voice ringing through the room. Not that we had much choice, given that they'd ambushed us at the front door. "I know we've had some challenges in the past weeks, but it's important that we remember who we are and what we do. We need to accept—even embrace—the fact that our world has changed and move forward proudly. To that effect, I would like to present a challenge. If we reach our productivity goals for the year before the holidays, everyone will receive a bonus."

The crowd cheered, and I had to give the old guy credit. He knew exactly how to motivate people: money. I wasn't sure where the hats and posters fit in, though. It seemed to me that he could have delivered the same message via e-mail.

"Now Mr. Gwaltney will take over," Merlin said, then stepped aside for Rod.

"Thank you, Mr. Mervyn," Rod said. His voice appeared to have been magically amplified, but it didn't have the same ringing quality to it that Merlin's had. "We're going to be working hard in the next couple of weeks, but we can also have some fun. We'll be conducting the first-ever company-wide treasure hunt. If you'll open your envelopes, you'll find out what team you're on, and you'll have a list of clues. The clues won't make sense until you match them up with the clues the rest of your team has. Then you can find all the items for the hunt, which are hidden around the building. The prize for best team will be given at the holiday party. Good luck, everyone!"

His last sentence was nearly drowned out by the sound of ripping paper as everyone tore open their envelopes. I watched to see how the group would react to the idea of having to work that closely with each other, and I was surprised by how many actually seemed okay with it. There were smiles and laughter—things I hadn't seen in weeks. I opened my own envelope to find that I was on the Unicorn team. The list of clues made no sense to me. They were like pieces of a jigsaw puzzle. I had to admit, Rod had come up with something clever that might actually work.

"Unicorns, over here!" I heard Isabel bellow. I joined the group gathered around her, where we made plans to meet for lunch to go over our clues. Then I made my escape up the stairs to my office.

Rod caught me at the top of the stairs. "What do you think?" he asked.

"Good idea, both the productivity bonus and the treasure hunt. They seem to be having fun, and it looks like we might even get through this without anyone killing each other. The hats might be overkill, though."

He grinned, and I swayed and had to catch myself on the banister. "The hats are enchanted," he said.

"They're what?"

"A subtle spell that gives a sense of well-being to the wearer. We thought about doing something to the building in general, but this is more direct and efficient."

I went up one step so I could move myself out of his sphere of influence and think more clearly. "So you put the whammy on the company?"

He gave a casual shrug that made my heart skip a beat. I moved up one more step. "It was Mr. Mervyn's idea, but I came up with the idea of doing ball caps. I notice you're not wearing yours."

"Hat hair avoidance," I explained.

"Not that the spell would affect you. Good luck on the hunt. You should have a good team."

I was glad I'd more or less ruled him out as a suspect, because his mention of my immunity made the little hairs on the back of my neck stand up. But unless he was veiling his real expression along with his real face, I didn't think he meant anything by it.

I got upstairs to find a grinning Merlin, still wearing his ball cap, waiting for me. "This plan of Mr. Gwaltney's should be quite entertaining," he said. "We always found that a good tournament helped keep the knights from killing each other between battles. This appears to work on the same principle."

"It is one of the better team-building activities I've seen. It might even be fun."

He gestured me toward his office, then once we were seated, he asked, "Now, how is your investigation progressing?"

"I've made absolutely no progress on finding the spy. I'm right where I started, and I feel like I'm going in circles."

"Someone must have thought you were close to have bothered attacking you the other night," he said mildly, raising one eyebrow.

"If I am close, I don't know it. I have no real suspects. I have no evidence. I'm at the point of hoping they do something else that will give me more clues. I've even resorted to wondering if maybe the attacks were personal, but I couldn't think of anything I have or anything I've done that would set someone off like that. Idris seems to want to make me quit, but I can't see where that would do him much good."

He remained unruffled, even as I was close to tears. "Let's consider the evidence you've gathered."

"That's just it, there is no evidence. Everyone in the company suspects everyone else, and nearly everyone could have had motive and opportunity if you look hard enough for it."

"Then let's see who had the most opportunity. Most of the damage was focused on the R and D department, right?"

"Yes. But that doesn't narrow it down much. It's the biggest department in the company."

"True. Did you say anything to anyone Friday that might have given them an impression you knew more than you really did?"

"I was in R and D, but for an entirely different reason," I said, hoping I didn't blush.

"I know you've been assigned as Santa for Mr. Palmer," he said gently. "That was at my suggestion. I felt he'd be more comfortable with someone he knew, and it would give you broader access for investigation."

"Well, while I was down there I talked to Ari and Jake, but a lot of others saw me and thought I was investigating. Or else they thought I was the spy."

"I propose you focus on that department. You have an excuse to be there." He smiled. "I believe Mr. Palmer is going to find himself awash in holiday treats in the days to come."

He was a sneaky old man, but as comfortable as I felt with him, I didn't dare say so to his face. I shouldn't have been surprised, though. He'd put kings on thrones. This was small potatoes to him.

"So, hanging out in R and D, then," I said, feeling a little better. If only I could deal with my magic problem the same way.

He took a flat crystal from his desk. "This should get you past security there. The spell is on the crystal, so you don't have to worry about a lack of magical ability." No, I just had to worry about wards I could no longer get through, but I didn't have a pressing need to get into Owen's office. "And I can keep Mr. Palmer busy so you'll be able to snoop without giving away your Santa identity."

I had the distinct feeling I was being manipulated, but I wasn't sure where he was going with it. I took the card-like crystal from him and put it in my pocket. "Thank you."

"I'd like a report at the end of the week, if you don't mind."

"No problem." In the meantime, it looked like I'd be doing more baking. Then there was the treasure hunt, which was the least of my worries. I handed my clues over to my team and made a couple of suggestions about deciphering them, but otherwise I let the people who were truly enjoying themselves play. I had bigger puzzles to solve.

That evening, as I baked another favorite family recipe, I reflected that I might actually be in better shape than the last time we'd had a crisis, despite what felt like a lack of progress. Before, we'd relied on my dating ability to save the world, and I was a much better cook than I was a potential girlfriend.

This batch of cookies I put in a plastic bag tied with ribbon, which I was able to hide easily in my tote bag. I waited until Owen arrived at Merlin's office for a meeting, then I headed down to R&D with the cookies and the crystal card. Along the way, I passed at least two teams of treasure hunters, all wearing their company caps. Everyone was laughing and smiling, which was a nice change of pace from the previous week, even if it was mostly because of magical company caps. One team had on matching outfits. The other stopped in the middle of the hallway to give their team cheer, which had something to do with how dominant the Dragons were. My team was going to lose. We hadn't even reached the point of looking for items. We definitely didn't have a cheer, a mission statement, or a team uniform.

As Merlin promised, the card got me easily through the front door at R&D. Ari was in her lab not too far from the entrance, her feet propped up on a table while she read a book. She wasn't wearing the company cap, which didn't surprise me. I suspected she was doing even less for her team than I was for mine. "Hi!" I said.

She looked up from her book. "Oh good, you're not one of those treasure hunt nutcases. I've had three people so far thinking something was hidden in my lab." She glanced at the bag I carried. "Let me guess, another Santa mission."

I tried my best to look vague. "Maybe."

"You're carrying a bag of cookies."

"That doesn't mean they're for my secret Santa."

She rolled her eyes. "Don't even try to lie. You totally suck at it. Coffee?"

"Yes, please." As usual, the cup popped into my hand. I was proud of how nonchalantly I handled it. "What are you reading?"

She held up the antique-looking book. "Love-spell book I swiped from Owen's lab. Somehow, I doubt he'll be using it anytime soon. He only has it because it's by some old wizard he's been studying. There's a spell in here for getting the attention of human men. I may have to give it a try—at the next full moon, I can take a canary feather and sprinkle it with rose essence, then wave it in the path of my target."

"Or you could say, 'Hi, come here often?' Even I manage to make that work sometimes."

"It also has spells to make people fall in love with each other. Want me to hook you up with anyone?"

That was the last thing I needed, magical interference in my shambles of a love life. "No thanks. Besides, remember, I'm immune." Well, I was once, and I hoped I would be again.

"Oh yeah. I keep forgetting that. But that doesn't mean the spell wouldn't work on him. What do you think? Wouldn't you like a real date with a certain dark-haired, blue-eyed someone who otherwise will never get around to asking anyone out?"

"I'll pass."

"Let me know if you change your mind."

I finished my coffee, put the cup down, and said, "Guess I'd better get back to my mission. Thanks for the coffee."

"Don't mention it."

As Merlin had no doubt arranged, the coast was clear in Owen's office and lab, so it was easy enough to drop off the cookies. But it looked like I wasn't the only person who'd taken advantage of Owen's absence. The place was a mess—not the comfortable clutter that was usually there, but a real mess. Someone had apparently been looking for something, or else had been causing destruction for its own sake. I left my cookies on a table, then ran back down the hall to report it.

I shot past Ari's lab on my way to the exit, then turned back. "Can I use your phone?" I asked.

"What is it?"

"I'll explain later." I dialed Trix's desk and said, "Tell the boss that he needs to get down here now." She promised to pass the word, and I hung up.

"Ah, so it was Owen's lab you were heading to," Ari said.

"What?" Only then did I remember the reason I'd supposedly

come down in the first place. "Oh, that. No, I accomplished my mission and thought I'd stop by to say hi to Owen."

"He's in a meeting."

"Really?" Then I remembered what she'd said about swiping a book from him. "You mentioned that you got that book from his office. Did you notice anything when you were in there?"

"I took this months ago. Sorry I can't help. What happened?"

"Our spy has been busy again."

"Hmm. Funny no one noticed. Owen hasn't even been gone that long. I saw him go past not ten minutes before you got here."

Owen and Merlin then went by. I caught up with them in the hallway. "Someone's been in your lab," I said to Owen, "and I'm not talking about your secret Santa. Well, your secret Santa seems to have been there, too, because it looks like something's been left, but someone else has been there."

By the time I finished rattling all that off, we were in the lab. "Can you tell if anything's missing or changed?" Merlin asked.

Owen ran a hand through his hair, making pieces of it stand on end. "I have no idea. I guess I'll have to start warding the lab, too, but that'll make it difficult to get much work done." Then he looked at me. "What are you doing down here, Katie?"

"You're not the only person in this department who has a secret Santa, you know. And I thought I'd drop by to say hi while I was in the neighborhood."

He went back to sorting through the books and papers that were on the floor. "You didn't see anything, did you?"

"Sorry. It was like this when I got here, and I called right away."

Another man then joined us. He was perhaps old enough to be Owen's father and was nearly a head shorter than Owen. "Did I hear there's been another break-in?" he asked.

Owen practically snapped to attention. "Yes, sir, I'm afraid so." I'd never seen him that deferential to anyone in a business setting, except sometimes to Merlin.

"What about all those security measures you've taken?" the newcomer demanded.

"They don't do any good if the culprit is within your department," Merlin said in his usual mild manner.

That didn't calm the newcomer. "Are you implying that my department is the problem?"

"Your department is clearly the target, and it would appear that someone in the department is the culprit, so yes, I'm saying we have a problem in your department," Merlin replied.

"I don't keep anything essential out here, so they can't have stolen anything worthwhile," Owen said. "It's more like vandalism."

"Well, report to me when you have more information," the other man said before turning to leave.

"Katie, you'll keep me updated?" Merlin asked.

I nodded. "I will when I figure something out."

He left, and I knelt by Owen to help him gather books and papers. "I should probably explain about Mr. Lansing," he said.

"Who?"

"The one who was just here. You probably saw him as a frog."

I bit my tongue before I blurted that I hadn't seen a frog.

"He's the departmental director for R and D. There was apparently an industrial accident a number of years ago. He doesn't come out much since maintaining that illusion is a drain on him, but he doesn't feel like he gets much respect as a frog."

"I can see where that would be a problem," I said, nodding. For once, I was grateful for my hopefully temporary lack of magical immunity. I'd have been totally freaked out if a frog had hopped into the room and started asking questions. "But don't you have ways of breaking the frog spell?"

"Trust me, he's kissed half the city. And we've tried everything. It was a pretty diabolical spell. I'm not even sure how it happened, but they've been working on breaking it for decades. We generally don't talk about it that much. I usually try to stay out of his way." He gathered a few more papers, then asked, "Was there something you needed to see me about?"

My cover stories were starting to need cover stories. Then I thought of something. "Did you ever find out where that camera was sending its signal?" I asked.

"Unfortunately, no," he said with a sigh. "The cord ran through the ceiling and stopped halfway down the hall, then was severed. Someone must have cut it before I managed to track it back. But I've reached the conclusion that this has more to do with chaos than it does with espionage. That would definitely be Phelan's style. And it may be a sign that he's as lost as we are. He must not have anything of substance up his sleeve if he's resorting to this sort of behavior. Otherwise, he'd be more focused on taking us on in the marketplace."

"So our best strategy might be to ignore it and hope it goes away."

"He might go away. I'm not sure his spy would."

"Yeah, anyone motivated enough to be willing to spy probably has personal reasons for doing so. Which brings me back to square one."

"Sorry I couldn't help more."

"And I'm sorry I haven't been able to do anything to stop this." I stood and dusted off my knees. "I guess I'd better get back to work. Let me know if you run across anything interesting."

I felt like an utter loser as I headed out of the department. I was letting everyone down. I passed Ari's lab, and she called out, "So, what was the sitch down there?"

I turned back and stood in her doorway. "The usual. Chaos and all that."

"As messy as he is, I don't know how he'd notice the difference with a few books and papers scattered. He looks like he'd be a neat freak, but he's such a pack rat."

I suddenly got a prickling feeling between my shoulder blades. No one had described the chaos in the lab to her, so how had she known? Fragments of conversations, facial expressions, and odd coincidences all crashed together at once in my brain—Ari on the phone just before the last attack, her apparently fruitless pursuit of Owen, her hounding me about him, her grilling me about what I did and didn't see, the camera cord that was cut halfway down the hall, right about where her lab was.

No, it couldn't be. Happy-go-lucky Ari couldn't be the spy. But she had access. She had information. She even had motivation, if her feelings about Owen ran deeper than she let on. I had no real evidence, though, just a hunch. That wasn't enough to risk our friendship by turning her in. I had to know more.

I tried to keep a straight face and an even voice as I said, "I think it was just enough to tick him off. You might want to stay away from that end of the hall for a while. He doesn't get angry often, but when he does, you'd better duck." Her eyes narrowed briefly at me. Did she sense that I knew? That would be bad. To cover my tracks, I added casually, "Oh, and you might want to warn Jake when he gets back before he says the wrong thing."

She laughed then, and I relaxed. She didn't sound like someone who knew the game was up. "Yeah, I'll keep an eye out for Jake. He drives Owen crazy at the best of times. We wouldn't want him walking into a hornet's nest."

My heart raced as I slipped out of the department. I didn't want to believe that one of my closest friends, one of the people who'd introduced me to the magical world in the first place, could be the spy. I really hated the idea of spying on her, but I told myself that I was looking for evidence to exonerate her, not hang her. I needed to eliminate her as a suspect, once and for all.

Before returning to my own office, I went to see Isabel. If anyone knew the whole story behind whatever ill-fated thing Ari had for Owen, it would be Isabel.

"Are you okay?" she asked me when I got to her office. "You look like you don't feel so well."

"I'm fine. I just wanted to brainstorm some on those treasure hunt clues." I sank into her comfortable guest chair, relieved to get off my watery legs.

Her face lit up. "I found something this morning." She pulled a small figurine out of her desk drawer. "We can cross off clue fourteen."

"Good work."

"I saw that one team had T-shirts. Do you think we need that?"

"Probably not." Then, because I didn't really have anything to say about the hunt, I dropped a piece of gossip I knew would sidetrack her completely. "Did you hear? There was another break-in in Owen's lab. He doesn't think anything's gone, but it's a mess in there."

"That poor boy. He hates it when people rearrange his clutter."

I licked my lips, trying to think of a delicate way to phrase what I needed to ask. "You know what Ari was saying the other night about having tried her luck with Owen? What do you know about that?"

"Why?" Then she grinned. "I knew it! You're interested in him yourself, aren't you?"

It looked like I was going to have to take one for the team. This was the only way I could think of to get the information without raising suspicions. If it made me the butt of office gossip, I'd have to get over that and hope Owen forgave me. Looking down at my lap, I said, "Yeah, maybe. But I don't want to do anything that would hurt Ari, and if she liked him, it would be a bad idea for me to go after him."

She beamed. "You two would be perfect for each other, and I still say he likes you—and not only as a friend." Leaning back in her seat and steepling her fingers, she said, "Let's see, it must have been back when she joined the company, before he was promoted. Gregor was still fully human. She pretty much fell for Owen at first sight—and can you blame her? He was focused on something else—I think that was when he was starting to get suspicious of Idris—and didn't even notice. She made the mistake of getting aggressive with him, which sent all the barriers up. Make a note of that: sneak into his heart. No full-frontal assault. But I think that's what you're already doing. He trusts you."

"So what happened?" I prodded.

"She got more and more aggressive, and he either didn't notice or pretended he didn't notice. I don't think she would have minded so much if he'd outright rejected her, but he neatly sidestepped every pass she threw at him, and that made her feel like she hadn't made any impact. After a while, she gave up."

"Do you think she really got over him, or does she still resent him?"

"I think she gives it another try every so often, just for kicks and to see what will happen. She wouldn't be happy if you ended up with him, but I think she'd also be the first one to say it was his choice, and you won fair and square. It's all a game to her, anyway. I'm not sure she would have liked him if she had caught him. She just wanted to be able to say she'd caught him."

"Catch-and-release dating, huh?" I had a sinking feeling Ari wouldn't be so happy about me ending up with Owen. Not that it was likely to happen. I gave Isabel my most beseeching look. "You won't say anything about this to Ari, will you? Or anyone else? You know how shy Owen is. If he knew I was interested, he'd probably clam up on me."

"My lips are sealed," she promised. I knew she meant it, but I also knew her good intentions tended to disintegrate when she had a really juicy piece of gossip.

I nearly ran head-on into Rod in the hallway outside the personnel office, and as usual, it took me a moment to remember that the gorgeous guy I saw was the Rod I knew. He steadied me with his hands on my shoulders, and I fought to resist the effects of that attraction spell. I took a couple of steps backward to get out of the spell's range.

"You okay?" he asked me.

"What? Oh, sorry, just a little distracted."

"Did you need me for something?" He waved toward the office I'd just left.

I shook my head. "No, I was discussing something with Isabel."

He grinned. "Ah, office gossip, then."

"Treasure hunt, actually."

"Of course. Then I'd better let you go on about your important business." He gave me a jaunty salute and a wink, and I grabbed the nearest door handle to anchor myself so my body wouldn't fly at him of its own accord. With that kind of pulling power, there was no wonder he never lacked for a date. It was a miracle he wasn't the Pied Piper of New York, with hordes of salivating women following him around town.

Before I could force my feet into motion so I could get farther from his enticing spell, he said, "Uh, Katie?"

"Yes?"

"I was wondering . . . I know things have been rough for you lately, what with this investigation, and then your parents, and Ethan, and that attack last weekend, and all. Would you like to have dinner this weekend? Don't worry, nothing romantic. I just feel like you could use a break, a no-stress night out."

My body shouted *Yes, yes!* but my mind knew better, reminding me that I had a huge crush on Rod's best friend, and I could kiss any future chance I might have with Owen good-bye if I got together with Rod. It was a persuasive argument, but my body wasn't quite ready to give up. My mouth compromised between body and brain with, "Can I get back to you? I need to check my calendar." Maybe once I got away from him I could think straight enough to decide if this was something I wanted to do. I suspected he meant exactly what he'd said. He had no way of knowing that I was influenced by his attraction spell.

"Sure. That would be fine."

I had a lot to think about when I finally got back to my office and fell wearily into my desk chair. In the plus column, I now had a real suspect, someone who had motive and opportunity. In the minus column, that suspect was one of my friends, and I didn't have a shred of hard evidence, just an instinct. It would be easy enough for her to rebut every charge I made, even if she really was guilty. I wasn't sure which column Rod's invitation fit into.

There was a light tap on my door, and I looked up to see Trix standing in my doorway. She looked timid, which was unusual for her. "Can I talk to you about something personal?" she asked.

"Sure. Come on in." She shut the door behind herself, then approached my desk.

"I know this is a terrible thing for a friend to do, but I did want to ask you first," she said, wringing her hands.

"What is it, Trix?"

"Ethan was just here to see the boss. And, well, he asked me out. And to be honest, I'd like to go. He seems nice. But I know you and he had that thing, and it ended not that long ago, but I don't know how much it still bothers you. So I thought I'd talk to you before I said anything. If you have a problem with it, I'll say no, and I'd understand completely."

My stomach twisted. I knew he'd said he was interested in exploring the magical world, but I hadn't realized how close to the mark I'd come when I said he wanted to date chicks with wings. Looking at Trix's face, though, I knew I couldn't be bitch enough to tell her she couldn't see him.

"You go ahead, please. It's not like we were engaged or even dating that long," I said. "Maybe you'll have better luck with him than I did."

She shot up into the air and spun around, then landed. "Thank you! You're the best friend I could imagine."

I watched her flutter back to her desk, wondering what she'd think if she knew I was going to try to bust her other friend. Then my eyes began stinging. I hadn't thought much about Ethan in a few days, but the realization that he'd already moved on hurt. Before I knew what I was doing, I'd picked up my phone and dialed Rod's extension. "Hi, it's me," I said when he answered. "I'd love to have dinner with you this weekend."

seventeen

"Really?" Rod sounded so overjoyed that I was glad I'd accepted his dinner invitation.

"Sure." I didn't have to tell him that it was mostly to strike back at Ethan for asking Trix out. Or maybe I was distracting myself. I wasn't sure which it was. I just knew I wanted to go out with somebody that weekend.

"How's Friday? Not right after work. I live close enough to you that I can pick you up at your place, say sevenish?"

"That works for me."

"Good. This is mostly for fun, but we could also discuss some of my morale-building ideas while we're at it."

"Okay. I'll see you Friday. And I guess I'll probably see you some before then, huh?"

He laughed. "I hope so. Thanks, Katie."

I realized as I hung up that I was actually looking forward to it, and that had nothing to do with his attraction spell, unless it was capable of carrying over the telephone. I'd have to ask about that.

I spent that evening frantically cross-stitching a Christmas ornament for Owen. I needed an excuse to go back to R&D to spy on Ari, and if I kept baking at my recent rate Owen would probably explode, no matter how often he went to the gym.

"What are you up to?" Gemma asked when she came home from work and found me watching TV while stitching.

"More secret Santa stuff."

"You're really going all-out."

"It's a long story, but this has nothing to do with the guy. There's this whole other reason, and I don't have nearly enough time to get into it."

"Mmm-hmm," she said, and I could tell from her tone that she didn't believe a word of it.

"Really. In fact, I happen to have a date with someone else Friday night."

"You're on a roll, aren't you? I knew all it would take was a little confidence for your luck to change."

"Yeah, a couple of good dates and now I'm the most desirable woman in New York." I still hadn't told her about the nightclub last weekend. I wasn't sure I believed it myself. I'd had plenty to drink that night, plus a big scare. The whole thing could have been a very vivid dream.

"Need help planning an outfit?"

"I've got something picked out—an old standby."

"Including the red shoes?"

I hadn't thought about it, but why not? It would make the strike back at Ethan complete if I wore the shoes I'd bought for him with someone else.

At work the next day, I put the ornament in my skirt pocket, got Merlin's crystal key, and headed down to R&D. Ari caught me in the hallway. "Let me guess, another Santa mission," she said with a smirk. "You've got one lucky secret pal."

"Just doing my part to spread the holiday spirit."

"I hear you're going out with Rod this weekend."

I wondered how that one had got around. Probably Isabel, who would have heard it from Rod. "Yeah, we're going to discuss some of these morale projects we're working on."

She snorted. "Yeah, right, like that's high on his agenda. Then again, I keep forgetting you don't see his illusion, and that love spell won't work on you. You might be okay. Watch yourself, though."

If she was our mole, she was good. Everything she said could have had a totally innocent meaning, or she could have been hinting that she knew I'd lost my immunity. "I'll be okay," I said with a cheerful smile. *Nope, nothing wrong here whatsoever,* I tried to project.

She snorted again as she returned to her lab. Oh, I so desperately needed to get some solid evidence on this, preferably evidence that Ari wasn't the one, even if that took me back to square one. I could hear Owen's voice coming from a lab near his, so I darted into his lab, hung the ornament on his office doorknob, then hurried away. I lingered in the hallway for a while, but it wasn't as though Ari was going to go out and sabotage something while I waited. Watching her probably wouldn't work very well. I'd have to find a way to set a trap and catch her red-handed, but you had to be pretty sneaky to catch a thief, and I'd never been that good at being sneaky. I was getting better, what with all the secret keeping I'd been doing lately, but I was still a novice compared with Ari.

By the time Friday rolled around, I was truly looking forward to going out with Rod. As I dressed for the date, I gave myself a stern lecture about not falling under the influence of whatever spell he threw at me. I had no magical defenses, but I retained at least a little bit of common sense, and if I knew there was magic at work, I stood a better chance than your average girl off the street.

For the finishing touch of my outfit, I slipped my feet into the red shoes. I couldn't hold back a smile as I thought that maybe he'd be the one having to resist me. I once more felt like the girl who'd snagged all the guys at the nightclub the previous weekend. The weather forecast threatened freezing rain and possibly snow, but it wasn't supposed to start until later that night. This was a simple dinner, so I should be home long before it got nasty. My shoes would be safe from the elements.

The door buzzer sounded, and I hurried to the intercom. "Hi, it's Rod," the voice crackled over the speaker.

"I'll be right down," I said. I grabbed my coat and my purse and headed out.

"I thought we'd stay more or less in the neighborhood," he said when I stepped out the front door. "With the weather the way it is, I didn't think we wanted to rely on cabs to get us home."

"Good thinking," I said.

He steered me down a nearby street to a modest, snug little restaurant. "This is one of my favorite places. I hope you like it," he said as he ushered me inside. So far, he was behaving like a perfect gentleman, as though this truly was a business dinner rather than a romantic date. I didn't even feel the dizzying effects of his attraction spell. Maybe he'd decided against wasting the energy on someone he didn't think would be affected and was gentleman enough not to use the spell on other women while he was with me.

Once we'd taken off our coats and settled ourselves with menus at a candlelit table, he smiled at me and said, "By the way, I didn't tell you how nice you look tonight."

"Thanks. You look nice, too." I didn't think it would be a good idea to tell him how much nicer than normal he looked to me. Or would he feel better knowing I saw him this way? His psyche would take Dr. Phil hours to untangle. If I ever managed to get Owen truly talking, I'd have to ask what it was in Rod's childhood that had made him so insecure.

"Do you want to get an appetizer? Preferably something warm?"

"Sounds good. Order what you want, and I'm sure I'll like it."

The dinner ended up being far more comfortable than I'd anticipated. Somewhere during the appetizer, I managed to forget about the disconnect between what I saw and the Rod I knew, and the man in front of me became just Rod. He was funny, smooth, and charming—the perfect dinner companion. As the waitress cleared our dinner plates, Rod said, "Do you mind if we don't order dessert? I've got something back at my place I thought we'd enjoy."

Ordinarily, my warning bells would have gone off, but in spite of Rod's reputation, he'd shown nothing more than a friendly, businesslike interest in me up to that point. If he was using his spell, it was too subtle for me to notice. I hadn't even once thought about what it would feel like to kiss him.

"That sounds nice," I said. Of course, the moment I thought about not thinking about kissing him, I couldn't help but think about kissing him. If that made any sense whatsoever. But it wasn't like I felt compelled to kiss him, just mildly curious.

"No thanks," he told the waitress when she brought the dessert menu. He paid the check, then we bundled up to brave the outdoors once more.

The temperature seemed to have dropped ten degrees while we were inside. I wished I'd been sensible and worn boots instead of being so vain as to wear a short skirt and the red stilettos. Rod put his arm around me, but I doubted he was making a move on me, and even if he was, I didn't mind because it made me that much warmer.

We hurried to his building, then both of us breathed a sigh of relief when we got inside the warm lobby. "I'd better not stay too late," I said, as we waited for an elevator. "It looks like that storm may hit early, and I don't want to have to go home through the snow."

"We'll keep an eye on the window, and on the clock," he said. An elevator arrived, and he gestured for me to go ahead of him. He lived near the top of the building, so it seemed like it took several minutes before we got to his floor. While we faced each other across the elevator, I felt a strange tension growing between us. It was an entirely different feeling from the ease I'd noticed in the restaurant, and it seemed to have come out of nowhere. Even as I tried to fight the feeling, my breathing grew faster.

I didn't think it was his attraction spell, though, or else it was affecting him the same way. He was practically panting. Could it be that we were really that attracted to each other? I'd never been the least bit turned on around Rod, except in the past couple of weeks when I'd noticed the effects of his attraction spell. This kind of thing didn't happen because of one good dinner, did it?

Both of us rushed for the door when the elevator finally came to a stop. The air seemed to have grown very heavy in there. I felt a little more normal once we were out in the hallway. Whatever it was eased up, so I felt almost relaxed again as I waited for him to unlock his apartment door.

He ushered me inside. "Have a seat, and I'll make some coffee," he said. I dropped my purse on the floor inside the doorway, then draped my coat across a chair and sat on the sofa. The last time I'd been in his apartment, I'd just been magically mugged. It hadn't changed much since then—a typical high-end bachelor pad with leather upholstery, blond wood, metal and glass, plus a great view of the city lights. "If you like, you can put on some music," he called from the kitchen.

I went to his entertainment center and looked through his CDs. I had to bite my lip to keep from laughing as I noticed the number of surefire seduction discs in his collection. He seemed to have the complete works of Barry White, as well as a broad collection of mellow jazz. Naturally, he had a recording of Ravel's Bolero. What Casanova didn't? I selected the least sultry jazz disc and put it in the player.

He emerged from the kitchen with two mugs of frothy coffee. "I hope this is good," he said. "I found it at the store and thought it looked interesting."

"You didn't have to go to all this trouble for me," I said, as he went back to the kitchen, only to return with a packet of cookies.

"You're worth the trouble. You should know that. But if it makes you feel better, I'm not putting these out on a plate. Just take some from the box."

"Now, that's more like it," I said with a laugh, as I took a couple of cookies out of the box. I felt that ease I'd enjoyed during dinner return. Whatever had happened in the elevator seemed to have dissipated.

"I wanted to thank you again for getting me involved in the morale-boosting effort," he said. "That's the main reason I asked you to dinner. For the first time, I feel like I'm really part of what's going on in the company."

"Of course I included you. It's your job."

"Funny how no one else seems to remember."

"Like I told you, Merlin doesn't understand modern stuff like human resources—though he's probably getting better with all those business books he's been reading. And you're doing a great job. Some of those teams have even made up T-shirts and cheers."

He laughed. "Yeah, and that's almost scary. We've had great results from the secret Santa program, too. Since it started, productivity has gone almost back to normal, after a serious drop from the time word about the spy got out."

"I'm glad to hear it."

He raised his cup for a toast, and I clinked mine against it. "To fighting the bad guys with whatever tools we've got," he said.

"Hear, hear!"

All of a sudden, the tension I'd felt in the elevator returned with a vengeance, so forcefully that I almost thought I could hear it rush in. His breath caught, and I knew he could feel it, too. Without a word, he set his cup on the coffee table, took my mug from me, and set it beside his. And then we all but fell on each other.

There was nothing cautious or gentle about this kiss. It was an all-out tongue-tangling lip-lock, like we couldn't get enough of each other. He bent me back so I was lying on the sofa, my head resting on the sofa arm and him lying on top of me. Things were getting very serious very fast, and I was impatient for more.

He trailed his fingers down my neck to my collarbone, then traced the neckline of my blouse. I felt a button open, then another. And then sanity returned. What on God's green earth was I doing?

I ducked the next kiss by turning my head aside, then I tried to wriggle out from under him. He responded by kissing my neck and tightening his hold on me. That meant I had to escalate. I put my hands against his chest and pushed with all my strength. When he grabbed my wrists with one hand and pinned them out of the way, I got scared. This wasn't fun anymore, by any definition of the word. It was serious.

That meant I had to get serious. First, a verbal warning. "Rod, no, please. Let's not do this," I gasped, but it didn't slow him down one bit. So I brought one knee up to hit him in a very sensitive place as hard as I could. That got his attention.

He released me enough that I was able to worm out from under him to land on the floor in front of the sofa, even as I mentally blessed the brother who'd taught me that particular move when a friend of his known for his octopus-like arm action had asked me out.

When Rod recovered from the initial impact, he looked at me in shock and horror. "Oh, God, Katie, I'm sorry. I don't know what happened," he said. I knew he had to be pretty stunned, for his illusion dropped entirely.

My head finally cleared enough for me to realize what had to be going on. "It's a spell," I said. "It has to be. Someone's trying to make you do something you would never do otherwise."

He closed his eyes and groaned. "That would explain it."

"I have to get out of here," I said, scuttling away from him. "For both our sakes." I grabbed my purse in the entryway, made it to my feet, and ran out of the apartment.

I reached the elevator bank and pushed the DOWN button repeatedly, hoping that this one time it defied logic and called an elevator faster. I'd just stepped onto an elevator when Rod came running out of his apartment after me. I hit the door CLOSE button as he shouted, "Katie!"

"I'll be okay," I called out between the closing doors. Only when I got outside did I realize I'd left my coat behind. It wouldn't be safe for either of us if I went back there, though, even if freezing rain was already falling. At least I had my purse, and therefore my keys. It wasn't that far to my own apartment, and if I ran I'd keep warm. The tears that insisted on spilling out of my eyes didn't help. It was cold enough that I was afraid they'd freeze on my face. I was in way over my head, and it was my own fault. If only I'd told someone about my loss of immunity so they'd know how vulnerable I was.

But the low point to my evening hadn't come yet. I felt the tingle of power that meant magic was in use nearby, but of course I couldn't see anything to know if I was under attack. Great, I was out in freezing rain without a coat, I was shaken up by a case of spell-induced seduction that had almost gone too far, and I was very possibly being attacked while I was too magically blind to know when to duck or get out of the way.

The only thing I could do was run the other way when I felt a buildup of magic and hope I could make it home in time. I put my head down and took off, then veered to the side when I felt the telltale tingle. I wondered if anyone would oblige me by shouting "Polo" if I yelled "Marco," but I doubted that people who grew up without ready access to swimming pools would know all the kids' swimming pool games. The tingle increased, and I spun around, swinging out with my purse and feeling a satisfying contact with something solid. Then I ran in the other direction.

I was in the clear for a little while, then felt it again, stronger than before. But before I could get away, something grabbed onto me, and I started to fight my way loose until I realized someone was saying my name over and over again, like he was soothing a troubled child. I looked up into Owen's concerned blue eyes.

"Katie, what's wrong?" he asked. "What are you doing out in this weather without a coat?"

I didn't have time to get into that at the moment. "I think there's someone after me," I sobbed as he wrapped me up in his overcoat, pulling me tighter against his chest. At any other time, I would have really enjoyed that, but I had other things to worry about at the moment.

"I think you may be right. We should get out of here," he said. Then he looked down at me, his eyes very serious. "Katie, do you trust me?"

I started to give him a flippant, lip-service reply, the same way you automatically say "fine" when someone asks you how you're doing, whether or not you're really fine. But I got the feeling he needed a real answer for this. "Yes, I trust you," I said at last.

He nodded. "Okay. This may be a little frightening. I think I can make it work, but I'm going to be more or less magically useless for the rest of the evening. Hold onto me."

If this was a scheme to get me into a compromising position, I could kill him later, I thought. For now, I just wanted out of the cold. I wanted to be safe. I wrapped my arms around his waist, and he tightened his hold on me. Then there was a lurching feeling, like I'd left my stomach behind at the top of a roller coaster. And then I was suddenly warm, with no cold rain falling on me. Owen held onto me for a second longer, steadying me, then he released me.

"That wasn't as bad as I thought it would be," he said, his voice a little rough, as if he'd been truly nervous.

I reluctantly released my death grip on him and stepped away, blinking as I tried to take stock of my surroundings. I was in a dark room, with dim light coming through a window. Owen waved a hand and the lights came on. Another wave of his hand and a fireplace sprang to life. "Okay, I think I'm now officially shot for the evening," he said, sounding stronger.

I looked around and realized I was in a room that appeared to be a combination living room and study. The study part was near the front window. A large wooden desk faced the window. The walls to either side of the window were covered in bookcases. Directly behind me was an overstuffed sofa in a dark, soft-looking material. Across from it was a marble fireplace, a fire blazing inside and Christmas stockings hanging from the mantel. On the wall at the other end of the room was a television set. A lit, decorated Christmas tree stood in the far corner of the room.

The room had the ornately carved crown moldings and door and window facings of an older building, and the floor was of polished wood with Oriental rugs scattered on it. It was a room where delicate antique furniture would have been entirely at home, but the heavier, more comfortable furnishings made it look cozy and livable, like a home rather than a museum. I didn't have to ask to know it was Owen's place. It looked exactly like I would have expected of him.

I finished studying the room and turned back to him, only to find him giving me a funny look and turning pink. "Um, Katie, your, uh," he said, fiddling with his collar. I looked down and saw that my blouse was still partially unbuttoned.

"Oh, oops," I said, hurrying to button up.

He looked intensely relieved. "Here, you should have a seat." He guided me to the sofa, then took an afghan off the back of the sofa and wrapped it around my shoulders. "You'll be safe here. This place is heavily warded, as well as physically secure. Now, what was going on that had you running through the streets on a night like this without a coat?"

I was still trying to think of a good answer when a white streak shot into the room. Owen caught it before it could jump up onto the sofa, and I then saw that it was a small white cat with big black spots. "A familiar?" I asked.

He shook his head, a wry grin on his lips. "No, just a pet." He addressed the cat he held, "Be good, Loony, Katie's a guest," then gently dropped the cat onto the sofa, where it proceeded to investigate me.

"You named your cat Loony?" I asked as I scratched it behind the ears and listened to the answering purr.

He slipped out of his overcoat and threw it over a nearby chair. "I named my cat Eluned, after a figure from Welsh mythology. Rod started calling her Loony, and it stuck."

I tried not to stiffen at the mention of Rod. "She's sweet," I said.

He sat beside me on the sofa, and the cat immediately turned from me to snuggle adoringly against him. He absently stroked her as he spoke. "She's not so bad. I'm not really much of a cat person. We always had dogs when I was growing up. But I found her in a gutter when she was a newborn. It looked like her mother had been hit by a car. I tried to save the whole litter, but she was the only one who made it."

Tears threatened to come once more, but I fought them back. Instead, I forced a laugh. "Are you for real? Seriously? You may not be ready to give your foster parents the Parent of the Year award, but they seem to have done a pretty good job with you. Please tell me you have some flaws, or are you not really human?"

He kept his attention on the cat as his face turned redder than I'd ever seen it. With him, the man who had an entire repertoire of blushes, that was saying something. "I'm human, with maybe a slight genetic variance. And I have plenty of flaws. For one thing, I'm lousy at talking to people. My house is a mess, too."

"I like it. It's cozy."

He didn't say anything for a while, and I joined him in petting Loony, who reveled in the attention. She might have adored her owner, but she didn't seem to see me as the other woman or a threat to her position in the household. I was simply someone else to fuss over her.

Then, just as I was getting comfortable with the silence, he asked again, "What happened tonight? It had to have been pretty bad to have you running out in this weather without a coat."

I scratched a purring Loony under her chin as I thought about how to respond. There wasn't an easy way to tell a guy you were in serious danger of falling in love with that you'd just run screaming away from his best friend. I finally said, "Can we table that discussion for later? I'm not ready to talk about it, and I think I need to process it a little more before I'd even know what to say."

He nodded. "Okay. Take all the time you need. Just know that you're safe here. You can relax."

"Thank you. And thank you for coming to my rescue. What were you doing there, anyway? Did you know something was wrong, or did you just happen to be in the neighborhood at the right time?"

"I had a feeling."

"Your ESP must have a twenty-four-hour Katie channel."

"Something like that. Maybe I'm attuned to you because we spend so much time together. I've never done much study on it. My precognition always seemed too erratic to analyze before." He looked up at me then, and his eyes softened. "Or maybe it has something to do with the fact that you're so utterly irresistible," he added, his voice not much more than a whisper.

My heart skipped a beat as he leaned forward and touched his lips to mine. This wasn't the hungry, possessive, all-out kiss that had happened between Rod and me, and I didn't sense any of the tension that had built up between us before that happened. This just felt right, like it was meant to happen.

It was the perfect first kiss, firm enough to be real, but still gentle and sweet. I felt surrounded by a warm, safe glow. At the same time, I wanted to shout for joy. All that time I'd had a crush on him, and it turned out that he'd felt the same way about me. This amazing, wonderful man—who also turned out to be a fantastically talented kisser—liked me in return. It was almost too good to be true.

Then, just as I was really getting into it, he pulled away from me with a gasp, and an expression of utter horror came across his face. "Oh, God," he breathed. I wanted to grab him and pull him back to me, but he was shaking his head, like he was trying to snap out of something.

"What is it?" I managed to choke.

He frowned as if in deep concentration, then looked down at my feet. Leaning over, he waved a hand over my feet, then turned back to me and said, "It's your shoes."

eighteen

"M y-my shoes?" I stammered, my brain still fuzzy from the kiss.

He moved off the sofa to kneel at my feet. "May I?" he asked. I knew he wasn't entirely normal, but I'd never figured Owen for a shoe fetishist. Then again, he seemed a lot more worried than turned on, which didn't say much for my kissing ability. "Sure," I said, even though I had no idea what he was talking about.

He slid my shoes off my feet, then held one and frowned some more. He looked up at me and said, "Hmm, it seems to be a Cinderella spell."

"A what?"

He went into business mode, all calm and articulate and like he hadn't just been kissing me. "You don't see it often, but it's a classic. It's a spell cast on footwear that renders the wearer irresistible and utterly attractive to others. It may also have an effect on the wearer— the spell can be what compels the wearer to purchase the shoes in the first place and can give the wearer a sense of artificial confidence. Of course, that wouldn't work on you, but it would definitely have an impact on those around you."

"That explains a lot," I said with a nod. In fact, it explained more than he realized. No wonder I'd been so quick to whip out my credit card and buy them. My immunity must have already been fading by then.

"Explains what?" he asked. The question seemed innocent enough, and obvious, if he was trying to get to the root of the situation, but a crease had formed between his eyes. Was he jealous? But no, he'd only been kissing me because he was affected by the shoes. Just my luck—the best kiss I'd ever had in my entire life, and it was meaningless.

"Some stupid stuff that's been happening to me lately. Like last weekend when we went out, I was a lot more popular than I've ever been. I had men buying me drinks and asking me to dance all night." I gave a bitter laugh. "I should have known it couldn't possibly have been real."

That should have been his cue to correct me and tell me I didn't need magical shoes to be irresistible. I wasn't fishing for compliments, but I would have welcomed one. He was apparently telling the truth about not being good at talking to people, though, for he didn't even try to say anything to make me feel better. I could feel my hopes deflating. The kiss hadn't meant anything to him, then.

"I think I can break this spell, but not tonight. I'm still too drained from the teleportation. In the meantime, I'd better put these in a safe place. I mean, a place where we'll both be safe. Well, they won't affect you, but, yeah, a place where we'll both be safe." Apparently, he'd fallen out of business mode and was back to his usual bashful self. He stood up, holding the shoes out at arm's length, like he was afraid they'd bite. "And we need to get you out of those wet clothes." He turned crimson as he realized what he'd said, then hurried to correct himself. "I mean, you need something warmer and drier to wear. Stay there. I'll be back."

As rattled as I was, I couldn't help but smile as he all but ran from the room. He was so adorable when he was flustered. So adorable, and he didn't like me as anything more than a friend, after all. I wished he'd never kissed me, for now I knew what I was missing. If I closed my eyes, I could still feel the touch of his lips on mine, still taste him. I doubted I'd forget it anytime soon.

I heard footsteps on stairs and soon he returned, holding a bundle of clothing. "These are probably too big for you, but they should work," he said, handing the clothes to me. "The sweatpants have a drawstring waist, and there's elastic at the ankles, so they may be baggy, but you won't trip over the hem. There's a bathroom under the stairs if you want to change and, um, freshen up. While you do that, I'll make some cocoa."

I got up from the sofa and followed him into the hallway, where he pointed out the bathroom before heading to the end of the hall, Loony following faithfully at his heels.

Safely locked inside the small half bathroom, I finally let myself break down and cry. This night had been one disaster after another, from the surprisingly fun date with Rod that had disintegrated into a nightmare to the miraculous kiss with Owen that turned out to have been nothing more than the result of a spell.

When I got myself under control, I washed my face, then got out of my wet clothes and put on the sweat suit he'd brought me. He was right about the pants being baggy, but they didn't fit much worse than any I might have worn at home, and I only had to push up the sleeves of the sweatshirt a little bit. It was an old, faded blue sweatshirt that said YALE on the front in cracked lettering that looked like it had been washed hundreds of times over the years. He'd also given me a pair of thick socks to warm my feet. I found a ponytail holder in my purse and pulled my hair back, then put on a little lip balm and almost felt human again when I left the bathroom.

The first doorway off the hall led to the living room, where we'd been. The next one opened into a formal dining room that didn't appear to be used often for its intended purpose, given the piles of books and papers on the dining table. The last door turned out to be the kitchen, where Owen stood at the stove, stirring something in a pot,

Loony sitting at his feet and staring up at him in all-out worship. I couldn't much blame her. He really was remarkable.

It was a typically small New York kitchen, but compared with mine it could have been a catering kitchen designed to feed thousands. He had actual counter space, as well as a nook for a small table for two. "I think I have kitchen envy," I said.

He turned around from the stove and gave me a shaky smile. "How did the sweats work out for you?" he asked.

"Fine. Thank you." I gestured toward the stove. "You're making real cocoa? I'm impressed."

I bit my lip to keep myself from smiling as the expected faint pink stain spread over his cheekbones. The poor guy had the bad luck to be so bashful and yet so fair-skinned. He kept his attention on the pot he was stirring as he said, "Gloria does not believe in shortcuts of any kind. Besides, I didn't have any mix handy."

He poured the cocoa into two mugs, then opened a cabinet over the stove and took out a bottle, from which he splashed a little liquid into each mug, then gave a stir. "I thought we could probably both use a dram of something extra," he explained, as he brought the mugs over to the table, his cat following him.

"Good idea," I said as I took a mug from him. We both sat at the table, and I suddenly felt self-conscious around him. Sleet rattling against the window punctuated the silence between us. I hoped the memory of that kiss faded quickly, for it would be hard to stay just friends with him when all I could think of when I looked at him was that kiss. On the other hand, though, I never wanted to forget such a perfect kiss.

"Sorry about, um, earlier," he said.

"It's okay. It wasn't your fault." I pondered whether or not I should tell him I'd actually kind of enjoyed it, but decided that would probably send him over the edge. "And, uh, you weren't the only one affected tonight."

"Is that what you were running from?"

I nodded and took a sip of cocoa. Whatever he'd added to it was pretty strong. It seemed to start a fire in my stomach that spread throughout my body, dispelling the last traces of cold and fear. Taking another sip of cocoa to steel myself, I said, "I went out to dinner with Rod tonight."

His eyes widened. "You did?"

"It wasn't a romantic date. He made that clear up front. I think he mostly felt sorry for me about the thing with Ethan, and I'll admit that was the main reason I accepted. He asked Trix out."

"Rod?"

"No, Ethan. Sorry. But anyway, Rod said he wanted to talk about some of those morale-building programs we've been working on, and that was what we did talk about at dinner. It was nice. And then he suggested we go to his place for dessert."

He shook his head with a smile that managed to be fond and disgusted at the same time. "Bad idea when you're with Rod."

"No, it was okay. I didn't get the slightest idea that he had any ulterior motives, and usually I can tell when he's pouring on the sleaze. But once we got to his place, it was like something came over us, and then it got out of hand, and then I realized where it was going and tried to stop, and then it got scary—and that's when I ran out of there and forgot my coat."

This time he didn't turn red. He went stark white and a muscle jumped in his jaw.

"I don't think he meant it," I hurried to add. "It wasn't him. It was probably the shoes—that spell, maybe even something worse. I know he can be a—" I groped for words that didn't sound too insulting to his best friend.

Apparently I didn't have to worry about being insulting. "—lech, satyr, sleazeball, lothario," he completed my sentence.

"Yeah, that. I know he can be like that, but he's never been like that with me. And he seemed pretty horrified when he realized what was happening. I got out of there to protect both of us."

He drained his cup, then got up from the table and went to put it in the sink. "You said you were both affected?" he asked, his back to me.

I mentally kicked myself. Either I could leave him with the impression that I wouldn't have minded a certain level of activity with Rod or I had to tell him about losing my immunity. But I'd kissed him back, too. Surely he had to have noticed that. And it's not like he cared all that much, anyway. "I don't know what was happening with me, to be honest," I said with a sad sigh. "I think I was all messed up about the Ethan thing and all these men throwing themselves at me."

He came back to the table and took my empty mug, then went back to the sink and proceeded to wash the dishes. "I'm curious about those shoes," he said as he worked. "They shouldn't have affected you, so why were you drawn to buy them?"

"My roommate suggested it. She said I had to have them." That was true, in a way, although Gemma's suggestion had nothing to do with my impulsive purchase. I had to stifle a groan when I realized that even if Ethan hadn't dumped me, the shoes would have done me no good with him. He was immune to their power. How ironic.

"But your roommate wasn't compelled to buy them for herself?"

I shook my head. "No. She loved them, but she said I had to have them."

"Hmm."

"Hmm, what?"

"It's possible that the spell was specifically targeted at you."

"You haven't met Gemma. She would have gone ape over those shoes even without magic."

"With the recent attacks on you and the activity within the company, it's not outside the realm of possibility that you were being targeted."

"So, what, someone was trying to undermine me by making me incredibly attractive? Please, torture me some more."

"It made for a distraction, and as you saw with both Rod and me, it could have served to totally undermine your trust in us."

"Oh," I breathed, as the realization hit me. It was going to be difficult enough to face Rod after this, even knowing what I knew. If I hadn't learned the secret of the shoes, if things had gone further with either Owen or Rod, how effectively could I have worked with either of them in the future? I was incredibly lucky that Owen was an even better wizard than he was a kisser.

I needed to get away from there. I needed to get back home where sanity prevailed, where I didn't have to look at him and wonder why he couldn't have waited a little while longer to figure out that my shoes were enchanted. "Thanks for the cocoa, and the rescue, and all," I said, "but I probably ought to head home."

"Have you looked outside? It's nasty out there."

"It's only a few blocks."

"And you're going to make it in what shoes?" He looked mildly amused, which was an improvement on the borderline anger he'd shown earlier.

"Oh, right."

"I have a guest room, so it won't be a bother. You'll probably be more comfortable than you would be at home. And then after we've both had some rest, we can tackle the problem of your enchanted shoes and see if we can get to the bottom of what's going on."

"I don't know," I hedged. Part of me was dying to accept his offer, while the saner side knew it might be a bad idea.

He headed toward the hallway. "Come on," he said, gesturing for me to follow. Loony and I trailed him down the hallway to the living room. "Look out the window," he said. I leaned on the desk to look and saw that snow was already drifting on the ground, and it was falling so hard I couldn't see the buildings across the very narrow street. "That's on top of a layer of ice and sleet," he pointed out.

"You don't mind?"

"You'd be making my life easier. If you decide to go home, I'd have to walk you, and then I'd have to walk back home in that. So please do me a favor and let us both stay inside, warm and dry tonight."

How could I resist that? He was too cute for words. "Okay, if you insist."

"The guest room has its own bathroom, and I keep some extra toothbrushes in there, along with a few other things. I've had enough occasions where people had to stay here unexpectedly when they couldn't get off the island, so I like to be prepared."

I nodded. "That's good."

"Not that I'm sending you off to bed if you're not ready. But the guest room is upstairs and to the right when you are ready. You can lock the door from inside, if that makes you feel better. I should warn you that you'd better shut the door if you don't want someone joining you in the middle of the night." He suddenly flushed bright pink and hurried to add, "I mean, the cat. She seems to like you."

I looked down to where Loony was wrapping herself around my ankles. "Better than clawing my eyes out."

He grinned. "That's how she greets Rod." Then he winced. "Sorry, didn't mean to bring that up."

"It's okay. I'm not going to faint when you mention his name." I looked around the warm, cozy room. It was so inviting, with its fire and Christmas tree. I'd be happy to curl up for hours in a room like that, but I wasn't sure I could stand being around Owen much longer. I might feel compelled to try that kiss again to see if it was as wonderful as I remembered. "If you don't mind, I think I will go to bed now. Everything's catching up with me at once."

"Go ahead. I'll see you in the morning."

"Thanks again for the hospitality."

He shrugged. "What are friends for?"

Loony followed me as I left the room. She paused at the doorway, as if asking Owen for permission. He gave her the slightest of nods, and she ran ahead to sit on the bottom step of the staircase. I stopped by the bathroom to collect my purse and my still-damp clothes, then followed Loony up the stairs.

The house was truly spectacular, the kind of New York showplace you see in movies and magazines. It might be only a few blocks from my apartment, but it might as well have been on another planet. When I reached the guest room, I realized Owen hadn't been kidding about being more comfortable there than at home. The guest bed was a big four-poster with a pile of pillows and a fluffy down comforter— a far cry from my narrow, hard twin bed at home.

Loony jumped up onto the bed and sat grooming herself. I went into the bathroom and draped my clothes over the shower curtain rod. I found a drawer full of toothbrushes and unwrapped one, then found another drawer filled with sample-size toiletries, from which I selected a tube of toothpaste. It looked like he more or less ran a bed-and-breakfast. I imagined that with a house like that and a spare room, he was very popular with friends and family from out of town.

I returned to the bedroom, leaving the door to the hallway open just slightly so Loony could leave if she wanted to, and to send a subtle signal to Owen that I did trust him. Then I pulled back the covers and crawled into bed. It was like lying on a cloud. Owen might have had to persuade me to stay, but after a night in that bed, he might have to force me to leave. When I got myself settled, Loony came to the head of the bed to join me, curling up against me. I wasn't much of a cat person, but I was glad for the company. It was like she knew I didn't want to be alone. I would have preferred her owner, but that would have been a very bad idea.

I slammed a fist into the pillow next to me. How stupid could I possibly be? I should have known that there was far more going on than my magical immunity being gone. Men never fell all over me like that, and I'd never had two men in one night kiss me. It had to have been supernatural, and I should have clued into that a long time ago. I consoled myself with the thought that the artificial confidence from the shoes must have kept me from seeing the truth. I wondered if the shoes were also the source of the libido surges, but I was not going to ask Owen that question.

I rolled onto my side and buried my fingers in Loony's soft fur. She purred in response. The big question was whether the shoes had been targeted directly at me and if they had anything to do with me losing my immunity. Was Ari behind it all? She had been at Bloomingdale's the day I first saw the shoes. That might not have been a coincidence, after all. Gemma had even shown her the shoes, and then I'd told everyone my holiday shopping plans.

The only conclusion I managed to reach was that I couldn't do this alone. If I kept trying to puzzle out the spy, my immunity problems, and now the mystery of the shoes all by myself, disaster was inevitable. I was going to have to tell someone everything that had happened. Owen was probably my best candidate. He was smart, powerful, and a truly good guy. He took in orphaned kittens, for crying out loud. Surely I could trust him with my problems.

I heard footsteps outside my bedroom door and held my breath as I listened to a nearby door open and close. I doubted I'd get much sleep so close to Owen. Closing my eyes, I allowed myself the luxury of reliving that kiss, from the first thrilling moment when I realized he was going to kiss me, to the initial contact, to the ever so gently increasing pressure and feather-soft touches between more serious kisses. It had been sheer heaven, right up to the point he recoiled in horror.

With a stifled groan, I rolled to my other side. He was the one who needed to lock his door for safety. I didn't know if I was still under the effects of any spell, but I wanted just one more kiss like that, only preferably without the horror at the end of it.

Loony climbed over me to get back into a position where I could stroke her properly. "What are we going to do about that guy of yours?" I whispered to her.

Sleep didn't come easily, and when it did come, it brought with it nightmares and disturbingly erotic dreams, some of which got tangled together so that I woke both terrified and turned on. I must have tossed and turned too much, for at some point in the night, Loony left me. When I woke the next morning, cold, dim light came through the curtains. The clock said it was nine. I hoped Owen wasn't sitting around wondering if I'd ever get up.

I went to the bathroom, brushed my teeth, washed my face, and tried to do something with my hair before I headed downstairs. I found Owen in the kitchen, standing at the stove. He wore jeans and a sweatshirt even more faded than the one he'd loaned me, and his hair was rumpled, as though he hadn't done much more than run a hand through it upon waking.

Loony was nibbling at her breakfast from a bowl near the refrigerator. She noticed me and greeted me with a happy "meow," which caused Owen to turn around and see me. There was a day's worth of dark stubble on his jaw, and he wore a pair of wire-rimmed glasses. I had to grab the back of the chair near me to steady myself at the sight. How was it that the more disheveled he got, the cuter he became?

"Good morning," he said, apparently oblivious to my total meltdown. "Did you sleep well?"

"It took me a while to get to sleep, but then I must have really conked out. Sorry I was such a slugabed."

"Don't worry about it. I wasn't up much earlier than you were. Do you like scrambled eggs?"

"Yeah. I can make them if you want me to."

He gave me a knee-weakening grin. "I can manage breakfast. There's fresh coffee in the pot if you want to get yourself some. Cups are in the cabinet above. There's milk in the refrigerator. No cream, sorry."

I followed his directions and poured myself a cup of coffee, then added milk and sugar. I leaned against the counter by the stove as I drank it and watched him cook. "Is there no end to your talents?" I teased, hoping it sounded like teasing instead of gushing. "Wizard, scholar, sleight-of-hand artist, spy, benefactor of orphaned animals, and now cook." I decided it would be best to leave out the part about him being an expert kisser.

"I was a decent fencer in college, but I haven't picked up a sword in years. But you're pretty multitalented yourself."

"What? Let's see, I can cook, shop, and come up with crazy schemes to save the world."

"All very valuable and important life skills." He dished eggs and bacon onto plates, then took toast from the nearby toaster as it popped up. "Breakfast is served."

We ate at the kitchen table, with Owen dropping the occasional bite of food to Loony, who sat patiently at his feet, ready to catch each morsel. "I have a few ideas about what to do with your shoes," he said. "I did some research last night, and it looks like this is a variant on the more common Cinderella spell, one that very likely could have been targeted at you, though I don't know how they could have been sure you'd buy those shoes, given your magical immunity."

I wasn't going to get a better opening than that. If I was going to tell him, it was now or never. "Um, actually, that's something I kind of need to talk to you about."

"What, your immunity?" He fed a bite of toast to Loony.

"Yeah. It's gone."

His attention snapped back to me. "It's what? Gone? Really?"

"Yeah, pretty much." Once I started the ball rolling, the story came pouring out of me. "I see illusions now—Rod looks totally different, and when we're away from work, Ari and Trix look like ordinary humans. The other night I didn't see you talking to that gargoyle. I didn't see any of the people who attacked me last weekend, and I only felt like magic was being used near me last night. The shoes did affect me. They did all the things you said they would, and I'm pretty sure I was as much under a spell last night as Rod was."

Behind his glasses, his eyes were full of concern. I noticed that they were as beautiful a dark blue as they ever were, so if he wore contact lenses most of the time, they weren't colored. "When did this happen?" he asked.

"I'm not sure exactly when it started, but I first noticed it Thanksgiving weekend. We ran into Rod and I didn't recognize him. It may have started sooner, though. Now that I think about it, it was like things were fading in and out sometimes. Mom saw a few things I didn't see. And then it was totally gone, and it hasn't come back at all."

"Why didn't you say something?"

I traced a pattern in my uneaten eggs with my fork. "I kept hoping it was just a glitch, that it would come back on its own. And then I got scared that it wouldn't, and then the company wouldn't want me anymore. I didn't want to have to face that until it was a last resort."

"If you'd told me, I could have helped you, and I would have kept your secret until we had a better sense of what was happening. Why did you tell me now?"

"Because I realized I was only going to get myself into more trouble if I didn't do something. So can we reverse it, or am I stuck this way?"

"It depends on the cause, but I have an idea. I'll get someone to look into it Monday morning, but in the meantime, don't drink the water at your home. Your water supply may have been tainted."

"That's how they were drugging me."

"You knew about that?"

"I did a little research, not that it did me much good. All I know is that there's a list of chemicals that supposedly dampen immunity. But I didn't know what they were or how I might have been affected."

He nodded. "You're right. The more recent versions of anti-psychotic and anti-depressant medications have a dampening effect on magical immunity. That's why it's so hard to find immunes these days. Someone says they're seeing things, they're given drugs, and then they're no longer seeing things."

"So you think someone put Prozac in the water supply, and presto, I'm no longer immune?" He nodded. "Come to think of it, my grouchy downstairs neighbor has been surprisingly nice lately. And Gemma and Marcia have been in a running fight about whose turn it is to buy bottled water, so I've been staying out of it by drinking out of the tap." I felt like someone had given me a jolt of Prozac with the weight that lifted from my shoulders.

"I'll have the water tested, and in the meantime, don't even brush your teeth with tap water at home, and then be very careful about who you accept food or drinks from, including at work." He winced. "That probably means you'd better not eat anything your secret Santa leaves you, not until you know more."

"That sounds ominous."

"I don't mean to scare you, but I do want you taking precautions." He put his fork down and shoved his plate aside. "I have to confess that I haven't been entirely honest with you, either."

nineteen

"Well, aren't we a secretive bunch," I said, even as I hoped his secret was that he would have wanted to kiss me even without a spell. "What have you been hiding from me?"

"You know those notes the spy apparently looked at?"

"Yet another counterspell to fight the enemy?"

He grinned and shook his head. "The secret is that there isn't any big project. It was a trap to see if Idris did have an inside spy. We made it as tempting as possible, too tempting for him to resist. If he had someone on the inside, he'd get them to look into it."

"So those papers that were in your desk, they were fake?"

"Oh, they were real, but they had nothing to do with anything, just an old spell that's all but irrelevant today."

"You really are the master spy, aren't you?"

I expected him to blush, but he looked somber instead. "I had no idea you'd end up caught in our scheme. I don't know if they came after you because you were onto something, or because they thought you were a good way of getting to me."

"It may be even more personal than that," I said, deciding that now was a good time to go whole hog and let him in on everything I knew or suspected.

"What do you mean?"

"I think I know who our spy is. I have no evidence, nothing more than a string of suspicious coincidences and a hunch or two, but the coincidences are adding up."

"Who is it?"

"Ari." I was surprised by how much it pained me to say it. "She's in the same department with you, so she has access, and she's been around every time something happened. She was the one who spread the rumor about the spy in the first place, back when you, Merlin, and I—and, of course, the spy—were the only ones who knew about it. She was even in Bloomingdale's that first time my roommate and I saw the shoes."

He chewed on his lower lip and frowned, like he was processing the information before reacting. The fact that he didn't immediately deny it seemed a good sign to me that I might be onto something. Eventually, he nodded and said, "I could see that. She and Phelan were fairly close when he worked at MSI. But I'm not sure why she'd be willing to turn on us."

This was where things became potentially uncomfortable. "It may be personal," I said, avoiding his eyes. "I don't know if you were even aware of it, but from what I've heard, she was pretty interested in you for a while and went to a great deal of effort to get you to notice her. She even confessed to throwing herself at you."

"She did? When?"

"You didn't even notice? Honestly, Owen, no wonder she's pissed off. That's a huge blow to the ego. In most people, it wouldn't inspire treachery and bad magic, but I think anyone would be irked." I took a deep breath and forced myself to continue. "She also seems to be jealous of me because you spend so much time with me, when you wouldn't spend time with her."

"But she's shrill and shallow, and you're not."

"Boy, do you know how to sweet-talk a girl."

He blushed at that and got up from the table. "There's one sure way to find out. When someone casts a spell, there's a signature left behind. Let's see who's been tinkering with your shoes."

I followed him to the hall closet, where he retrieved the shoes and carried them to the living room. There were already some books scattered around the floor in front of the fireplace, where he must have done his research the night before. He set the shoes down among the books and sat on the floor. I joined him.

"Since you're not wearing the shoes at the moment and haven't worn them in hours, the spell shouldn't have much of an effect," he said. "But try to avoid the temptation to touch them, please."

I scooted back a few inches and sat on my hands. The siren call of the shoes wasn't nearly as strong as it had been in the past, but I still wanted to put them on.

"I'll need one of your hands," he said, reaching out to me. I hesitated, and he added, "It's okay. Nothing will happen to you, but I need to see if this spell is specific to you or if it's a more general spell simply meant to enhance these shoes."

I tentatively reached my left hand out to him. He laced his fingers through mine, and I thought I'd die on the spot. Did he have any idea what he did to me? When this was over, I'd have to avoid him for a while or risk spontaneous human combustion.

His eyes went unfocused as he held his other hand over the shoes. He blinked, then smiled. "It looks like you were right, it's definitely Ari, and the spell is specific to you. Which means she, or someone she was working with, knew you were going to lose your immunity. I think there's even a transmitter in there, too. That could be how you and Rod were affected last night. As long as you were wearing those shoes, they could influence you and the people around you."

"So that's evidence, then?"

He nodded. "Unfortunately, that means I can't disenchant your shoes yet. I'll need to take them to the office Monday and document everything."

I sighed. "That's okay. It's not like I have anywhere to wear them anytime soon."

"What size do you wear? I may be able to come up with something you can wear home."

"Seven. Don't tell me you keep ladies' shoes lying around the house."

"No, but my downstairs neighbor should have something you can borrow. She doesn't get out much anymore, so it's not as though she'll be needing snow boots." He got up and picked up the red shoes. "In the meantime, I'd better put these away where they'll be safe."

As he went out into the hallway, I leaned my back against the sofa and wondered what would happen next. I hoped his mention of shoes to wear home didn't mean he wanted me to leave. This place already felt more like home to me than my own home did. Maybe it was the fireplace, or the Christmas tree, or even the cat, who got up from her spot in front of the fireplace and crawled into my lap. Then Owen came back into the room and I knew what it was that made this place feel like home. It was the man who lived there.

I felt disloyal for even thinking it, since my roommates had been my friends for so long, but in the months I'd worked at MSI, he'd become my closest friend in so many ways. He was the only person I didn't have to hide things from, especially now that I'd told him all my secrets—all, that is, except the one big secret of how I really felt about him. I didn't know what to do about that one.

"I like your Christmas tree," I said, as he sat next to me.

He turned a lovely shade of rose. "Oh, that. Gloria had me help her put up her decorations at Thanksgiving, and that made my place look bare when I got back home. Normally I don't put much of anything up."

"We don't have room to put anything up." I glanced around the spacious living room, which was the size of our whole apartment. "This is such a great place."

"Thank you. I was lucky to find it. If you think it seems big now, it was originally built as a single town house. Now it's two units, two floors each. My downstairs neighbor used to own the building. When her husband died, I bought it from her, and now I lease her home to her."

If I knew him, he probably rented it to her at a fraction of what he could get from any other tenant. Was he trying to make me fall in love with him? "I still don't think you're for real," I said.

He groaned. "Don't start that again, please. I'm just on my best behavior with you."

I liked the sound of that, even though I doubted he meant anything by it. I played with the fringe on the Oriental rug we were sitting on. "So, what now? We have our suspect and our evidence. Do we bust her, or what?"

"I don't think so, not yet. All we have is proof that she was targeting you. It makes sense that she's also our spy and that she therefore works for Idris. But we don't have that evidence."

"We'll have to set a trap," I said, thinking aloud. "We'll have to goad her into acting."

"Now that we know who it is, we can be much more specific in what we set up," he said, nodding in agreement.

"The trick will be thinking of a trap."

He looked over at me. "Do you have any plans for the rest of the day?"

It was like he'd read my mind. I could think of nothing I'd rather do on a snowy Saturday than spend the day strategizing ways to save the company while snuggling in front of a fireplace with a man I was crazy about. Okay, so snuggling wasn't likely, given that he seemed reluctant to touch me except under extreme circumstances, but a girl could hope.

While he washed the breakfast dishes and I dried, he thought out loud. "I don't think you should let on that you're getting your immunity back once it starts coming back. Make her think you're still affected." He handed me a plate to dry. "Do you think you could fake being affected while pretending not to be affected? You did a good enough job of fooling most of us."

"I may not have to fake it. I don't know how long it'll take to come back."

"And you definitely shouldn't let on that you know about the shoes."

"Yeah, but how are we going to get every man in sight to follow me around acting all besotted?"

"Easy. We set our trap for the company Christmas party Friday night. Trust me, after a couple of hours at one of our parties, all kinds of strange things start to happen." He suddenly grinned. "In fact, I believe I have an idea."

I loved his idea, and hated it at the same time. It gave me everything I'd ever wanted, but with the hollow awareness that it was all for show. By the time he bundled me up in a pair of his neighbor's snow boots and one of his old coats and walked me home that afternoon, I had a date for the company party and an excuse to wear my new dress. I also had a better sense of how devious he could be beneath that angelic face. I almost had to pity the bad guy dumb enough to take on Owen Palmer.

He met me in front of my building Monday morning with my coat over his arm and a Starbucks cup in one hand. I'd followed his instructions to use bottled water even to brush my teeth, so I was dying for the coffee. I was patient, though, and let him help me put the coat on before I grabbed the coffee from him. I noticed as I did so that his knuckles looked bruised. I had a sinking feeling that had something to do with him having the coat I'd left at Rod's place.

As we walked to the subway station, I rehearsed our plan for the day between sips of coffee. "So, I try to act like I accept everything that happened to me on face value, and like I'm happy with it, right?"

"Right. That should drive her nuts, especially if her plan was to ruin your life."

"Then you'll do your part to drive her nuts. Somehow I doubt it was part of her scheme to send me straight into your arms." That was the part of the plan I both loved and hated. I had a feeling that by the end of this week, Ari wouldn't be the only one driven insane.

The plan kicked into gear when I got to my office. "How was your weekend?" Trix asked.

All I had to do was think of that kiss, and I knew I got the appropriate dreamy look. "Better than I could have anticipated," I answered. "What about your date with Ethan?"

"It was fun. But I want to hear about what happened with you. Shall I convene the lunch bunch?"

"Sure. I should be free." As soon as I got to my desk, I sent Owen a "mission accomplished" e-mail. My secret Santa had left a box of chocolates on my desk, and I was tempted to celebrate with one, until I remembered Owen's warning. I shoved the box to the far corner of my desk so I wouldn't forget and reach for one.

At lunchtime, I took the sack lunch I'd brought from home, just in case, and gathered in a conference room with Ari, Trix, and Isabel. I hated having to snow Trix and Isabel, but I was sure they'd understand later. "So," Trix began, "what was it about your weekend that made you so starry-eyed?"

"You went out with Rod, didn't you?" Ari asked.

"Yeah, but that's not who I ended up with." I took a deliberate bite of my sandwich as they all leaned forward with great interest.

"Who did you end up with?" Isabel prodded.

I finished chewing, swallowed, then took a sip of my drink. "Well, I left Rod pretty early, and as I was heading home, I ran right into Owen, and let me tell you, he really loosens up away from work."

"Owen?" Ari blurted. I had to bite my tongue to keep from grinning. She'd taken the bait.

"Yeah, it was the weirdest thing. He's so shy and reserved at work, but Friday night, well, he was very, very different. I don't know what came over him. Anyway, let's just say I now have a date for the party Friday night."

The others congratulated me, but I thought I saw steam coming out of Ari's ears. Round one seemed to have gone to the illustrious team of Palmer and Chandler.

On my way back from lunch, I ran into Rod in the hallway. Even though I knew the truth about what had happened, that didn't make me any more eager to see him. It didn't help that my immunity still wasn't back, so I saw the illusion that played a central role in my most cringe-inducing flashbacks. He must not have felt much better about it than I did, for he merely nodded at me as he passed. Out of the corner of my eye, I saw his real face for a fraction of a second, and I was fairly sure he had a split, swollen lip. I suspected it had something to do with the bruises on Owen's knuckles.

Then I reminded myself that it wasn't his fault. I stopped, turned around, and said, "Rod?"

He stopped walking, stood motionless for a long moment, then finally turned around, his face totally still, like he was guarding his feelings.

I took a deep breath. "Look, about the other night. It wasn't your fault. Both of us were under a spell." I never thought I'd be in a situation where I'd have to give the "we were both drunk" speech, but he looked like his mood was lifting ever so slightly, so I kept going. "Even worse, I knew I was susceptible to being enchanted, which you didn't know, so it's probably more my fault than it is yours. I should have realized something was going on."

He gave me a wry, sad smile. "I guess we were both pretty stupid. I should never have put us in that position. You're my friend, and I shouldn't have crossed that line."

"So we're still friends?"

"Yeah, we're still friends—if you still want me as a friend."

"I do," I said, realizing that I truly meant it. Rod had his problems, but he was basically a good guy.

He gave me a goofy smile that would have been a lot more at home on his real face than it was on his illusion. "I'm glad. I really like you." He winced, then clarified, "And by 'like' I mean like a friend, not anything else."

"I know what you mean," I hurried to assure him. "And I like you, too—in the same way."

He stepped forward with his arms open to hug me, but just before we made contact, I felt the draw of his attraction spell and took a quick step back. "Uh, maybe we'd better not go there," I said. "Not until I'm back to normal. We don't want to risk going through this all over again."

He took an even larger step backward. "Good idea."

I felt like we still needed some way to seal the deal, so I stepped forward to where he was just within reach and gave him an awkward punch on his shoulder, like my brothers did to each other when they wanted to be affectionate but were too macho for bodily contact that didn't look violent. "Well, see you around," I said.

I turned to go, but he called after me. "Katie?" I looked back over my shoulder. "Thanks," he said. "This makes me feel a lot better."

"Me, too." I fought for a carefree grin. "Give us a few weeks, and we'll probably be laughing about it."

Owen came to my office later that afternoon. "I got the test results back on the water at your building," he said. "We were right, you were being drugged. We're getting something done about that, but in the meantime, don't drink the water."

"I think I'm already getting the immunity back, just little flashes every so often, but it is coming back. And you didn't have to hit Rod."

He turned red and rubbed his bruised knuckles. "Just carrying through on a promise I made him a while ago. He should have known better, spell or not."

"Well, now Ari thinks you were the one her spell affected and that I didn't mind you mauling me one bit."

He reached for the box of chocolates my secret Santa had left on my desk, then frowned. "Don't eat those," he warned.

"Let me guess, they're enchanted?"

"Yeah. And it might still affect you, could even prolong the effects of the drug. Once the drug weakened your immunity, they were able to hit you with spells to make it worse."

"I guess I need a magical food taster now."

"You should run things by me until we get this resolved."

"But will it be resolved? All we're going to do is reveal Ari and then try to get the rest of the company on track. Idris will still be out there."

"We can only deal with each problem as it comes along."

"He's got to be up to something bigger if he's trying to distract us."

"Or he's just enjoying watching us run around like rats in a maze. But we'll worry about that when we get through the immediate crisis. Relax, Katie, everything will be okay."

It was easy for him to say. He had all his magical powers at his disposal. I didn't even have reliable nonpowers. I couldn't be sure if someone was affecting me magically or not, and if they were, I couldn't do anything about it.

In the meantime, I had to find one more secret Santa gift for Owen, the one I'd give to him in person at the party Friday night, the party I was going to as his fake date.

On the way home from work, I stopped by the Union Square Barnes & Noble store and found a history of espionage that sounded interesting. I was sure he'd like it, and it even made for a nice inside joke between us. I would have enjoyed it more if we weren't playing lovers. If we couldn't be together for real, I'd have preferred to be just friends for real. Our relationship felt as fake as Rod's illusion, and I hated that.

My unease must have been obvious, for when I got home, Gemma asked, "What's wrong?"

There was no way I could begin to explain it to her, but I needed to talk. "It's that guy, the one from work."

"Didn't you say you were going to the office party with him?"

"Yeah, but it's not a real date."

"Define 'real date.' You're going with him, aren't you?"

I couldn't get into the stuff about a company spy who'd tried stealing my nonmagical powers from me. Instead, I oversimplified the situation. "There's this girl he works with who's become all crazy-stalker obsessed with him. He's too nice to be mean to her and really break her heart, but she's not getting the message that he's not interested. So he asked me to play girlfriend at the office party so she'd realize he wasn't available." It was sort of true, in a twisted, backward way.

She didn't look like she bought it. "That's what he told you?"

"Sort of."

"And let's see, this is the guy who suggests that you grab dinner on the way home and who asks you to help him with his Christmas shopping—the same one who sheltered you from the snowstorm and insisted on you staying at his place overnight?"

"In his guest room," I reminded her. "He was a perfect gentleman."

"And you say that this guy is extremely shy, can barely talk to people without stammering and blushing?"

"Yeah. It's kind of cute. Most of the time, he doesn't seem to have that problem with me, which is why I don't think he likes me that way. I'm like his sister, someone who doesn't fluster him."

"Honey, I've got news for you. You're being stealth-dated."

"What?"

"He's taking you out, so it's like a date, but without that scary asking-you-out part. He's managing to date you under the radar, no pressure for either of you. Next thing you know, you'll be an established couple without ever having had an official date."

I shook my head. "No way. For one thing, he never touches me, not even when he has an excuse to. If he was doing this stealth-dating thing, wouldn't he manage to accidentally brush against me, or take my arm to guide me somewhere, and then not let go?"

"Hmm. It depends on the guy. He might not trust himself with you. That might be the only way he can stay comfortable with you. He might have to choose between getting physical or getting to know you, and for now he's chosen to get to know you."

I could certainly see that after the kiss, but he'd been that way before he had any reason to be afraid of me. I wished Gemma was right, but I was afraid she was wrong about this one. You'd think that magic would make everything easier—a flick of the wrist and you can have anything you want—but it only seemed to complicate things.

That didn't stop me from being nearly breathless with anticipation Friday night as I finished getting dressed in my new velvet dress and my now disenchanted red shoes. Gemma helped me pin my hair up. "You look fantastic," she said. "Even if he wasn't really crazy about you before, he will be after he gets a good look at you." As much as I hoped she was right about that, a part of me wished I could have kept some of the enchantment on the red shoes, at least the part that gave me confidence if not the part that would make Owen want to kiss me.

I didn't want to subject the poor guy to my roommates, so I ran downstairs to meet him after he rang the buzzer instead of making him come up to get me. He had a cab waiting at the curb, and he was impossibly gorgeous in a classic black tuxedo. "Are you up for this?" he asked as he helped me into the cab.

"You're the one who has the acting job," I replied. That was supposed to be his cue to say that he didn't have to pretend to be totally enchanted by me, but this was Owen I was dealing with, so I shouldn't have been surprised when he didn't give me the smooth comeback.

Instead, he said, "You'll have some acting of your own to do." Then he looked at me, concern in his eyes. "Don't you?"

I sighed and hoped our cabdriver was one of the many whose English was sketchy at best. "Not that much," I admitted. "It is coming back, but it's still iffy. I catch things out of the corner of my eye from time to time, but I'm not a hundred percent yet."

"That's going to make tonight extremely interesting." It was his typical understatement.

"Have you let the boss in on what you have planned tonight?"

"No, it's probably best if he doesn't know."

I turned to stare at him in shock. "I thought you showed him the shoes, for evidence."

"I documented the spell. There are ways of recording those things.

But I believe it's best if he's surprised tonight. I didn't want to risk even the slightest hint of a rumor getting out."

"I believe I've found your flaw. You're insane."

"I have everything under control." He sounded as calm as he usually did, but I recognized the edge under his words and shivered. Owen was usually so mild-mannered that it was easy to forget how very powerful he was—so powerful that, according to Rod, he'd actually been brought up to be shy and unassuming so he wouldn't become a dangerous megalomaniac. I couldn't help but wonder how much of Rod's warning hadn't been mere jealousy, after all.

The party was being held in the building's soaring, cathedral-like lobby. I'd thought that was an odd place to hold a company party, but it had been transformed in the few hours since the close of business that afternoon. At any other company, it would have taken a team of decorators a week to carry out a transformation like that. At MSI, it probably took a few people a wave of a hand.

Lush green garlands hung from the balcony railings over the lobby. Tiny lights twinkled among the branches, and I had a feeling there were no cords involved. Star lights like larger versions of the ones that had been put in my office floated beneath the ceiling. The room itself was surrounded by Christmas trees, with the largest reaching almost to the roof, in the middle of the room where the doorman usually sat. Scattered among the trees were tables loaded with food and drink. A string quartet—the instruments playing themselves—sat at the top of the stairs.

"This is fantastic," I said.

"We do some of the best decoration spells around," Owen remarked, as he helped me out of my coat. "They're very popular at this time of year." He pointed to one of the smaller trees, which had the effect of snow-covered branches sparkling on a moonlit night. "That's one of mine, something I came up with while I was still in school. Royalties from that one paid for my house, more or less."

"It's beautiful. Beats the heck out of the foil icicles we put on our tree back home."

He handed our coats over to the coat check, then we put our secret Santa gifts under the huge central Christmas tree. I noticed that if I looked at some of the trees out of the corner of my eye, they disappeared or looked bare, and I was grateful that I'd been given at least a brief glimpse of their glory, even if my lack of immunity was a problem. I stood on tiptoe and whispered to Owen, "How much of this is real and how much is illusion?"

"The good ones are real. Illusion is a shortcut."

"So I'll still be able to see your tree when it comes back to me?"

He gave my hand a reassuring squeeze. "Yes, you will."

"You know, this whole experience has certainly given me a new perspective on things. I may even miss some of it."

"Let's hope you have a chance to miss it. Is it any better?"

"It's so gradual, it's hard to tell."

A short, balding man then came over to join us. I recognized Owen's boss, Mr. Lansing, the one who was supposedly a frog. He stuck a hand out to me. "Arthur J. Lansing, director of Research and Development. I don't believe we've met formally."

I took his hand and had to make an effort not to flinch when it turned out to be cold and smooth—like shaking hands with a frog, as a matter of fact. "Nice to meet you," I said. "I'm Katie Chandler, the CEO's assistant."

"Yes, I know. I normally send the boy here to any meetings. Don't get out much, you know."

I smiled and turned to Owen, prepared to say something about those meetings, then almost jumped when the man became a frog, right before my eyes. There was a giant frog wearing a tuxedo and glasses standing in front of me. It took all my self-control not to leap out of the way and scream in shock. Instead, I smiled and said, "You probably get so much more done without all those meetings."

"Well, I'm getting empty." He gestured with his glass. "Off for a refill, nice chatting with you." Then he hopped away and I had to bite my tongue to keep from giggling.

"Let me guess, it's starting to come back," Owen whispered in my ear.

"Oh yeah, and interesting timing, too. What is the deal with frogs, anyway? There are way too many of them in my life these days."

He shrugged. "It's a classic. Those never go out of style. I wish I could figure out a way of undoing that one. That's no way to live. Should we get something to drink?"

"A drink sounds wonderful."

With his hand on my waist, he guided me to a nearby champagne fountain, where he handed me a glass before filling one for himself. For someone who normally showed no signs of romantic interest, he was doing a good job of acting like he couldn't take his eyes off me.

I saw Isabel's head approach through the crowd. When she reached us, she hugged me and patted Owen on the shoulder. "You're wearing the fabulous shoes again!" she boomed. "Love them!" Then she gave me a sly wink as she gestured toward Owen with her chin. "And nice work. You go, girl!"

I smiled back at her and made a mental note to let her in on the real story when all was said and done. That would be the most effective way of spreading the word companywide that Owen and I were not, in fact, a real item. Pity.

While we got food and made small talk with the various people we ran into, I scanned the room constantly, looking for Ari. "Are you sure she's coming?" Owen asked when half an hour had gone by with no sign of her.

"She said she was. She's probably being fashionably late. She'll want to make a big entrance."

Just then, the front doors opened and Ari swept in on the arm of a tall, lanky man. He looked unfamiliar at first, but as I focused on him, his appearance shifted, blurred, then solidified into something all too familiar to me. "Speak of the devil," I breathed, "and you'll never believe who she brought as her date."

twenty

"Who is it?" Owen hissed into my ear. His warm breath on my cheek made me momentarily forget the urgency of the situation, but I forced myself to focus.

"Guess," I whispered back to him.

"Katie." There was a warning tone in his voice.

"She brought Phelan Idris. He's wearing an illusion."

"And you can see him?"

"He just came into full focus. Looks like I was cured in the nick of time. But how could she possibly hope to get away with that? There are people here who can see him."

"Not a lot of the verifiers show up for these parties, and few of those would have the slightest idea who he is. And remember, she thinks you can't see him."

"There's Ethan," I pointed out. "He knows Idris, and he's an immune."

"Is he even here?"

"I haven't seen him yet, but I can't imagine Mr. 'I want to explore magic' staying away. I think he's supposed to be coming with Trix."

"Hmm, I haven't seen her, either. I hope they're okay."

Ari and Idris approached us, both of them smiling smugly. "Play it cool," Owen whispered. I wondered if he was talking to me or to himself.

"Hey," I said to Ari. "Love your dress." Then I smiled at Idris and said, "Hi, I'm Katie."

"This is my friend, Fred," Ari said. He darted a funny look at her, like that wasn't the cover name he'd have chosen. It seemed she couldn't resist making even her evil allies uncomfortable. "And this is Owen and Katie. We work together."

Now that I knew what was going on, I recognized the cat-who-ate-the-canary look in her eyes. I should have suspected earlier that she was up to something, but she always looked like she was up to something, or was at least thinking about being up to something.

"It's good to meet you, Fred," I said with faked sincerity as I kicked Owen in the ankle. He was quivering with barely suppressed hostility. Owen kept a carefully blank face, though, going only a little bit pale. I couldn't resist giving the verbal knife a little twist. "I can't believe Ari hasn't told us anything about you. She usually doesn't have much of a problem with kissing and telling."

I was rewarded by a fleeting look of panic in her eyes. "Fred's just a friend," she said. "All my other potential dates vanished. Well, gotta mingle. Catch you later."

Owen's champagne glass shattered in his hand, then disappeared in midair before it hit the floor. "I'm going to kill him," he said with calm certainty. "But unfortunately, I don't think it'll be tonight."

"All our players appear to be onstage, so now what?" I asked.

"We play our roles and see what happens. I can break his illusion, but it'll be easier if he's off-guard, and much, much more effective if I do it at the right moment. But let's first give her enough rope to really hang herself. Bringing him as her date is probably enough evidence, but let's see what else she does."

It was hard to focus on party small talk when I knew a major battle could take place at any moment. Then we ran into Rod. Now that my immunity had returned, he was the same old Rod I'd always known, which made it easier for me to face him. I could pretend those things that had happened between us had involved some stranger I'd never see again, and in time maybe I'd be able to forget it entirely. For now, though, his split lip served as a vivid reminder of what had happened.

Rod gave me one of his more charming smiles, and Owen responded by putting his arm around my waist and pulling me roughly against him. "Back off," he said with quiet intensity. "How many times do I have to warn you to leave her alone?"

"At least I had the stones to make a move. And shouldn't the lady have the right to decide who she wants to be with?"

"She's here with me."

I'd had enough of two otherwise sane, rational men acting like rutting stags over me. "Would you two cut it out, please?" I begged. "Let's put it behind us, okay?"

Owen's mouth twitched, then he whispered to me, "Play along."

While I was still gaping at him, Psychodrama Theater continued to play, drawing a growing audience. "Please," Rod said. "Like you'd even know what to do with her."

"And you did such a good job that she ran away from you and went straight to me."

I wondered what my role in this little play was supposed to be. Was I supposed to be horrified, or was I supposed to enjoy the attention? It would have helped if they'd shared the script with me, but I had a feeling they were making it up as they went along, based on a lifetime of being practically brothers who knew each other well enough to anticipate every thought or action. I finally decided that I should go with the way things were when the shoes were working on me and everyone else around me. That had to have been the intent of the scene. They were making Ari think the shoes still worked.

I tried to put on the attitude of a woman who could have any man she wanted. That was something of a stretch. I could, however, fake not knowing why men were acting so weird around me. "Seriously, cut it out, you two," I said. "You've been friends forever, and I don't want that to end on my account. Besides, we don't want to ruin the party for everyone else."

Rod glared at Owen for a second longer, then turned and stalked away. Owen pulled me to the other side of the room with a possessive arm still around my waist. Oh, but that felt good. I chanced a glance at Ari, who seemed to have enjoyed the entertainment immensely.

"Would it have killed you to let me in on that?" I asked Owen when we were out of earshot of everyone else.

"I thought it would be more authentic if you didn't know."

"So you two are okay now? You're friends again?"

"At least enough to cooperate on this."

"You really hit him, then? Or was that part of the plan?"

"I hit him, and then we came up with the plan. You're the only one who can see what I presume is a fat lip."

"Owen! You didn't have to do that."

He flexed his right hand. "Yes, I did. He promised me that you were off-limits, and I promised what I'd do if he broke that promise. He wasn't supposed to ask you out, and the spell wouldn't have been a factor if he'd kept that promise."

"What were you doing making him make that promise?" I asked, hardly daring hope it meant he had any interest in me.

"You've seen the way he is with women. We agreed that you weren't a candidate to be one of his conquests."

"He needs professional help. Seriously."

"Tell me about it. Now it's almost time for act two."

"What's act two?"

He gestured behind me, and I turned to see Merlin appear at the top of the stairs. "Ladies and gentlebeings," the ancient wizard boomed in a voice that seemed too strong to come from someone so old and seemingly fragile.

"Oh, act two," I said, nodding with realization. "And you're not going to tell him what's going on?"

"We didn't have enough evidence going in to say anything, and now we don't have time. Come on." With his arm still around my waist, he tugged me toward the front of the crowd that was forming at the foot of the stairs. The instruments stopped playing and hung suspended and still in midair. Ari and Idris were also near the front of the crowd. Rod wasn't too far from them. I still hadn't spotted Ethan or Trix.

Once he had everyone's attention, Merlin began speaking. "This is my first such celebration to share with all of you, and I deem it a great honor to do so," he said. "We are facing troubled times, but I believe we can prevail if we face them together, if we remember the purpose behind this company and the role it plays in the magical world."

I knew I should have been paying attention to my boss, but I couldn't help watching Idris. He rolled his eyes and made mocking expressions, which I presumed were covered by the illusion he wore.

Merlin continued, "In recent weeks, we've been forced to focus inward due to the disloyalty of one of our own. I believe we've moved past that now and can work together toward our common goal. The perpetrator will be caught, and we will protect ourselves from the forces of chaos who seek to undermine us."

Now I noticed that Rod was looking right at us. "Showtime," Owen whispered. "Watch my back." He released my waist, and I felt the tingle of powerful magic building near me. The hair on the back of my neck stood on end, and there was an audible *zap* followed by a gasp from the crowd.

Merlin froze, then he dropped any pretense of being a kindly elder statesman. "You," he said, his voice a whisper, but one that cut through the silence like a knife.

Only then did Idris apparently realize he'd been exposed. He glanced over his shoulder, like he was looking for an exit, and panic washed over his features when he found his way blocked by the entire workforce of MSI. Only then did he assume the cocky pose that was so familiar to those of us who'd faced him in the last battle we'd fought.

At that, Owen stepped in front of me. The crowd between Owen and Idris took a collective stride backward, leaving the space clear between them. Merlin made his way slowly down the stairs.

"Nice trick," Idris said to Owen.

"Thank you," Owen replied, sounding calm and casual.

"How'd you know it was me?"

"You give off an unmistakable odor." Muffled laughter rippled through the crowd.

Idris crossed his arms over his chest and looked up at Merlin. "So, what are you going to do about it, old man? I'm here as an invited guest. That's not against the law. Or are you going to get your pet lawyer to file for a restraining order? Where is your lawyer, anyway? I haven't seen him here tonight."

Ethan wasn't my favorite person in the world at the moment, but that didn't mean I wanted to see something bad happen to him, so I immediately became worried.

"Whose guest are you?" Merlin asked.

"I came here with one of your own employees," Idris said with a smirk. "Says a lot about your company loyalty, doesn't it?"

While watching Idris for signs of treachery, I noticed Ari's wings moving away. The little rat was trying to sneak out of this. Not on my watch, I vowed. I slipped through the crowd toward her, trying to keep an eye on her while also watching for any illusions or other magic that might be a danger to Owen or Merlin. The bitch had taken my powers, enchanted me, and screwed around with my life. She was not going to get away with it.

"It says something about that particular employee," Merlin said. "Don't assume it says anything about the rest of us." His eyes scanned the crowd, like he was looking for who the traitor might be. Ari moved faster.

I knew I couldn't keep up with her if she used her wings, and if she got away without being exposed, we'd be right back to the widespread paranoia and suspicion that had swamped the company when we first learned we had a traitor. "Hold it right there!" I shouted to her back. "Stop her!"

Isabel was standing closest to Ari, and she looked at me in shock and horror. "Katie?" she asked softly, and I could feel every head in the room swivel to look at me.

Ari, ever the schemer, turned to look at me with wide, innocent eyes. "What are you talking about, Katie? You aren't trying to create a distraction, are you?"

That was a low blow, even for her, one I hadn't been anticipating. "Wha—?" was all I could say.

"Who would have guessed it of sweet little Katie? Investigating the traitor, when the whole time, you're the one stirring up trouble. It seems like in the last month, you've dated half the company, broken up a lifelong friendship, and now you're trying to frame me?" With an air of affronted innocence, she looked around at the enthralled crowd. "Maybe you should ask her where she got those pretty red shoes, and what she's doing with them. How else do you think she got all those men interested in her? She's had her eyes on Owen Palmer since before she joined the company, and she's stopped at nothing to get him, even if it takes getting someone to put a Cinderella spell on her shoes to make him want her."

By this time, I was well over my shock and on my way to anger. "How would you know the shoes are enchanted?" I asked.

"Please! Like he'd see someone like you any other way? I wish I'd thought of it. If you didn't have him under a spell, he wouldn't notice if you threw yourself at him."

I kicked off my shoes and tossed them at two nearby people. "Do they seem enchanted to you?" I asked them. I felt a lot shorter in my stocking feet, but I was also better prepared to run if I had to give chase.

She wasn't done, though. In fact, she seemed surprisingly confident, probably because she knew for a fact that the shoes had been enchanted. "You may not have noticed the enchantment, since you're immune. Or are you? Maybe you've been lying about that, too."

The crowd parted, and soon Merlin was standing beside me. "Katie, is this true?"

Wishing I'd been honest with him sooner, I said, "Yes, sir. It was.

I completely lost my immunity for a couple of weeks. It turned out someone had been drugging me. The water in my building was tainted, and then the effect was reinforced with enchanted candy sent to me by my secret Santa."

"Ari!" Isabel blurted out, moving to block any possible path for Ari to escape. Then she turned to Merlin. "It was Ari. I assigned her to Katie because I thought it would be fun among friends."

"But now I'm okay," I added. "Totally back to normal."

"Why didn't you say something?" Merlin asked me, sounding disappointed.

"I was afraid I'd lose my job, so I kept waiting and hoping it was temporary. And then, once we found the source, well, we figured that the only person who'd know about it would be the one who did it."

"That was my idea, sir," Owen's voice called out from behind us, loud and clear. Every head in the room turned. Most of them had probably never heard Owen speak before tonight, let alone speak that loudly and firmly. "It was part of our plan."

Now Merlin looked amused. "Your plan? Please, let's discuss this."

Ari tried to back away. "You're going to believe her? She was lying to you."

"At least she wasn't conking people on the head and leaving them tied up in a broom closet," a male voice said from the top of the stairs. I turned, along with everyone else in the room, to see Ethan and Trix at the top of the stairs. Both of them looked bedraggled and dazed.

Trix held up a small figure of a fairy. "But on the bright side, we found the last treasure hunt item, which I think means the Dragon team wins."

The Dragon team launched into its cheer, which fizzled away a couple of seconds later when they realized that it wasn't the right time for that sort of thing.

"What's Idris doing here?" Ethan added.

"Are you sure who did it?" Merlin asked.

"Ari asked us to meet her before we left to get ready for the party," Trix said, straightening her skirt.

I'd had enough. I stepped forward and grabbed one of Ari's

wings. She yelped. "Does that hurt?" I asked. She nodded. "Good," I said, and dragged her forward to the foot of the stairs. That position made it easier for me to keep an eye on Idris and still run the inquisition on Ari.

"Now, would someone please explain the enchanted shoes to me?" Merlin said.

"What enchanted shoes?" Ethan asked. "Did we miss something? What's going on?"

"There's no spell on these shoes," one of the bystanders I'd tossed my shoes to shouted.

Ari whirled in surprise. "Yes, there was!" she blurted.

I grabbed her wing again. "And how would you know?"

"They were enchanted," Owen said. "They were affected by a rather powerful, layered spell that not only altered the perceptions of people around Katie, but also gave the caster some degree of control over her and served as a way of transmitting other spells to her and others around her. I broke it, of course. I can provide the documentation, but I will say that Ari's fingerprints were all over it."

The shoes were passed forward through the crowd. Owen took them and handed them to me. I put them back on, and this time they didn't have to be enchanted to make me feel confident and powerful. I faced her and said, "You were my friend. How could you?"

"Like I'd ever really be friends with you," she said with a haughty sniff. "It was all an act, and you bought it."

"Yeah, stupid, nonmagical me. But why is it that if I'm such a weakling, you had to resort to magic and removing my abilities in order to come even close to getting in my way?"

I realized as I said it how true it was. I had my own power, and it was maybe even more powerful than magic. I held myself taller and continued, "You may think I'm a pushover because I'm nice, but being nice means people like me, and they're willing to trust me even when I've been afraid to trust them." I couldn't help but glance at Owen when I said that. "They're willing to talk to me and listen to me, and they stay at my side no matter what. You have no idea how much power my friends give me." Owen's smile at that moment reinforced what I'd just said, and I felt a surge of strength.

"You probably wouldn't think much of my father. He's a simple Texas farmer, totally unmagical, but he taught me how to read a person's eyes to look into her heart. I don't need to be able to see past illusion to see the truth. I've had that skill all along. In fact, I had you nailed as our traitor even when I'd totally lost my immunity, while you were drugging me and putting the whammy on me. Something about you didn't add up, and in my gut I knew the truth. I just didn't have the evidence to pin it on you. But now, thanks to you, I do."

I turned to Merlin. "Wouldn't you consider much of what she's said here a confession?"

"She does seem to know too much for someone who wasn't involved," he agreed. "Security, please take Miss Ariel into custody."

Sam and some of his colleagues flew in and grabbed Ari. "Are you going to let them do this to me?" she shouted at Idris as they dragged her away.

We all turned, prepared for a fight. I noticed Owen flexing his wrists. But Idris simply shrugged. "Hey, all that was her deal. I was just her date. I thought it was only a little prank. And I think I'll be leaving now." He put his hands in his pockets and sauntered away.

I turned to Merlin. "You're not going to let him get away, are you?"

"He's right. He's done nothing."

"And he was very careful to keep his fingerprints off Ari's work," Owen added. "I wouldn't be surprised if he was the one who devised that particular variant on the Cinderella spell, mostly because that kind of work is beyond her abilities, but she was certainly the one who cast it."

"So we're letting him go?" I couldn't believe this.

"This time," Merlin said. "We have no reason to hold him. If we did, we'd be guilty of the kind of chaotic inattention to the law that he usually practices, and we might even aid in his cause to draw others away from order. Now, if you'll excuse me, I have a speech to finish."

He climbed back to the top of the stairs. "As I was saying before I was so rudely interrupted," he began, and the employees gave an answering murmur of laughter. "We have much to celebrate this year, but much work ahead of us. For tonight, let us enjoy ourselves. Greet your fellow workers and know that you're not merely employees of Magic, Spells, and Illusions, Incorporated, you're also the vanguard in the effort to maintain the ancient standards and purity of magical use. Let us all continue to find ways to use our power to serve not only our community, but also the greater good of all humankind. And by the way, we met our targets, so you will all be receiving bonuses."

The employees burst into applause and cheers, and I joined in, truly feeling like part of the group. I felt an arm around my shoulders and turned to see Owen smiling down at me. "Good work," he said. "I didn't anticipate her trying to frame you, but you handled it well."

"Like I said, I've got my own powers."

"You really do. And it looks like we got rid of at least one headache by exposing our spy."

I shook my head. "No, it means we could have an even bigger headache. Idris may be in it for the chaos, but Ari's a lot more focused, and with her it's personal now. Plus, she has an attention span that lasts longer than your average commercial break."

He frowned. "So the two of them really are working together . . ."

"Fasten your seat belt," I said with a nod.

"Fortunately, she'll be in custody for a while."

"Let's hope so, or we're in trouble. You don't want to give her a chance to pull his strings."

Merlin waved his hand for attention once more. "I believe we have one additional portion of our celebration to carry out. This season we've attempted to pull together as a company by doing kind things for each other. Tonight, we'll all learn the identities of our benefactors. Each of you was instructed to bring a gift tonight to present in person. Please take your gifts from beneath the tree and reveal your identities to your friends."

"I guess I'll be coming up short tonight," I muttered as everyone swarmed to the tree. "Not that I'd want anything she gave me." I shuddered, trying to imagine what it might have been.

I let the crowd around the tree die down, in part because I was enjoying watching others surprise their co-workers. The delighted hugs and handshakes warmed my heart. There might have been a few hitches—most of them involving me—but it looked like it had worked overall. There was a family feel to this gathering that certainly hadn't been there at my old job working for Mimi.

While Owen gave his gift to his pal, I took the book from under the tree and waited on the sidelines. Merlin came up to stand next to me. "I'm sorry I didn't tell you," I said. "I was so afraid."

"Your employment with me is not contingent on your magical abilities, or lack of abilities, as the case may be." His eyes twinkled. "In fact, you made a rather accurate summation of your true skills for the position. You must have great discernment if you were able to carry out your duties even without your magical immunity in place."

"It would have gone a lot easier if I'd trusted someone sooner."

"You've learned some valuable lessons from this experience. Don't forget them."

Jake, almost unrecognizable with his hair combed, approached Merlin shyly with an elaborately decorated package. "Um, sir? I have something for you."

They moved away, and I watched others open fantastic magical gifts that soared, sparkled, and sang. It was enough to make me want to hide my book behind my back and play dumb, but then that would have negated that little lesson I'd learned about trust. Owen was my friend and had never failed to be gracious about anything. I could trust him to see the spirit of my gift.

Finally, I found the nerve to approach him. He was still a bit pink from having to carry on a nonbusiness conversation with his secret Santa, someone he didn't know, but he looked happy. "This has gone really well," he said.

"Yeah, if you don't count all my dirty little secrets being aired in front of the whole company."

"You weren't the only one dragged through the mud tonight," he reminded me. I remembered what Ari had said about it taking an enchantment for him to notice someone and winced on his behalf, even if it was kind of true.

"Well, anyway, I have something for you, which I'm sure you've already guessed by now." I handed him the book. "Merry Christmas from your secret Santa. You did know, didn't you?"

"Well," he hedged, not quite looking me in the eye.

"Owen, I thought we were going to be honest with each other."

"Okay, then, yes, I knew. Who else was going to go to that much effort? But you did a good job covering your tracks." He then looked me in the eye, turning pink, but keeping eye contact steady. "And I was glad it was you. I can have magical things anytime I want. But I almost never get the kinds of things you did for me. Thank you."

I felt myself turning almost as red as he was. "Aren't you going to open it?" I asked.

He tapped the wrapping paper with his index finger and made it disappear. Then he grinned. "This is great, thanks! You do pay attention, don't you?"

"Well, I may not have ESP with a twenty-four-hour Owen channel, but I do what I can."

"Thank you. I know I'm going to love this."

I noticed that he didn't hug me or otherwise touch me. Now that the game was over, it appeared that we were going to go back to being just friends. It was a disappointment, but I wouldn't want to lose his friendship now that I knew how much it meant to me. "And thank you for everything," I said. "You got me through this. Without your help, this wouldn't have worked out at all."

"That's what friends are for, right?"

I forced a smile even though I wanted to cry. "Right."

He put the book down on a nearby table. "Actually, I haven't been entirely honest with you." He turned a shade of pink I'd never seen before, then it faded to white, leaving his cheeks rosy. He seemed to search for words, then finally blurted out, "It wasn't just the shoes, you know."

"What?"

"Ari was wrong. It didn't take the shoes for me to find you interesting. That twenty-four-hour Katie channel has been tuned to that frequency pretty much since the moment I first saw you."

I was so shocked I forgot to breathe. "Oh," I managed to gasp. "But I thought—all this time—you didn't even— Why didn't you say something? Or do something?"

"You mean other than walk you to work every morning, ask you to dinner, talk to you more than I talk to anyone? And you kept talking about being friends."

I laughed. "That's because I thought that's what you wanted. I didn't want to scare you."

He pulled me to him and held me against him. I could feel the laughter rumbling in his chest. "We're so clueless, I think we deserve each other," he murmured in my ear.

I was glad he was holding onto me because I felt so dizzy I was afraid my knees would buckle under me. "It's funny, but I seemed to interpret all those clues that you liked me as clues that you didn't like me, or maybe that you liked me, but only liked me. I was trying so hard just to be your friend, and you made it more and more difficult by being perfect." I looked up at him. "And what does someone like you want with someone like me, anyway? You're like a superwizard and I'm Miss Ordinary."

"Katie, shut up." He said it kindly with a fond smile on his lips. "Don't talk yourself out of this."

I groaned and leaned my head against his chest. "See what I mean? You take in homeless cats and keep old ladies in their homes, and you're brilliant and powerful and did I mention gorgeous, and here I am—"

He proceeded then to shut me up very thoroughly. It turned out that first perfect kiss was no fluke caused by a pair of enchanted shoes. The second was even better, and this time it was for real.

SHANNA SWENDSON has written category romance novels (as Samantha Carter), radio scripts, marketing brochures, annual reports, newsletter articles, and too many news releases to count. She has been a finalist for awards given by organizations ranging from *Romantic Times* magazine to the Dallas Press Club. She lives in Texas, but loves to play Southern belle in New York as often as possible. She is the author of *Enchanted, Inc.* Visit her website at www.shanna swendson.com.